Her eyes widened. What was he talking about? If Atlantis had a special interest in elemental mages, wouldn't she have heard about it? Not a single elemental mage she knew had ever attracted Atlantis's attention simply by being an elemental mage. "Every circus has a dozen mages who can do what I do. Why should Atlantis pay any mind to me?"

"Because you are younger and have far more potential."

Two thousand years ago she would not have questioned him. Differences among realms then had been settled by wars of elemental magic. Good elemental mages had been highly prized, and great elemental mages, well, they'd been considered Angels incarnate. But that was two thousand years ago.

"Potential for what?"

"For greatness."

# THE BURNING SKY

## SHERRY THOMAS

BALZER + BRAY
*An Imprint of* HarperCollins*Publishers*

Balzer + Bray is an imprint of HarperCollins Publishers.

The Burning Sky
Copyright © 2013 by Sherry Thomas
www.epicreads.com

Library of Congress Cataloging-in-Publication Data
Thomas, Sherry (Sherry M.)
 The burning sky / Sherry Thomas. — First edition.
  pages cm
 Summary: "A young elemental mage named Iolanthe Seabourne discovers her shocking
power and destiny when she is thrown together with a prince to lead a rebellion against a
tyrant."—Provided by publisher.
 ISBN 978-0-06-220730-2
 [1. Fantasy.] I. Title.
PZ7.T3694533Bu 2013                                                    2013014504
[Fic]—dc23                                                                      CIP
                                                                                      AC

Typography by Erin Fitzsimmons
15 16 17 18   PC/RRDC   10 9 8 7 6 5 4 3 2
❖
First paperback edition, 2014

*To J, who is as kind, smart, and hilarious as he is gorgeous,*
*and who has loved this story since it was but a blob*

JUST BEFORE THE START OF Summer Half, in April 1883, a very minor event took place at Eton College, that venerable and illustrious English public school for boys. A sixteen-year-old pupil named Archer Fairfax returned from a three-month absence, caused by a fractured femur, to resume his education.

Almost every word in the preceding sentence is false. Archer Fairfax had not suffered a broken limb. He had never before set foot in Eton. His name was not Archer Fairfax. And he was not, in fact, even a he.

This is the story of a girl who fooled a thousand boys, a boy who fooled an entire country, a partnership that would change the fate of realms, and a power to challenge the greatest tyrant the world had ever known.

Expect magic.

## CHAPTER 1

FIRE WAS EASY.

In fact, there was nothing easier.

They said that when an elemental mage called forth flame, she stole a little from every fire in the world. That would make Iolanthe Seabourne quite the thief, gathering millions of sparks into one great combustion.

That flame she sculpted into a perfect sphere ten feet across, suspended above the rushing currents of the River Woe.

She beckoned with her fingers. Streams of water shot up and arced over the fireball. Stray droplets gleamed briefly under the sun before falling into the flame, releasing sizzles of steam.

Master Haywood, her guardian, used to love watching her play with fire. He had not been alone in his fascination. Everyone, from neighbors to classmates, had wanted her to show them how she made little fireballs dance upon her palm, the same way Iolanthe, as a child, had asked Master Haywood to wiggle his ears, clapping and laughing with delight.

Master Haywood's interest, however, had run far deeper. Unlike others who simply wished to be entertained, he'd challenge her to make intricate, difficult patterns and draw entire landscapes with filaments of fire. And he'd say, *My, but that is beautiful*, and shake his head with wonder—and sometimes, something that felt almost like unease.

But before she could ask him what was the matter, he'd ruffle her hair and tell her he was taking her out for ices. There had been two years during which they'd had many, many cups of ices together, lumenberry for him and pinemelon for her, sitting by the window of Mrs. Hinderstone's sweets shop on University Avenue, just a five-minute walk from their house on the campus of the Conservatory of Magical Arts and Sciences, the most prestigious institution of higher learning in the entire Domain.

Iolanthe hadn't had pinemelon ice in years, but she could still taste its tart, fresh tingle on her tongue.

"My, but that is beautiful."

Iolanthe started. But the voice belonged to a woman—Mrs. Needles, in fact, who cooked and cleaned for Master Haywood three days a week here in Little Grind-on-Woe, about as far from the Conservatory as one could get without leaving the shores of the Domain. Not that Master Haywood earned enough to hire help anymore, but some housekeeping had been included as part of his compensation.

Iolanthe dissipated the fireball still hovering in the air above the fast, white-foamed river. She didn't mind juggling apple-sized handfuls of fire for the children, or providing a few garlands of dancing flames at Little Grind's solstice ball, but it embarrassed her to display her abilities to this extent, with enough fire on hand to burn down the entire village.

*Unless you are actually performing at the Majestic Circus,* Master Haywood had always urged her, *think twice about exhibiting your powers. You never want to appear a braggart—or worse, a freak.*

She turned around and smiled at the housekeeper. "Thank you, Mrs. Needles. I was just practicing for the wedding."

"I had no idea you were such a mighty elemental mage, Miss Seabourne," marveled Mrs. Needles.

In the Old Millennia, when elemental mages decided the fate of realms, no one would have given Iolanthe's middling powers a second glance. But these were the end days of elemental magic.[1] Compared to the majority of elemental mages, who could barely call forth enough fire for a night-light—or enough water to wash their own hands— Iolanthe supposed her powers would indeed be considered mightier than average.

"Mrs. Oakbluff and Rosie—and all their new in-laws—will be so impressed," continued Mrs. Needles, setting down a small picnic basket. "And Master Haywood, of course. Has he seen your performance yet?"

"He was the one who gave me the idea for the big fireball," Iolanthe lied.

The villagers might suspect Master Haywood to be a merixida

addict who neglected his sixteen-year-old ward, but she refused to portray him as anything other than a most solicitous, attentive father figure.

In the seven years since his troubles started, she'd developed a certain demeanor, a second personality that she wore like an exoskeleton. The Iolanthe who faced the public was a darling: a confident, outgoing girl who was also wonderfully sweet and helpful—the result of having been deeply cherished her entire life, of course.

She had grown so accustomed to this exterior that she didn't always remember what truly lay underneath. Nor did she particularly want to. Why fester in disillusion, bewilderment, and anger when she could float above and pretend to be this sunny, charming girl instead?

"And how are you today, Mrs. Needles?" she turned the questioning around. Given a choice, most people preferred to talk about themselves. "How's the hip?"

"So much better, ever since you gave me that joint-easing ointment."

"That's wonderful, but I can't take all the credit. Master Haywood helped me make it—he's always hovering about when I've a cauldron before me."

Or perhaps he'd locked himself in his room for an entire day, ignoring Iolanthe's knocks and the trays of food she'd left outside his door. But Mrs. Needles didn't need to know that.

No one needed to know that.

"Oh, he's lucky to have you, he is," said Mrs. Needles.

Iolanthe's cheer faltered a little—did she ever fool anyone, in the end? But she remained resolutely in character. "For running a few errands now and then, maybe. But there are far easier ways of getting chores done than raising an elemental mage for it."

They chuckled over that, Mrs. Needles good-naturedly, Iolanthe doggedly.

"Well, I brought you some lunch, miss." Mrs. Needles nudged the picnic basket closer to Iolanthe.

"Thank you, Mrs. Needles. And if you'd like to leave early today to get ready for the wedding, by all means, take as much time as you need."

That would get Mrs. Needles away from the house before Master Haywood awakened testy and disoriented from his merixida-induced stupor.

Mrs. Needles placed a hand over her heart. "That'd be nice! I do love a wedding, and I want to look my best in front of all those fancy city folks."

Rosie Oakbluff's wedding was to take place in Meadswell, the provincial capital sixty miles away. At the wedding, Iolanthe would light the path on which the bride and groom would walk arm in arm toward the altar. It was considered good luck for the lighting of the path to be performed by a friend of the bride rather than a hired elemental mage, and no one minded too much that Iolanthe was less a friend to the bride than someone trying to bribe the mother of the bride.

"I will see you at the wedding," she said to Mrs. Needles.

Mrs. Needles waved, then vaulted, leaving behind a faint distortion in the air that quickly cleared. Iolanthe checked her watch—quarter to one in the afternoon. She was running behind.

Not just for the wedding. She was at least half a term behind in her academic reading. Her clarifying potions kept failing. Every last spell from *Archival Magic* fought tooth and nail against her efforts at mastery.

And the first round of qualifying exams for upper academies began in five weeks.

Elemental magic was elder magic, a direct, primordial connection between the mage and the universe, needing no words or procedures as intermediaries. For millennia subtle magic had been the pale imitation, trying without coming close to matching the power and majesty of elemental magic.

But at some point the tide had turned. Now subtle magic possessed the depth and flexibility to suit every need, and elemental magic was its clunky, primitive country cousin, ill-adapted to the demands of modern life. Who needed fire-wielding elemental mages when lighting, heating, and cooking were all done with much safer, much more convenient flameless magic these days?

Without a sound education in subtle magic, elemental mages had pitifully few choices in careers: the circuses, the foundries, or the quarries, none of which appealed to Iolanthe. And without stellar results on the qualifying exams and the grants they'd bring, she would not be able to afford an upper academy education at all.

She checked her watch again. She'd run through her routine for the lighting of the path one more time, then she needed to check on the light elixir in the schoolroom.

A snap of her fingers brought a fresh sphere of fire five feet across. Another snap, the fireball doubled in diameter, a miniature sun rising against the steep, treeless cliffs of the opposite bank.

Fire was such a pleasure. *Power* was such a pleasure. Would that she could bend Master Haywood to her will just as easily. She laced her fingers, then yanked them apart. The fireball separated into sixteen trails of flame, darting through the air like a school of fish, taking fast turns in unison.

She clasped her palms together. The streams of fire formed again into a perfect sphere. A flick of her wrist had the fireball leap high in the air and spin, tossing out countless sparks. Now her hands pressed down, half submerging the fireball into the river, sending up a huge plume of hissing steam—there was a large reflecting pool at the wedding venue, and she planned to take full advantage of it.

"Stop," said a voice behind her. "Stop this moment."

She stilled in surprise. Master Haywood—he was up early. Dismissing the fire, she turned around.

He used to be a handsome man, her guardian, golden and fit. No more. Limp hair hung about his pale face. Bags drooped under his eyes. His thin frame—he sometimes reminded her of a marionette—looked as if it might rattle apart with the least exertion. It never *not* hurt to see him like this, a shadow of his former self.

But a part of her couldn't help being thrilled that he had come to watch her rehearse. He hadn't shown much interest in her in a long time. Perhaps she could also get him to help her on some of her coursework. He'd promised to homeschool her, but she'd had to teach herself, and she had so many unanswered questions.

But first, "Afternoon. Have you had anything to eat?"

He shouldn't have vaulted on an empty stomach.

"You cannot perform at the wedding," he said.

Her ears felt as if they'd been stung by bees. *This* was what he'd come to tell her? "I beg your pardon?"

"Rosie Oakbluff is marrying into a family of collaborators."

The Greymoors of Meadswell were rumored to have turned in more than a hundred rebels during and after the January Uprising. Everyone knew that. "Yes, she is."

"I did not realize," said Master Haywood. He leaned against a boulder, his face tired and tense. "I thought she was marrying a Grey*more*—from the clan of artists. Mrs. Needles corrected my mistake just now, and I cannot let agents of Atlantis see you manipulate the elements. They would take you away."

Her eyes widened. What was he talking about? If Atlantis had a special interest in elemental mages, wouldn't she have heard about it? Not a single elemental mage she knew had ever attracted Atlantis's attention simply by being an elemental mage. "Every circus has a dozen mages who can do what I do. Why should Atlantis pay any mind to me?"

"Because you are younger and have far more potential."

Two thousand years ago she would not have questioned him. Differences among realms then had been settled by wars of elemental magic. Good elemental mages had been highly prized, and great elemental mages, well, they'd been considered Angels incarnate. But that was two thousand years ago.

"Potential for what?"

"For greatness."

Iolanthe bit the inside of her lower lip. Merixida, in sufficient quantities, caused delusion and paranoia. But she'd always secretly adulterated Master Haywood's homemade distillate with sugar syrup. Did he have a stash somewhere she didn't know about? "I'd love to be a great elemental mage, but there hasn't been a single Great for the last five hundred years anywhere on earth. And you forget that I can't manipulate air—no one can be a Great without having control over all four elements."

Master Haywood shook his head. "That is not true."

"What is not true?"

He did not answer her question, but only said, "You must listen to me. You will be in great danger if Atlantis becomes aware of your power."

Iolanthe had volunteered to light the path at the wedding. She could only imagine what the bride's mother, Mrs. Oakbluff, would think were Iolanthe to suddenly announce, hours before the ceremony, that she had thought better of it.

Her pocket watch throbbed. "Excuse me. I need to take the light elixir out of the cauldron."

She'd also volunteered to take care of the wedding illumination. Silver light elixir was the current craze; but a light elixir that emitted a true silver light without any tinge of blue was both difficult and time-consuming to make—and once mature, radiated for precisely seven hours.

The entire enterprise was fraught with the possibility of failure. Iolanthe had started with five batches, and only one had survived the curing process. But the risk was worth it. The Oakbluffs wanted to show their much wealthier in-laws that they were capable of putting on an impressively elegant wedding, and a successful batch of silver light elixir went a long way toward achieving that goal.

Iolanthe vaulted, hoping Master Haywood wouldn't follow.

It was spring holiday; the schoolroom was empty of pupils and their usual clutter. The equipment for the practicals was located at the far end, underneath a portrait of the prince. She uncovered the biggest cauldron and gave its contents a stir. The elixir stuck to the spatula, thick and opaque like a sky about to rain. Perfect. Three hours of cooling and it should begin to radiate.

"Have you heard anything I said?" Master Haywood's voice again came behind her.

He didn't sound angry, only weary. Her heart pinched as she

unpacked the sterling ewer Mrs. Oakbluff had given her for the light elixir. She didn't know why, but she'd always felt a nagging suspicion that she was somehow responsible for his condition—a suspicion that went deeper than mere guilt at not being able to take care of him as she would like to. "You should eat something. Your headaches get worse when you don't eat on time."

"I don't need to eat. I need you to listen."

He rarely sounded parental these days—she couldn't remember the last time. She turned around. "I'm listening. But please remember, a claim as extraordinary as yours—that I'll be in danger from Atlantis by doing something as commonplace as lighting a wedding path—needs extraordinary proof."

He was the one who'd introduced her to the concept that extraordinary claims needed extraordinary proofs. Such a sponge she'd been, soaking up every one of his words, giddy and proud to be the closest thing to a daughter to this eloquent, erudite man.

That was before his mistakes and lies had cost him position after position, and the brilliant scholar once destined for greatness was now a village schoolmaster—one in danger of being sacked, at that.

He shook his head. "I don't need proof. All I need is to rescind my permission for you to go to Meadswell for the wedding."

The only reason she was going to Meadswell in the first place was to save his employment. Rumor was that parents who'd soured on his inattentiveness to their children were urging Mrs. Oakbluff, the village registrar, to dismiss him. Iolanthe hoped that by providing a spectacular lighting of the path, not to mention the silver light elixir, Mrs. Oakbluff might be persuaded to tilt her decision in Master Haywood's favor.

If even a remote village in desperate need of a schoolmaster wouldn't retain him, who would?

"You forget," she reminded him. "The laws are very clear that when a ward turns sixteen, she no longer needs her guardian's permission for her freedom of movement."

She could have left him more than six months ago.

He pulled a flask out of his pocket and took a gulp. The sickly sweet scent of merixida wafted to her nostrils. She pretended not to notice, when she'd have preferred to yank the bottle from his hand and throw it out of a window.

But they were no longer the kind of family whose members raged honestly at one another. Instead, they were strangers conducting themselves according to a peculiar set of rules: no reference to his addiction, no mention of the past, and no planning for any kind of a future.

"Then you will simply have to trust me," he said, his voice heavy. "We must keep you safe. We must keep you away from the eyes and ears of Atlantis. Will you trust me, Iola? Please."

She wanted to. After all his lies—*No, this is not match fixing. No, this is not plagiarism. No, these are not bribes*—she still wanted to trust him the way she once had, implicitly, completely.

"I'm sorry," she said. "I can't."

She'd never before acknowledged openly that she had only herself to rely on.

He recoiled and stared at her. Was he searching for the child who'd adored him unabashedly? Who would have followed him to the end of the world? That girl was still here, she wanted to tell him. If he would only pull himself together, she would gladly let him take care of her, for a change.

He bowed his head. "Forgive me, Iolanthe."

This was not an answer she'd expected. Her breath quickened. Did he really mean to apologize for everything that had led her to lose faith in him?

He moved all of a sudden, marching toward the cauldrons while unscrewing the cap of his flask.

"What are you—"

He poured all the merixida that remained in the flask into the light elixir on which she'd slaved for a fortnight. Then he turned around and pulled a mute, openmouthed Iolanthe into his arms and hugged her hard. "I have sworn to keep you safe, and I will."

By the time she comprehended what he'd done, he was already walking out of the schoolroom. "I will inform Mrs. Oakbluff that you will not be able to perform the lighting of the path this evening, because you are too ashamed that your light elixir failed."

Iolanthe stared at the ruined light elixir, a flat, mildew-green puddle without any hint of viscosity. Silver light elixir she'd promised Mrs.

Oakbluff, but silver light elixir could not be had for love or money at the last minute.

Despair swamped her, a bitter tide. Why did she try so hard? Why bother saving his post when no one else cared, least of all he himself?

But she was too accustomed to brushing aside her self-pity and dealing with the aftermath of Master Haywood's actions. Already she was at the bookshelves, pulling out titles that might help. *The Novice Potionmaker* did not deal with light elixirs. *The Quick Solution: A Classroom Handbook to Potionmaking Mistakes* provided only guidance for light elixirs that emitted a foul smell, solidified, or wouldn't stop fizzing. *The Potionmaster's Guide to Common and Uncommon Draughts* gave her a lengthy historical perspective and nothing else.

In desperation she turned to *The Complete Potion*.

Master Haywood loved *The Complete Potion*. She had no idea why—it was the world's most pretentious doorstop. In the section on light elixirs, beyond the introductory paragraphs, the text was in cuneiform.

She kept flipping the pages, hoping for something in Latin, which she read well, or Greek, which she could manage with a lexicon, if she had to. But the only passages not in cuneiform were in hieroglyphs.

Then, all of a sudden, in the margins, a handwritten note she could read: *There is no light elixir, however tainted, that cannot be revived by a thunderbolt.*

She blinked—and hastily tilted her head back: she had no idea there were tears in her eyes. And what kind of advice was this? Placing any elixir in a downpour would cause irreversible damage to the elixir, defeating any hope of repairing it.

Unless . . . unless the writer of the note had meant something else, a *summoned* thunderbolt.

Helgira the Merciless had wielded lightning.

But Helgira was a folkloric character. Iolanthe had read all four volumes and twelve hundred pages of *The Lives and Deeds of Great Elemental Mages*. No real elemental mage, not even any of the Greats, had ever mastered lightning.

*There is no light elixir, however tainted, that cannot be revived by a thunderbolt.*

The author of those words certainly had no doubt it could be done. The swirls and dashes of the penmanship brimmed with a jaunty confidence. As she looked up, however, the prince in his portrait expressed nothing but disdain for her wild idea.

She chewed on the inside of her cheek for a minute. Then she pulled on a pair of thick gloves and grabbed the cauldron.

What did she have to lose?

The prince was about to kiss Sleeping Beauty.

He was tattered and sweaty, still bleeding from the wound on his arm. She, his reward for battling the dragons that guarded her castle, was pristine and beautiful—if blandly so.

He walked toward her, his boots sinking ankle-deep in dust. All about the garret, in the gray light that filtered past the grime on the window, cobwebs hung as thick as theatrical curtains.

He was the one who had put the details in the room. It had mattered to him, when he was thirteen, that the interior of the garret accurately reflect a century's neglect. But now, three years later, he wished he had given Sleeping Beauty better dialogue instead.

If only he knew what he wanted a girl to say to him. Or vice versa.

He knelt down beside her bed.

"Your Highness," his valet's voice echoed upon the stone walls. "You asked to be awakened at this time."

As he thought, he had taken too long with the dragons. He sighed. "And they lived happily ever after."

The prince did not believe in happily-ever-after, but that was the password to exit the Crucible.

The fairy tale faded—Sleeping Beauty, garret, dust, and cobwebs. He closed his eyes before the nothingness. When he opened them again, he was back in his own chamber, sprawled on the bed, his hand atop a very old book of children's tales.

His head was groggy. His right arm throbbed where the wyvern's tail had sliced through. But the sensations of pain were only his mind playing tricks. Injuries sustained in the imaginary realm of the Crucible did not carry over to the real one.

He sat up. His canary, in its jeweled cage, chittered. He pushed off the bed and passed his fingers over the bars of the bird's prison. As he walked out to the balcony, he glanced at the grand, gilded clock in the corner of the chamber: fourteen minutes past two o'clock, the exact time mentioned in his mother's vision—and therefore always the time he asked to be awakened from his seeming naps.

In the real world, his home, built on a high spur of the Labyrinthine Mountains, was the most famous castle in all the mage realms, far grander and more beautiful than anything Sleeping Beauty ever occupied. The balcony commanded splendid views: ribbon-slender waterfalls cascading thousands of feet, blue foothills dotted by hundreds of snow-fed lakes, and in the distance, the fertile plains that were the breadbasket of his realm.

But he barely noticed the view. The balcony made him tense, for it was here, or so it had been foretold, that he would come into his destiny. The beginning of the end, for his prophesied role was that of a mentor, a stepping-stone—the one who did not survive to the end of the quest.

Behind him, his attendants gathered, feet shuffling, silk over-robes swishing.

"Would you care for some refreshments, sire?" said Giltbrace, the head attendant, his voice oily.

"No. Prepare for my departure."

"We thought Your Highness departed tomorrow morning."

"I changed my mind." Half his attendants were in Atlantis's pay. He inconvenienced them at every turn and changed his mind a great deal. It was necessary they believe him a capricious creature who cared for only himself. "Leave."

The attendants retreated to the edge of the balcony but kept watch. Outside of the prince's bedchamber and bath, he was almost always watched.

He scanned the horizon, waiting for—and dreading—this yet-to-transpire event that had already dictated the entire course of his life.

Iolanthe chose the top of Sunset Cliff, a rock face several miles east of Little Grind-on-Woe.

She and Master Haywood had been at the village for eight months, almost an entire academic year, yet the rugged terrain of the Midsouth March—deep gorges, precipitous slopes, and swift blue torrents—still took her breath away. For miles around, the village was the only outpost of civilization against an unbroken sweep of wild nature.

Atop Sunset Cliff, the highest point in the vicinity, the villagers had erected a flagpole to fly the standard of the Domain. The sapphire banner streamed in the wind, the silver phoenix at its center gleaming under the sun.

As Iolanthe knelt, her knee pressed into something cold and hard. Parting the grass around the base of the flagpole revealed a small bronze plaque set into the ground, bearing the inscription DUM SPIRO, SPERO.

"While I breathe, I hope," she murmured, translating to herself.

Then she noticed the date on the plaque, 3 April 1021. The day that saw Baroness Sorren's execution and Baron Wintervale's exile—events that marked the end of the January Uprising, the first and only time the subjects of the Domain had taken up arms against the de facto rule of Atlantis.

The flying of the banner was not in itself particularly remarkable—that, at least, Atlantis hadn't outlawed yet. But the plaque commemorating the rebellion was an act of defiance here in this little-known corner of the Domain.

She'd been six at the time of the uprising. Master Haywood had taken her and joined the exodus fleeing Delamer, the capital city. For weeks, they'd lived in a makeshift refugee camp on the far side of the Serpentine Hills. The grown-ups had whispered and fretted. The children had played with an almost frantic intensity.

The return to normalcy had been abrupt and strange. No one talked about the repairs at the Conservatory to replace damaged roofs and toppled statues. No one talked about *anything* that had happened.

The one time Iolanthe had run into a girl she'd met at the refugee camp, they'd waved awkwardly at each other and then turned away embarrassed, as if there had been something shameful in that interlude.

In the years since, Atlantis had tightened its grip on the Domain, cutting off contact with the outside world and extending its reach of power via a vast network of open collaborators and secret spies inside the realm.

From time to time, she heard rumors of trouble closer to home: the loss of an acquaintance's livelihood on suspicion of activities unfavorable to the interests of Atlantis, the disappearance of a classmate's relative into the Inquisitory, the sudden relocation of an entire family down the street to one of the more distant outlying islands of the Domain.

There were also rumors of a new rebellion brewing. Thankfully, Master Haywood showed no interest. Atlantis was like the weather, or the lay of the land. One didn't try to change anything; one coped, that was all.

She lowered and folded the banner, setting it aside to avoid damage. For a moment she wondered whether she could truly endanger herself by putting on a display of fire and water. No, she didn't believe it. During the first two years after Master Haywood had lost his professorship at the Conservatory, they'd lived next door to a family of small-time collaborators, and he had never objected to her showing fire tricks to the children.

She nudged the cauldron so that its metal belly was snug against the pole, the better to absorb the jolt of the lightning. Then she measured fifty big strides away from the pole, for safety.

Just in case.

That she was preparing for anything at all to happen amazed her. Yes, she was a fine elemental mage by current standards, but she was nothing compared to the Greats. What made her think she'd accomplish a feat unheard of except in legends?

She gazed up at the cloudless sky and took a deep breath. She could not say why, but she knew in her gut that the anonymous advice in *The Complete Potion* was correct. She only needed the lightning.

But how did one summon lightning?

"Lightning!" she shouted, jabbing her index finger skyward.

Nothing. Not that she'd expected anything on her first try, but still she was a little deflated. Perhaps visualization might help. She closed her eyes and pictured a bolt of sizzle connecting sky and earth.

Again nothing.

She pushed back the sleeves of her blouse and drew her wand from her pocket. Her heart pumped faster; she'd never before used her wand for elemental magic.

A wand was an amplifier of a mage's power; the greater the power, the greater the amplification. If she failed again, it would be a resounding failure. But if she should succeed . . .

Her hand trembled as she raised the wand to point it directly overhead. She inhaled as deeply as she could.

"Smite that cauldron, will you? I haven't got all day!"

The first gleam appeared extraordinarily high in the atmosphere, and seemingly a continent away. A line of white fire zipped across the arc of the sky, curving gracefully against that deep, cloudless blue.

It plummeted toward her—searing, bright death.

# CHAPTER · 2

A COLUMN OF PURE WHITE light, so distant it was barely more than a thread, so brilliant it nearly blinded the prince, burst into existence.

He stood mute and amazed for an entire minute before something kicked him hard in the chest, the realization that this was the very sign for which he had waited half his life.

His hand tightened into a fist: the prophecy had come true. He was not ready. He would never be ready.

But ready or not, he acted.

"Why do you look so awed?" He sneered at his attendants. "Are you yokels who have never seen a bolt of lightning in your lives?"

"But, sire—"

"Do not stand there. My departure does not ready itself." Then, to Giltbrace specifically, "I am going to my study. Make sure I am not disturbed."

"Yes, sire."

His attendants had learned to leave him alone when he wished it—they did not enjoy being sent to clean the palace guards' boots, haul kitchen slops, or rake out the stables.

He counted on their attention returning immediately to the burning sky. A glance backward told him that they were indeed again riveted to the extraordinary, endless lightning.

There were secret passages in the castle known only to the family. He was before the doors of his study in thirty seconds. Inside the study, he pulled out a tube from the center drawer of his desk and whistled into it. The sound would magnify as it traveled, eventually reaching his trusted steed in the stables.

Next he drew an heirloom field glass from its display case. The field glass pinpointed the location of anything that could be sighted within its range—and its range extended to not only every corner of the Domain but a hundred miles beyond in any direction.

His fingers shaking only slightly, he adjusted the knobs of the field glass to bring the lightning into sharper focus. It had struck far away, near the southern tip of the Labyrinthine Mountains.

He grabbed a pair of riding gloves and a saddlebag from the lower drawers of the desk and murmured the necessary words. The next instant he was sliding down a smooth stone chute at a near vertical angle, the acceleration so dizzying he might as well be in free fall.

He braced himself. Still, the impact of slamming onto Marble's waiting back was like running into a wall. He swallowed a grunt of pain and groped in the dark for the handles mounted on the old girl's shoulders. With his knees he nudged her forward.

They were at the mouth of a hidden expedited way cut into the mountain. The moment the invisible boundary was crossed, they hurtled through a tunnel twelve feet in diameter—barely wide enough for Marble to fit through with her wings folded.

The darkness was complete; the air pressed heavy and damp against his skin. They shot upward, so fast his eardrums popped and popped again. Then, a pinprick of light, which grew swiftly into a flood of sunshine, and they were out in the open, above an uninhabited peak well away from the castle.

Marble opened her great wings and slid into a long swoop. The prince closed his eyes and called to mind what he had seen in the field glass: a village as ordinary as a sparrow, and about as small.

It would have been preferable to vault alone. But vaulting such a great distance on visual cue, rather than personal memory, was an imprecise business. And he did not have the luxury of proceeding on foot once he reached his destination.

He leaned forward and whispered into Marble's ear.

They vaulted.


Iolanthe was flat on her back, blind, her face burning, her ears ringing like the bells on New Year's Eve.

She must still be alive then. Groaning, she rolled over, pushed onto her knees, and clamped her hands over her ears.

After a while, she opened her eyes to a fuzzy spread of green cloth—her skirt. She raised her head a little and looked at her hand, which slowly swam into focus. There was a scratch but no blood. She sighed in relief. She'd feared that her ears had bled and that she'd find bits of brain on her palm.

But the grass around her was brown. Strange, the moor atop the cliff had recently turned a boisterous green with the arrival of spring. Her gaze followed the expanse of withered grass and—

The flagpole had disappeared. Where it once stood, black smoke rose from an equally black pit.

She struggled to her feet, stuck her wand back into her pocket, and tottered toward the crater, feeling as if her legs were made of mush. The smoke made her eyes water. Grass, dry as tinder, crunched beneath the soles of her boots.

The crater was ten feet wide and as deep as she was tall; the flagpole lay drunkenly across the top. This was mad. When the lightning struck, its electrical charge should have safely dissipated into the ground.

Then she spied the cauldron, sitting upright at the very bottom of the crater, filled with the most beautiful elixir she'd ever seen, like distilled starlight.

A laugh tore from her throat. For once, Fortune had smiled upon her. The wedding illumination would be perfect. Her performance would be perfect—oh, she was going to perform, all right. And Mrs. Oakbluff just might forgive Master Haywood for the prank he'd pulled on her, telling her—ha!—that there would be no silver light elixir for her daughter's wedding.

A whoosh overhead made her look up. A winged beast, something of a cross between a dragon and a horse, shot past her. It had come from the north, flying with astonishing speed toward the coast. But as she watched, its wings flapped vertically to reduce its forward momentum.

Then it swung around to face her.

The prince could not believe his eyes.

He had vaulted quite close to where the lightning had actually struck, but Marble had flown by too fast for him to get a good look at the mage atop the blackened cliff. But now that he had turned Marble around . . .

The long dark hair, half of it standing up from electrical shock, the ruffled white blouse, the green skirt. There was no mistaking it: the elemental mage who had brought down lightning was a girl.

A girl.

Archer Fairfax could not be a girl. What in the blazes was he to do with a girl?

The next moment the girl was no longer alone. A man in a black robe materialized and sprinted toward her.

Iolanthe stared at the winged beast. It was iridescent blue, with sharp, barely branched antlers on its equine head and a spiked, crimson-tipped tail.

A Barbary Coast peryton.

They were very fashionable in the cities, but not in the hinterlands. What was one doing here, immediately after she'd summoned a bolt of lightning?

"What have you done?"

Master Haywood! His black schoolmaster's robe billowed behind him as he raced toward her.

"I repaired the light elixir," she said. "And you don't need to worry about the crater, I'll take care of it—and put the flagpole back where it belongs."

She commanded earth, too, if not quite as well as she commanded fire and water—and lightning.

"My goodness, what happened here?" Mrs. Greenfield, a villager, also appeared. "Are you all right, Miss Iolanthe? You look a fright."

Master Haywood drew his wand, yanked Iolanthe behind him, and pointed the wand at Mrs. Greenfield.

"*Obliviscere!*" he shouted. "*Obliviscere! Obliviscere!*"

*Obliviscere* was the most powerful spell of forgetfulness—and illegal for mages without a medical license to use. Mrs. Greenfield would lose six months, if not a year, of memories.

"What are you doing?" Iolanthe cried.

Mrs. Greenfield dropped to her knees and vomited. Iolanthe started toward her. Master Haywood caught Iolanthe's sleeve. "You come with me."

"But Mrs.—"

He had a death grip on her arm. "You come with me this moment if you want to live!"

"What?"

They both startled at the sound of wings beating above—the peryton. It carried a rider. She squinted for a better look. But the next moment, she was looking at her own front door.

Master Haywood shoved her inside. She stumbled.

Mrs. Needles poked her head into the vestibule. "Master Haywood, Miss Seabourne—"

"Get out!" Master Haywood bellowed. "Leave this instant."

"I beg your—"

Master Haywood pushed Mrs. Needles out of the house and slammed the door shut. He dragged Iolanthe into the parlor and pointed his wand at the ceiling. The tip of the wand shook.

She swallowed. "Tell me what is going on!"

A satchel fell from nowhere into his arms. "I already told you. Atlantis is coming after you."

From the open windows came the sound of the peryton's wing beats. The hairs on the back of Iolanthe's neck stood up.

"What should I do?" she asked, her voice barely above a whisper, her hand clenched about her wand.

A loud knock struck the front door. She jumped.

"Master Haywood, open the door this minute!" The voice belonged to Mrs. Oakbluff, who also served as the village constable. "You are under arrest for the assault on Mrs. Greenfield, as witnessed by Mr. Greenfield and myself. Miss Seabourne, you come with me too."

Master Haywood thrust the satchel into Iolanthe's arms. "Ignore her. You need to leave."

She hurried after him. The satchel was heavy. "What's in the bag?"

"I don't know. I've never opened it."

*Why not?*

In a corner of his bedchamber stood a large trunk, which had followed them through many moves. As he unlocked the trunk and lifted the lid, she saw its inside for the first time. It was completely empty—a portal trunk. "Where am I going?"

"I don't know that either."

Her stomach twisted. "What *do* you know?"

"That you have put yourself in terrible danger." He closed his eyes briefly. "Now get inside."

The house exploded. Walls caved; debris hurtled. She screamed, threw herself down, and shielded her head with the satchel. Chunks of brick and plaster pummeled her everywhere else.

When the chaos had died down a little, she looked around for Master Haywood. He was flat on the floor among the wreckage, bleeding from a head wound. She rushed to his side.

"Are you all right, Master Haywood? Can you hear me?"

His eyelids fluttered open. He looked at her, his gaze unfocused.

"It's me, Iolanthe. Are you all right?"

"Why are you still here?" he shouted, struggling to his feet. "Get in the trunk! Get in!"

He grabbed the satchel from her and tossed it into the trunk. She took a deep breath and hauled herself over the trunk's high sides. He pulled on the lid. She held it open with the palm of her hand. "Wait, aren't you coming w—"

He crumpled to the floor.

"Master Haywood!"

Through the chalky air, a matronly figure advanced. Mrs. Oakbluff waved her wand. Master Haywood's inert body went flying, landing with a thud in the next room and missing being impaled upon a broken beam by mere inches.

Mrs. Oakbluff came at Iolanthe.

Where had they vaulted?

The village was not big, but it still had some forty, fifty dwellings of varying sizes. The villagers stopped what they were doing to gawk at Marble, her shadow gliding on rooftops and cobbled streets like a harbinger of doom.

The prince assessed the situation. Were he the father or the guardian—who obviously understood the implications of what the girl had done—would he have already gone on the run? Unlikely. He would want to return to their home nearby, where he had a bag packed for just such an emergency and a swift means to safety.

But where was home?

The prince had zoomed past the small house that sat apart from the rest of the village when a movement caught his eye. He turned his head, hoping it was the man and the girl rematerializing. Only one mage, however, stood before the house—not the long-haired girl, but a squat woman.

Disappointed, he continued his search. Only to see, a minute later, the same house shaking violently before collapsing on itself.

He reined Marble as close to a full stop as he dared and vaulted for the now crooked front steps of the house.

"What are you doing?" Iolanthe wanted to shout in indignation, but her voice was barely above a whimper.

"Impressive, isn't it?" Mrs. Oakbluff smiled, but her square face was without its usual rustic goodwill. "Did you know I once worked in demolition?"

"You destroyed our house because I damaged the flagpole?"

"No, because you resisted arrest. And I need the credit for your arrest, young lady—I've been in this wretched place too long."

Credit for *her* arrest, not Master Haywood's. Mrs. Oakbluff, soon-to-be in-law of Atlantis's staunchest collaborators in all of Midsouth March, clearly believed seizing Iolanthe would bring her special rewards.

The fear that had been welling up in Iolanthe suddenly boiled over. She yanked on the lid of the trunk, but it refused to lower.

"Oh, no, I'm not letting you go so easily," said Mrs. Oakbluff.

She raised her wand toward Iolanthe. Without thinking, Iolanthe reacted. A wall of fire roared toward Mrs. Oakbluff.

The prince first secured the house with an impassable circle to keep out other intruders. The front door still stood more or less intact, but the wall around it had crumbled. He stepped over the debris strewn across the vestibule, and barely had time to duck as a tongue of fire roared in his direction.

But the fire did not reach him. Instead it pivoted midair and shot back where it had come from. He followed it toward the back of the house and stopped in his tracks.

A dozen trails of hissing, crackling flames, vicious as serpents, attacked the housebreaker, who frantically shouted shielding charms. The girl, now covered in plaster dust, stood in a tall trunk, her arms waving, her face a scowl of concentration.

Some of the housebreaker's shielding charms took. Behind their barricade, she pointed her wand at the girl.

The prince raised his own wand. The housebreaker fell to the broken floor. The girl gawked at him a moment, raised both hands, and pushed them out. Fire hurtled toward him.

"*Fiat praesidium!*" The air before him hardened to take the brunt of the fire. "Recall your flames. I am not here to harm you."

"Then leave."

With a turn of her wrists, the wall of flame reconfigured into a battering ram.

Good thing he had fought so many dragons. *"Aura circumvallet."*

Air closed around the fire. She waved her hands, trying to make her fire obey her, but it remained contained.

She snapped her finger to call forth more fire.

*"Omnis ignis unus,"* he murmured. *All fire is one fire.*

The new burst of flame she wanted materialized *inside* the prison he had already made.

He approached the trunk. Sunlight slanted through the broken walls into the room, sparkling where it caught specks of plaster in the air. One particular ray lit a thin streak of blood at her temple.

She yanked at the trunk lid. He set his own hand against it. "I am not here to harm you," he repeated. "Come with me. I will get you to safety."

She glowered. "Come with you? I don't even know who . . ."

Her voice trailed off; her head jerked with recognition. He was Titus VII, the Master of the Domain.[2] His profile adorned the coins of the realm. His portraits hung in schools and public buildings — even though he was not yet of age and would not rule in his own right for another seventeen months.

"Your Highness, forgive my discourtesy." Her hand loosened its grip on the trunk's lid; her gaze, however, remained on guard. "Are you here at Atlantis's behest?"

So she knew from which quarter danger came. "No," he answered. "The Inquisitor would have to step over my dead body to get to you."

The girl swallowed. "The *Inquisitor* wants me?"

"Badly."

"Why?"

"I will tell you later. We need to go."

"Where?"

He appreciated her wariness: better wary than naive. But this was no time for detailed answers. Each passing second diminished their chances of getting out unseen.

"The mountains, for now. Tomorrow I will take you out of the Domain."

"But I can't leave my guardian behind. He—"

Too late. Overhead Marble emitted a high, keening call: she had sighted the Inquisitor. He untwisted the pendant he wore around his neck and pressed its lower half into her hand.

"I will find you. Now go."

"But what about Master—"

He pushed her down and slammed the trunk shut.

The moment the trunk closed, its bottom dropped out from underneath Iolanthe. She fell into utter darkness, flailing.

# CHAPTER · 3

THERE WAS NO TIME TO bring down Marble. Titus had two choices: he could let the Inquisitor see Marble, catch her, and realize that Titus's personal steed was loose in the vicinity; or he could vault onto the beast, with the latter in midflight.

It was stupid to vault onto a moving object. It was suicidal when the moving object was two hundred feet in the air. But if his presence was to be deduced no matter what, then he preferred to be caught flying, which would allow him to claim that he had never set foot on the ground.

He sighted Marble, sucked in a deep breath, and vaulted where he hoped she would be.

He rematerialized in thin air, with nothing under him. His heart stopped. A fraction of a second later, he crashed onto something hard—Marble's back. Relief tore through him. But there was no time to indulge in the shaking exhaustion of having cheated death. He was too far aft. Shouting at Marble to keep steady, he scrambled forward along her smooth spine, even as he pointed his wand at the house to erase the impassable circle.

Already there had been a cluster of villagers gathered outside the circle, discussing among themselves whether they ought to go in. The removal of the circle lifted all such inhibitions. The villagers rushed into the house.

Titus had no sooner grabbed the reins than the Inquisitor and her entourage arrived. A moment later, her second in command raised a formal hail.

Titus took his time descending, applying miscellaneous cleaning spells to his person as he did so: it would defeat the purpose of his stunt to appear before the Inquisitor with the detritus of the house still clinging to him.

There was an open field behind the house. Marble's wings swept close to the ground, forcing the Inquisitor's retainers to throw themselves down, lest they be impaled by the spikes that protruded from the front of those wings—natural spikes that Titus's grooms had polished into stiletto-sharp points.

Marble was now on her feet, but Titus did not dismount: the Inquisitor, in a deliberate slight, was not yet present to receive him. He took out two apples from the saddlebag, tossed one to Marble, and took a bite of the other. His heart, which had not yet slowed to normal, began to beat faster again.

The Inquisitor was an extractor of secrets, and he had too many of them.

Out of the corner of his eye, he saw the Inquisitor emerge from the rear door of the house. Marble hissed—of course a beast as intelligent as Marble would hate the Inquisitor. Titus kept on eating the apple—at a leisurely pace—and dismounted only after he tossed aside the core.

The Inquisitor bowed.

Appearances were still kept—Atlantis enjoyed pretending that it was not a tyrant, but merely first among equals. Therefore Titus, despite not having a dram of real power, reigned nevertheless as the Master of the Domain; and the Inquisitor, a representative of Atlantis, was officially of no more importance than any other ambassador from any other realm.

"Madam Inquisitor, an unexpected pleasure," he addressed her.

His palms perspired, but he kept his tone haughty. His was a lineage that stretched back a thousand years to Titus the Great, unifier of the Domain and one of the greatest mages to ever wield a wand. The Inquisitor's parents had been, if he was not mistaken, traders of antique goods—and not necessarily genuine ones.

Ancestry was an indicator of little importance when it came to a mage's individual abilities—archmages often came from families of otherwise middling accomplishment. But ancestry mattered to the average mage, and it especially mattered to the Inquisitor, though she was no average mage. Titus reminded her as often as he could that he was a vain, self-important boy who would have been nothing and no one had he not been born into the once-illustrious House of Elberon.

"Unexpected indeed, Your Highness," replied the Inquisitor.

"The Midsouth March is remote from your usual haunts."

She was in her early forties, pale, with thin, red lips, almost invisible eyebrows, and eerily colorless eyes. He had first received her at age eight and had been frightened of her ever since.

He forced himself to hold her gaze. "I saw the sustained lightning from the castle and had to have a look, naturally."

"You arrived fast. How did you locate the precise spot of the lightning so quickly?"

Her tone was even, but her eyes bore into his. He blamed his mother. By all means the Inquisitor should believe in Titus's frivolousness, but for the fact that the late Princess Ariadne too had once been deemed docile—and had proved anything but.

"My grandfather's field glass, of course."

"Of course," said the Inquisitor. "Your Highness's vaulting range is commendable."

"It runs in the family, but you are correct that mine is particularly extensive."

His immodest self-congratulation brought a twitch to the Inquisitor's face. Fortunately for him, the ability to vault was considered analogous to the ability to sing: a talent that had no bearing on a mage's capacity for subtle magic.

"What do you think of the person who brought down the lightning bolt?" asked the Inquisitor.

"A person brought down the lightning?" He rolled his eyes. "Have you been reading too many children's tales?"

"It is elemental magic, Your Highness."

"Rubbish. The elements are fire, air, water, and earth. Lightning is none of them."

"One could say lightning is the marriage of fire and air."

"One could say mud is the marriage of water and earth," he said dismissively.

The Inquisitor's jaw tightened. A bead of sweat rolled down Titus's back. He played a perilous game. There was a fine line between irritating the Inquisitor and angering her outright.

He set his tone slightly less pompous. "And what is Atlantis's interest in all this, Madam Inquisitor?"

"Atlantis is interested in all unusual phenomena, Your Highness."

"What have your people discovered about this unusual phenomenon?"

The Inquisitor had come out of the house. So she would have seen the interior already.

"Not very much."

He began to walk toward the house.

"Your Highness, I advise against it. The house is structurally unstable."

"If it is not too unstable for you, it is not too unstable for me," he said blithely.

Besides, he had no choice. In his earlier hurry to get out, he had not had time to remove all traces he might have left behind. He must go back in and walk about, in case his previous set of boot prints had not been sufficiently trampled by the villagers.

The January Uprising had failed for many different reasons, not the least of which was that its leaders had not been nearly meticulous enough. He could not afford to make the same mistakes.

The Inquisitor in tow, he strolled through the house. Except for the number of books, there was nothing remarkable about it. The Inquisitor's agents swarmed, checking walls and floors, pulling open drawers and cabinets. Nearly half a dozen agents crowded around the trunk, which, thankfully, seemed to be a one-time portal that kept its destination to itself.

On the front lawn, guarded by more agents, the girl's guardian and the housebreaker were laid out, both still unconscious.

"Are they dead?" he asked.

"No, they are both very much alive."

"They need medical attention, in that case."

"Which they will receive in due time—at the Inquisitory."

"They are *my* subjects. Why are they being taken to the Inquisitory?"

He made sure he sounded peevish, concerned not so much about his subjects but about his own lack of power.

"We merely wish to question them, Your Highness. Representatives of the Crown are welcome at any time to see them while they remain in our care," said the Inquisitor.

No representatives of the Crown had been allowed into the Inquisitory in a decade.

"And may I call on you this evening, Your Highness," continued the Inquisitor, "to discuss what you have seen?"

Another drop of sweat crept down Titus's spine. So she did suspect him—of *something*.

"I have already mentioned everything I saw. Besides, my holidays have ended. I return to school later today."

"I thought you weren't leaving until tomorrow morning."

"And *I* thought I was quite at liberty to come and go as I wish, as I am the master of all I survey," he snapped.

They were there in her eyes, the atrocities she wanted to commit, to reduce him to a witless imbecile.

She would not. The pleasure she would derive from destroying him was not worth the trouble it would incite, given that he was, after all, the Master of the Domain.

Or so Titus told himself.

The Inquisitor smiled. He hated her smiles almost more than her stares.

"Of course you may shape your itinerary as you wish, Your Highness," she said.

He had been let go. He tried not to exhale too loudly in relief.

When they were once again on the field behind the house, she bowed. He remounted Marble. Marble spread her wings and pushed off the ground.

But even after they were airborne, he still felt the Inquisitor's unwavering gaze on his back.

This was no instantaneous transportation. Iolanthe kept dropping. She screamed for a while and stopped when she realized that no air rushed past her to indicate speed. She might as well have been suspended in place, only thinking that she was falling because there was nothing underneath her.

Suddenly there was. She thudded onto her bottom and grunted with the skeleton-jarring impact.

It remained pitch-black. Her hands touched soft things that smelled of dust and faded lavender—folded clothes. Digging beneath the clothes, she found a lining of smooth, stretched leather. The solid material under the leather was probably wood. Wary of making any unnecessary sounds, she did not knock to find out.

She continued to explore her new surroundings. Action kept fear—and jumbled emotions—at bay. If she tried to make sense of the events of the afternoon, she might howl in bewilderment. And if she thought about Master Haywood, she'd crumble from panic. Or pure guilt.

He had not been deluded by merixida. He had not even exaggerated. And she had chosen not to believe him.

Leather-covered walls rose shoulder-height about her, ending in a padded, tufted leather ceiling: she was inside another trunk.

The trunk seemed tightly closed. She decided to risk a flicker of fire. It shed a dim, coppery light that illuminated a sturdy latch below the seam of the lid.

The implication of the latch was discomfiting: it was for her to keep the trunk shut. To either side of the latch was a round disc of wood, one marked with an eye, the other, an ear. Reconnoitering was clearly recommended.

She extinguished the fire in her palm—its light might give her away—and felt for the discs.

The first one she found was the ear hole, which conveyed only silence. She moved to the peephole but likewise saw nothing. The room that contained her trunk was as dark as the bottom of the ocean, without even the telltale nimbus of light around a curtained window.

Wherever she was, she seemed to be completely alone. She found and released the latch. Placing her palms against the lid of the trunk, she applied a gentle pressure.

The lid moved a fraction of an inch and stopped. She pushed harder and heard a metallic scrape, but the lid did not lift any higher. Frowning, she put the latch back and tried again. This time, the lid moved not at all. So the latch in place prevented the trunk from opening. What had caused the trunk to open only a crack *after* the latch had been released?

The tips of her fingers turned cold. The trunk was secured *from the outside*.

A second vault in such a short time unsettled even a steed as disciplined as Marble. She screeched as they materialized above the

Labyrinthine Mountains, her eyes shut tight in distress. Titus had to yank the reins with all his strength to avoid crashing into a peak that suddenly reared in their path—the constant motion of the mountains meant that even one as familiar with them as he must always take care.

"Shhhhhh," he murmured, his own heart pounding hard at the near miss. "Shhhhh, old girl. It is all right."

He guided her higher, clear of any summits that might decide to sprout additional spurs. She obeyed his commands, her prodigious muscles contracting with each rise of her wings.

Beneath him, the Domain stretched in all directions, the Labyrinthine Mountains bisecting the island like the plated spine ridge of a prehistoric monster. To either side of the great mountain range, the countryside was a fresh, luminous green dotted by the pinks and creams of orchards in bloom.

*You are the steward of this land and its people now, Titus,* Prince Gaius, his grandfather, had said on his deathbed. *Do not fail them as I did. Do not fail your mother as I did.*

Had he known then what he knew now, he would have told the old bastard, *You chose to put your own interests above that of this land and its people. You chose to fail my mother. I hope you suffer long and hard where you are going.*

Quite the family, the House of Elberon.

Since the Inquisitor already knew he had visited the location of the lightning strike, there was no more need to be stealthy. As the castle came into sight, he wheeled Marble directly toward the landing arch at the top.

Marble cried plaintively at his dismount. He gave the rubbery skin of her wing a quick caress. "I will have the grooms take you for more exercise. Go now, my love."

Strong winds buffeted the pinnacle of the castle. Titus fought his way inside and sprinted down two flights of stairs into his apartment.

He greeted the usual huddle of attendants with a snarled, "Am I ready to depart yet?" and waved away those still foolhardy enough to follow him.

The apartment was vast. Even with the aid of secret passages, it still took him another minute to emerge in the globe room, where a representation of the Earth, fourteen feet across, hovered in midair.

With a swish of his wand, doors shut, drapes drew, and a dense fog rose from the floor. Only the air between the globe and his person remained transparent. Carefully, he touched the half pendant he still wore to the globe. His fingers brushed against something hot and grainy—the Kalahari Desert, probably.

A pulse passed between the pendant and the globe. He drew back and looked up. A bright red dot appeared on the globe, a thousand miles east northeast of where he stood—and very much in the middle of a nonmage realm.

To limit the influence of Exiles,[3] Atlantis had placed a chokehold on travel between mage realms and nonmage realms. Most portals would have been rendered useless. The girl's trunk must employ startlingly unusual magic—or someone had made sure a loophole had been left open for it.

She could have been taken anywhere. But Fortune smiled upon him today, and her current location was within twenty-five miles of his school. With luck, he would find her in the next hour.

Waving away the fog, he summoned Dalbert, his valet and personal spymaster. He must leave immediately, before the Inquisitor put more agents on his tail.

"Your Highness." Dalbert appeared at the door, a middle-aged man whose round, pleasant face hid a ferocious talent for intelligence gathering.

He had supplied facts and rumors to Titus in a timely and discreet manner for the past eight years, keeping his master apprised of everything that went on in the Domain and around the world while looking after Titus's personal comforts. The prince, however, had never taken Dalbert into his confidence.

"There is a train getting into Slough in twenty minutes. I plan to be on it. Make it happen."

"Yes, sire. And, sire, Prince Alectus and Lady Callista await below. They request an audience with Your Highness."

The regent and his mistress resided in Delamer, the capital, and rarely called upon Titus's mountain keep.

Titus swore under his breath. "Show them into the throne room—and have Woodkin exercise Marble."

Dalbert hurried off. Titus took himself two levels below, shrugging into a day coat as he went. He rarely entered the throne room except on the most public of occasions—it was ridiculous for him, essentially a puppet, to be in a room meant to symbolize the justness and might of his position. But today he wished to get rid of his visitors fast, and the throne room discouraged small talk.

The ceiling of the throne room rose fifty feet on two rows of white marble pillars. The obsidian throne was set upon a waist-high dais. Titus walked past it to the arched windows. Beneath him was a drop of a thousand feet to a ravine cut by a blue, glacier-fed river. Beyond, purple peaks shifted like slow waves.

Alectus and Lady Callista appeared on two of the four low pedestals that transported audience seekers from the reception room to the throne room.

Alectus was the youngest brother of Titus's grandfather, a handsome, morally flexible man of fifty-eight. Lady Callista was a beauty witch—the greatest beauty witch of her generation. Of the last three hundred years, it had been argued.[4]

She was on the brink of forty. Unlike many other beauty witches, she had not resorted to questionable magic to keep herself looking half her age. Instead, she had aged gracefully, allowing a few wrinkles to spread here and there while maintaining her sway over legions of hearts.

Ever since Alectus had been appointed regent, she had been his mistress. Some whispered that Alectus had even proposed to her, but she had declined. She was the capital's leading hostess, its arbiter of style, a generous patron of the arts—and an agent of Atlantis.

Alectus bowed. Lady Callista curtsied.

"To what do I owe the pleasure of this visit?" asked Titus, offering neither seats nor refreshment.

His bluntness surprised Alectus, who looked toward his mistress: Alectus had no appetite for confrontation, or any kind of unpleasantness.

Lady Callista smiled. It was said that to this day, love letters arrived for her by the wheelbarrowful. There was a great deal of skill in her smile, a smile meant to make a boy who had done nothing with his life feel accomplished and remarkable—virile, even.

Titus felt only revulsion—she was most likely the one who had betrayed his mother, informing the Inquisitor of the latter's secret participation in the January Uprising.

"We received a note from the Inquisitor," she said, her voice a dulcet murmur. "Her Excellency is concerned that she doesn't see enough of you. She's quite fond of you, Your Highness."

Titus rolled his eyes. "She is getting above herself. What do I care whether she is fond of me? She was a nobody before the Bane plucked her out of obscurity."

"But now she is the Inquisitor, and can cause much unpleasantness."

"Why would she do that? Does she wish to incite a new uprising?"

At the word "uprising," Lady Callista's smile faltered slightly, but she was quickly all warmth and concern again. "Your Highness, of course she does not want that. Once you come of age, the two of you will see a great deal of each other. She hopes for a respectful, productive, and mutually beneficial association."

"I appreciate your diplomacy," he said, "but there is no use gilding a turd. I cannot stand that upstart, and she is jealous and resentful of me. Save me the time and tell me what she really wants."

Alectus choked at Titus's language. Alectus never had problems being deferential to the Inquisitor. He was ill suited to wield power himself, but he yearned toward it as a vine reaches for a higher branch. And parasite that he was, he was probably happier the more powers the Inquisitor concentrated onto herself.

Lady Callista's next smile was strained. Had the Inquisitor been nasty to her? Usually Lady Callista's smiles were entirely effortless.

"The Inquisitor would like to speak to you about what you saw this afternoon."

"I saw nothing—I already told her."

"Nevertheless, she believes that with her help, you might remember more."

"Will I still be continent when I emerge from her 'help'?" The Inquisitor's methods were widely feared.

"I'm sure she would treat you with utmost courtesy and consideration, sire."

Titus assessed his situation. He must leave without delay. Yet the Inquisitor must also be placated somehow.

"Your spring gala is to take place in a few days. I will attend as the guest of honor. You may invite the Inquisitor. I will grant her a brief audience during the course of the evening."

He made appearances at various state and charitable functions during the year, usually those involving children and young people. A gala was not quite the same thing, but he would stir curiosity, not controversy.

Lady Callista opened her mouth. Titus preempted her. "I trust you are grateful that I will take the trouble."

It was time she remembered that he was still her sovereign.

"Of course," she murmured, conjuring another smile.

Now they were down to mere formalities before he dismissed them. "Is there anything else that requires my attention?"

"My choice of a new overrobe for the gala," said Alectus, jolly now that his task had been discharged by his mistress. "I cannot make up my mind, and Lady Callista claims to be far too busy."

"Thousands of details need to be seen to before the gala," said Lady Callista, in her you-silly-man-but-of-course-I-love-you-madly tone.

"Close your eyes and make a random selection," Titus said, forcing himself not to sound too impatient.

"Indeed, indeed," Alectus agreed, "as good a method as any."

"I wish you both a good day," said Titus, his jaw hurting with the strain of remaining civil.

Alectus bowed. Lady Callista curtsied. They stepped on the

pedestals and disappeared to the reception room below.

Titus let out a breath. He glanced at his watch: still ten minutes to make the train.

But Lady Callista reappeared, looking suitably apologetic. "I beg your pardon, sire, I seem to have left my fan behind. Ah, there it is."

What did she want *now*?

"Do you know what curious news I just heard, sire?" she asked. "That by the bolt of lightning you saw, a great elemental mage has revealed herself—a girl of about your age."

Of course she would ask him about the girl—what good minion of the Inquisitor's would not? He acted bored. "Should I care?"

"She could be very important, this girl."

"To whom?"

"Atlantis does not expend its wherewithal on needless concerns. If the Inquisitor is after the girl, she must be valuable in some way."

"And why are you telling me this, my lady?"

Lady Callista approached him and placed a hand on his arm. This close she smelled of the subtle yet potent fragrance of narcissus. "Does it not concern you, sire, that the Inquisitor is halfway to finding this possibly very significant young woman?"

Very few of his subjects touched him without express permission. Lady Callista dared take the liberty because she had once been Princess Ariadne's dearest friend. Her touch was warm and maternal, her person present and interested in a way that his perpetually preoccupied mother had never been.

Titus yanked away. "Madam, if you seek someone to stand up to the Inquisitor, you are looking at quite the wrong man. I am the heir of a princely house well past its hour of glory. That is burden enough. I am not going to spearhead some quixotic cause for which I have neither the desire nor the talent."

Lady Callista laughed softly. "Don't be silly, sire. I'm looking for nothing of the sort. My goodness, why should I want anything to destabilize the current situation, which favors me so?"

She walked backward until she was on the pedestal and curtsied again. "However, should you ever decide to spearhead a quixotic cause, sire, you must let me know. Stability does grow tedious after a while."

CHAPTER·4

A CURIOUS VEHICLE OCCUPIED THE highest garret of the castle: a black-lacquered private rail coach. Inside, the walls of the coach were covered in sky-blue silk. A pair of padded chairs were upholstered in cream brocade. A porcelain tea service, with steam curling from the spout of the teapot, sat on a side table.

Canary cage in hand, Titus entered the rail coach, the link to his other life. He could almost smell the coal burning at the heart of the yet-distant steam engine, feel the rumble of the wheels on the tracks.

Dalbert brought his luggage, then closed the door of the coach. "Something to drink for the journey, sire?"

"Thank you, but hardly necessary."

Dalbert glanced at his watch. "Brace yourself, sire."

He pulled a large lever. The coach shook. The next moment it was no longer in placid storage in the castle's uppermost reach, but a thousand miles away on English soil, part of a train that had departed from Mansion House station, London, three quarters of an hour before.

"Slough in five minutes, sire."

"Thank you, Dalbert."

Titus rose from his seat to stand before the window. Outside it drizzled—another wet English spring. The land was green and foggy, the train's motions rhythmic, almost hypnotic.

How strange that when he had first arrived in this nonmage realm, he had hated everything about it—the sooty, offensive smells, the flavorless food, the inexplicable customs. Yet now, after nearly four years at his nonmage school, this world had become a refuge, a place to escape, as far as escape was possible, from the oppression of Atlantis.

And the oppression of his destiny.

Two shrill steam blasts announced the train's arrival in Slough. Dalbert pulled down the window shades and handed Titus his satchel.

"May Fortune walk with you, sire."

"May Fortune heed your wish," replied Titus.

Dalbert bowed. Titus inclined his head—and vaulted.

None of the opening spells Iolanthe knew worked. She did not have power over wood. Water was useless here, as was fire. She could keep herself safe from fire, but were she to set the trunk aflame, either from inside or outside, she'd still succumb to smoke inhalation.

Unless someone freed her, she was stuck.

She didn't often give in to panic, but she could feel hysteria rising in her lungs, squeezing out air, squeezing out everything but the need to start screaming and never stop.

She forced her mind to go blank instead, to breathe slowly and try for a measure of calm.

*The* Inquisitor *wants me?*

*Badly.*

The Inquisitor was the Bane's de facto viceroy to the Domain. Once, when Iolanthe had been much younger, she'd asked Master Haywood why mages were so afraid of the Inquisitor. His answer she'd never forgotten: *Because sometimes fear is the only appropriate response.*

She shuddered. If only she'd listened to Master Haywood. Then the light elixir would have been safe—and she'd never have brought down the lightning.

She dropped her face into her hands. Something cold and heavy pressed into the space between her brows: the pendant the prince had given her before he shoved her on her way.

A new smidgen of fire revealed the pendant to be a half oval made of a gleaming silver-white metal, with faint tracery on its surface. At first it remained icy to the touch—proximity to her fire made no difference. Then, for no reason she could discern, it warmed to room temperature.

The prince's presence had to be one of the most puzzling aspects of the day, second only to Master Haywood's anguished ignorance.

Master Haywood had known that she should be kept away from

the prying eyes of Atlantis. He had prepared a satchel in the event of an emergency evacuation. How could he not know then where she was going or what was in the satchel?

The satchel!

She shoved the pendant into her pocket, called for more fire—taking care that it didn't come near her hair or her clothes—and searched inside the satchel. Her fingers encountered fabric, leather, a silky pouch with jingling coins, and at last, an envelope.

The envelope contained a letter.

*My dearest Iolanthe,*

*I have just come from your room. You are a week short of your second birthday, sleeping with a sweet gusto under the singing blanket that was still crooning softly to you as I closed the door behind me.*

*I want a secure, uneventful future for you. It fills me with dread to think of you someday reading this letter, still a child, yet utterly alone, as you must be.*

*(I can't help but wonder how your power would have manifested itself. By causing the Delamer River to flow in reverse? Or shearing the air of a sunny day into a cyclone?)*

*Nightly I pray that we will never come to it. But it has been agreed that for the sake of everyone's safety, I will give up my knowledge of certain events to a memory keeper. After tomorrow, I will only know that I must guard the extent of your powers from the notice of*

Atlantis, and that if I were to fail, to distance you from immediate harm.

You no doubt crave explanations. Yet explanations I dare not set down in writing, for fear that this letter falls into the wrong hands, despite all my precautions. Only remember this: keep away from any and all agents of Atlantis. Every last mage in pursuit of you seeks to abuse and exploit your powers.

Trust no one.

Trust no one, that is, except the memory keeper. She will find you. And she will protect you to her dying breath.

To help her, remain where you are for as long as you can—I have been assured that the end-portal will be kept at a secure location. But by all means use caution. You cannot be careful enough. And whatever you do, do not repeat the action that brought you to Atlantis's notice in the first place.

Be careful, Iolanthe. Be careful. But do not despair. Help will reach you.

I want nothing more than to take you into my arms and assure you that all will be well.

But I can only pray ardently that Fortune walks with you, that you discover hitherto unimagined strength in yourself and encounter unexpected friends along this perilous path that you must now tread.

All my love,
Horatio

*P.S. I have applied an Irreproducible Charm to you. No one can capture your likeness—and therefore Atlantis will not be able to disseminate your image.*

*P.P.S. Do not worry about me.*

How could she not worry about him? The Inquisitor would be furious when she realized that he'd deliberately given up his memories to foil her. And if—

A thump in the floor—a vibration that shot up Iolanthe's spine—scattered her thoughts. She shoved the letter back into the satchel and extinguished her fire. For a moment she could hear nothing, and then it came again, the thump. Her fingers closed around her wand.

She lifted the disc covering the peephole. Part of the floor lifted. A trapdoor—she was in an attic. Light wafted up from the opening, illuminating crates, chests, and shelves upon which crowded ranks and rows of dusty curiosities.

The trapdoor rose farther, accompanied by a squeak of the hinge. A lantern made its way into the attic, followed by a woman with a wand. She raised the lantern. It glowed brighter and brighter, rivaling the blinding brilliance of noonday.

Iolanthe squinted against the glare. The woman was about forty and quite lovely: deep-set eyes, high cheekbones, and wide lips. Her hair was very fair, almost white in the eye-watering light, swept up to the top of her head. Her pale-blue gown was of a fashion Iolanthe had never seen. It buttoned all the way to her chin and cinched to a tiny handspan at the waist, with tight sleeves that ended below her elbows in swishes of lace.

Who was the woman? Was she, by happy chance, the memory keeper who *should* find Iolanthe?

"So, you are finally here," the woman said, speaking as if through clenched teeth.

Iolanthe's stomach dropped. The woman's tone was grim, hostile even.

The woman pointed her wand at the trunk. Things snapped and clanked to the floor. Locks? No, chains. Iolanthe could see thick metal links from the peephole.

"*Aperi,*" said the woman, using the simplest opening spell now that the restraints had been removed.

Some deep-seated instinct made Iolanthe clutch at the latch. She had not moved three times in seven years without learning a thing or two about reading people: whoever this woman was, she did not mean well.

The latch twitched against Iolanthe's hand, but she kept it in place.

"*Aperi,*" the woman repeated.

Again the latch fidgeted.

The woman frowned. "*Aperi maxime.*"

This time the latch twisted and bucked like a caught animal bent on escape. Iolanthe's fingers hurt with the strain of keeping it from disengaging.

At last the latch stilled. But she barely caught a breath before the woman called, *"Frangare!"*

*Frangare* was a mason's spell, used for cleaving boulders in two. The trunk must have been protected: it did not crack open, not even the smallest of fractures.

*"Frangare!"* the woman cried again. *"Frangare! Frangare! Frangare!"*

Iolanthe's fingers were icy with fear. The trunk remained intact. But for how much longer? She tried to vault—and moved not an inch: no self-respecting mage dwellings allowed vaulting within its perimeters.[5]

The woman set down the lantern and clutched the bodice of her dress, as if exhausted. "I forgot," she said slowly. "He made the trunk indestructible so I could not get rid of it."

So there was a man about. Could *he* help Iolanthe?

"On his deathbed he asked me to swear a blood oath that I would protect you as I would my own child, from the moment I first saw you," the woman said softly. Then she laughed, a sound that chilled Iolanthe's blood. "He wanted much, did he not?"

The woman lifted her head; her face was cold and blank, her eyes burning with fervor. "For you he gave up his honor," she said. "For you he destroyed us all."

Who *was* this madwoman? And why had anyone believed this house to be a secure location?

The woman raised her wand. The chains slammed back into place around the trunk. Her lips moved silently, as if she were praying.

Iolanthe held her breath. For a long minute, nothing seemed to happen. Then the ends of her hair fluttered. The trunk was shut, she herself was still—how could air move? Yet it moved. In only one direction: out of the trunk.

The woman intended to suffocate Iolanthe right in the trunk.

And air was the only element over which Iolanthe had no control whatsoever.

Titus's pendant had warmed appreciably as he reached England. It had warmed further after he materialized in London.

Many Exiles from the Domain, accustomed to the urban life of Delamer, had chosen to settle in London, the closest thing Britain had to an equivalent. The girl had likely arrived at the home of an Exile.

The city was in the throes of one of its infamous fogs. He saw well enough with his fog glasses, but no one on the ground could spot him on his flying carpet.

Flying carpets were once the fastest, most comfortable, and most luxurious mode of travel. In this age of expedited channels, however, they had become antiques, much admired but little used. Titus's carpet, measuring four feet in length, two in width, and barely a quarter of an inch in thickness, was actually a toy—and not meant for any child to ride on, but for dolls.

He flew over the town house of Rosemary Alhambra, the Exiles' leader, but the pendant did not react further. Next he tried the house of the Heathmoors, considered the most powerful mages among the Exiles—still nothing. He was on his way to the home of Alhambra's lieutenant when the pendant heated abruptly.

He had just passed Hyde Park Corner. The only mage family who lived nearby were the Wintervales. *Surely not.* No one in their right mind would entrust this girl to Lady Wintervale.

But as he circled above the Wintervale house, the pendant grew so hot he had to pull it outside his shirt so it would not scald his skin.

Wintervale House was one of the most tightly secured private dwellings Titus knew. Fortunately—most fortunately—Leander Wintervale, the son of the house, was Titus's schoolmate, and there was a way to access the house from the former's room at school.

Titus landed on a nearby roof, took off his fog glasses, and rolled the carpet into a tight bundle to carry under his arm. From there he vaulted to his resident house at school. Specifically, into Archer Fairfax's perennially unoccupied room.

A glance out of Fairfax's window showed Wintervale and Mohandas Kashkari, an Indian boy and Wintervale's good friend, behind the house. The rain had reduced to a mist. Kashkari, the calmer of the two, stood in place; Wintervale paced around him, talking and gesticulating.

Excellent—now Titus did not need to devise a way to get Wintervale away from his room. He opened Fairfax's door a fraction of an inch and peered out.

Many of the boys had returned. A cluster stood talking at the far end of the passage. But they decided to go to Atkins' to buy some foodstuff and stomped down the stairs.

Once the corridor was empty, Titus dropped the flying carpet on the floor of his own room—after much tinkering he had fortified it enough to carry his weight, but the combined weight of both himself and the girl would keep the carpet grounded. Next he slipped into Wintervale's room four doors down, squeezed inside Wintervale's narrow wardrobe, and closed the door.

"*Fidus et audax.*"

He opened the wardrobe again to step into Wintervale's room at the family's London town house. The corridor outside was empty. He made for the stairs. Descending turned the pendant cooler. Ascending, hotter.

He sprinted up the steps.

There was still air in the trunk; it whished softly as it left. But breathing already felt like heaving a boulder with her lungs.

Soon the madwoman would have Iolanthe sealed in a vacuum. Her fingers shook. She looked out of the peephole, searching frantically for something she could use to help herself.

There! On a shelf in the recesses of the attic, among dusty metal instruments, stood one lone statuette of stone.

She could not manipulate ceramic—cooking the earth changed its properties—but she did have power over stone. She elevated the statuette. It hovered a few inches above the shelf. She swung her arm. The statuette smashed into the back of the woman's head.

The woman cried. Her wand clattered to the floor. She did not, however, lose consciousness as Iolanthe had hoped, but only stumbled until she banged into crates piled against the wall.

Iolanthe hesitated. Should she attack the woman again in the latter's weakened state?

But the woman already had her wand back in her hand. *"Exstinguare."*

The stone statuette turned into dust. "Now what are you going to use?" said the woman, with a chilling smile.

Suddenly the air inside the trunk was so thin Iolanthe became light-headed. It felt as if someone had pushed her face into wet cement. Try as she did, she could not draw a single breath.

Faintly, very faintly, she became aware that something burned against her left thigh. Then everything went black.


As he arrived below the open trapdoor, Titus heard Lady Wintervale speaking.

"What have you done?" Her voice was low yet frantic. "Never again, remember? You were never, *never* to kill again."

A blade of fear plunged into Titus's heart. Lady Wintervale's paranoia ran deep, and her sanity was not always reliable. Was he too late?

He wrapped a muffling spell about the rickety steps and climbed up. The moment he had Lady Wintervale in view, he pointed his wand. *Tempus congelet,* he mouthed, not wanting her to hear his voice before the time-freeze spell took effect.

*If* the spell took effect. He had never used it in the real world.

Lady Wintervale stilled. He darted past her to the trunk.

"Are you there? Are you all right?"

The trunk was as silent as a coffin.

He swore. The chains did not respond to the first few spells he tried. He swore again. If he had more time, he could coax the chains. But there *was* no time: the time-freeze spell lasted three minutes at most. And the girl, if she was still alive, must be let out right away.

He looked about. There was nothing he could use. A moment later, however, he saw that the chains did not go around the trunk all the way, but were instead fastened to plates bolted to the side of the trunk. And the magic that anchored the plates to the trunk was ordinary enough that a stronger-than-usual unfastening cant did the trick.

He flung back the chains, but the trunk lid lifted only a fraction of an inch. What more obstacles stood in his way?

*"Aperi."*

The sound of something unlatching. He hoisted up the lid. The girl was slumped over, her face invisible beneath her still-wild hair.

His mind went blank. She could not possibly be dead. Could she?

Reaching inside, he lifted a limp wrist and searched for a pulse. His heart thudded as he encountered a feeble throb in her vein.

"*Revisce!*"

No reaction.

"*Revisce forte!*"

Her entire person shuddered. Her head slowly rose. Her eyes opened. "Highness," she mumbled.

He was weak with relief. But again, no time to indulge. "Hold still, I will get you out. *Omnia interiora vos elevate.*"

Everything in the trunk floated: the girl, who gasped and thrashed to find herself airborne; her wand; her satchel; and a great many items of clothing that must have been packed before the trunk was closed the first time. Not a single piece of clothing was nonmage. If the trunk had been entrusted to the Wintervales, it would have been before their exile.

He caught the girl, her wand, and her satchel, and let everything else fall back into the trunk. A quick swish closed the trunk. An undo spell set the plates and the chains back into place. Then he was easing the two of them out the trapdoor, with an "*Omnia deleantur*" tossed behind him to erase his footprints and any other traces he might have left in the dust of the attic.

"Did she hurt you?" he asked at the first stair landing.

"She siphoned all the air from the trunk."

He looked down at the girl in his arms. Her breathing was

labored, but she hung on to her composure remarkably well for someone who had just endured an attempt on her life—or perhaps she was simply too breathless for hysteria.

"Why did she want to kill me?" she rasped.

"I do not know. But she is disturbed—she lost her father and her sister in the uprising. Her husband also died young."

Back in Wintervale's room two stories below, he sat her on the bed and opened the opposite window. Fog rushed in.

"What's that smell?"

"London."

"London, *England*?"

He was glad that she had some knowledge of nonmage geography. "Yes. Here. Let me—"

The unmistakable sound of someone arriving in the wardrobe. Lady Wintervale must have come out of the time freeze, found the trunk empty, and summoned her son. Titus shut the window, yanked the girl off the bed, and pushed her flat against the wall in the blind spot behind the wardrobe.

She had the sense to keep still and silent.

The wardrobe opened. Wintervale leaped down. Titus's heart imploded: the girl's satchel was in plain sight under the windowsill—he had set it down earlier to open the window. But Wintervale paid no attention to the contents of his room and rushed out to the corridor.

Titus allowed himself a moment to calm down. "Hurry."

The window was set deep in the facade of the house. He reopened the window and lifted the girl to the ledge. Next, her satchel in hand, he climbed out, closed the window, and latched it with a locking charm.

The fog was pervasive. She was lost in the thick, mustard-colored miasma. He felt for her but only came across a tumble of her hair.

"Where is your hand?"

She placed her hand in his, her fingers cold but steady. "I didn't expect you'd really come."

He exhaled. "Then you do not know me very well."

He vaulted them both.

## CHAPTER 5

VAULTING HAD NEVER BEEN A problem for Iolanthe before, whether on her own or hitching along with someone else. But this particular vault was like being crushed between two boulders. She shut her eyes and swallowed a scream of pain.

At the other end, she stumbled.

The prince caught her. "I am sorry. I knew vaulting might be difficult for you just now, but I had to get you to safety right away."

He shouldn't apologize. If they were safe, then nothing else mattered.

They were in some sort of an anteroom. There was a mirror, a console table, two doors, and nothing else. He pointed his wand at the door in front of them. It opened silently, revealing a room beyond with dark-red wallpaper, pale-yellow chairs, and a large, empty grate, before which stood a wrought-iron screen with curling vines and clusters of grapes.

He lifted her again and carried her to a reclining chaise. "I might have a remedy for you," he said, setting her down.

He crossed the room to another door. *"Aut viam inveniam aut faciam."* *I will either find a way or make one.*

The door opened. He walked into a room lined with drawers and shelves as far as she could see, shelves holding books, shelves holding vials, jars, and bottles, shelves holding instruments both familiar and exotic. A caged canary sat upon a long table at the center of the room. Also on the table were two valises, one brown, the second a dull red.

He disappeared briefly from her sight. She heard the sound of drawers opening and closing. He returned, sat down next to her, and cradled her head in the crook of his arm. The bitter tang of the fog clung to the wool of his jacket.

"That fog," she mumbled, "is it natural?"

It had been thick enough to cut with a knife, alarmingly yellow in color, and foul like pig swill.

"There is no magic behind it, but it is not entirely natural either— a consequence of Britain's industrialization. Here: this is to relieve the effects of vaulting."

The prince held a vial with a fine midnight-blue powder inside. He took her by the chin, his fingers warm and strong, and tipped the blue powder into her mouth. The flavor reminded her of seawater.

"There is no counter-remedy for suffocation, exactly, but this is good for your general well-being."

He held out a second vial. The wellness remedy, silver-gray granules, tasted unexpectedly of oranges.

"Thank you, Your Highness," she murmured.

He was already walking away, back into the room full of shelves.

"What is that room, sire?" she asked.

"My laboratory," he answered, opening a drawer.

"What do you do there, if I may ask?"

"What anyone does in a laboratory—potions, distillations, elixirs, things of that sort."

She conducted practicals at the village school for Master Haywood—practicals, in one form or another, were compulsory until a pupil reached fourteen. But it wasn't as if mages made their own potions at home. Commercial distilleries and potion manufacturers adequately supplied their needs. In fact, many households didn't even possess the necessary implements to make the recipes she taught.

Was it just princely eccentricity that had him equip an entire laboratory for himself, or was it something else?

The prince came out of the laboratory and closed the door behind him. He was tall and lean—not thin, but tightly built. When she first saw him in her collapsed house, he'd had on a plain blue tunic and dark trousers tucked into knee-high boots. Simple country attire, nothing like the elaborate state robes he donned for his official portraits.

Now he wore a black jacket with a hunter-green waistcoat, black trousers, and shoes of highly polished black leather—the jacket was more formfitting than the tunics men wore in the

Domain, the trousers, less so.

Her gaze returned to his face. Official portraits were notoriously unreliable. But in this case, the pictures hadn't lied. He *was* handsome—dark hair, deep eyes, and high cheekbones.

In his portraits he always sneered. She had once remarked to a classmate that he came across as mean-spirited, the kind of boy who would not only tell a girl she looked like a bumpkin but deliberately spill a drink on her. In person he appeared less cynical. There was a freshness to his features, an appealing boyishness, and—as far as she could see—no malice at all.

Their eyes met. Her stomach fluttered.

Without a word, he opened the door behind him again. But instead of the laboratory, he walked into what appeared to be a bathroom.

"What happened to the laboratory, sire?"

Sound of water running. "That is a folded space, not part of this hotel suite."

"Is that where we are, in a hotel?" She'd thought, for some reason, that they were at one of his lesser estates, a hunting lodge or a summer cabin.

The sound of even more water running. "We are less than two miles from where you were when you came out of the trunk."

"We are still in *London*?"

"Very much so."

Now that he mentioned it, she saw that real flame—rather than light elixir—shone behind the frosted glass mantles of the wall sconces. She'd have noticed sooner had she been less preoccupied.

He emerged from the bath with a towel. Crouching before her, he pressed the damp towel against her temple.

"Oww!"

"Sorry. The blood is a bit caked on by now. But you should not need more than a good cleaning."

She endured the discomfort. "Your Highness, will you please tell me what's going on?"

Why was she here? Why was he here? Why was the sky falling today of all days?

"Later. I would be remiss as your host if I did not offer you the use of a tub first."

She'd forgotten the state she must be in, dirty and battered.

"Your bath is filling as we speak. You will be all right in there by yourself?"

He'd asked a perfectly legitimate question, given that he'd had to carry her a great deal of late. But all the same, what a thing to ask.

"And if I'm not all right, sire?"

She immediately regretted her question. It was far too cheeky. And before her sovereign, no less. She might not have received much parental guidance of late, but she still liked to think of herself as better brought up than that.

He tapped his fingers against the armrest of the chaise. "Then I suppose I will have to watch over you."

There was no inflection to his tone; not even a flicker of anything in his expression. Yet the air between them drew taut. She heated.

"Now, will you be all right—or will you not?" asked the prince.

She became aware for the first time that his eyes were blue gray, the color of distant hills.

Now she had no choice but to brazen it out. "I'm sure I will be fine," she answered. "But should I need you, sire, please don't hesitate."

The gaze of her sovereign swept over her. She'd seen that look of interest from boys. But his was so swift that she wasn't quite certain she hadn't imagined it.

Then he inclined his head, all pomp and formality. "I am at your service, madam."

Even without the caked blood, when Iolanthe finally caught sight of herself in a mirror, she still flinched. She looked awful, her face filthy and scratched, her hair coated in dust and bits of plaster, her once-white blouse the color of an old rag.

At least she was safe. Master Haywood . . . Her heart tightened. Her intuition had been exactly right: it *had* been on her account that everything had gone wrong for him.

She washed quickly. Afterward, she dressed in the change of clothes the prince had supplied—slippers, undergarments, a blue flannel shirt, and a pair of matching trousers, everything for a boy four inches taller and a stone and a half heavier.

When she came out of the bath, her battered clothes in a bundle in her hand, there was a tray of food waiting in the parlor and a fire in the grate. So it really was true, fireplaces were not mere decorations in the nonmage world.

The prince looked at her oddly, as if seeing her for the first time. "Have we met before? You look . . . familiar."

Every year there were children selected to meet him, but she'd never been among the chosen. "No, we haven't, sire. I'd have remembered."

"I could have sworn . . ."

"You are probably thinking of someone else, sire." She extended her hand. "Here's your pendant."

"Thank you." The prince shook his head, as if to clear it. He pointed at her clothes. "If you do not mind, we need to destroy them—I would prefer as little evidence of your mage origins lying about as possible. Same with the contents of the satchel. Is there anything you particularly wish to keep?"

A reminder that she wasn't quite as safe as she would like to be. She didn't know how the prince remained so calm. But she was grateful for his aplomb—it made her less afraid.

He motioned her to sit down and handed her the satchel. Master Haywood's letter she set aside. Digging through the clothes, she found the pouch of coins she'd felt earlier—pure Cathay gold, acceptable tender in every mage realm.

"I think there is a false bottom," she said, feeling along the linings, her fingers discerning the shape of something cylindrical.

The prince produced a spell that neatly removed the cover of the false bottom to reveal a hidden tube.

He astounded her—not so much the spell, though it was deft, but his demeanor. Had he been an orphan who'd had to fend for himself from the youngest age, perhaps she would not be surprised at his maturity and helpfulness. But his must have been the most privileged upbringing in all the Domain; yet here he was, always thinking one step ahead, always anticipating her needs.

"Thank you, sire," she said.

Could he detect the admiration in her voice? *She* did, and it embarrassed her. Hurriedly she reached for the tube, which contained her rolled-up birth chart—she recognized the elaborate painted night sky at the top of the scroll.

She put the letter, the pouch of coins, and the birth chart back into the satchel. He scooped up everything else. "May I ask why you called down the lightning today?"

*I needed to keep my guardian employed and a roof over our heads.*

"I was trying to correct a batch of light elixir. I found in my guardian's copy of *The Complete Potion* a note that said a bolt of lightning could right any light elixir, no matter how badly tainted."

He walked toward the fireplace, his arms full. "Who wrote that note?"

"I don't know, sire."

He tossed her discards into the grate. *"Extinguamini. Tollamini."*

Her things turned to dust. The dust rose in a column up the flue. The prince braced his elbow on the mantel and waited for all the evidence of destruction to depart. He was all long, elegant lines and—

She realized she was staring at him, in a way she could not remember ever looking at anyone else. Hastily she dropped her gaze.

"It is bizarre that anyone would counsel that," he said. "Lightning plays no role in potion making. How old is that copy of *The Complete Potion*?"

"I'm not sure, sire. My guardian always had it."

He returned to the door of the laboratory, repeated the password, and went inside. "Mine is a first edition. It was published during the Millennium Year."

The Millennium Year celebrated one thousand years of the House of Elberon—his house. It was currently Year of the Domain 1031, which meant the copy in Little Grind was at most thirty-one years old. She'd thought the book much older. "Do we need to find out who wrote the note, sire?"

*We.* Her use of the word further embarrassed her. She was assuming a great deal of common purpose with her sovereign.

"I doubt we would be able to, even if we tried," said the prince. "Are you well enough to eat something?"

"I think so." Her stomach had settled down and she *was* famished, having not touched a bite of the luncheon Mrs. Needles had brought her.

He poured her a cup of tea. "What is your name?"

It so surprised her that he did not already know that she forgot to thank him for the tea. "Seabourne, sire. Iolanthe Seabourne."

"Pleased to meet you, Miss Seabourne."

"Long may Fortune uphold your banner, sire."

That was what a subject said upon meeting the Master of the Domain. But perhaps she also ought to kneel. Most likely she should curtsy.

As if he read her thoughts, the prince said, "Do not worry about niceties. And no need to keep calling me 'sire.' We are not in the Domain, and no one will chastise us for not observing court etiquette."

*So . . . he is also gracious.*

Enough. She didn't even know what had happened to Master Haywood, and here she was, very close to hero-worshipping some-one she'd barely met. "Thank you, sire—I mean, thank you. And may I impose upon you to tell me, Your Highness, what happened to my guardian after I left?"

"He is in the Inquisitor's custody now," said the prince, sitting down opposite her.

Even the pleasure of his nearness could not dilute her dismay. "So the Inquisitor did come?"

"Not even half a minute after you left."

She clasped her hands together. That she was in real danger still shocked her.

"You have not touched your tea, Miss Seabourne. Cream or sugar?"

Usually she liked her tea full of sugar and cream, but such a rich beverage no longer appealed. She took a sip of the black tea. The prince pushed a plate of sandwiches in her direction.

"Eat. Hiding from the Inquisitor is hard work. You need to keep up your strength."

She took a bite of the sandwich—it had an unexpectedly curried taste. "So the Inquisitor wants me."

"More precisely, the Bane wants you."[6]

She recoiled. She couldn't recall when or where she'd first learned of the Bane, whose official title was Lord High Commander of the Great Realm of New Atlantis. Unlike the Inquisitor, whom people did talk about, if in hushed whispers, regarding the Bane there was a conspicuous silence.

"What does the Bane want me for?"

"For your powers," said the prince.

It was the most ridiculous thing anyone had ever said to her. "But the Bane is already the most powerful mage on earth."

"And he would like to remain so—which is only possible with you," said the prince. "You are crushing your sandwich, by the way."

She willed her stiff fingers to unclench. "How? How do I have anything to do with the Bane remaining powerful?"

"Do you know how old he is?"

She shook her head and raised her teacup to her lips. She needed something to wash down the sandwich in her mouth, which had become a dry paste she couldn't quite swallow.

"Close to two hundred. Possibly more."

She stared at him, the tea forgotten. "Can anyone live that long?"

"Not by natural means. Agents of Atlantis watch all the realms under their control for unusually powerful elemental mages. When they locate such a mage, he or she is secretly shipped to Atlantis, never to be heard from again. I am ignorant of how exactly the Bane makes use of those elemental mages, but I do not doubt that he does make use of them."

If she clutched her teacup any harder, the handle would break. She set it down. "What precisely is the definition of an unusually powerful elemental mage? I have no control over air."

The prince leaned forward in his chair. "Are you sure? When was the last time you tried to manipulate air?"

She frowned: she couldn't remember. "Someone tried to kill me by removing all the air from the end portal. If I had any affinity for air, I'd have stopped it, wouldn't I?"

It became his turn to frown. "Were you not born on either the thirteenth or fourteenth of November 1866—I mean, Year of the Domain 1014?"

"No, I was born earlier, in September."

Her birthday was a day after his, in fact. It had been fun, when she'd been small, to pretend that the festivities surrounding his birthday had been for her also.

"Show me your birth chart."

A birth chart plotted the precise alignment of stars and planets at the moment of a mage's birth. It was once a crucial document, for everything from the choice of school to the choice of mate: the stars must align. In recent years it had become fashionable in places like Delamer to break with tradition and leave one's birth chart to molder. But not so in Little Grind. When Iolanthe had volunteered to contribute the fire hazards for the village's annual obstacle course run last autumn, her chart, along with those of all the participants, had been requisitioned to determine the most auspicious date on which to hold the competition.

As she dug the cylindrical container out of the mostly empty satchel, it occurred to her that if she had used her birth chart only months ago, then it could not possibly be in the satchel, the contents of which hadn't been disturbed in more than a decade.

She'd unrolled only the top six inches of the birth chart earlier, when she'd checked to see that it *was* a birth chart. Fully unfurled, the three-foot-long chart had no name at the center, only the time of birth, five minutes past two o'clock in the morning on the fourteenth of November, YD 1014.

Something gonged in her ears. "But I was born in September. I've seen my chart before—many times—and it's not this one."

"And yet this is the one that had been packed, for when the truth came out and you were forced to leave," said the prince.

"Are you saying that my guardian counterfeited the other? Why?"

"There was a meteor storm that night. Stars fell like rain. Seers from every realm on earth predicted the birth of a great elemental mage. Were I your guardian, I would have most certainly *not* let it be known that you were born on that night."

She'd read about that night, when one could not see the sky for all the golden streaks of plummeting stars.

"You think I'm that great elemental mage?" she asked, barely able to hear her own voice.

She couldn't be. She wanted no part of what was happening now.

"Until you, there has never been anyone who can command lightning."

"But lightning is useless. I almost killed myself when I called it down."

"The Bane just might know what to do with such power," said the prince.

She didn't know why the idea should make her more frightened than she was already, but it did.

"It has been an exhausting day for you. Take some rest," the prince suggested. "I must go now, but I will return in a few hours to check on you."

Go? He was leaving her all alone?

"Are you going back to the Domain?" She sounded weak and afraid to her own ears.

"I am going to my school."

"I thought you were educated at the castle." More precisely, at a monastic lodge farther up the Labyrinthine Mountains that was used only for a young prince or princess's education, or so Iolanthe had learned at school.

"No, I attend an English school not far from London."

She couldn't have heard him right. "You can't be serious."

"I am. The Bane wished it."

"But you are our prince. You are supposed to be one of our better mages. You won't get any proper training at such a school."

"You understand the Bane's purpose perfectly," he said lightly.

She was appalled. "I can't believe the regent didn't object. Or the prime minister."

His eyes were clear and direct. "You overestimate the courage of those in power. They are often more interested in holding on to that power than in doing anything worthwhile with it."

He did not sound bitter, only matter-of-fact. How had he handled it, the utter insult of having the Bane dictate his movements, when he was, on paper at least, the Bane's peer in power and privilege?

"So . . . what should I do while you are at school?"

"I was hoping to take you to school with me, but it is a boys' school." He shrugged. "We will make new plans."

He couldn't have been more cordial about it, but she had the distinct sensation it did not please him to have to make new plans.

"I can come with you. I went to a girls' school for a while, and every term I had the male lead role in the school play. My voice is low, and I do a good imitation of the way a boy walks and talks."

She'd acquitted herself so well some of her classmates' parents had thought a boy had been brought in to act the part. "Not to mention I can fight."

Unlike most magelings, who were taught to refrain from violence, elemental magelings were actively encouraged to use their fists—far better they punched someone than set the latter on fire.[7]

"I am sure you can knock boys out left and right. And I am sure you are perfectly proficient on stage. But playing a boy for a few hours each term is quite different from playing one twenty-four hours a day, day after day, to an audience of agents."

"I beg your pardon?"

"There are agents of Atlantis at my school," he said. "I am watched."

She gripped the armrests of her chair. "You live under Atlantis's surveillance?"

Somehow she'd thought he must be exempt from it.

"I am better off at school than at home—the castle is riddled with the Inquisitor's informants—but that is no help to us now."

She could not imagine the life he led.

"You are safer here," he continued. "The vestibule is accessible by the hotel staff—that is where we vaulted in—but the rest of the suite is protected by anti-intrusion spells."

Anti-intrusion spells were no guarantee of safety—her house in Little Grind had had its share of those.

"You are entirely anonymous," he further reassured her. "Atlantis, great as it is, cannot hope to locate you so easily in a city of millions. And should anything alarm you, go into the laboratory and wait. You already know the password; the countersign is the first paragraph on page ten of the book on the demilune table."[8]

She would prefer that he quit school to stand guard beside her. If he should be wrong, if Atlantis proved quicker and cleverer than he believed, she would be all too easy a target. He had to stay with her. She'd reason with him—beg him, if she must. Bar the door with her person.

She opened her mouth and out came "All right."

Her life hung in the balance and here she was, trying to appear brave and stalwart before this boy.

"Thank you," he said, and briefly touched her on the arm.

He *was* impressed. The bright happiness that flared inside her was almost enough to dispel her fear of his absence.

He disappeared a moment inside the laboratory and returned with the brown valise she'd seen earlier and a round-crowned hat. "I will be back after lights-out at school. In the meanwhile, eat and rest. It has been a great deal of trouble finding you; I do not intend to lose you any time soon."

He had been searching for her? She longed to know more, but that would have to wait until his return.

"May Fortune walk with you, Your Highness." She dipped into a small curtsy.

He shook his head. "No need to curtsy. And may Fortune abide with you, Miss Seabourne."

He set the hat on his head and made for the door.

If she hadn't been staring so intently at him, she wouldn't have noticed the small, flat disk on his sleeve. She hesitated. Perhaps it was the fashion in England to have such decorations on one's jacket.

But what had Master Haywood said? *You cannot be careful enough.*

"One moment, Your Highness. There is something on your left sleeve."

His expression instantly sobered. He looked down at his arm. "Where?"

She turned her own arm to show him. It was placed at a spot above his elbow where it would be difficult for both he himself and someone else to see it, unless that person was looking squarely at him when he had his arm elevated.

He found the disk by touch, ripped it off, and stared at it, his eyes shadowed.

Closing his fist, he said, "We are in trouble."

# CHAPTER ⋅ 6

TITUS YANKED OPEN THE DOOR of the water closet, threw the penny-sized disk into the commode, and tugged a cord to flush.

"What kind of trouble are we in?" asked Miss Seabourne behind him. Her voice was unsteady, but to her credit, she showed no signs of falling apart.

"I have been tracked."

Lady Callista. He remembered now: She had put her hand on his arm before she took leave of him. And he had been in too much of a hurry to notice.

If they were lucky—and they had been quite lucky so far this day—then Lady Callista's lackeys would have a frustrating time following the disk as it traveled through London's sewers.

But they had run out of luck. Murmurs rose outside the front door and outside the French doors that opened to a narrow balcony.

He beckoned Miss Seabourne to come to him. She did not hesitate. To her further credit, she already had in hand not only her own satchel, but also the valise he had dropped in his haste to get rid of the disk.

He pulled her into the laboratory, closed the door, and listened. All too soon, there were footsteps in the suite.

"What of your anti-intrusion spells?" she whispered.

"They were to keep nonmages away." The suite's anonymity had been his best defense against Atlantis.

Agents of Atlantis would not find anything belonging to him in the suite—he had always been excruciatingly careful about that. And they would not so easily discover a folded space. All the same, the suite's safety had been hopelessly compromised.

*"Exstinguatur ostium,"* he said, destroying the connection that anchored the laboratory to the suite.

They were safe, for now. But what would have happened to her had he already left? Yes, she was alert. She would have escaped into the laboratory. She would not, however, have been able to sever the connection. By the time he returned, after lights-out at school, Atlantis's agents might very well have broken through.

"I apologize." The words burned his throat. "I should have . . ."

The very first day, and already he had very nearly lost her to Atlantis.

"I should have caught the device before I left the Domain. I thought I had planned for every contingency, but I did not plan for my own carelessness."

She was tense, her knuckles white about her wand, but she had herself well under control and seemed to be taking their hasty retreat better than he. "How did you know to prepare for anything at all?"

"The prophecies about you—I never doubted their accuracy." He pulled out a stool for her. "Have a seat."

She sat down and, betraying more emotion than he had seen from her so far, squeezed her head between her palms. "When I woke up this morning, I mattered to no one except myself. Would that nothing had changed."

"Fortune cares little for the will of mortals."

"So I have learned." Her face still lowered, she said, "Please don't let me keep you from returning to school."

Dalbert was required to note the time of Titus's departure from the Domain. The Inquisitor and her agents knew what time Titus should arrive at school—and he was already running late.

But he could not simply leave the girl in the laboratory, a place that had no food or water, no lavatory, and nowhere for her to lie down and rest except atop the workbench.

She pushed her hair back from her face. She had used the Pears soap the hotel provided, with its subtle fragrance of an English meadow. The laboratory was small; he stood quite close to her. For a moment he was completely distracted by her scent—and the ripple of her still-damp hair.

He had seen her before. Where had he seen her before?

She looked up, her eyes dark as ink. "You don't need to go anymore?"

"I cannot leave you here."

The laboratory had two other exits. One led to Cape Wrath in the Scottish Highlands, where he sometimes visited in warmer weather, the other to an abandoned barn in Kent. Either way, by taking her out of the laboratory, he would be bowing to the inevitable.

He pulled open a drawer and took out a vial of green powder.

"It seems we will be following the original plan after all, Miss Seabourne," he said. "I hope you enjoy the company of boys."

The barn was more or less the same as when Titus had seen it last. Fallen beams, missing doors, patches of gray sky visible through the dilapidated roof. Rain puddled on the floor. The smell of rotting wood and ancient muck assailed his nose.

A stiff breeze stirred. Her hair blew about her face. She looked tousled, as if she had just rolled out of bed, the warmth of the quilt still clinging to her. "Where are we?"

He closed the laboratory door behind him. The door promptly disappeared—it let the occupants of the laboratory out, but could not be used to gain entrance. "Southeast England."

"You don't have an exit that takes you directly to school?"

"In case the laboratory is breached, I do not want it easily traced to me. Can you vault more than once in a day?"[9]

"Yes, but I haven't much of a range. I've never tried to vault more than a few miles."

He took her hand and tapped out a small mound of the green

powder into her palm. "Take this vaulting aid. We have to go fifty miles, but you do not need as big a range when you hitch a vault."

She swallowed the vaulting aid. "You have a fifty-mile range?"

He had a three-hundred-mile range, practically unheard of. She put her hand on his arm, and the next moment they were in Fairfax's room.

Either his vaulting aid was superlatively effective, or her natural range measured far greater than a few miles: she neither bent over in pain nor stumbled about, disoriented. As if they had merely climbed up a flight of stairs and walked through the door, she let go of his arm and looked about.

Thirty-five pupils, ranging in age from thirteen to nineteen, lived in this house. The junior boys had the smaller rooms on the upper floors. The senior boys enjoyed bigger, better accommodation right above the ground floor.

Fairfax's room, like those of other senior boys, measured eight feet by ten feet. A writing desk and a chair had been placed near the fireplace. A set of shelves beside the window held books on top and various sporting equipment on the bottom. A chest of drawers and a spare chair by the door rounded out the collection of furniture.

An oval-framed picture of Queen Victoria, looking puffy and dis-approving, hung on the blue-papered wall. Six postcards of ocean liners had been arranged in a semicircle under the queen's image. Scattered about the rest of the room were photographs and etchings of Africa: wavelike dunes, grazing gnus, a leopard at a watering hole, and a round, thatched hut beside a listing shepherd's tree.

He drew a soundproof circle. "Welcome to Eton College. We are in Mrs. Dawlish's house. And this is your room."

"Who's Mrs. Dawlish? And why do I have a room here?"

"Boys at Eton live in resident houses—this particular house is run by Mrs. Dawlish. You have a room here because you are a pupil here. Your name is Archer Fairfax, and you have been home these past three months with a broken femur. Your family has a home in Shropshire, but you have spent most of your life in Bechuanaland—an area near the Kalahari Realm."

"Where is the real Archer Fairfax?" She sounded alarmed.

"There was never a real Archer Fairfax. Since I had to be here, I made a place for you—when I thought you were a boy."

She frowned. "And people here know me, even though I have never set foot here?"

"Yes."

"That's impressive," she murmured.

He seldom impressed anyone on his merits alone—the sensation was more than a little dizzying.

"We need to cut your hair now," he said rather abruptly, not wanting her to sense his headiness.

She expelled a breath. "Right."

He stepped behind her, gathered her hair, lifted it—it was smooth and surprisingly heavy—and lopped it off at the nape with a severing spell. "Sorry."

"Hair grows back."

A shame they would need to keep it short for the foreseeable future. He trimmed the remainder of her hair as best as he could, leaving it just long enough so that the wound at her temple would not be visible. She did not quite look like a boy. But then neither was she obviously a girl.

He collected the shorn hair and destroyed it in the unlit fireplace. From the chest of drawers he brought out the items of an Eton boy's uniform.

"You have prepared for everything."

"Hardly. If I had any foresight at all, I would have prepared for a girl."

The vision of his death had mentioned a boy by his side, lamenting his passing. Such was the peril of visions—they must be interpreted by the seer and were therefore subject to human errors. In this case a short-haired girl had been mistaken for a boy. And despite all Titus's preparations, he now found himself swimming in uncertainty.

He knocked on what looked like wall cabinets and a narrow bed flipped down, startling her. From the sheet he ripped a long white strip of linen, hemmed it with a quick spell, and handed it to her.

"For . . . resizing your person," he said as he rehemmed the sheet with another spell.

How else to describe something meant to bind her chest?

She cleared her throat. "Thank you."

"Once you are ready, the clothes are not that tricky." He spoke briskly to cover his own embarrassment. And to think, this was only the beginning of the complications of bringing a girl to an all-boys school. "The shirt studs go into the buttonholes. Everything else is as you would expect."

He turned around to give her privacy. Behind him came the soft shushing of her disrobing. There was no reason for his pulse to accelerate. Nothing was going to happen, and henceforth he would treat her as just another boy. In fact, for her safety and his, he would not even *think* of her as anything but Archer Fairfax, school chum.

All the same, his pulse raced, as if he had just sprinted the length of a playing field.

Then he glanced up and saw her reflection in the small mirror on the door. She stood with her back to him, naked to the top of her pajama trousers, her head bent, puzzling over her binding cloth. The contour of her slender neck, the smoothness of her back, the tapering of her waist—he jerked his head away and stared at the spare chair.

After what seemed an eternity—an eternity during which he forgot all about what the agents of Atlantis would think of his continued absence—she asked, "How should I hold it in place, the binding cloth?"

"Say *Serpens caudam mordens*. It is a simple spell—no need for a wand."[10]

"Not even for the first time?"

"No."

"All right then." She did not sound convinced. *"Serpens caudam mordens."*

A long moment of silence. He had by now completely memorized the form of the lyre-shaped slat on the back of the spare chair.

*"Serpens caudam mordens,"* she said again. "It's not working."

There was no time for her to keep trying. He took a deep breath and turned around. She was now facing him, holding on to the ends of the binding cloth that she had wrapped about her chest. He lowered his gaze: above the too-loose pajama trousers, her waist indented sharply; her navel was deep and perfectly round.

He was going to step closer to her, but now he changed his mind. Remaining precisely where he was, he said, *"Serpens caudam mordens."*

The cloth visibly tautened. She emitted a muffled grunt. "Thank you. That's perfect."

She had not flattened to anything resembling a plane. "Once more," he said.

"No, no more. I can barely breathe."

"You are sure it is tight enough?"

"Yes, absolutely."

He should not, but his eyes again dipped to her navel. He realized what he was doing and looked up, only to see her flush. She had caught him staring.

He turned away to examine the chair some more. "Move and make sure it stays in place."

The next time she called him, she already had on the white shirt and the black trousers he had handed her. As expected, the clothes did not fit her. He set to work with an assortment of spells. The shirt needed its sleeves shortened and the width of the shoulders taken in. For the trousers he nipped the waist and raised the cuffs three inches—he had acquired everything big, as it was much easier to make clothing smaller than the other way around.

"If all else fails, you can always find employment as a tailor," she murmured while he knelt on one knee before her, making sure the trouser cuffs were even.

"You should see my lacework," he said. "As fine as a spiderweb."

Above him she laughed softly. "I didn't know you had a sense of humor."

"Not often," he said, with more candor than usual.

Perhaps he would not need to lie to her, the way he lied to everyone else.

He rose to his feet. The waistcoat came with straps on the back and was easily enough cinched to fit her. The jacket required its armholes shrunk, the bagginess at the shoulders and the middle taken in.

But that was not the end of it. The shirt needed a collar attached and the necktie had to be fastened. Because she had no experience with either, he put them on for her.

They stood nose to nose, so close he could see the small pulse at her throat. The clothes smelled of the lavender sachets he had put in Fairfax's drawers. Her breath brushed the tops of his fingers.

As he pulled her necktie into shape, his knuckles grazed the underside of her chin. She bit her lower lip. Something in him shifted out of place: his concentration.

He took two steps back. "Let me get your shoes."

"How much practice with tailoring spells have you had?" she asked.

"Hundreds of hours." And half again as much on cobbling. He made a pair of too-big black leather oxfords fit her and handed her a derby hat. "Here in England you never go anywhere without headgear."

Did she pass for a boy? He was not entirely confident. But assumption was a powerful thing, especially such a big-belief assumption.

She examined herself in the mirror on the door, adjusting the angle of her hat. Suddenly she swiveled around.

"What is it?"

She opened her mouth, only to press her lips together again. "Never mind."

But he knew what she had realized. That he could have watched her undress in the mirror. They stared at each other. She dropped her eyes and turned her attention back to the mirror.

He walked to the window, parted the curtains a sliver, and looked out. The clouds had begun to dissipate. A few rays of pallid sunlight reached the small meadow behind the house. There were no boys or house staff about—it was near teatime, and everyone must have returned inside.

She came to stand next to him.

"Vault out from here to behind those trees," he instructed. "Then come through the front door of the house. I will meet you in the entry hall."

He did not want her out of his sight. But there was nothing for it: Fairfax's return had to be seen as an event entirely unrelated to the disappearance of one Iolanthe Seabourne. If he produced Fairfax from nowhere, they would both look more suspicious to agents of Atlantis.

"And the other boys will know who I am?"

"When they hear me say your name they will." He turned toward her. "I know it is my fault you are here. But please be convincing as a boy—or I will have prepared in vain."

She glanced at him, her gaze half-admiring, half-mystified. "You have prepared a great deal."

*You have no idea.* "And therefore you will not fail me."

It was as much a prayer as it was a command.


Mrs. Dawlish's house was built of weathered red brick, the outlines neat and solid. Above the ground floor, behind a window at the southern end, stood the prince, watching her.

Had he also watched her when she had stripped down nearly to her skin? Was it her imagination or had he looked at her differently afterward? The underside of her chin, where he'd accidentally brushed her, scorched anew at the thought.

He raised his hand in a silent salute and disappeared. All at once she felt exposed. She'd thought her former life precarious; she'd had no idea how sheltered she'd been, protected at an impossible cost to Master Haywood.

She must remain safe, if only so that his sacrifice would not be in vain.

It had rained earlier in this place—everything was soaked. A watery light shone on the damp landscape. In the distance she could make out a grander building than the rest—the school? Farther away, in a different direction, the hulking shadows of what looked to be a squat castle.

She didn't seem to be in a city—there was too much tree and grass and sky. Nor did she seem to be in isolated countryside. There were other houses. Carriages clattered down a nearby street, carriages drawn by—were they?—she squinted—yes, horses.

Real horses, without wings or a horn on the forehead, their hooves clacking wetly. She couldn't help smiling, reminded of the picture books she'd loved as a child, stories of nonmage children who had nothing but their wits, their swords, and their loyal horses to accompany them on their adventures.

The carriages were black and closed, some with curtains drawn. The pedestrians in blacks, browns, and drab blues were entirely preoccupied with their own affairs, with no idea that a fugitive was among them, pursued with the full might of the greatest empire on the face of the earth.

The thought was almost comforting: at least no one paid her any attention.

A breeze almost made off with her hat; she clamped it down and began walking. Her new clothes did not move well—too many layers, the cut restrictive, the material inelastic. And without her hair, her head felt oddly light, nearly weightless.

Gingerly, and trying not to look like a foreigner, she stepped onto the sidewalk, only to be immediately accosted by a grimy boy of indeterminate age, waving pieces of printed paper in the air.

She leaped back, primed to run the other way.

"More details from John Brown's funeral! You want to know about 'em, guv?"

"Ah . . ." *Did she?*

"Read all about Her Majesty's sorrow. Read it for a penny."

She found her breath. A newspaper, that was what the boy was waving—newspapers in the Domain hadn't used actual paper for a very long time.

"Sorry. Never cared for the man," she said truthfully.

The boy shrugged and continued peddling his wares down the narrow street, which was squeezed in by tightly packed brick houses with steep, pitched roofs.

She came to a stop before the front door of Mrs. Dawlish's house, black and unassuming beneath an arched doorway. There, she'd made it. Now she only had to pass herself off as a boy. For the foreseeable future.

And under the watchful eyes of Atlantis.

❖ ❖

Titus changed into his school uniform in his own room. As he stepped out into the passage, Wintervale's door opened.

"When did you get here?" asked Wintervale, surprised.

"A while ago," said Titus. "I have been in my room."

"Why didn't you join Kashkari and myself?"

"I was in a foul mood—ran into the Inquisitor today. You do not look too pleased either. What is the matter?"

"My mother. I had to go back home just now."

Titus asked the obvious. "Does she not usually leave for Aix-les-Bains as soon as you return here?"

"Baden-Baden this time, but she hasn't left yet. I found her in the attic in a state. She kept saying she'd killed someone and that this time there would be no forgiveness from the Angels. I checked the house from top to bottom: nothing. If she had truly killed someone, you'd think I'd have found a corpse."

It was not easy being Lady Wintervale's son. She was not consistently insane. But at times she came close enough.

"Is she still at home?"

"She's gone to stay with the Alhambras." Wintervale knocked the back of his head against the wall behind him. "Atlantis did this to her. When are you going to lead us to overthrow them?"

Titus shrugged. "You will have to organize the revolt, cousin. If I could, I wouldn't be here."

Lying to Lady Callista and the Inquisitor was a perennial necessity—Titus took pride in rarely speaking a true word before those two. But lying to his second cousin, equally necessary, had always bothered him. He wished Wintervale were not so trusting.

"Why do you think I'm trying to get into Sandhurst?" said Wintervale. "The British fight lots of wars. Maybe there is something to be learned from them."

Titus also wished Lady Wintervale had not adamantly adhered to the tradition of having a child from one of the Domain's grandest families study alongside the heir of the House of Elberon. Lady Callista had been his mother's companion—look how well that had turned out.

"Try not to get yourself killed in one of Britain's colonial wars," he told Wintervale. "It would be the ultimate irony."

"Do I hear mentions of colonial wars?" said Kashkari, joining them, dapper in his impeccably turned-out uniform and sleek black hair. "Is your stomachache gone, Wintervale? You look better."

"I'm fine now," said Wintervale.

Lady Wintervale's unpredictable mental state and penchant for relying on her only child meant that Wintervale often had to invent sudden pains to go back to his room—or clear his room—to use the wardrobe portal.

"Do the two of you want some tea?" Wintervale issued his usual invitation.

"Why not?" said Kashkari.

"I will join you in a minute. I think I saw Fairfax from my window. Let me go down to make sure it is really him."

"Fairfax!" exclaimed Wintervale. "Are you sure?"

"But your window doesn't face the street. How did you see him?" asked Kashkari.

"He was walking across the grass. Who knows? Maybe he wants to refamiliarize himself with everything."

"About time," said Wintervale. "We need him to play."

"He still does not feel the strength in his leg," said Titus, moving toward the stairs. The otherwise charm he had created before he first stepped into the school was fairly watertight: no one doubted that Fairfax existed.[11] All the same, he had better reach the ground floor soon. The boys would not recognize her as Fairfax unless someone said the name aloud; and only Titus could do that. "Who knows whether he will still be any good at sports after an injury like that?"

Wintervale's other passion, besides returning the barony of Wintervale to its former glory, was cricket. He had convinced himself—and a fair number of other boys—that Archer Fairfax was the veriest cricket prodigy whose return would propel the house team to the school cup.

"Strange. He's been gone only three months, and already I can't remember what he looks like," said Wintervale.

"Lucky you," said Titus. "Fairfax is one of the most ferociously ugly blokes I have ever met."

Kashkari chuckled, catching up with Titus on the steps down. "I'll tell him you said that."

"Please do."

Mrs. Dawlish's house, despite its overwhelming majority of male occupants, had been decorated to suit Mrs. Dawlish's tastes. The wallpaper in the stairwell was rose-and-ivy. Frames of embroidered daisies and hyacinths hung everywhere.

The stairs led down to the entry hall, with poppy-chintz-covered chairs and green muslin curtains. A vase of orange tulips nodded on the console table beneath an antique mirror—a boy was required to examine himself in the mirror before he left the house, lest his appearance disgrace Mrs. Dawlish.

Titus was two steps above the newel post when Fairfax came into the entry hall, a slim, tall-enough figure in the distinctive tailed jacket of an Eton senior boy. Immediately he was appalled by his abysmal judgment. She did not look like a boy at all. She was much, much too pretty: her eyes, wide-set and long-lashed; her skin, needlessly smooth; her lips, red and full and all but shouting girlishness.

She saw him and smiled in relief. The smile was the worst yet: it brought out deep dimples he had not even suspected she possessed.

Dread engulfed him. Any moment now someone was going to shout, *What is a girl doing here?* And since everyone knew Fairfax as his closest friend, it would take no time for the agents stationed at Eton to put two and two together and conclude that there was far more than just cross-dressing going on.

"Fairfax," he heard himself speak—his voice almost did not quiver. "We thought you were never coming back."

Almost immediately Kashkari said, "My goodness, it *is* you, Fairfax!"

"Welcome back, Fairfax!" hollered Wintervale.

With the repetition of her name, other boys swarmed out of the woodwork and took up the chorus of "Look, Fairfax is back!"

At the sight of so many boys, her smile disintegrated. She did not say anything, but looked from face to face, her hand tightening upon the handle of the valise. Titus could not breathe. For eight years he had lived in a state of slow-simmering panic. But he had never known real terror until this moment. He had always depended on himself; now everything depended on her.

*Come on, Fairfax,* he implored under his breath. But he knew it. It was too much. She was going to drop the valise and bolt. All hell would break loose, eight years of work would circle the drain, and his mother would have died for nothing.

She cleared her throat and beamed, a smug, lopsided grin. "It's good to see all your ugly faces again."

Her voice. Lurching from one emergency to another, he had paid no mind. Now he truly heard it for the first time: rich, low-pitched, and slightly gravelly.

But it was her grin, rather than her voice, that steadied his heartbeat. There was no mistaking the cockiness of that grin, absolutely the expression of a sixteen-year-old boy who had never known the taste of defeat.

Wintervale bounced down the rest of the steps and shook her

hand. "You haven't changed a bit, Fairfax, as charming as His Highness here. No wonder you two were always thick as thieves."

Her brow lifted at the way Wintervale addressed Titus. Wintervale knew who Titus was, but to the rest of the school, Titus was a minor Continental prince.

"Do not encourage him, Wintervale," said Titus. "Fairfax is insufferable enough as it is."

She looked askance at him. "Takes one to know one."

Wintervale whistled and slapped her on the arm. "How's the leg, Fairfax?"

One of Wintervale's thwacks could snap a young tree. She managed not to topple over. "Good as new."

"And is your Latin still as terrible as your bowling?"

The boys snickered good-naturedly.

"My Latin is fine. It's my Greek that's as ghastly as your love-making," she retorted. The boys howled, including Titus, who laughed out of sheer shock—and relief.

She was good.

Brilliant, in fact.

CHAPTER ✦ 7

AFTER RUNNING THE GAUNTLET OF handshakes, backslaps, and general greet-and-insults, Iolanthe hoped for a moment to breathe. But it was not to be.

"Benton!" Wintervale called. "Take Fairfax's bag to his room. And make sure you light a good fire there. Fairfax, come with us for tea."

A smallish boy, wearing not a tailed coat but one that stopped at the waist, whisked the valise away.

"Work him hard." Wintervale smiled at her. He was as tall as the prince, blond and strapping, almost spinning in place with nervous energy. "Benton hasn't done much in your absence."

She didn't ask why she had to work Benton hard—the prince would explain everything later. She only grinned at Wintervale. "I'll make him regret that I ever came back."

Before Little Grind, Master Haywood had taught at a school for boys. Each evening, after sports practice, a group of them would walk past Iolanthe's window, chatting loudly. She'd paid particular attention to the most popular boy, carefully noting his cheerful swagger and good-natured insults.

Now she was acting the part of that happy, affably cocky boy.

The prince, walking a pace before her, turned his head and slanted her an approving look. Her heart skipped a beat. She didn't think he was the kind to approve easily.

Entering Wintervale's room, however, stopped her dead. On his windowsill bloomed a sizable weathervine—terribly useful for knowing when an umbrella would be required for the day.

Only it couldn't be a weathervine, could it? The weathervine was a mage plant. What was it doing in—

The prince put his arm about her shoulder. "Forgot what Wintervale's room looks like?"

She let him ease her inside, knowing that she shouldn't have stopped to gawk. "I was just wondering whether the walls were always so green."

"No, they weren't," said Wintervale. "I changed the wallpaper just before the end of the last Half."

"You are lucky—and good," the prince whispered in her ear.

His breath against her skin sent a jolt of heat through her entire person. She couldn't quite look at him.

The room was soon filled to capacity. Two small boys crouched before the fire, one making tea, the other scrambling eggs with surprising expertise. A third delivered buttered toast and baked beans.

She observed the goings-on carefully: the young boys, no question about it, acted as minions to the older boys.

Benton, who'd earlier been tasked with taking her valise to her room, now returned with a plate of still-sizzling sausages.

"You didn't burn them again, did you, Benton?" Wintervale asked.

"I almost never burn them," Benton responded indignantly.

Wintervale poked Iolanthe with his elbow. "The new boys, they do get so ornery by the third Half."

His elbow rammed a very tender spot in her chest. She would always be proud that she only sucked in a breath in reaction. "They'll learn their places yet."

She walked to the plant and fingered its soft, ferny leaves. A weathervine, no doubt about it. "Did you always have this?"

"I raised it from a seedling," Wintervale answered. "It was probably only three inches tall when you went home with the broken limb."

Perhaps the prince gave one to him? "It doesn't seem as if I've been gone quite that long."

"How was Somerset?" Kashkari asked.

*Somerset?* Instinctively she moved closer to the prince, as if his proximity made her less likely to make mistakes. "You mean Shropshire?"

The prince, who'd taken a place on Wintervale's bed, gave her another approving look.

Acacia Lucas, one of Master Haywood's pupils in Little Grind, had been quite keen to marry the prince. One day, during a practical under Iolanthe's supervision, Acacia had pointed at his portrait and whispered to her friend, *He has the face of an Angel*. Iolanthe had looked up at the prince's coldly haughty features and snorted to herself.

Acacia was not entirely right—or entirely wrong. He was nothing like a sublimated Angel. But a sublunary one, perhaps: the dangerous kind that made those gazing upon them see only what they wished to see.

She saw a stalwart protector. But was that what he truly was, or merely what she desperately wanted? As much as she did not wish to, somewhere deep inside she understood that he had not risked everything purely out of the goodness of his heart.

"Sorry, is it Shropshire?" Kashkari shook his head. "How was Shropshire then?"

He had straight blue-black hair, olive skin, intelligent eyes, and an elegant, if slightly forlorn mouth—an outstandingly handsome boy.

"Cold and wet for the most part," said Iolanthe, figuring that was always an acceptable weather for spring on a North Atlantic island. And then, remembering herself, "But of course I spent all of my time inside, driving our housekeeper batty."

"How was Derbyshire?" the prince asked Kashkari, moving the topic away from Archer Fairfax.

Iolanthe let out the breath she'd been holding. The prince had shown remarkable foresight in making Fairfax someone who'd spent most of his life abroad: it could be used to excuse his lack of knowledge concerning Britain. But it was the barest piece of luck that she'd remembered his mention of Shropshire. No matter how unfamiliar with England an expatriate was, he should still know where he lived.

"I wish there were enough time between terms for me to go back to Hyderabad. Derbyshire is beautiful, but life in a country house becomes repetitive after a while," Kashkari replied.

"Good thing you are back in school now," said the prince.

"True, school is more unpredictable."

"Is that so? School is predictable for me, and I like it that way," said Wintervale. "We should have a toast. To school, may it always be what we want it to be."

Tea was ready. Wintervale shooed out the young lackeys and poured for his guests. They clinked their teacups. "To dear old school."

Tea at home was usually accompanied by a few bites of pastry. But here tea—the table was laden with eggs, sausages, beans, and toast—constituted a meal on its own. Iolanthe hoped this meant that the boys would concentrate on their food. Any more questions and she was bound to betray herself.

"Make sure you eat enough," said Wintervale. "We need you ready for cricket."

What cricket? Grasshopper? "Ah—I'm as ready as I will ever be."

"Excellent," said Wintervale. "We are in desperate need of a superior bowler."

A what? At least Wintervale did not expect her to define what a bowler was. He only extended his hand to her. "To a season to remember."

She shook his hand. "A season to remember."

"That's the spirit," said Kashkari.

The prince did not look nearly as thrilled. What exactly had she committed herself to with that handshake? But before she could pull him aside and ask, Kashkari had another question for her.

"I don't know why, Fairfax," he said, "but I have a hard time remembering how you broke your leg."

Her stomach plunged. How did she fudge a question like that?

"He—" Wintervale and the prince began at the same time.

"Go ahead," the prince said to Wintervale.

She drank from her cup, trying not to appear too obviously relieved. Of course the prince would take care of her.

"He climbed the tree at the edge of our playing field and fell off," Wintervale answered. "The prince had to carry him back here. Didn't you, Your Highness?"

"I did," said the prince, "with Fairfax crying like a girl all the way."

Oh, she did, did she? "If I wept, it was only because you were so pitiful. I weigh barely nine stone. But one'd think I were an elephant the way Your Highness moaned. 'Oh, Fairfax, I cannot take another step.' 'Oh, Fairfax, my legs are turning into pudding.' 'Oh, Fairfax, my knees are buckling. And you are crushing my delicate toes.'"

Kashkari and Wintervale chuckled.

"My back is still hurting to this day," said the prince. "And you weighed as much as the Rock of Gibraltar."

Their exchange was almost flirtatious. But she could not help notice that in the midst of the general jollity, he remained apart— had she never met him she'd have considered him moody. She wondered why he was utterly alone when he was among mates.

Her, of course, she realized with a start. *She* was the reason. She was his great secret.

And now they were in this secret together.

She flashed him a smile. "What are friends for, prince?"


"I am sorry I did not have the time to tell you that Wintervale is an Exile," Titus said. "He is an elemental mage, in fact, but any non-mage with a match can produce a more impressive flame than he."

They stood some distance from the house, near the banks of the brown and silent Thames. Titus had rowed on the river for years. The repetition, the perspiration, and the good, clean exhaustion quieted his mind beautifully.

Eton was not always a pleasant place: many boys had a difficult time finding their place in the hierarchy, and there were senior boys who roundly abused their powers. But for him, the school, with its drafty classrooms, its grueling sports, its thousand boys—and even its agents of Atlantis—was the closest thing to normalcy he had ever known.

"Are there other mages here?" she asked.

The day was fleeing. And so were the clouds, leaving behind a clear sky that had turned a deep twilight blue, except for the western horizon, still glowing with the last embers of sunset.

"Besides Wintervale, only the agents of Atlantis."

She had been almost giddy with relief upon leaving Wintervale's room, but this reminder of Atlantis's omnipresence sobered her mood. Her eyes lowered. Her shoulders hunched. She seemed to grow smaller before his eyes.

"Afraid?"

"Yes."

"You will become accustomed to it." Not true at all. He never had, but learned to carry on in spite of it.

She took a deep breath, snapped a leaf from a weeping willow, and rolled it into a green tube in her hand. Her fingers were slender and delicate—very much a girl's.

"Wintervale calls you 'Your Highness' and nobody bats an eye. Do they all know who you are?"

"Wintervale does. But to everyone else, I am a minor Germanic princeling from the House of Saxe-Limburg."

"Is there such a house?"

"No, but anyone who has ever heard of the name will find it on a map and in history books as a principality of Prussia—the regent's mage-in-chief made sure of it."

"That is a highly illegal otherwise spell, it is not?"

"Then do not tell anybody that is also how I made a place for Archer Fairfax here."

This earned him a long glance from her, half-approving, half-disquieted.

At the edge of the river they stopped. The water was a dark ripple, with a few daubs of reddish gold.

"The Thames," he said. "We row on it, those of us who do not play cricket."

He thought she might ask what exactly cricket was, but she only nodded slowly.

"Across the river is Windsor Castle, one of the English queen's homes," he added.

She looked south for a moment at the ramparts that dominated the skyline. He had the distinct feeling that she was only half listening to him.

"Is there something on your mind?" he asked.

She glanced at him again, reluctant admiration in her eyes. He rarely cared what others thought of him. But with this girl who observed him carefully and unobtrusively, who was as perceptive as she was capable . . .

"We spoke of my guardian earlier, did we not?"

Her decision to confide in him pleased him—and turned him oddly anxious. "We did, at the hotel."

She dropped the willow leaf into the river; it swirled in a small eddy. "For the past several years I have been frustrated with him. He had been a scholar of great promise. But then he made one terrible mistake after another and became a nobody in the middle of nowhere.

"I learned today that, fourteen years ago, to keep me safe, he gave up certain crucial memories of his past to a memory keeper. Since then he has lived without knowing the events that brought him to where he was."

Titus could scarcely imagine how the man had managed for so many years. It was the current medical consensus that memory escrow was eminently unsuitable for the long term. After a few years the mind started to hunt for the missing memories. They became an obsession.

"That was probably the reason he turned to merixida," she went on. "Now that I think about it, all those choices that cost him his career and even his respectability—he must have been trying, however subconsciously, to force the memory keeper to intervene."

She picked up a pebble from the ground and tossed it with a flick of her wrist. The pebble skipped four times on the surface of the river before disappearing beneath the currents. She watched the river a moment longer, then squared her shoulders and stood taller, as if she had come to an important decision.

"My case is different, of course. I'm in full possession of my memories. But like him, I'm in the dark. And I don't want to be."

"Am I keeping you in the dark?"

She bit her lower lip. "Please don't mistake me. I am enormously grateful for everything you've done. Were I a better person, I'd let myself be guided by gratitude and only gratitude. But I have to ask, why? Why have you placed yourself at such risk? Why do you defy the Inquisitor? Why are you involved at all?"

She was embarrassed to be asking these questions—her foot scuffed the soft ground of the bank, as fidgety as he had ever seen her. But all the same, her voice was wary.

The exchange he would ask for had always seemed fair and simple to him. He kept the elemental mage safe; and in return, the elemental mage lent him the great powers he needed. But would *she* see it that way?

Perhaps he needed to use her guardian as a bargaining chip: she could not infiltrate the Inquisitory on her own. Neither could he, but she did not know that.

He, however, did know. He was a liar by necessity, but could he lie to her, knowing that he was very possibly asking for her life in return?

That he did not answer immediately discomfited her. She ran her hand through her hair, only to pull her fingers back in surprise, as if she had forgotten that most of her hair had been shorn and destroyed.

She shook her head slightly, her eyes wistful. He stared at her, this girl who would never again be safe anywhere.

No, he would not lie, not to her. Going forward, it would be the two of them against the world, an alliance that would define what remained of his days on this earth.

And be his only chance for something true and meaningful.

For a minute Iolanthe thought the prince would not tell her anything at all. Then he made a double impassable circle around them.

One did not make a double impassable circle unless one absolutely did not want to be overheard. The breeze coming off the river suddenly felt raw.

The prince gazed across the water at a narrow strip of an island. His profile was familiar—it graced every coin of the realm—yet she couldn't look away. Handsome boys she'd met before. He was more than handsome; he was striking. And there was a nobility to his bearing that had little to do with his bloodline and everything to do with the sense of purpose he radiated.

"I am going to bring down the Bane."

His quiet words brushed over her and departed on a cold gust. She shivered and waited for him to tell her that it was a joke—since he did have a sense of humor.

He met her eyes squarely, his gaze unwavering.

This was mad. He might as well bring down the Labyrinthine Mountains—it would be easier. The Bane was invincible. Untouchable.

"Why?" Her voice was hoarse.

"Because that is what I am meant to do."

Despite her incredulity—or perhaps because of it—she found his conviction awe-inspiring.

"How—how do you know that is what you are meant to do?"

"My mother told me so."

When people talked about Princess Ariadne, it was usually to speculate on the mysterious liaison that had produced the prince. No one could recall another instance in the whole history of the House of Elberon when a ruling prince's paternity remained unknown.[12]

"Was your mother a seer?"

"She was." What was the emotion underlying his reply? Anger, resignation, sadness—or a mix of all three? "At her wish, it was never revealed to the public."

True seers were few and far between. "What did she prophesy that has come true?"

Without bending down he had a pebble in hand. He weighed it. "Twenty-five years ago, she and my grandfather received a delegation of Atlantean youth. There was a girl of seventeen who was not a delegate, but a mere assistant. My mother pointed out the girl to my grandfather and said that one day the girl would be the most powerful person in the Domain."

"The Inquisitor?"

He tossed the pebble. It skipped far. "The Inquisitor."

That was scarily impressive. "What else?"

"She knew the exact date of Baroness Sorren's funeral, years before the baroness even took up the charge against Atlantis."

This unnerved Iolanthe. No wonder Princess Ariadne hadn't wanted it known that she was a seer, if funeral dates were the sort of things she foresaw.

The prince skipped another pebble. "She also said that it was on my balcony that I would first learn of your existence. And so it was."

A flicker of hope ignited in Iolanthe's heart. "And she said that you would bring down the Bane?"

He did not answer immediately.

"Did she or did she not?"

"She said that I must be the one to try, to set things into motion."

"That's not a guarantee of success, is it?"

"No. But we will never accomplish anything worthwhile in life if we require the guarantee of success at the onset."

His audacity took her breath away. Compared to him, she had lived on the smallest scale, concerned only with the well-being of herself and Master Haywood. While he, who could have led a life of unimaginable luxury and privilege, was willing to give it all up for the sake of the greater good.

"What is my part in your plan?"

"I need you," he said simply. "Only with a great elemental mage by my side will I have a prayer of a chance."

When she'd been a child, enthralled by her reading of *The Lives and Deeds of Great Elemental Mages*, she'd wondered what it would be like for her own powers to grow to such fearsome immensity, to hold the fate of entire realms in the palm of her hand. Listening to him, she felt a stirring of that old excitement, that electric charge of limitless possibilities.

"Are you really sure I am that great elemental mage?"

The certainty in his eyes was absolute. "Yes."

If he was convinced, and Atlantis too, and Master Haywood so much so as to give up his memories—she supposed they could not all be wrong. "So . . . how will we bring down the Bane?"

"We will have to pit ourselves against him someday."

She felt dizzy. Surely they could find some clever way of defeating the Bane from a distance.

"Face-to-face?" Her voice quavered.

"Yes."

The froth of imagined valor in her heart dissipated, leaving behind only dregs of stark fear.

But the prince thought so highly of her. And risked so much. She'd hate for him be disappointed in her. She'd hate for *her* to be disappointed in her. In the four *Great Adventures* and all seven *Grand Epics*, books she'd cherished as a child, this was the moment the protagonist rose to the occasion and embarked on the legendary journey. No one in the stories ever said, *Thank you, but no thank you, this really isn't for me.*

Yet this really wasn't for her. Thoughts of heroics might stir her soul for a minute, but no more than that. She didn't want to go anywhere near the Bane, let alone take part in some sort of match to the death.

If she were dead, she'd never become a professor at the Conservatory and live on that beautiful campus again.

Besides, the Domain had long been under the shadow of Atlantis.

She was inured to the reality of it. She had no burning desire to topple the Bane and no wish—unless it was to free Master Haywood—to ever cross paths with the Inquisitor.

"I thought—I thought I was here to hide," she said, hating how feeble she sounded.

"You cannot hide forever from Atlantis."

She would be found one day, he meant, and must fight or die.

She wanted to muster her courage, but she might as well pluck diamonds out of thin air. Her feet felt as if they were dissolving; her lungs, as if they'd been filled with mercury.

"How exactly am I supposed to—defeat the Bane?"

"I am not sure. I have been reading about elemental magic for years, but I have yet to discover how to harness the power of a great elemental mage—and only by harnessing the power of a great elemental mage can one defeat the Bane, according to my mother."

"Harnessing the power of a great elemental mage . . ." she echoed slowly. "You mean, as the Bane does."

"No, not the way he does."

"Then how?"

"I do not know yet."

She was confused. "So you are going to experiment on me?"

"No, I am going to experiment *with* you, not on you. We are in this together."

She wanted desperately to trust this boy who looked as if he'd been born under the wings of the Angels, beautifully unafraid. But they were *not* in this together. To help him achieve his goal of altering the course of history, she would have to give up her entire purpose of survival.

And great elemental mage or not, she was no great heroine, just an ordinary girl trembling in a pair of nonmage shoes that pinched slightly at the toes.

Her desire to impress him, however, still warred with her need to save herself. "Perhaps—I'm only supposed to help you in an advisory capacity."

She was a coward, but better cowardly than dead.

He shook his head. "No, you are the most essential part."

Each word fell on her like a knife. "But if I don't know what to do and you don't know what to do—"

"I will find out, eventually. In the meantime I will train you to better channel your powers. Potential is not enough; you must achieve mastery. Only then can you face the Bane."

Her lips quivered. She could no longer deny the truth. "I don't want to face the Bane."

"No one does, but you cannot escape your destiny."

Did she believe in destiny, she who shamelessly curried favor with a lowly village official, just so she could stay in one place until her qualifying exams? "I don't have a destiny," she said weakly.

"Maybe you did not learn about it until today, but you do and you always did."

His voice was urgent, his gaze intense. Were she any kind of a dreamer, the force of his conviction would have carried her away. "I'm not this brave soul you think I am. I came with you because you offered sanctuary. I don't have what it takes to shoulder what you ask."

He was silent for a moment; something flickered in his eyes. "What of your guardian? You can rescue him on your own?"

His questions agonized her for nearly a full minute before she recognized them for what they were: manipulation. He was not above using her anxiety for Master Haywood to get his way.

*Every last mage in pursuit of you seeks to abuse and exploit your powers.*
*Trust no one.*

Why hadn't she understood it sooner? For all the prince's seeming majesty, he was monumentally ambitious and wanted her only as a means to his own ends.

Dismay spread unchecked in her heart. "This is beneath you, Your Highness. My guardian did not make his sacrifices so that I could throw away my life on a wild quest doomed to fail. He would be apoplectic if I allowed myself to be exploited this way."

The prince's jaw tightened. "I am not exploiting you. I have saved you two times, offered you as much security as you will find anywhere on this earth, and put myself at abysmal risk. It is a fair enough exchange to ask for some help from you for a good cause— for as worthy a cause as there ever was."

Unlike her, he had not raised his voice. But he sounded defensive.

"So a steer should head willingly to slaughter because the farmer has fed and housed it? How many would make this bargain if they only knew what would happen to them in the end? You are asking me to give up everything for a cause that isn't mine. I don't want to be part of any revolution. I just want to live."

"To live like this, never knowing what it is like to be free?" His voice was tight.

"I will know nothing when I'm dead!"

Her anger was all the more bitter because she had stood ready to place her faith and hope in him. To rely on him as her anchor in this new, turbulent life. And to repay his kindness to the utmost of her ability.

Only to be told that he wanted her to die for him.


Back in Archer Fairfax's room, Iolanthe lifted the dull-red valise the prince had given her to carry as her own and placed it on the desk. Inside were boy's clothes, unfamiliar-looking coins, a map of London, a map of the Eton-Windsor area, and a book called *Bradshaw's Monthly Railway Guide*.

"Please reconsider," said the prince.

She spun around sharply. She had no idea when he'd vaulted into the room.

He stood with his back against the wall, his expression blank. "You do not even know where to go."

But she did. The prince had said that his school was not far from London. She needed to be back in London. Master Haywood had advised her to wait near the end portal for as long as possible, for the arrival of the memory keeper. The move had its risks. But she did not plan to go back inside the madwoman's house. She could monitor the house from outside, a nearby rooftop, perhaps—

"I would not even think about it."

Her heart missed a beat, but she turned back to the valise, pocketed the coins, and pretended to check what else it contained.

"That woman in the attic knows who you are—or what you are, at least. She will have consulted other Exiles. There are informants among the Exiles. Atlantis will have the entire neighborhood under surveillance by now. The agents will strip the house of its protections for you to vault in, if you are desperate enough to try. Do it, and it will be the last anyone sees of you."

She felt nauseous. "Britain is a large realm. My options are nearly endless. As you yourself said earlier, Atlantis, great as it is, cannot hope to locate me so easily in a land of millions."

"You are not as anonymous as you think. Your jacket is part of the Eton uniform. It will mark you anywhere as an Eton boy. The natives will wonder why you roam about when you should be at school instead—and they will remember you."

She broke into a sweat. She could reveal herself so easily, without even being aware of it. "All I have to do is to change."

She exchanged the jacket for a brown one from the valise.

"If only it were so easy. In the countryside, where everyone knows one another, you will be too conspicuous. So you must go into cities, where anonymity is possible. But you do not know which parts of a city are safe for a well-dressed young man, and which will get you robbed and possibly beaten. And before you reassure me again how handy you are with your fists, how many grown men can you take on at once, without resorting to elemental powers?"

"If you aim to convince me that every place out there is dangerous for me," she retorted, "you have not succeeded."

But he was coming awfully close.

"Every place out there *is* dangerous for you. Have you not realized this yet?"

She wished he wouldn't speak so quietly and reasonably. "More dangerous than here? You will lead me to my death."

"I will lay down my life for you. Do you know anyone else who will do that?"

*I will lay down my life for you.* The words had a strange effect on her, a pain almost like a wasp sting to the heart. She shut the valise. "Can you promise me I will live? No? I thought not."

He was quiet. Saddened. She had not perceived it earlier, but now she saw that there was always a trace of melancholy to him, a heavy-heartedness that came of being entrusted with too great a burden.

"I'm sorry," she said, unable to help herself.

He walked to the window and looked toward the darkening sky. His left hand tightened on the curtain. She could not be completely sure, but it seemed that he shivered.

"What is it?" she asked.

He remained silent for some more time. "The stars are out. They will be quite beautiful tonight."

He turned around and came toward her, his wand raised. She took a step back, uncertain of his intentions. But he only tailored the brown jacket to fit her.

"Thank you," she mumbled.

"If you are going to be caught by Atlantis, you might as well look your best."

She wanted to snort coolly, but could do nothing of the sort. She seemed to have a ball of sawdust in her throat.

"So . . . this is good-bye."

"It does not need to be."

She shook her head. "You took the risks for a reason. Since I can't give you what you want, I shouldn't put you at further risk."

"Let me decide how much risk I am willing to bear," he said softly.

This almost undid her altogether. If he would shelter her even when she would not help him . . .

No, she must not let herself become starry-eyed again. "I can't stay, but thank you, in any case, for telling me the truth."

A shadow darkened his eyes before his face quickly became unreadable. He placed a hand on her shoulder. For a moment she thought he would pull her in and kiss her, but he only drew the pad of his thumb across her forehead, a princely benediction.

"May Fortune walk with you," he said, and let go of her.

# CHAPTER · 8

*DÉJÀ VU.*

It seemed only moments ago that Iolanthe last stood in the same spot behind Mrs. Dawlish's house, looking up at Fairfax's window. Except then she was going toward safety. Now she was leaving for unknown dangers.

There was no movement behind the curtain, but the light remained on, a golden rectangle of comfort and refuge. She ought to be off, but she kept watching the window, hoping for things she had no more right to expect.

If only she didn't feel so small and alone out here, like a lost child, in desperate need of a helping hand.

The hotel suite was out of the question. The ruined barn, then. The memory of its leaky, muddy interiors did not appeal, but she closed her eyes and willed herself to traverse the distance.

The displacement did not happen. She tried again; still no use. The distance must be greater than her vaulting range. And since she didn't know any places en route, she could not break the journey into smaller segments.

She kicked the nearest tree in frustration. Could her retreat be any more inept? She should have considered her course of action with much better care. Should have had an achievable destination in mind. And failing that, should have at least swiped the prince's vaulting aid.

And put on a warmer jacket. Now that night had fallen, the temperature had taken a tumble. The brown jacket she had changed into was not quite thick enough to shield her from the chill. She hugged herself with her free hand.

The cold also made her realize she was hungry. She'd hardly eaten anything this entire day; her stomach was emptier than a midnight street.

If nothing else, she had to find some food.

She took one last look at Fairfax's brightly lit window. If something were to happen to her, would the prince feel a tug of loss?

She shivered. She told herself it was only the cold. Besides, she didn't need to go back to a place she'd already been. She'd put the English coins from the valise into her pocket. By walking along the streets of Eton, she'd probably find an inn where she could buy something to eat and a bed for the night.

In the morning things wouldn't look so dire.

She inhaled deeply, shifted her valise to her left hand, and headed for the street. But she'd barely taken two steps when something made her look up.

The sky was a deep, cavernous blue. The prince was right: the stars were out, brilliant and countless. Leo. Virgo. Gemini. And there, Polaris, the North Star, anchoring the great celestial compass.

But what were those black dots high above, almost invisible against the darkness of the night? She squinted. Birds didn't fly in a perfect diamond formation, did they?

The birds headed east and disappeared in the distance. Before she could breathe a sigh of relief, however, another group approached from the west, again in a perfect diamond formation.

This time, as they passed overhead, three birds broke formation. They circled, descending as they did so, until she saw the dull metallic glint of their bellies.

They were not birds, but the infamous armored chariots of Atlantis, aerial vehicles that could convey a single visiting dignitary, or shower rains of death upon mutinous populations.[13]

What had the prince said? That once news of her arrival spread, Atlantis would have the madwoman's entire district surrounded, on the chance that Iolanthe might return.

If this was Atlantis mobilizing, then the prince had, if anything, understated the ferocity of its response.

The rush of blood was loud in her ears. She dug frantically into every pocket for her wand. It wasn't until she was almost in tears that she remembered she'd left it behind in the laboratory, after the prince advised her not to have anything on her person that might identify her as an escapee from a mage realm.

Now she was caught in the open without a wand.

She tried to reason with herself. Atlantis did not know her precise location—here in Britain she was but a single speck of sand on a mile-long beach. Besides, Atlantis sought a girl, and dozens of boys had failed to recognize her as one.

But the three armored chariots above her continued to descend. She scurried into a coppice of trees, her hands trembling, her heart careening.

Two hundred feet above the ground, the armored chariots stopped, suspended in air.

She gripped the nearest trunk for support.

A moment later, a cluster of mages at least a dozen strong appeared on the lawn behind Mrs. Dawlish's house.

In hindsight, her reaction had been entirely predictable. Why would anyone want to embrace such a hopeless cause? Titus himself hated it with a passion, this albatross around his neck.

But he had been deluded by his own sentiments. His entire life had been defined by secrecy and subterfuge. With her he yearned for a true partnership, a rapport of trust, understanding, and good will—everything he had never experienced before.

Stupid, of course. But stupid did not mean he wanted it less badly.

He left the window and sat down on the spare chair, a sturdy Windsor with a thick, tufted cushion in gray-and-white-striped cloth. The chair he had selected himself, the fabric for the seat cushion likewise. He had also chosen the blue wallpaper and the white curtains. He knew very little of decor, but he had wanted to make the room calm and comforting, knowing that the events leading to Fairfax's arrival at Eton were inevitably going to be traumatic.

Opposite him on the shelves were books he had collected with the express purpose of familiarizing Fairfax with the nonmage world: a handbook of Britain for foreigners, several almanacs and encyclopedias, a guide to Eton written by a former pupil, a volume on etiquette, another on rules for the most popular games and pastimes, among dozens of others.

So much thought, so much effort, so much futility.

He should have bent his mind to duplicity. He was the best actor of his generation, was he not? He could have said that he must protect her at whatever cost because she had been prophesied to be the love of his life. There, an easy, marvelous lie, perfect for deceiving a girl. She would have stayed, and he would have proceeded with her training, no further questions asked.

But she had wanted truth and he, in a fit of derangement, had wanted honesty and fair dealing. And truth, honesty, and fair dealing had brought him to this fine wreck.

He bolted out of the chair. That sound, what was it? He turned off the light and rushed to the window.

Bloody hell—as his classmates would say.

*Bloody hell.*

He vaulted for it.

One of the mages pointed in Iolanthe's direction. They all loped toward the coppice.

She panted, the sound of her fear fracturing the silence.

Could she take on all the mages come to hunt her? Or was it better to vault back to the hotel and hope that fewer agents of Atlantis awaited her there? And did she dare throw all caution to the wind and call down a second bolt of lightning, if it should come to that?

Another mage materialized on the lawn, a woman in nonmage clothes. Iolanthe shrank farther inside the coppice. The woman strode purposefully toward the agents of Atlantis.

They spoke softly. Iolanthe could not make out their conversation, except to note that despite their low voices, they exchanged some heated words.

At last the Atlantean agents vaulted away, probably back into the armored chariots. And the woman, with a final look around, also disappeared.

Someone tapped her on her shoulder. She leaped in sheer terror. But it was only the prince.

"They are gone for now. I am not sure if they will remain gone. Leave fast if you want to leave."

*Ask me to stay, just a few days, until the worst passes.*

He did nothing of the sort. And why should he? She'd made it abundantly clear that nothing could induce her to stay.

"What happened just now?" she asked, her voice holding more or less even, as if she weren't still petrified.

"A jurisdictional dispute."

She bit the inside of her cheek. "What does that mean?"

"It means that the mages from the chariots were dispatched by the Inquisitor. But Mrs. Hancock here has her orders directly from Atlantis's Department of Overseas Administration, and she does not care for the Inquisitor's minions barging in on her territory without express invitation. They knew it, which was why they tried to conceal themselves right here, where you are."

Her heart pounded even more violently than before.

"Go," he said.

She had no choice but to admit the obvious. "I don't know where to go."

He took her hand and placed it on his arm. The next moment they were on a brightly lit street, across from a long, pillared building with curved mansard roofs.

"Where are we?"

"Slough, a mile and a half north of Eton. That is the railway station." He pointed at the long building. "You have a timetable in your bag and more than enough money to go anywhere. Take a steamer to the Americas if you want."

He was angry with her, but he was still helping her. Somehow that made a future without him even bleaker. Her heart was full of strange pains she could not begin to name.

He turned her around. She now faced a squat two-story house.

"That is an inn. You can buy your supper there and stay the night if you prefer to leave in the morning. Make sure you monitor what goes on outside and know the location of the rear exit."

"Thank you," she said, not quite looking him in the eye.

"And take this."

He pressed a wand into her hand.

"But it's yours."

"Of course not—it is an unmarked spare. I cannot have my wand in your possession when you are captured."

Not if, but *when*.

She raised her head. But he'd already disappeared.

The inn was small, but cheerfully lit and scrupulously clean. A fire blazed in the taproom. The aroma was of strong ale and hot stew.

Mrs. Needles often railed against the evils of an empty stomach: it sapped warmth, drained courage, and decimated clear thinking. Iolanthe had been cold, confused, and disheartened when she pushed open the doors of the inn. But now, with her supper laid out on the table before her—chunks of beef and carrots swimming in gravy, slices of freshly baked bread with a huge mound of butter, and the promise of a pudding to come later—she felt slightly more herself.

She had selected a table next to the window, within view of the back door, which led out to an alley. Upstairs a spare but decent room awaited her. And in front of her, the railway timetable. She had already circled the train—a very crude form of expedited highway, from what she could gather—she intended to take in the morning.

She reached for a slice of bread and slathered it with butter. At his resident house, the prince would soon also be sitting down to supper. Would he think of her, as she thought of him? Or would he secretly rejoice, relieved not to have to take on the Bane?

Master Haywood would be pleased that she'd wisely turned away from the prince's extravagant schemes to concentrate on her own survival. She stared at the bread in her hand, glistening with melting butter, and wondered whether the food offered to Master Haywood in the Inquisitory was as palatable. And would the agents of Atlantis do anything for him when symptoms of merixida withdrawal began? Or would they simply let him suffer?

"What are you thinking, you handsome lad?"

Iolanthe jumped. But it was only the barmaid, smiling at her.

Smiling *flirtatiously.*

"Ah . . . a brimming mug of ale, served by the prettiest girl in the room?"

The girl giggled. "I will fetch that ale for you."

Iolanthe stared at the barmaid's retreating back, wondering how to keep her away. She couldn't afford even the possibility of a situation where someone might find out she wasn't such a handsome *lad* after all.

The barmaid glanced over her shoulder and winked. Iolanthe hastily looked out the window. At home a hub of the expedited highways usually had more than one inn. Perhaps she'd see some-thing else nearby.

Across the street, high above the railway station, hovered two armored chariots. On the ground, a team of agents—easy to dis-tinguish from the startled English pedestrians by their uniform tunics—fanned out from the station. Several of them headed directly for the inn.

The fear that seized her made time itself stretch and dilate. The man reading a timetable under a streetlamp yawned, his mouth opening endlessly. The diner at the next table asked his mate to "Pass the salt," each syllable as drawn out as pulled taffy. The mate, moving as if he were inside a vat of glue, set his fingers on a pewter dish with a small spoon inside and pushed it across.

With a loud thump, a great tankard of ale was plunked down before Iolanthe, the froth high and spilling. She jerked and glanced up at the barmaid, who winked again meaningfully. "Anything else for you, sir?"

Her illusion of freedom crumbled.

She was not safe here. She was not safe anywhere. And she had no choices except between dying now or dying slightly later.

She threw a handful of coins beside her largely untouched supper and ran for the back door.

He was a bastard. Of course he was: he lied, cheated, and manipulated.

She would not like him very much when she realized what he had done.

It did not matter, Titus told himself. He did not walk this path for flowers and hugs. The only thing that mattered was that she should come back. The hollow feeling in his chest he ignored entirely.

He turned on the light in Fairfax's room and waited. A quarter hour passed. And there she was, her face pale, her eyes wild.

"If you are looking for your hat, it is on the hook over there," he said as casually as he could manage. "Pay me no mind; I am just here to forge a good-bye note from you."

She dropped her valise, pulled out the chair at her desk, and sank into it, her face buried in her hands.

In the last few weeks of his mother's life, she too had often sat like this, her face in her hands. Impatient with her anguish, he used to yank at her sleeve and demand that she play with him.

After her death, for months he could think of nothing but whether she would have still decided on the same course of action had he been different, had he patted her on the back and stroked her hair and brought her cups of tea.

He moved forward slowly, cautiously, as if the girl before him were a sleeping dragon.

Against his better judgment, he laid a hand on her shoulder.

She shook, as if caught in a nightmare.

He had always considered himself cold-blooded. Sangfroid was a trait highly prized by the House of Elberon. His grandfather had especially insisted on it: one was permitted to lose one's life, but never one's detachment.

Now, however, his detachment cracked. Somewhere inside him, he shook too, with the force of her fear, her confusion, and her vulnerability—an empathy that shocked him with its depth and enormity.

He yanked back his hand.

"They were there." Her voice sounded ghostly, disembodied. "They were at the railway station. Two of those armored chariots in the air and—and agents were headed for the inn."

Of course they had been there. He had told Mrs. Hancock that if Atlantis really thought the girl was nearby, they should watch the rail stations, since she would not know Britain well enough to vault far.

"Did you vault here directly from your dining table?"

"No, from the alley behind. I hope I left enough coins for supper—I was in too much of a hurry."

"Now is hardly the time to worry about the innkeeper's profit."

"I know." She turned her face toward the ceiling and blinked rapidly. He was shocked to realize that she was on the verge of tears. "It's stupid. Of everything that happened today, I don't know why this is the one thing that—"

She passed the base of her palm over her eyes. "I'm sorry."

The thing to do now would be to pull her into his arms for a reassuring embrace, perhaps even to kiss her on her hair. Offer her the comfort she craved and convince her that she had made the right choice to return.

He could not do it. If anything, he took a step back.

She glanced up at him. "Can I still be Archer Fairfax?"

He clasped his hands behind his back. "You understand what you are to give in return?"

Her lips twisted. "Yes."

"I require an oath."

She exhaled slowly. "What do you want me to swear on?"

"Let me clarify. I require a blood oath."[14]

She was on her feet. "What?"

"The only meaningful oath is one that can be enforced. Your life is not the only one at stake here."

She trembled, but she met his gaze. "For a blood oath I want more. You will always tell me the truth. You will free my guardian. And we will make one and only one attempt on the Bane. Whether we succeed or fail, you will release me from this oath."

As if there would ever be a second attempt.

"Granted," he said.

He found a plate, set it on the desk, and aimed his wand at the plate. *"Flamma viridis."*

A green flame flared. He opened his pocketknife, passed the blade through the fire, cut open the center of his left palm, and let three drops of blood fall on the flame. The fire crackled, turning a more brilliant emerald hue. He lowered the knife into the flame again and passed it to her. "Your turn."

She winced, but copied his action. The fire devoured her blood and turned the color of a midnight forest. He gripped her still bleeding hand with his and plunged their joined hands directly into the cold, cold flame.

"Should either of us renege on the oath, this fire will spread in the veins of the oath breaker. It will not be so cool then."

The fire abruptly turned a brilliant white and burned. She hissed. He sucked in a breath against the scalding pain.

Just as abruptly, the flame went out, leaving no trace of having ever been there. She pulled her hand back and examined it anxiously. But her skin was perfectly smooth and intact; even the self-inflicted wound at the center of her palm had disappeared.

"A little taste of what awaits the oath breaker," he said, perhaps unnecessarily.

"You've thought of everything, haven't—"

Her voice trailed off.

The curtains were securely drawn. From where she stood, she could not see out. Yet she stared at the window, disbelief in her eyes. Her denial made the hollow feeling in his chest return with a vengeance. She still wanted to believe he was better than this.

But it was inevitable. She was too sharp, and he had been too hurried to be subtle.

Her already pale face turned ashen, her jaw hardened, she

scratched a nail down the center of her palm, where the cut had been.

"You saw them in the sky, didn't you, the armored chariots? That was why you told me about the stars, so that I'd be sure to look up and see them."

Her voice was unnaturally even. He thought of her thanking him for his honesty. She had to be thinking of the same thing, knowing that even as she spoke those words, he was already planning to betray her trust.

He said nothing.

"You couldn't have had the decency to tell me that they were out there and that I should wait a quarter hour before venturing out?"

"Decency is not a virtue in a prince."

She laughed bitterly. "The house in London, is it really surrounded by agents of Atlantis?"

He might have exaggerated the likelihood that Lady Wintervale would speak of her arrival to other Exiles. Lady Wintervale was inclined toward secrecy, not confessions.

"Did you also have something to do with the armored chariots at Slough, the ones that sent me scrambling back to you?"

He shrugged.

She laughed again. "So what then, exactly, is the difference between you and Atlantis?"

"I still gave you a choice. You came back here of your own will."

"No, I came back here because you cornered me. You played fast and loose with my life. You—"

She fell back against the wall, her face contorted by pain.

"Thinking of reneging on the oath already?" He could only imagine the agony that slashed through her.

She looked as if she could scarcely breathe. Her voice was hoarse. "This cannot be a valid pact. Release me now!"

"No."

*Never.*

She closed her eyes briefly. When she opened them again, they were full of cold fury. "What kind of person are you, to live without honor or integrity?"

His nails dug into his palm. "Obviously, the kind chosen for what others are too decent to do."

He wanted to come across as flippant, but instead he sounded harsh and angry.

She clenched her hand. "I liked you much, much better when I didn't know you."

It did not matter. He had what he wanted from her. What she thought of him was henceforth irrelevant.

He had to draw a deep breath before he could reply. "Your affection is not required in this endeavor, Fairfax, only your cooperation."

She stared at him. Suddenly she was right before him. Her fist struck him hard low in the abdomen.

He grunted. The girl knew how to hurt someone.

"You bastard," she snarled.

An irrelevant thought gripped him: he should have kissed her when he still had the chance.

He straightened with some effort. "Supper is in half an hour, Fairfax. And next time, tell me something I do not already know."

# CHAPTER · 9

EVERY THOUGHT BROUGHT AGONY.

Iolanthe didn't know when she collapsed on the floor, but it was as good a place as any to suffer.

The pain was unlike any she'd ever known—messy and brutal, dirty, rusty blades scraping along her every nerve ending. She almost prayed for the clean blackness of suffocation.

It took her a long, long time to find ways to think that did not renew the torture. It was painless to picture the prince's eventual wife cuckolding him with every attendant in the castle. It was also all right to imagine his children detesting him. And most satisfying of all, it did not hurt to envision the entire population of Delamer spitting on his casket, for his funeral to turn into a farce and a riot.

She didn't need to be a historian to know that the House of Elberon had been in decline. No doubt he wanted to revive its fortunes and make his mark. No doubt he wanted to be the next great prince. She was but a pawn in his plan, just as for the Bane she was but a thing to be sucked dry and discarded.

She felt raw and depleted, as if she'd come through a terrible illness. She almost could not believe that when she'd awakened this day, her biggest concern had been Rosie Oakbluff's wedding. That seemed years ago, a different lifetime altogether.

Holding on to the edge of the desk, she pulled herself upright.

Somehow this was not too unknown a place, being barely on her feet while the world reeled around her. In fact, there was an eerie familiarity to it: each time Master Haywood had lost his post, she'd thought they'd come to an abyss from which they'd never emerge.

Except this time, it really was the abyss, the end of life as she knew it.

What should she do?

As if to answer her question, her stomach grumbled—she'd been too nervous at tea and too distracted by her thoughts in the inn. She almost laughed. She was still alive, so she must eat—and downstairs supper awaited.

This she was accustomed to: carrying on no matter what; making the best of a terrible situation.

What else was there to do?


Titus knocked on her door and received no answer.

"You do not want supper?"

Still no answer.

He went down by himself. To his surprise, when he arrived outside the dining room, she was already there, deep in conversation with Wintervale. Or rather, Wintervale analyzed the strengths and weaknesses of rival houses' cricket teams, and she listened attentively.

Wintervale must have said something funny. She threw back her head and laughed. The sight stopped Titus cold: she was terrifyingly pretty. He did not understand how Wintervale could stand so close and not realize a thing.

Wintervale continued talking. She gazed upon him with a frank appreciation. The urge came upon Titus to smash Wintervale into a china cabinet. It was difficult to believe that he had known her only mere hours: she had already turned his life upside down.

He approached them. She gave him a cursory nod before returning her attention to Wintervale. Kashkari arrived beside Titus, and they spent a minute talking of the liquefaction of oxygen, a new non-mage scientific achievement about which Kashkari had just read in the papers.

The dining room's door opened. With pushes and shoves, the boys entered, then settled themselves at two long tables, self-segregated by age. Mrs. Dawlish sat down at the head of the senior boys' table, Mrs. Hancock, the junior boys' table.

"Will you say grace, Mrs. Hancock?" Mrs. Dawlish asked.

At the mention of Mrs. Hancock's name, Fairfax, across the table from Titus, tensed. Titus could see that she wanted to turn around and have a good look at Mrs. Hancock, but she was careful enough to imitate the other boys and bow her head instead.

"Our Heavenly Father," began Mrs. Hancock, "assist us in your boundless mercy as we embark on a new Half in this ancient and splendid school. Guide the boys to be industrious and fruitful in their studies. Keep them strong and healthy in body and mind. And may 1883 be the year you bless them at last with victories upon the cricket pitch—for Almighty Lord, you know how sorely we have been tried in Summer Halves past."

The boys groaned and snickered. Mrs. Dawlish, half smiling herself, shushed them.

Fairfax raised her head, surprise written all over her face. Did she imagine that the agents of Atlantis could not be perfectly charming individuals? Mrs. Hancock was beloved in this house, almost more so than Mrs. Dawlish.

"We give our thanks for the bounty of this meal, O Lord," continued Mrs. Hancock. "For Mrs. Dawlish, our stalwart dame. Even for the boys, whom we love dearly but, if history is any indication, will wish to throttle with our bare hands before the week is out."

More laughter.

"All the same we are overjoyed that all of our boys have returned safely to us, especially Fairfax. May he refrain from climbing trees this Half."

Fairfax's hands tightened on the table. She bowed her head again, as if to hide her unease at being singled out by an enemy.

"But above all other things may we attain the knowledge of thee, O Lord, and serve thee with every breath and every deed. For thine is the kingdom, and the power, and the glory, for ever and ever. Amen."

"Amen," echoed the boys.

Fried smelts, asparagus, and orange jelly were served—what must be strange food to Fairfax. She ate sparingly. Three minutes into supper, she dropped her napkin. She turned in her seat, picked up the napkin, and, as she straightened, finally glanced toward Mrs. Hancock.

Mrs. Hancock was, in Titus's opinion, a more attractive woman than she let on. She favored shapeless dresses in infinite varieties of dull brown and always kept her hair covered with a large white cap. But it was the buckteeth that really left a lasting impression—teeth that Titus did not believe to be naturally overlarge.

To his relief, Mrs. Hancock, speaking with a boy on her left, did not appear to notice Fairfax's attention. To his further relief, Fairfax did not stare long. In fact, did not stare at all. If Titus had not been specifically looking for it, he might not even have noticed that she had peeked at Mrs. Hancock.

Fairfax resumed her non-eating, chewing a spear of asparagus as if it were a piece of firewood. *Now* Mrs. Hancock turned—and gazed at the back of Fairfax's head.

Titus quickly looked down. His heart pounded. It was possible a woman would realize sooner that Fairfax was a girl. Did Mrs. Hancock already suspect something, or did she pay attention because Fairfax was nominally Titus's best friend and must be kept under close watch?

"Would you pass me the salt?" Wintervale asked Fairfax.

The saltcellar was right next to Fairfax, a small pewter dish. But dishes from any self-respecting kitchen in the Domain would already be seasoned just right for each person at the table. Unless she helped with the cooking, she would not even know what salt looked like.

But before he could act, she reached out with perfect assurance, took a pinch of salt to sprinkle on her fried smelt, and handed the saltcellar to Wintervale.

Titus stared at her in astonishment. The look she returned was one of pure contempt.

Soon she and Wintervale were again chin-deep in cricket talk. Titus managed to carry on a creditable conversation with Kashkari. But he could not concentrate, his awareness saturated with the sound of Fairfax and Wintervale relishing each other's company.

That, and the more-than-occasional looks Mrs. Hancock cast their way.

The cricket talk did not stop at the end of supper, but continued in Fairfax's room, a chat to which Titus was emphatically not invited.

He opened a cabinet next to his bed. Inside the cabinet was a late-model Hansen writing ball, a typewriter that resembled a mechanical porcupine, with keys arranged on a brass hemisphere. He loaded a sheet of paper into the semicylindrical frame beneath the hemisphere.

The keys began moving, driving the short pistons beneath them to form the words and sentences that made up Dalbert's daily report to Titus.

The report, partly in shorthand, partly in code, would have made no sense to Titus's schoolmates—or most mages, for that matter. But to Titus, a half page conveyed as much information as an entire English broadsheet.

Usually he was informed about the decisions of the government, but tonight there were no mentions of the regent or the prime minister. Instead Dalbert supplied what information he had gathered on Fairfax and her guardian.

Haywood had been born on the largest of the Siren Isles, a picturesque archipelago southwest of mainland Domain. His father had been the owner of a commercial fishing fleet, his mother a fishery conservation expert. The couple had three children: Helena, who died in childhood, Hyperion, who ran away from home at an early age, and at last Horatio, the high-achieving offspring to make any parent proud.

The records of his education were typical enough for a gifted and ambitious young man, culminating in his admission to the Conservatory, where his brilliance stood out even among a brilliant crowd. At the end of his third year, his parents passed away in rapid succession, and he began to run with a fast set. There were numerous minor infractions on his record, though his academic success remained undiminished.

The wildness came to an abrupt end when he assumed guardianship of an eleven-month-old baby named Iolanthe Seabourne. The little orphan had been under the care of an elderly great-great-aunt. When the old woman became ill, she had contacted the person named next in the late Seabournes' will to take charge of the girl.

Interestingly enough, the guardianship had not been without minor controversy. Another friend of the Seabournes' had stepped forward and claimed that before the child had been born, the Seabournes had asked to put her name in their will, as the one to care for their child in the unlikely event of their demise.

The will was brought out. Haywood's name was in it, hers was not, and that was the end of the matter.

Everything seemed fine for a while, but seven years ago, Haywood was caught match-fixing intercollegiate polo games. He was relegated to a position at the Institute of Archival Magic, where he plagiarized one of the better-known research papers in recent memory. After he lost *that* post, he found work teaching at a second-tier school. Still unchastened, he accepted bribes from pupils in exchange for better marks.

Outrageous actions on his part, yet the memory keeper had not intervened.

As for the girl, she was a registered Elemental Mage III, uncommon but still far less rare than an Elemental Mage IV, one who controlled all four elements. Judging by her academic record, she had no intention of becoming a street busker—the choice of many elemental mages these days, eating fire before tourists for a living.

And interestingly enough, the deeper Haywood got himself into trouble, the better her marks became and the more effusive the praise from her schoolmasters. A desirable trait, this, the ability to subsume fear and frustration into a singular focus.

His door opened, and in charged Wintervale.

Titus crumpled the report and threw it into the grate. "We do not knock anymore?"

Wintervale grabbed him by the arm and dragged him to the window. "What the hell are those?"

The armored chariots were still there, motionless in the night air.

"Atlantis's aerial vehicles. They have been there since before supper."

"Why are they here?"

"I told you I met the Inquisitor today—must have run afoul of her," said Titus. "Go ahead. Throw a rock at them and start your revolution."

"I would if I could throw a rock that high. Aren't they worried about being seen?"

"Why should they be? If anything, the English will think the Germans are up to no good."

Wintervale shook his head. "I'd better go check on my mother again."

"Give her my best."

Titus waited a minute, then left his room to knock on Fairfax's door. "Titus."

"Come in," she said, to his surprise.

She was in a long nightshirt, sitting barefoot on her bed, her back against the wall, playing with fire. The fire was in the form of a Chinese puzzle ball, one openwork sphere nestled inside another, and yet again another.

"You should not play with fire," he said.

"Neither should you." She did not look up. "I assume you are here to discuss freeing my guardian?"

Her voice was even. There was an almost preternatural calm about her, as if she knew precisely what she wanted to do with him.

When he was nowhere as certain what to do with her.

"Are you?" she pressed the point.

He had to remind himself that having sworn a blood oath to always tell the truth, he could no longer lie to her—at least not when asked a direct question.

"I came to get my spare wand back and to discuss your training. But we can talk about your guardian, too."

She pulled the wand out from under her mattress and tossed it at him. "So let's talk about him."

"I am going back to the Domain in a few days. While I am there, I will arrange a visit to the Inquisitory to see how he is getting along."

"Why don't you order him released?"

She had asked the question to needle him. He had no such

powers, not even if he were of age. "My influence over the Inquisitor is severely limited."

"What can you do then?"

"I need to first see whether he is still in rescuable shape—he may or may not be, depending on what the Inquisitor has done to him."

"What do you define as not being in rescuable shape?"

"If his mind has been completely destroyed, I will not run the risk of physically removing him from the Inquisitory. You will have to accept that you have lost him."

"And if he is still all right?"

"Then I will need to plan—my goal has been to stay out of the Inquisitory, not to get in."

"You can find out what you need easily enough, can't you?"

"I can. But I would rather not be known to ask about it."

"You don't have anyone you can trust?"

He hesitated. "Not about you or any plans involving you—everyone has something to gain by betraying us."

"I imagine a deceitful person such as you would see deceit everywhere," she said, her voice sweet. "I can also imagine why no one would voluntarily risk anything for you."

Her words pierced deep, like arrows from an English longbow.

Part of him wanted to shout that he longed for nothing more than trust and solidarity. But he could not deny the truth of her words. He was a creature of lies, his entire life defined by what others did not and could not know of him.

But things were supposed to be different with her—with Fairfax. They were to be comrades, their bond forged by shared dangers and a shared destiny. And now of all the people who despised him, she despised him the most.

"You see the difficulties involved in removing your guardian from the Inquisitory then," he answered, hating how stiff he sounded. "That is, if he is found to be still sentient."

"*I* will decide whether he still has enough mental capacity left to warrant a rescue."

"And how will *you* do that?"

"I will accompany you to the Inquisitory. You must have ready means to transport me back to the Domain—otherwise where would you stow Fairfax during school holidays?"

"You do understand you could be walking into a trap, to enter the Inquisitory so baldly?"

"I will take that risk," she said calmly.

He realized with a flash of insight that he was dealing with no ordinary girl. Of course, with her potential, she had never been ordinary. But the ability to manipulate the elements was an athletic gift—almost. Great elemental power did not always coincide with great presence of mind.

But this girl had that force of personality, that steeliness. At a time when a less hardy girl—or boy, for that matter—would have been wrecked by the calamity, or incoherently angry, she had decided to push back against him, and to take charge of as much of the situation as possible.

She would have made a formidable ally—and an equally formidable foe.

"All right," he said. "We will go together."

"Good," she said. "Now what did you want to tell me about my training?"

"That we must begin soon—tomorrow morning, to be exact—and that you should expect it to be arduous."

"Why so soon and why so arduous?"

"Because we do not have time. An elemental mage has control of as many elements in adulthood as she has at the end of adolescence. Are you still growing?"

"How can I know for certain?"

"Precisely. We have no time. Since today has been a difficult day, I will expect you at six o'clock in the morning. Day after tomorrow it moves to half past five. And then, five for the rest of the Half."

She said nothing.

"It will be to your advantage to get up early. You do not want to use the lavatory when everyone else is there."

Her lips thinned; she again said nothing. But the fire in her hand merged into a solid ball, and then a ball full of barbs. No doubt she wished to shove it down his throat.

"As for bathing, you might want to stay away from the communal baths. I will tell Benton you want hot water in your room."

"How kind of you," she murmured.

"My munificence knows no bounds. I also brought you something to eat." He dropped a paper-wrapped package on her desk. She had not eaten much either at tea or at supper, and he did not imagine it would have been very different at the inn. "Good-night cake—eat it and you will have no trouble sleeping."

The cake was for his insomnia. It would be a long night for him.

"Right," she said. "So that I won't have trouble waking up for the training."

Abruptly she jerked, her shoulders bracing forward as if she had been punched in the stomach. Her fingers clawed into fists. The fireball turned the blue of pure flame.

"Thinking about how you will slack off during your training?"

The oath called for her to do her utmost.

She grimaced and straightened, saying nothing.

He could not afford to have her bottled up like this. Much better that she took it out on him periodically.

A thought occurred to him. "I know you want to punish me, so here is your permission. Do your worst."

"I will only punish myself."

"Not when you have my consent. Think about burning me to cinders every minute of the day, if it pleases you. And as long as you do not actually kill me, you can think and mete out whatever abuses you want."

She snorted. "What's the catch?"

"The catch is that I am allowed to defend myself. You want to hurt me? You have to be good enough."

She looked up at him for the first time, her eyes alight with speculation.

"Go ahead, try it."

She hesitated a second, then her index finger moved in a circle. The fireball transformed into a firebird, shot high in the air, and swooped down at him.

"*Fiat ventus.*"

The firebird's wings beat valiantly, but could not advance against the air current generated by his spell.

She snapped her finger and the firebird quadrupled in size: she took all the fire from the fireplace.

"*Ignis remittatur.*"

His spell sent the fire back to the grate.

Her eyes narrowed. "And what would you do now, bring out the old shield charm again?"

The entire room was suddenly ablaze.

"*Ignis suffocetur.*" The fire went out, suffocated under the weight of the spell.

He flicked a nonexistent speck of ash from his sleeve. "There is more than one way to snap a wand, Fairfax."

She had underestimated him.

He was cunning and ruthless. But she'd failed to perceive that he was also a mage of great ability. An elemental mage's fire was not easy to divert by subtle magic, and yet he did it effortlessly—without even the aid of a wand.

*You seem to have prepared a great deal for this.* She'd had no idea how much. He was not a normal boy of sixteen, but a demi-demon in a school uniform.

"You are no match for me yet, Fairfax. But you will be, someday. And the more diligently you train, the sooner you can penalize me at will. Think about it: the fearful look in my eyes when I beg for mercy."

She was being very adroitly maneuvered. He wanted her to slave for his goal, holding out his debasement as a carrot before her. But that wasn't what she wanted. She wanted only to—

She yanked sharply away from any thought of freedom.

"Please leave," she said.

He pulled out his wand. *"Ignis."*

A small fireball blazed into being. He waved it toward her. "Your fire, Fairfax. I will see you in the morning."

## CHAPTER 10

THE LAVATORY WAS NOT, THANKFULLY, as nasty a place as the prince had led Iolanthe to believe. Still, one look at the long urinal trough and she resolved to visit as infrequently as possible.

The corridor, like the rest of the house, had walls papered in ivy and roses. The lavatories and the baths occupied the northern end. Directly opposite the stair landing was a large common room. South of the common room were the individual rooms for the sixteen senior boys—fifteen senior boys and Iolanthe.

She and the prince occupied two adjacent rooms at the southern end of the floor. Across from their rooms was a smaller common room reserved for the house captain and his lieutenants. And just north of the prince's room was the galley where the junior boys did some of the cooking for the senior boys' afternoon tea. As a result, she and the prince were isolated from the rest of the floor.

As he'd intended, no doubt.

A seam of light shone underneath his door. Memories came unbidden: herself in the dark, looking up at the window of her room, yearning for the light. For him.

She reentered her room, closed the door, and dressed. The evening before, she'd disrobed with excruciating care, extricating the shirt studs, studying the attachment of the collar, and making sure she could duplicate the same knot with her necktie. She did not go to bed until she'd managed the *serpens caudam mordens* spell seven consecutive times.

No trouble with it this morning: the figurative serpent that was the binding cloth bit into itself and tightened to the limits of her endurance. The rest of the clothes went on easily enough. The necktie refused to look as crisply knotted as it had earlier, but it was acceptable.

When she was done, she checked her appearance in the mirror.

She'd always thought that if one looked carefully, it was possible to detect the cynicism beneath her sunny buoyancy. Now there was no need to look carefully at all. Mistrust and anger burned in her eyes.

She was not the same girl she had been twenty-four hours ago. And she never would be again.

The prince knelt before the grate, already dressed. At her entrance, he pulled a kettle from the fire.

"Did you sleep well?"

She shrugged.

He glanced at her, then bent to pour water into a teapot. For a moment he appeared strangely normal—young and sleep-tousled—and it made her acutely unhappy.

She looked away from him. Unlike her room, which had been carefully decorated to convey Archer Fairfax's colonial upbringing, his was plain except for a flag on the wall, which featured a sable-and-argent coat of arms with a dragon, a phoenix, a griffin, and a unicorn occupying the quadrants.

"That is the flag of Saxe-Limburg." He pointed to a map on the opposite wall. "You will find it as part of Prussia."

A golden tack, embossed with the same heraldic designs as the coat of arms, marked a tiny squiggle of land. She walked past the map to the window, lifted the curtain a fraction of an inch, and looked up.

The armored chariots were gone.

"They left at quarter past two," he said. "And they are probably not coming back—an order from Atlantis supersedes an order from the Inquisitor."

She resented that he'd read her thoughts.

"Give me that, would you?" He pointed to a small, plain box on his desk.

She handed the box to him. She thought he'd open the box, but instead he put it away in a cabinet that contained plates, mugs, and foodstuff before handing her a cup of tea.

The tea was hot and fragrant. How did he learn to make a perfect cup? When he'd been a junior boy, had he too carried luggage, lit fires, and cooked for senior boys?

She refused to ask him any personal questions. They drank their tea in silence. He finished first and inspected her, while she pretended not to notice it.

"Good," he said. "Except for the cuff links."

He showed her what cuff links were on his own sleeves. Pesky things: she'd thought them part of the previous day's shirt.

When she looked up from her cuffs, he was still studying her. "What is it?"

"Nothing."

"You are to always tell me the truth."

"The truth as it relates to our mission. I am not obliged to inform you of my every thought, just because you happen to ask."

"You snake," she said.

"What can I say? Prince Charming only exists in fairy tales. And speaking of fairy tales —"

From a bookshelf next to the window, he lifted a small stone bust, pulled out the volume beneath, and set it on his desk. The book looked very old. The leather binding, once probably a brilliant scarlet, had faded to a reddish brown. The gold embossing on the title had smudged away almost entirely, but she managed to make out the words *A Book of Instructional Tales*.

"This is the Crucible," he said.

"What is a Crucible?"

"I will show you. Sit down."

She did. He took a seat on the other side of the desk and placed his hand on the book.

"Now put your hand on the book."

She followed his direction, half-reluctant, half-curious.

He was silent for more than a minute—must be quite the long password. Then he tapped the book with his wand. Her hand was suddenly numb to the elbow. Something yanked her forward. She opened her mouth to shout as the desk rose to meet her forehead with alarming speed.

She landed on her knees in tall grass. The prince offered her his hand, but she ignored him and pulled herself to her feet. All about her was a large meadow bathed in early morning light. At one end of the meadow, the beginning of rolling hills covered in a dense forest. At the other end, a good several miles away, a castle on a high knoll, its white walls tinted rose and gold by the sunrise.

"So it's a portal, the Crucible."

"That is not how it is used. Everything you see is an illusion."[15]

"What do you mean, illusion?"

It could not be. She scooped her hand into the tall grass. Small, white, five-petaled flowers nodded in the morning breeze. The blades of grass were rough against her skin. And when she broke a blade and brought it to her nose, the smell was the fresh and mildly acrid scent of plant sap.

"It means none of this is real."

A pair of long-tailed birds flew overhead, their feathers iridescent.

A herd of cattle masticated near the edge of the meadow. Her hand was wet with dew. She shook her head: she could not accept that all this was make-believe.

"If you walk ten miles in any direction, you will find you can go no farther—as if this world is but a terrarium under a giant bell jar. Since we do not have time to walk ten miles . . ."

He led her a hundred yards to the north and pointed toward the eastern horizon. "That is Sleeping Beauty's castle—you will battle dragons there someday. Do you see the second sun?"

The castle obscured most of the second sun, but an edge of it was visible, a pale circle in the sky, the same size and elevation as the sun, but two degrees farther south—no doubt put there to remind bumpkins like her that the Crucible was not real, after all.

"Think about it. Dreams are not real; but when you are inside a dream, it is real to you. The Crucible operates the same way. Except unlike dreams, it follows the physical and magical principles of the real world. Whatever works out there, works in here, and vice versa."

She touched her face. Her skin felt no different than it did in the real world. "Where is my person then?"

"Our bodies are in my room, probably looking as if we are taking a nap, our heads down on the desk."

This was extraordinary magic. "How did you get this book?"

"It is a family heirloom."

He turned toward the castle, pointed his own wand at it, then tossed her a wand. "At the ready."

"What did you just do?"

"Nothing."

"You pointed your wand at the castle."

"Oh, that. I cast a spell to break a window."

"Why?"

"Habit. I used to have trouble getting into the castle because of the dragons. So I broke windows from outside to annoy them."

"But that castle is three miles away. How can you break a window from this far?"

"Distance spell-casting. Use a far-seeing spell if you do not believe me."

She did. With the far-seeing spell, the castle was almost close enough to touch—and all its windows perfectly intact. She was about to call him on his bluff when a window blew apart in a shower of glass shards. A low roar rumbled, followed by a huge plume of fire that came from somewhere near the castle gate.

She scowled. "Are you training to be an assassin? Who uses such spells?"

"My mother had a vision in which she saw me practicing them. So I learned them."

"You should have your psyche examined. Most sixteen-year-old boys don't follow Mama's directions so slavishly."

"Most mothers are not seers," he answered simply. "Now, are you ready?"

"To do what?" She did not like the look on his face.

"You like flowers? *Decapitentur flores. Eleventur.*"

Thousands of white blossoms leaped into the air, impossibly pretty in the liquid light.

"Your training starts. *En garde.*" The prince raised his wand. "*Ventus.*"

A squall of flowers hit her with the force of thrown pebbles.

"Divert them," said the prince.

She waved the wand in her hand and imagined parting the tide of flowers. All she got for her trouble was a greater battering. Annoyed, she sent out a plume of fire. Immediately, something much bigger smacked her on the upper arm.

"What the—"

"Just cow dung. Now concentrate. I should not have to remind you this exercise is for air only."

*Just* cow dung?

And what did he know about elemental magic? Elemental mages didn't exercise. They either had an affinity for a particular element or they didn't. She'd known from the earliest moment of awareness that she could manipulate fire, water, and earth. And she did so, if not effortlessly—earth always required some exertion—then at least easily enough.

She ducked as a particularly large cluster of flowers careened toward her. "You are going to poke my eyes out."

"Do not let me."

She sent a huge spray of water his way, only to have it all thrown back at her, followed by a cowpat that hit her solidly in the rib cage.

She hurled her wand at him.

He stepped aside. "You have a good arm. Maybe Wintervale will get his wish after all."

She wiped her wet face with her hand. "What do you care?"

"I do not."

Her wand flew back at her. Flowers continued to batter her. And they hurt where they hit. She did her best to push them all back at him and pockmark his smug face. But nothing happened.

His lips moved. Blades of grass, a forest of them, rose straight up. His lips moved again. The blades of grass turned in midair, to point their sharp ends at her.

Blood drained from her face. The flowers had only hurt. The blades of grass, with their sharply serrated edges, would shred her.

They sped toward her. Instinctively she threw up a wall of fire to burn them to cinders. He put out her fire. She called for fresh fire. He made a prison for it.

She commanded the ground about her to rise up into an earthen wall. He shattered the wall before it had reached a foot in height.

"This is not about thwarting me," he said.

"Then don't try to hurt me."

"If you do not feel strongly about it, you will not be able to unblock whatever it is that makes you unable to command air."

"Maybe I don't want to unblock it. Not for you, you rat."

The vivisection-by-dull-knife pain of the blood oath came back with a vengeance. She swayed with the intensity of it. But she would not humiliate herself before him by collapsing to the ground. She would not. She would remain standing and defiant.

The grass scratched her face as she fell.

She burned with the force of her anger.

Her hand, of its own will, rose. Her wand pointed to the sky; her mind issued the command.

Before Titus quite understood what she intended, he had already jabbed his wand above his head. *"Praesidium maximum!"*

He had tested this shield against fire, but never lightning.

The sound of the lightning striking his shield was like that of grinding glass. The force of it was bone-snapping. He could barely keep his arm raised, barely scrape together enough strength to sustain the shield, which gave away inch by inch beneath the brilliant onslaught that made dots dance in his vision.

He grunted with the strain of keeping his wand aloft. The muscles of his shoulders and arms screamed in pain. He wanted to shut his eyes against the unbearable light.

How could lightning that came out of nowhere go on and on? How much more could his shield take? He felt it in his humerus, the obliteration of the shield, the cracking and splintering, air returning to being just air, and no protection at all.

The shield split altogether. His heart rammed up his throat. But the lightning, too, had spent itself. The air sputtered with remnant electricity.

He had survived a lightning strike.

"You will need to do better," he said—and hoped that his voice did not sound as limp as the rest of him felt. "When I went to Black Bastion, Helgira's lightning killed me outright."

She slowly came to her feet. "Helgira's been dead thousands of years, if she ever lived."

"Her tale is one of the training grounds in the Crucible—one of the more advanced ones."

Her lips pulled tight. "You can die in the Crucible?"

"Of course."

"With no consequences to your real person?"

"It is not pleasant. You die in the Crucible, and it will give you a deep aversion to going back to the scene of your death."

"You are in the Crucible now."

"True, but I have no plans to ever visit Black Bastion again. Someday, though, I might send you there for a battle royal against Helgira."

She shrugged. "Just because you fear her doesn't mean I will."

Titus had not slept much the night before, waiting for the

armored chariots to depart. As he stared at their barely visible metallic underbellies, he had gone over the events of the day again and again, knowing his actions had crossed a line—and knowing that he would have done exactly the same if he had to again.

At some point he had stopped defending himself. She was right: he was a villain who would stop at nothing to achieve his ends. And looking at her now, drenched, dirt-smeared, but unbowed, he realized had further to go yet.

If anyone could find a way to break a blood oath, she would. He must find some other way of holding her fast.

Or even better, find a way so that she would not wish to leave, even if she could.

But he could think of nothing—yet.

"That is enough for today," he said, pocketing his wand. "Time for school."

It was a sunny morning. Uniformed pupils exited resident houses in a steady stream. Along the way, junior boys clustered around various holes-in-the-wall—sock shops, the prince called them—buying coffee and freshly baked buns.

He took her to a bigger place, not exactly a proper restaurant but an establishment with two interconnected dining rooms, catering exclusively to senior boys. She ate a buttered bun and observed—it never hurt to know who was popular, who had information to share, and whom to avoid.

But even as she assessed her new surroundings, she felt herself similarly appraised. This was not new. From the moment they met, the prince had watched her intensely—after all, he believed her to be the means to his impossible ends. But since their exit from the Crucible, his gaze had seemed more . . . personal.

"What do you want now, Your Highness?"

He raised a brow. "I already have you. Should I want anything else?"

She pushed away her empty plate. "You have that scheming look in your eyes."

He turned the handle of his own coffee cup, from which he'd yet to take a sip. "That is terrible. I should only ever sport a condescending look. We never want to give the impression that I am capable of—or interested in—strategizing."

"You're fudging your answers, prince. I want the truth."

The corners of his lips turned up barely perceptibly. "I was thinking of how to best hold on to you, my dear Fairfax who would leave me at the first opportunity."

She narrowed her eyes. "Since when is a blood oath not enough to keep a mage enslaved?"

"You are right, of course. I should not doubt my own success."

"Then why do you doubt your own success?"

He looked her in the eye. "Only because you are infinitely precious to me, Fairfax, and the loss of you would be devastating."

He was speaking of her as a tool to be deployed against the Bane.

She didn't know why she should feel both a surge of heat and a ripple of pain in her heart.

She rose. "I'm finished here."

The school was old, a collection of faded, crenellated redbrick buildings around a quadrangle, at the center of which stood a bronze statue of a man who must have once been someone important. The cobblestones of the courtyard had been worn smooth from centuries of shuffling feet. The window frames looked as if they could use another coat of paint—or perhaps some fresh lumber altogether.

"I expected something more elegant," Iolanthe said. She'd attended grander, lovelier schools.

"Eton has a tendency to make do. They used to stuff seventy pupils in a broom cupboard and conduct class with the door open in winter."

She could not understand. "Why this school? Why a nonmage school at all? Why not just stick you in the monastery and give you incompetent tutors?"

"The Bane has his own seer. Or had—I have not received intelligence on the seer in my lifetime. But apparently he once saw me attend Eton in a vision."

The first principle in dealing with visions was that one never tampered with a future that had already been revealed.

"Destiny, then?"

"Oh, I am destiny's darling."

Something in his tone made her glance sharply at him. But before she could say anything, several boys came around and shook her hand.

"Heard you were back, Fairfax."

"All healed, Fairfax?"

She grinned and answered the greetings, trying not to betray the fact that she had no idea who anyone was. The boys went on their way. The prince was listing their names for her to remember when she was jostled from behind.

"What the—"

Two beefy boys chortled to each other. "Look, it's Fairfax," said one of them. "His Highness has his bumboy back."

Iolanthe's jaw dropped. His Highness, however, was not the least bit flustered. "Is that any way to refer to my dearest friend, pretty as he is? Or perhaps you are just jealous, Trumper, since your own dearest friend is as hideous as a crushed turnip."

So Trumper was the thick-necked one and Hogg the one with a broad, pale, and somewhat squashed-looking face.

"Who are you calling a crushed turnip, you limp-wristed, mollycoddled Prussian?" bellowed Hogg.

"You, you big, virile Englishman, of course," said the prince. He placed his arm around Iolanthe's shoulders. "Come, Fairfax, we are running late."

"Who are they?" she asked when they were out of hearing.

"A pair of common bullies."

"Are they alone in thinking that we share this particular relationship?"

"What do you care?"

"Of course I care. I have to live among these boys. The last thing I want is to be known as your . . . anything."

"Nobody has to know, Fairfax," he whispered. "It can be our little secret."

The way he looked, between irony and wickedness, made something go awry inside her. "The unvarnished truth, if you would."

He dropped his arm. "The general consensus is that you are my friend because you are poor and I am wealthy."

"Well, that I can believe, since I'm sure no one wants to be your friend otherwise."

He was silent. She hoped she'd injured his feelings—assuming he had feelings to injure in the first place.

"Friendship is untenable for people in our position," he said, his tone smooth, almost nonchalant. "Either we suffer for it, or our friends suffer for it. Remember that, Fairfax, before you become best chums with everyone around."

Early school, as the first class of the day was called, was taught by a master named Evanston, a frail, white-haired man who all but disappeared underneath his black master's robe. As it was the beginning of the Half, Evanston started on a new work, *Tristia*, by a Roman poet named Ovid. To Iolanthe's relief, her Latin was more than sufficient for the coursework.

Early school was followed by chapel. After the religious service, which she found slow and mournful, the prince took her back to Mrs. Dawlish's house, where, to her surprise, a hearty breakfast was laid out. The boys, many of whom she'd seen buying breakfast outside earlier, wolfed down a second one as if they'd been starving for three days.

After breakfast, they returned to classes—called divisions—until the midday meal back at Mrs. Dawlish's. Mrs. Hancock, who had not been there at breakfast, was now present. Again, it was she who said grace. This time she did not mention Fairfax by name, but Iolanthe still felt her sharp-eyed gaze.

She didn't know what made her do it. At the end of the meal, when the boys were filing out, she broke rank and approached Mrs. Hancock.

"My parents asked me to tell you, ma'am, that I'll be less trouble this Half," she said.

If Mrs. Hancock was taken aback by Iolanthe's maneuver, she did not show it. She only chuckled. "Well, in that case, I hope you are listening to your parents."

Iolanthe grinned, even though her palms were damp. "They are hoping so too. Good day, ma'am."

The prince waited for her at the door. She was surprised to see his expression of sullen impatience—it was unlike his controlled, reticent person. He didn't speak to her as they left the dining room.

But when they were outside Mrs. Dawlish's house, he said softly, "Well done."

She glanced at him. "Was that why you looked as if you'd like to hit me with something?"

"She would be that much more watchful of you if she believed our friendship to be genuine." His lips curled slightly, a halfhearted sneer. "Much better that she sees me as an arrogant prick and you an opportunist."

*Friendship is untenable for people in our position.*

She never wanted to feel sympathy for him. But she did, that moment.

Titus was curious to see her reaction to their afternoon divisions.

They had Latin again, conducted by a tutor named Frampton, a man with a big beak of a nose and fleshy lips. One rather expected Frampton to speak wetly, but he enunciated with nothing less than oratorical perfection as he lectured on Ovid's banishment from Rome and read from *Tristia*.

Fairfax seemed mesmerized by Frampton's master-thespian voice. Then she bit her lower lip, and Titus realized that she was not listening only to Frampton's voice, but also to Ovid's words of longing.

She too was now an Exile.

They were almost a quarter hour into the division before she saw Frampton for what he was. As he read, Frampton passed by her desk. She glanced up and seized in shock: the design on Frampton's stickpin was a stylized whirlpool, the infamous Atlantean maelstrom. Immediately she bent her head and scribbled in her notebook, not looking at Frampton again until he had returned to the front of the classroom.

After dismissal, she all but shoved Titus into the cloister behind the quadrangle, her grip hard on his arm.

"Why didn't you tell me?"

"He is obvious. You would have to be blind not to see."

"Are there agents who don't wear the emblem?"

"What do you think?"

She inhaled. "How many?"

"I wish I knew. Then I would not need to suspect everyone."

She pushed away from him. "I'm going to walk back by myself."

"Enjoy your stroll."

She turned to leave; then, as if she had remembered something, pivoted back to face him. "What else are you keeping from me?"

"How much can you handle knowing?"

Sometimes ignorance truly was bliss.

Her eyes narrowed, but she left without further questions.


Iolanthe didn't return to Mrs. Dawlish's directly, but walked northeast, along the road before the school gate. To the left of the road was a large green field; to the right a high brick wall twice as tall as she.

Hawkers lined this wall. An old woman in a much-patched dress tried to sell Iolanthe a dormouse. A sun-browned man waved a tray of glistening sausages. Other hawkers peddled pies, pastries, fruits, and everything else that could be consumed without plates or silver-ware. Around each hawker, junior boys congregated like ants on a picnic, some buying, the rest salivating.

The normalcy of the scene only made Iolanthe feel more out of place. For these boys, this *was* their life. She was only passing through, pretending.

"Fairfax."

Kashkari. She inhaled: Kashkari made her nervous. He seemed to be the rare person who asked a question and actually paid atten-tion to the answer.

"Where are you going?" Kashkari asked as he crossed the street and came to stand next to her.

"Reacquainting myself with the lay of the land."

"I don't think that much has changed since you were here last. Ah, I see old Joby is back with his ha'penny sherbet drinks. Fancy one?"

Iolanthe shook her head. "The weather's a bit cool for it."

But she followed Kashkari to a gaunt-looking hawker. Kashkari bought a handful of toasted walnuts and held out his palm to her.

"Look, it's Turban Boy and Bumboy together."

Iolanthe whipped around. Trumper and Hogg.

"Bumboy, is Turban Boy your coolie now?" sniggered Trumper.

Her reputation obviously had not preceded her here. Few school-children in any mage realm deliberately chose to provoke elemental mages, as by the time latter were old enough to attend school, they would have had years of conditioning, directing their anger into physical, rather than magical, responses. And also because an elemental mage was almost never considered at fault, as long as the school hadn't burned down at the end of a fight.

Kashkari must have seen the belligerence in her face. "Ignore them. They feel more accomplished when you rise to the bait."

"I hate to pass on good fisticuffs." She took a few toasted walnuts from him. "But after you."

The walnuts were sweet and crunchy. They walked on. Trumper and Hogg shouted insults and slurs for another minute before giving up.

"I was surprised you came back," said Kashkari. "Word went around that you might depart with your parents to Bechuanaland."

There were a number of Atlanteans in the Domain, especially in the bigger cities. But as far as Iolanthe knew, all of them, even the lowest clerks and guards, sent their children home for schooling. She had to assume the British weren't that different.

"My parents might go back. But they want me to finish my education here."

Kashkari nodded. So her answer was acceptable. She let out a breath.

"Do you miss Bechuanaland?"

What had she learned about the Kalahari Realm at school? It was the seat of a great civilization, its music, art, and literature much admired. Its legal system had been copied in many a mage realm around the world. And it was famous for the beauty of its gentlemen mages—this last, obviously, gleaned from somewhere other than geography lessons.

She popped a piece of walnut into her mouth to buy herself some time. "I do miss the weather when it gets too drizzly here. And of course the big-game hunting."

"Are the natives friendly?"

She was beginning to perspire. She had to believe that if her non-existent parents would return there, the situation could not be too dire. "No more hostile than they are elsewhere, I suppose."

"In India the population isn't always happy about the British presence. In my father's youth, there was a great mutiny."

How had he drawn her into a discussion about the political situation of the nonmage world, of which she had only the sketchiest of ideas? What she did know was that the mage realms of the subcontinent had also risen up against Atlantis, twice in the past forty years.

"An occupier should always consider itself despised," she said. "Is there ever a population that is happy to be subjugated?"

Kashkari stopped midstride. She tensed. What had she said?

"You have very enlightened views," he mused, "especially for someone who grew up in the colonies."

Unsure whether she'd put her foot in her mouth, she decided to brazen it out. "That's what I think."

"You two! I've been looking for you."

Iolanthe looked up, surprised to find herself only fifteen feet from Mrs. Dawlish's front door.

Wintervale leaned out of his open window. "Change quickly. I've already rounded up the other lads. Time to play cricket."

There was a book in Iolanthe's room that gave the rules of popular games. The night before, she'd skimmed through the section on cricket. But she'd been so tired and distracted, nothing had made any sense.

"Come on," said Kashkari.

She was doomed. It was one thing to nod and pretend to be engrossed as Wintervale pontificated on the game, quite another to pass herself off as an experienced cricketer. The moment she stepped on the pitch—that was what a playing ground was called, wasn't it?—it would be obvious she had no idea what to do.

All too soon, she arrived upstairs. Wintervale was in the corridor, dressed in a light-colored shirt of sturdy material and similarly light-colored trousers.

"Hurry," he said.

The prince was nowhere in sight. Kashkari was already shrugging out of his coat and waistcoat. Iolanthe had no choice but to also start unbuttoning, although she kept all her clothes firmly *on* until she was behind closed doors.

In her wardrobe she found garments similar to those worn by Wintervale. They fit her well, as did a pair of rugged brogues. When had the prince altered them? Never mind, she had more pressing concerns.

Wintervale knocked on her door. "What's taking you so long, Fairfax?"

She opened the door a crack, her hand tight on the doorknob. "My trousers are ripped. I need to patch them. You go on, I'll catch up with you."

"Hanson is handy with a needle." Wintervale pointed at a shorter boy behind him. "Want him to help?"

"Last time he helped me, he used my left testicle for a pincushion," she said.

The boys in the passage laughed and left, stomping down the stairs like a herd of rhinoceros.

She slipped into Wintervale's room to see the direction the boys went. Then she knocked on the prince's door. No one answered. She opened the door to an empty room.

Where was he when she needed him?

She could pretend to fall victim to a sudden abdominal complaint, but what if Wintervale, or someone else in the house—Mrs. Hancock, for instance—insisted on medical attention for her? The last thing she wanted was a scrutiny of her body.

She paced in the prince's room, torn. If she didn't go soon, Wintervale might send someone to fetch her—another undesirable outcome.

Had she the opportunity to spy on the game for some time, she might grasp its essence. But what if the playing field was entirely open, with nowhere for her to conceal herself?

There was no perfect solution. She'd better return to her room and study the rules of cricket again—if she could study with her heart hammering away—and then try to approach the pitch unobserved.

But as she stepped back into the corridor, Kashkari came out from his room.

"Shall we go then?" he asked amiably.

She was caught.

# CHAPTER ✦ 11

TITUS RAN.

He hated unanticipated events. The unanticipated should happen only to the *unanticipating*. It was not fair that he, who spent all his waking hours actively preparing for everything the future could lob at him, should be caught short like this.

Yet from the moment Fairfax burst into his life, he had lurched from one unforeseen event to the next. He should have told her to walk around with a limp, well enough to attend school but not eligible for sports.

It had come as a shock to him, his first Summer Half at Eton, hearing Fairfax discussed as a cricketer. But with the popular consensus already formed, it was too late for him to intervene and convince the other boys that Fairfax was instead a rower.

He had meant to give her a few surreptitious lessons in cricket, but there had not been time. And damn it, Wintervale was not supposed to call a practice today.

His lungs hurt, but he forced himself to run even faster. She had no idea what to do. She would flounder and betray her ignorance.

Wintervale might begin to question things. Of course he would not immediately conclude that Fairfax had never existed before yesterday, but it was dangerous to have anyone question anything.

When the individuals on the pitch became distinguishable, he saw that it was Kashkari bowling. Kashkari took a short run, wound his arm, and bowled. The ball flew fast, but Wintervale, at the crease, was ready for it. He knocked it low and straight, toward the exact middle of the gap between the mid-wicket fielder and the square-leg fielder.

It was a good hit. The ball would zip past the fielders and roll out of bounds, giving Wintervale's team an automatic four runs.

A white blur: someone sprinting at tremendous speed. That someone dove to the grass. When he again stood straight, he lifted his hand to show that he had scooped the ball out of midair.

Fairfax! And by catching the ball before it had landed, she had dismissed Wintervale, one of the best batsmen in the entire school.

Wintervale emitted a jubilant shout. "What did I tell you? What did I tell you? All we needed was for Fairfax to come back."

Titus belatedly realized that Wintervale was addressing *him*. He had stopped running at some point and was staring, agape. He gathered himself and shouted back, "One lucky catch does not a cricket prodigy make!"

This earned him a disdainful glance from Fairfax. For some reason, his heart beat even faster than a minute ago, when he had feared that his entire scheme would be going up in smoke.

The practice resumed. Not even two overs later—each over being a set of six balls bowled consecutively—she dismissed Sutherland by striking one of the bails above the stumps while he was still running.

Wintervale was beside himself. He had Fairfax replace Kashkari as the bowler and set Kashkari to bat. The moment the ball left Fairfax's hand, everyone on the field knew that the team at last had the bowler they desperately needed: she threw with an astonishing velocity.

Kashkari, not expecting the ball to hurtle at him so swiftly, barely managed to hit it. A fielder near him quickly scooped up the ball, and Kashkari could not score any runs.

Wintervale shouted directions at Fairfax. "Higher!" "Lower!" "Put some spin to it."

She spun the ball very decently for someone with such attack to her throw. Kashkari wiped his brow as she readied herself to bowl again.

"Take him out, Fairfax," Titus heard himself yelling, enthused beyond what he had ever thought possible for cricket. "Take him out!"

She did, by knocking off one of the bails above the stumps of the wicket. The team roared with approval. Titus shook his head in amazement. She was gifted: fast, strong, and marvelously coordinated.

Of course she was. How could he have forgotten that elemental mages were almost invariably great athletes?

She turned around to face Titus, raised her right hand, and, with her forefinger and middle finger pressed together, passed her hand before her face.

It was a boasting gesture. But there were boasting gestures and there were boasting gestures. She had just told him to go bugger himself.

He laughed, then his laughter froze. Had Wintervale seen the gesture, by any chance? It was emphatically not one used in the non-mage world, at least not in this country.

No, Wintervale was behind her, thank goodness. She turned to shake hands with Kashkari, that most gracious of sportsmen.

The practice resumed. She continued to excel, so much so that when the teams switched sides and she took her turn at bat, she could laugh off her otherwise grievous mistake of using the wrong side of the bat—the side with the slight V in profile rather than the flat one—as the result of too much excitement.

They carried on until the college clock sounded for evening chapel. At which point every boy grabbed his equipment and broke into a run—lockup was in ten minutes.

It was a festive rush, the boys ribbing one another for mistakes made during practice. Fairfax wisely refrained—except to chortle when expected.

They were within sight of Mrs. Dawlish's house when Wintervale suddenly exclaimed, "What the hell!"

Titus had already seen them. Fairfax glanced up. By the tightening of her expression, he knew she had spied the formation of armored chariots. They were almost invisible now, disappearing into the darkening eastern sky.

"What is it?" asked several of the boys.

Wintervale shook his head. "Never mind. Just the clouds. My eyes were playing a trick on me."

"What did you think you saw?" Kashkari persisted.

"Your sister kissing the chai-wallah," said Wintervale.

Kashkari punched Wintervale in the arm. The other boys laughed, and that was the end of it.

Except for Fairfax. She had been both exhausted and exulted; now she looked only exhausted.

*You will become accustomed to it,* the prince had said to her.

She had not yet. The feeling of naked vulnerability was an iron fist at her throat.

"Are you all right?" asked the prince. They'd made it back to Mrs. Dawlish's before lockup. He'd slipped into her room with her.

She shrugged. At least she didn't need to pretend with him—the boys had not dispersed immediately upon reaching the house, forcing her to maintain her cheery facade for another quarter hour.

"I lied," he said softly. "The truth is you will never get used to it. The taste of fear always chokes."

She flattened her lips. "That isn't what I need to hear now. You should have kept lying."

"Believe me, I would like to. Nothing sounds more unsettling than truth rolling off my tongue." He put a kettle in the grate, opened her cupboard, lifted out a tin box, and pressed a piece of cake into her hand. "I had the foodstuff delivered today. Eat—you will be less afraid on a full stomach."

She took a bite of the cake. She didn't know whether it made her less afraid, but at least it was moist and buttery, everything a cake ought to be.

"How did you learn to play cricket so quickly?" he asked.

She had suggested to Kashkari that they run to catch up with the other boys. She then pretended, as they reached the pitch, to suffer from a muscle cramp. That bought her time to sit on the sidelines. Watching the other boys, her hasty reading on cricket the evening before began to make sense. The terminology of cricket had confused her, but the game in play was a bat-and-ball game, and she was familiar with those.

She rested her hip against the edge of her desk and shrugged again. "It isn't that hard."

He flipped down her cot and took a seat, his back against the wall, his hands behind his head. "Lucky for us. Wintervale was convinced you were an exceptional player. That was the problem with my trick: the mind finds ways to fill a blank—and Archer Fairfax was a perfect blank."

She almost didn't hear what he was saying. The way he sat, all strong shoulders and long limbs—it was . . . distracting. "Is that why Kashkari thinks I'm going back to Bechuanaland with my parents?"

"That is the least alarming of misconceptions. You will be surprised what people thought of you. Last year there was a rumor going around that you had not hurt your leg at all, but had been sent away because you had impregnated a maid."

*"What?"*

"I know," said the prince with a straight face. "I was impressed by the extent of your virility."

Then he smiled, overcome by the humor of the situation. Bright mischief lit his face and he was just a gorgeous boy, enjoying one hell of a joke.

It was a few seconds before she realized that, astounded by his transformation, she'd stopped chewing. She swallowed awkwardly. "Kashkari asked me a great number of questions."

This sobered him. The smile, like a brief glimpse of the sun in rainy season, disappeared. "What kind of questions?"

She was almost relieved not to see his smile anymore. "He wanted to know what I thought of the relationship between the British Empire and lands under her influence abroad."

"Ah." He relaxed visibly. "Kashkari would want to know your opinions."

"Why?"

The kettle sang. He rose, lifted it off its hook, poured boiling water into a teapot, and swished the teapot. "Kashkari has ambitions. He does not state it, but he wants to free India from British rule in his lifetime. Wintervale is sympathetic. I am known to be apolitical, so he is secure in the knowledge that at least I am not antagonistic toward his goals. But he is less sure about you."

"Wouldn't he have conjured Fairfax as someone more sympathetic to his views, the way Wintervale believes I'd help him win cricket games?"

He discarded the water from the warmed teapot, tossed in some tea leaves, and poured more boiling water on top. "Fairfax was born and brought up overseas. There are other such boys here at school, and they are the most fervent imperialists of all. Kashkari had no reason to think you would be different."

He set aside the kettle and placed the lid on the teapot for the tea to steep. "So what *did* you think of the relationship between the empire and her colonies?"

She still couldn't quite comprehend the sight of the Master of the Domain making tea—for her. "I said an empire shouldn't be too surprised that her colonies are unhappy with their overlord."

"And Kashkari was pleasantly surprised by your attitude, no doubt."

"He thought my thinking very unusual."

"It is. And do not broadcast it. The last thing we want is to have you labeled as a radical."

"What is that?"

"Someone whose parents had better explain why their son thinks

as he does. Imagine an Atlantean youth piping up at school and saying that Atlantis should let go of all the realms under its control. The
reaction here probably would not be quite as extreme, but better not
test it."

She nodded—she saw the point.

He filled a teacup and brought it to her. She wasn't sure whether
she wanted him so near. "Thank you, though you don't need to ply
me with food and drink all the time."

"You would do the same for the most important person in your
life."

She set down the teacup harder than she needed to. In the wake
of that resounding thud, an uneasy silence spread—uneasy for her,
at least, caught between the dark allure of his words and the harsh-
ness of her own common sense. And he was so close, she could smell
the silver moss with which his clothes had been stored, the clean,
crisp scent of it made just slightly peppery by the heat of his body.

"I need to go back to the laboratory," he said, taking a step back.
"Stay safe in my absence."

From his laboratory, Titus returned to Mrs. Dawlish's for supper,
then to his own room to test the trial he planned for Fairfax. He
emerged from the Crucible disoriented and nauseous, to knocks on
his door.

Wintervale charged in. "What the hell is going on out there? Why
are there armored chariots everywhere all of a sudden? Is there a war

going on I haven't heard about?"

Titus gulped down a glass of water. "No."

"Then what? *Something* is going on."

Wintervale's family, even in exile, was well-connected. He would learn sooner or later. And if Titus lied to a direct question, it would appear as if he were hiding something.

"Atlantis is hunting for an elemental mage who brought down a bolt of lightning."

"You mean, like Helgira?"

The name still made Titus squeamish. "You could say that."

"That's poppycock. No one can do that. What's next? Mages riding comets?"

A burst of masculine laughter came from Fairfax's room next door. Who else had become her friend now?

*Friends,* he mentally corrected himself, as more boys joined in the uproarious laughter.

"You know what I think?" Wintervale set two fingers under his chin. "I think it's just an excuse for Atlantis to get rid of some Exiles they don't like. I'd better tell my mother to be extra careful."

"We can all stand to be a bit more careful."

"You are right," said Wintervale.

Now why could Fairfax not be more like Wintervale, respectful and willing to take advice?

"How is Lady Wintervale, by the way?" he asked.

"Gone to her spas. I hope they calm her down. I haven't seen her so jumpy in a while."

Wintervale left only when it was nearly lights-out. But Fairfax's room, when Titus pushed open her door, was still full. She sat cross-legged on her bed, Sutherland next to her, Rogers and Cooper, two other boys from the house cricket squad, straddling chairs pulled up to the bed. They were playing cards.

"Come and help me, prince," she said casually. "I'm terrible at cards."

"He really is," said Sutherland.

"Good thing I'm a brilliant athlete *and* handsome as a god," she said, with that affable cockiness she did so astonishingly well.

The boys laughed and booed.

"Full of ourselves, aren't we?" asked Rogers.

"My mother taught me false modesty is a sin," she said, smirking.

Titus had cautioned her against making friends. But the sharp feeling in his heart was not concern, but a stab of envy. Even if his circumstances had allowed friends, he would not have had them so easily. There was something about him that discouraged contact, let alone intimacy.

"It is almost lights-out," he said.

Cooper, always awed by Titus, immediately set down his cards. "Better get back to my room then."

More reluctantly, Sutherland and Rogers followed.

As Titus closed the door behind them, she shuffled the cards. "You're very good at dispersing a party, Your Highness. Must have taken you years of practice."

"Incorrect—I was born this talented. But you, it must have taken *you* years to perfect your act."

"You refer to my innate and splendid charm?"

"Your charm is about as innate as my truthfulness."

She gathered the deck in her right hand. The cards flew out of her fingers and landed neatly in the palm of her left hand. "Did you have something to tell me?"

He had not come with any particular purpose. But as her question fell, his answer sprang readily, as if he had been mulling it over for a while. "I have been reading about your guardian. He has not made your life easy."

"His own life was made impossibly difficult because of me."

"Relax—I do not question his character. I only want to let you know that you took very good care of him. You have a good heart."

Her glance, when it came, was as cold as a mountain stream. "I took care of him because I love him—and because I can never do as much for him as he has done for me by taking me in and giving me a home. Your compliments will not earn you greater devotion from my part. I will do as much as the blood oath stipulates and nothing more."

Clever girl. She made him feel almost transparent.

"Good night, Your Highness."

Grand, too, dismissing him as if he were a subject of hers, instead of the other way around.

He vaulted the few feet that separated them, kissed her on the cheek, and, before she could quite react, vaulted back to his place by the door. "Good night, Fairfax."

# CHAPTER · 12

THE PRINCE WAS MANIPULATING HER, Iolanthe was sure. But to what goal? Did he think that telling her that she was infinitely precious to him, complimenting her on her good heart, or kissing her on the cheek would make her willingly embrace mortal danger for his sake?

Nothing would make her willingly embrace mortal danger for his sake.

But still she tossed and turned for a long time before she fell asleep, the imprint of his cool lips a burn upon her cheek.

The next morning her training plunged her into a story called "Batea and the Flood," where she had a grueling time holding back a swollen river. More grueling yet was an afternoon division called Greek Testament. Master Haywood had never quite understood her trouble with ancient Greek, pointing out that it was not much more morphologically complex than Latin. But whereas Latin she found no more difficult to master than fire, Greek had always felt like lifting mountains.

By the time she returned to Mrs. Dawlish's house, she was ready to lie down for a few minutes in her room. But the prince wasn't done with her.

"Come with me."

"We already trained for the day."

"Today is a shorter day at school. On those days, you will have an afternoon session, too."

She said nothing as she followed him into his room.

"I know you are tired." He closed the door behind him and directed a keep-away charm at it. "But I also know you are strong—far stronger than you, or perhaps even I, can comprehend."

She did not feel strong, only trapped.

"Always remember," he said, as he placed his hand on the Crucible, "that someday your strength will overturn the world as we know it."

They landed in a part of the Crucible she hadn't seen before: an apple orchard, the branches heavy with pink-and-white flowers, the air cool and sweet. She shaded her eyes with her hand and looked toward the second sun, pale and barely there. She was peeved at the extra session and angry at everything else in her life, but she couldn't quite help her fascination with the Crucible. It made her feel as if she were on a different world altogether.

"What story are we in?"

"'The Greedy Beekeeper.'"

No wonder the buzz of bees echoed in her ears. "What happens in it?"

"You will see."

She did not like that answer.

Side by side they walked deeper into the orchard. At one point a boulder jutted up from the ground. The prince leaped lightly on top and held out a hand toward her. She ignored him and made her own way across.

"It is only courtesy on my part, Fairfax. You need not worry that taking my hand will bind you more inextricably to me."

"Perhaps not in any magical manner. But with you, Your Highness, there's no such thing as simple courtesy. You extend a hand because you want something in return. Maybe not today, maybe not tomorrow, but someday you deem that your premeditated kindnesses will add up to something."

His response was a slight smile and an admiring gaze. Calculated, all calculated, she reminded herself. All the same, warmth pooled deep inside her.

They came to a clearing in the orchard. She frowned. "Is that a beehive?"

The hive was the familiar round, tapered shape of a skep, but it was three stories tall and measured at least twenty feet across at its base.

"That is the beekeeper's house."

He opened the door and ushered her in. The inside of the house, except for its shape, looked typical for a rustic dwelling: planked floors, unvarnished furniture, and honey-yellow curtains on the small windows.

He pushed a chest of drawers to the center of the house, set a chair on top of the chest, and climbed onto the chair to place something on a crossbeam.

"What's that?"

"A piece of paper with the exit password for the Crucible. It will not respond to a summons, but will obey a breeze."

He leaped down and, with the *exstinctio* spell, destroyed all the furniture. "The beekeeper keeps his bees in old-fashioned skeps. To get to the honey, he kills the bees each time. The bees have finally had enough."

"And?" She was beginning to be nervous.

"And I wish we had met under different circumstances." He pressed his spare wand into her hand. "Good luck."

He left. She stared at the door for a minute before glancing up at the crossbeam again. It was at least twelve feet in the air, too high for her to jump. He'd left nothing that could give her a lift. And since one couldn't vault in the Crucible, she'd have to do this either honestly or not at all.

She sighed, raised her face to the ceiling, and closed her eyes to concentrate.

Something wet and sticky splattered onto her face.

"What the—" She leaped back, her lids flying open.

A golden, viscous liquid dripped down from—everywhere. Every inch of the wall was now a honeycomb, each hexagon seeping honey.

Seeping turned into drizzling. Drizzling turned into pouring. Honey flowed down the wall. Thick ropes of it tumbled from the domed ceiling.

The only place that wasn't directly assaulted was the exact spot where he'd placed the password—the house had an opening at the very center of the roof, which served as a chimney.

Puddles gathered. She stepped around them for the door. But the door had disappeared behind six inches of hard wax. The windows, when she ripped away the curtains, were similarly inaccessible.

If honey continued to inundate the room, she'd be submerged.

She cursed him. Of course he would think of something so nefarious. She cursed some more and implored the air in the room to cooperate. *Please. Just this once.*

The honey cascaded faster and faster, rising to her ankles, then to her knees, so thick she could barely move her feet. The aroma overwhelmed her, too sweet, too cloying. She stood under the beam for shelter. But still honey slimed her, plastering her hair to her head. She had to wipe it away from her brows so it wouldn't get into her eyes. Even the wand had become coated, at once gluey and slippery.

She wanted that password. How she wanted it. But air ignored her attempts to control it. Like shouting at the deaf, or waving her hands before the blind.

The honey was now waist-high. Her chest hurt with panic.

Perhaps she ought to move out from directly underneath the crossbeam. She'd be able to see the piece of paper, and perhaps that might help.

But when she tried to do so, she lost her footing avoiding a huge glob of honey falling toward her and listed sideways. Like a fly caught in tree sap, she couldn't right herself. She was sucked downward—a horrifying sensation.

It occurred to her that she could drown in honey—and that *this* was precisely the brink toward which he meant to push her.

She flailed and sank deeper into the honey. Her toes hit the floor. She gasped, struggled upright, and dug her wand out of the honey. "I'm going to break your wand hand," she shouted. "And your skull, too."

The honey had risen as high as her chest, the pressure heavy against her sternum. She panted. A dribble of honey fell into her mouth. She'd thought she liked honey, but now its taste turned her stomach.

She spat and tried again to concentrate. She had never needed to concentrate for any of the other elements: her dealings with them were as straightforward as breathing. Wrestling with air was like—well, wrestling with air, struggling with an entity that could not be seen, let alone pinned down.

The honey swelled ever higher. Past her lips, creeping toward her nose. She tried to push herself up, to float. But she couldn't kick her legs high enough to turn herself horizontal. Thrashing about—if her molasses-slow motion could be called thrashing—only pulled her deeper into the mire.

She could no longer breathe. Her lungs burned. Instinct forced her to open her mouth. Honey poured in. She coughed, the raw pain of honey going down her air pipe indescribable.

Only her hand was above the honey now. She waved her wand, livid and desperate. Had she done it? She could not open her eyes. Her lungs imploded.

The next moment all the honey was gone and she was surrounded by the clean weightlessness of air. She fell to the floor—the floor of the prince's room—and panted, filling her lungs with the ineffable sweetness of oxygen.

Rationally, she knew she had never, not for a moment, been in real danger. And therefore there was no reason for her to shake and gasp with the relief of survival.

Which only made her loathe him more.

"Are you all right?" he asked.

Her arm shot out, wrapped around his ankles, and yanked. He went down hard, hitting his shoulder on the corner of the table. She leaped on top of him and took a swing at his face. He raised his arm in defense. Her fist connected with his forearm, a solid smash that jarred her entire person.

She swung her other fist. He blocked her again. She lifted her knee, intending to drive it somewhere debilitating.

The next thing she knew he'd heaved her off his person. She immediately relaunched herself at him. He'd just got to his feet; she knocked him back down.

"That is enough, Fairfax."

"I will tell you when it's enough, you scum!" She slammed her elbow toward his teeth.

Foiled again.

She grunted in frustration and head-butted him. He caught her face in his hands. Since both his hands were busy, she finally landed a blow at his temple.

He winced—and retaliated by pulling her head down and kissing her.

Shock paralyzed her. The sensations were huge and electric, as if she had called a bolt of lightning upon her own head. He tasted angry, famished, and—

She leaped up, knocking over a chair. He remained on the floor, his eyes on her, eyes as hungry as his kiss. She swallowed. Her fist clenched, but she couldn't quite hit him again.

He rose to his feet with a grimace. "I know how you feel. I was in there last night, in honey above my head."

She stared at him.

"Why do you look so surprised? I said I would experiment *with* you, not *on* you. Everything I try on you, I try on myself first."

Of course she was shocked. The idea that anyone would

voluntarily subject himself to such torture . . .

He was suddenly at the door, listening.

"What is it?"

"Mrs. Hancock. She is outside, talking to someone."

A minute later—just enough time for him to do something about the cut at his temple and Iolanthe to right the fallen chair and a few other things knocked askew by their scuffle—a rap came on the door. The prince, with a tilt of his head, gestured for Iolanthe to open the door.

"Why me?"

"Because that is the nature of our friendship."

She twisted her mouth and went.

Mrs. Hancock stood at the door, smiling. "Ah, Fairfax, I need to speak to you, too. I have a letter for you from your parents."

It took Iolanthe a full second to grasp what Mrs. Hancock was saying. Fairfax's nonexistent parents had sent a letter.

With slightly numb fingers she accepted the envelope. The paper inside was faintly lavender in color and smelled of attar of rose. The words were written in a pretty hand.

> *My dearest Archer,*
> *Ever since you left for school, Sissy has not been feeling well. She must have become accustomed to your presence at home during your convalescence.*

*Will you be so kind as to come home this Saturday after class? Sissy*
*will be thrilled to see you. And I am sure that will make her feel herself*
*again in no time.*

*Love,*

*Mother*

"My parents want me to go home on Saturday," Iolanthe said to no one in particular. Where was she supposed to go? And who was behind this letter?

"Yes, they also sent a letter to Mrs. Dawlish to that effect," answered Mrs. Hancock. "You may take a short leave, if you wish."

"Bother," said Iolanthe. "Sissy was perfectly fine when I left. I'll bet she's only pretending."

That seemed like something a boy of sixteen who'd been stuck home for three months with his little sister might say.

"Then stay here," said the prince. "Besides, you are supposed to help me with my critical paper Saturday."

He sounded enormously peevish.

"I'm afraid you won't have time Saturday for your critical paper, Your Highness," said Mrs. Hancock. "The embassy has requested leave for you, too. There is a function they would like you to attend."

"God's teeth, why do they insist on this charade? I rule nothing, isn't that punishment enough? Why must I attend their functions and be paraded around?"

"Come, prince, how terrible can it be?" Iolanthe said, playing the part of the affable friend. "There will be champagne and ladies."

The prince released his bed and plunked himself down on it. "That shows how much *you* know, Fairfax."

She knew he was playacting, but still she shot him an irate glance. Mrs. Hancock's sharp eyes took it all in—no doubt exactly as the prince intended.

Iolanthe mustered a smile for Mrs. Hancock. "I'm sure by tomorrow His Highness will be in a more receptive mood. Thank you for coming all the way to give me my letter, ma'am."

"Oh, it was nothing at all, Fairfax. And good day to you too, Your Highness."

After she left, neither of them spoke for a while.

Then the prince slowly let out a breath. "Saturday evening I meet with the Inquisitor."

CHAPTER ᛫ 13

IOLANTHE AND THE PRINCE UNDERTOOK a battery of test vaults and determined that she had a solo range of twenty-seven miles, enough to cover the distance between London and Eton in one vault.

Saturday afternoon, to keep up the pretense of heading home to Shropshire, she took the train to London. From there she vaulted to a broom cupboard at school, where the prince waited.

"Anyone following you?"

She shook her head.

The prince gave her a dose of vaulting aid. "Let us go then."

Their first vault took them to a musty-smelling, cramped space not very different from the broom cupboard they'd left behind.

"Where are we?"

"Somewhere inside the bell tower of a cathedral in Birmingham. Let me know if you need a few minutes."

She shook her head, determined not to show any weakness. She lasted two more such vaults before her head spun. It didn't matter where she was now—another long-disused room by the look of it.

She leaned against the wall and fought her nausea.

He checked her pulse, his fingers warm and light on her wrist. Then he gave her a powder as sweet as pure sugar.

"What is it?" she mumbled.

"Something that will make my kisses taste like chocolate."

Until now, neither of them had referred to the kiss. She had been trying not to remember it—the imminent meeting with the Inquisitor meant she would finally see Master Haywood, and that was plenty to occupy her mind.

But she *had* relived the kiss. And every time she had, lightning had shot through her.

*I wish we had met under different circumstances,* he'd said.

Did he wish daily—hourly—that he'd been born someone else, and not burdened with this crushing purpose? She would, but she could not tell about him. His true emotions were buried at the depth of an ocean trench, undetectable to anyone but himself.

"Your kisses will only ever taste like wet dog."

"Know a lot about that, do you?" he said amicably.

*What kind of person are you, to live without honor or integrity?*

*Obviously, the kind chosen for what others are too decent to do.*

She signaled that she was ready to vault again. After two more vaults, despite the remedy, her head pounded in agony.

He helped her sit down. "Put your head between your knees."

"Why are you still standing?" she asked, grumpily envious, her eyes half-closed.

They were outdoors. The grass beneath her was soft and green, the air cool and moist, with the distinct, salty tang of the sea.

"You might be handsome as a god, but I vault like one."

She wished she had the energy to glower at him, even though she felt strangely like smiling. "Where are we?"

"Cape Wrath, Scotland."

"Where is that?"

"The very north of Britain, five hundred some miles from Eton."

No wonder she felt so awful. Five hundred miles was generally considered the upper limit on daily vaulting range. For them to have come so far in less than a quarter of an hour was something marvelous—and possibly fatal.

She lifted her face. They were on a craggy headland overlooking a gray, restless sea. The wind was so strong she had to remove her hat. Her short hair blew about wildly.

He crouched down, held her chin between his fingers, and peered into her eyes. She knew he was only checking the size of her pupils, but the act was still overwhelmingly intimate, one long locked gaze.

If she weren't careful, she might delude herself into believing that she could see all the way into his soul.

She drew back from his hand. "Where is the entrance to your laboratory?"

"Over there." He tilted his head toward a lighthouse in the distance.

She came to her feet with a wobble. "What are we waiting for?"

The last time they were both in his laboratory, she still had her hair, and her opinion had not yet turned against him. Titus did not miss her hair, but he did miss the way she had looked at him, full of trust and reliance.

She lifted a hand and touched a jar of pearls. Her face was tilted up—he remembered putting on her necktie and brushing the underside of her chin. He remembered the sensation of heat rushing along his nerves, the softness of her skin.

She turned around. "Where's your canary?" she asked, pointing at the unoccupied birdcage.

He pretended to stir the potion before him. "I sold it at the songbird market in London. It was a prop; I do not need it when I am at school."

"A prop for what?"

He handed her the potion. It had matured well, the alarming purple goo of the night before now oatmeal-like in color and smelling pleasantly of nutmeg. "For you."

She eyed the potion warily. "You aren't trying to turn me into a canary, are you? Human transmogrification spells are hugely unstable, not to mention dangerous to the subject."[16]

"I have a workable transmogrification spell."

"Tested on yourself too?"

"Of course."

The glance she cast him—he had experienced a great deal of her displeasure of late, but this time she was not angry or averse. Instead she looked . . . pained, almost.

"Are you all right? I promise you it is safe. You know I would never let any harm come to you and—"

"I'm fine." She took the potion from him and drained it. "Why am I not a canary yet?"

He poured a vial of bright red powder into a glass of water. The water turned vermilion, then clear again. "You need to also drink this."

She did. Then she glanced at the empty birdcage. "Is it going to be painful?"

"Yes."

"You could have lied here, too." She smiled slightly, not looking at him. "I'm ready."

He pulled out his wand and pointed it at her. *"Verte in avem."*

The transformation was sudden and wrenching. He knew it well, having gone through it five times. She flailed. He caught her. A moment later he was holding only a bundle of clothes.

A canary, chirping, almost wailing, streaked about the room, its wings flapping madly.

"Come to me, Fairfax."

She flew straight into him. He barely caught her.

She lay still and stunned in his palms. He passed his fingers over her wings. "You did well, nothing broken. The first time I tried this, I gave myself a concussion and fractured my elbow."

He placed her in the cage, atop layers of clean newspaper. "Rest for a few minutes, then we need to go."

He went around the room gathering what he needed. She wobbled toward the water cup.

"Drink the water if you are thirsty, but do not eat anything from the feed cup. You may look like a bird, but you are not one. You cannot fly very well, and you most certainly cannot digest raw seeds."

She dipped her beak into the water, drank, and hopped around a little more in her cage.

The door of the cage was still open. He held out his hand. "Come here."

Her little bird head cocked to one side, looking almost as suspicious as her human self. But she hopped onto his palm. He raised her to his lips and kissed the top of her downy head.

"It will be you and me against the world, Fairfax," he murmured. "You and me."

Dalbert was on time, as always.

"Your Highness." Dalbert bowed from the waist.

He held open the door of the private rail coach. Titus nodded, gave his satchel to the valet, and mounted the steps into the coach with the birdcage in his hand.

Dalbert brought Titus a glass of hippocras and tipped some waterose seeds into Fairfax's feed cup.

"Hullo there, Miss Buttercup."

Titus watched her. She dipped her beak into the feed cup and took out a seed. But when Dalbert had smiled in satisfaction and turned to putter elsewhere in the coach, she dropped the seed back into the feed cup.

Titus breathed again. All the literature had insisted that a mage in a transmogrified state clearly understands language and instructions, but this was the first time he had been able to test the claim for himself.

The train's whistle shrieked. Its wheels ground against the tracks. They were on their way.

They remained on the rails for only a few minutes. The prince used the time to throw on a tunic and change into a pair of knee-high boots. Then Iolanthe was no longer looking at the English countryside, but at distant mountain peaks.

Which turned out not to be real mountain peaks, but a large mural that adorned the circular room in which the private rail coach now stood.

The prince rose from his seat. In her current size, he appeared immense, his hand the size of a door. He lifted her cage and alit, followed by his manservant.

A set of heavy, tall double doors swung open. She'd anticipated a great room of some sort on the other side, but it was only the stairwell, lit by sconces that emitted a remarkably pure white light.

They descended a long flight of circular stairs—the rail coach was parked at the top of a tower. Another set of doors opened, and they walked down a wide corridor with open arches, looking out to a garden terrace that hung several hundred feet above the courtyard below.

The corridor turned, split, turned again. Now there were attendants everywhere, bowing and scraping as the prince walked by. They went up a few steps, passed a library, an indoor garden with a sculpture fountain in the middle, and a large aviary filled with birds of all descriptions.

When they finally entered the prince's apartment, she found it rather sparsely furnished—Master Haywood had a more impressive parlor when he was still at the university. Or so Iolanthe thought, until her gaze landed on the tri-panel screen before the window. Inside each translucent panel, silver-azure butterflies fluttered. As she watched, one butterfly's color changed into a vibrant yellow, another to a delicate shade of violet, and yet a third an intricate pattern of green and black.

The butterflies must be made from blue argent, a priceless elixir sensitive to the least changes in the heat and intensity of the sun. The prince paid no attention at all to his incalculably precious screen, but charged past. In the next room she caught a glimpse of an enormous vase of ice roses, their pale-blue petals like blown glass. The room after that housed a huge spinning globe. She couldn't be sure, but she thought she saw a thunderstorm going on somewhere in the tropics, with tiny flashes of lightning. The prince ducked under the moon as he marched on.

In his bedchamber he stopped to pull off his boots; then they were in an enormous bathroom that boasted a tub carved out of a single block of amethyst, with fittings and claw-feet of pure gold. Steam curled above the tub, petals and herbs floated atop the water—she smelled orange blossom and mint.

She used to relish long soaks. It had been one of the most enjoyable applications of her elemental power, a gentle fire beneath the tub to keep the water at a constant temperature, while she made elaborate, fanciful sculptures with water droplets in the air.

The prince set her down and dismissed his valet. The latter left with a bow and closed the door. Leaning against the wall, the prince pulled off his stockings. As he walked toward the amethyst tub, he yanked his shirt over his head.

He was lean and tightly sinewed. Her little bird heart thudded.

He glanced at her, his lips curved in not quite a smile. The next thing she knew, his shirt had flown through the air and landed on the cage, blocking her view toward the bathtub.

"Sorry, sweetheart. I am shy."

She chirped indignantly. It was *not* as if she would have continued to watch him disrobe beyond a certain point.

"I know you would rather inspect my superlative form, but may I recommend admiring the tapestry behind you instead?" continued the prince. "It is a depiction of Hesperia the Magnificent destroying the Usurper's stronghold. Rumpelstiltskin himself wove the tapestry. Do you know the nonmages have turned him into a villain in their tales? Poor fellow, they have him forcing some poor innocent to spin gold from straw."

A splash of water, then a sigh as he settled himself in the tub.

She closed her eyes, the absurdity of the situation momentarily overwhelming her. She was a bird in a cage. The prince was stark naked not six feet from her. And the saintly Rumpelstiltskin, who had willed his life's savings to help indigent children, slandered as a greedy boor.

He sighed again. "Why am I talking to you? You will not remember anything from your time spent in bird form." He paused. "I have just answered my own question.

"Do you know what I did one time? I decided to record my time in bird form. In Morse code—a nonmage means of transmitting messages, with dots and dashes to represent letters. I had it all planned: I would use my beak to punch small holes in the paper to represent a dot, and make scratches with my claw for dashes.

"Except when I came to, the sheet of paper was in shreds. So much for that idea." He was silent for a moment. "And you will draw a similar blank come tomorrow."

Did this mean he was about to tell her something he wouldn't normally? Her ears perked—figuratively, since her ears were now feather-covered holes in the sides of her head.

He laughed softly. "You know, you are almost enjoyable to talk to, when you do not say anything back."

She willed the water in the tub to strike him in the face.

There was a loud splash. "Hey!" He sounded surprised, but not unpleasantly so. "Interesting. You are still capable of elemental powers. But stop—or I will feed you to the castle cats."

She struck him again.

"All right, all right. I take it back. You are almost enjoyable to talk to, even when you do talk back."

She wished he would stop speaking—she did not want this glimpse of the kind of rapport they could have had, had things been different.

*Say more,* thought a less sensible part of her.

He obliged. "You know what I should be worried about? Your inability to control air. Lightning is very dramatic, but armored chariots are built to withstand lightning strikes. You need to generate a cyclone to have a chance against them. It is no good when you cannot create a breeze to save your life."

Her wings quivered. She was supposed to fight against those machines of death?

"I should be thinking about new and better ways to break through your block. But I cannot think at all when the Inquisitor is going to question me tonight."

She'd never before heard fear in his voice. So he did experience it. Good. It was a sign of madness to not be afraid when one ought to be.

"The first time I met her face-to-face, I was eight." He spoke quietly; she had to strain to hear. "My grandfather had died two months before, and my coronation was the next day.

"When you are born to the House of Elberon, you are trained to act serene and superior no matter what you feel. But the Inquisitor was—she has frightening eyes. I tried, and I could not make myself look at her. So as she spoke, I looked down at my cat.

"Minos was actually my mother's cat, as gentle and sweet as she. After she died, he went everywhere with me and slept in my bed at night.

"That day he was on my lap. I scratched his head and he purred. At some point he stopped purring. But it was not until the end of the audience, when the Inquisitor rose to take her leave, that I noticed he was—he was dead."

The catch in his voice shot her through with a violent emotion she could not name.

"I wanted to cry. But because she was watching, I tossed Minos aside and said, the way my grandfather would, 'One would think a cat of the House of Elberon would have more breeding than to die before an esteemed guest. My apologies.'

"I have only kept birds ever since—birds and reptiles are immune to a mind mage's powers.[17] And I have been terrified of the Inquisitor ever since."

He fell silent.

She turned around and stared at the tapestry, willing herself to feel no sympathy for him.

And not succeeding.

## CHAPTER 14

TITUS DROVE HIMSELF, ACCOMPANIED BY a phalanx of mounted guards. A team of four Pacific golden phoenixes pulled his chariot—the head of the House of Elberon being the only mage in the Domain entitled to use phoenixes as beasts of burden.

There was a possibility, thought Titus, that the edict had been set down so that the ruling prince or princess would not be distracted from the task of governing by the need to invent ever more ostentatious ways to show up at a Delamer gala.

Lady Callista's spring gala was the worst. One year some idiots decided to arrive in a chariot drawn by hundreds of butterflies, each the size of a handspan. The butterflies began dropping of exhaustion as the chariot approached the landing platform, causing a nasty crash.

The year before that a group of guests came on turuls—giant Magyar falcons. Another set of lords and ladies brought along a pair of imported Chinese water dragons. As it turned out, turuls and Chinese water dragons despised each other with a white-hot passion. A messy spectacle had ensued.

Titus's cavalcade approached the expedited airway, built two hundred years ago during the reign of Apollonia III to facilitate travel between the castle and the capital. Fairfax had been perched on his shoulder, her claws digging lightly into his overrobe. But now he took her in hand and tucked her inside his tunic. "I would hold you," he said, "but I need both of my hands."

Phoenixes were fractious animals and cared not the least for expedited airways.

"Brace yourself. It will be a hard slam," he warned her. Probably unnecessarily. As a native of Delamer, she would have daily used the city's vast network of expedited ways, both on the ground and in the air. And if not daily, certainly more than he, with his upbringing in the mountains.

The thrust came suddenly. He could not breathe. His lungs grew emptier and emptier. Just when he thought he could stand it no more, the chariot was spat out the other end of the airway.

The phoenixes cawed harshly. He yanked them under control, reached for Fairfax, and set her on his shoulder again.

"You all right?"

She was busy gawking at the city that had once been her home.

Delamer was one of the greatest mage metropolises on earth, a glittering spread of pink-marble palaces and stately gardens, from the heights of the Serpentine Hills to the edge of the cool blue sea, aglow in the last rays of sunset.

Its beauty, however, was marred by patches of dense wood that resembled fungal growth from above. Quick pines, they were called: they were not pines at all, but certainly quick, achieving as much height and girth in two years as most trees did in five decades, bred by Atlantis's botanists to camouflage the blights left behind by death rains.

A familiar column of red smoke rose into the sky, marking the location of the Inquisitory. The Fire of Atlantis had burned steadily since the end of the uprising.

The hour of his meeting with the Inquisitor drew ever nearer.

He turned his face away. They were headed directly into the sunset. The west coast as a whole was rocky and wave-pummeled, especially the stretch along Delamer. Naturally an ambitious, wealthy capital of a great dynasty, full of mages who had enjoyed the balmy pleasures of the Mediterranean realms, had decided to make improvements.

During the reign of Hesperia the Magnificent, the city built five peninsulas, collectively known as the Right Hand of Titus. The peninsulas were rugged in appearance— so as not to look out of place against the craggy coast—but their seeming roughness hid a wealth of gentle slopes and beach enclaves, around which sprang hundreds of blue-roofed villas.

Three of the peninsulas comprised some of the most expensive land in all the mage world. One was a beloved public park. And the remaining one, the ring finger, was a princely preserve upon which stood Hesperia's Citadel.

The original citadel still rose at the center, but the complex had grown into a sprawling palace with vast gardens, ninety-nine fountains, and dozens of floating balconies.

Soon the Inquisitor would find Titus on one of those balconies.

He steered his chariot in the direction of the landing platform. He was not alone: from all points of the sky, chariots converged toward the Citadel. No turuls or Chinese water dragons this year, just the usual assortment of griffins and mock dragons.

Two young men performed flips and somersaults on a beam held aloft by four massive flights of doves. Beneath the beam hung a swing, with a young female acrobat sitting insouciantly upon it.

Titus wanted to enjoy the view—a fine view even for a prince. But already he had to work to keep his breath even and his hands steady.

The young woman recognized him. She pulled herself to her feet and performed a very creditable curtsy. Titus, as befitting his arrogant and ill-tempered public persona, ignored her altogether.

The path to the landing platform was demarcated with floating torches. Other guests had pulled aside to clear the way for their sovereign. As Titus's chariot drew to a stop, every single person on the platform bowed.

Alectus and Lady Callista were at the front of the crowd to welcome him. Titus swept past them without slowing down. But he knew that Lady Callista raised her head from her deep curtsy and regarded him with narrowed eyes.

Her device had followed him to a London hotel where he had no business being. How would he explain not only his presence, but also his precipitous departure, leaving behind a half-consumed tray of tea?

Lady Callista caught up to him. "I see you have brought Miss Buttercup, Your Highness."

"She is more tolerable company than most."

Fairfax chirped obligingly.

"And how is she enjoying England?"

"Better than I, no doubt. The very air is noxious."

"Does she like school?"

"School? One of the boys on my floor has a ferret in his trunk. A *ferret*. Buttercup lives in fear of her life. She is much happier at my mistress's."

Fairfax stopped chirping.

Lady Callista blinked. "I beg your pardon?"

"What do you not understand? Surely you, of all people, know what a kept woman is."

"I did not know that Your Highness had such an arrangement."

"And why should you? She does not cost me nearly as much as you cost Alectus, and she does not host soirees for me. In fact, she bores me already; I plan to replace her with a livelier girl, one whose tastes in lovemaking are not quite so pedestrian. Now if you will excuse me, I need a drink."

He pushed past her before she could summon one of the floating trays of sparkling blue beverages. Almost immediately, he was being bowed to by the prime minister and several not-so-prime ministers.

"I thought you did not care for such frivolous events," Titus said to the prime minister.

"Indeed I do not, sire. But I hear the Inquisitor herself is going to attend, and I hope to speak with her concerning the records," answered the prime minister. "There has been no progress at all on the talks. Unless we come to an agreement, the Inquisitory will begin to destroy records by the fourth week of June. Ten years of records, most likely including information concerning thousands of your subjects who disappeared after the uprising."

"How awful," Titus said, and brushed past.

Not that he was entirely unsympathetic, but what did the prime minister think fueled the Fire of Atlantis, the smoke of which rose so steadily from the Inquisitory?

He was next accosted by the current archmage and her two leading disciples, and a steady stream of matrons who wanted to know whether he would deign to appear at their charitable functions.

The first young woman to approach him was a beauty witch.

"Your Highness," she said with a bright smile.

"Have we met?"

"Diana Fairmyth, Your Highness."

He was wary of beauty witches; anyone who tried to seduce him could also be spying on him. "What is a girl like you doing at this dreadful party?"

She laughed. "Oh, is it dreadful? I haven't noticed yet."

"Alas, you are very beautiful, but I see our tastes diverge too much."

A few more young women tried, but he dispensed of them with similar efficiency. Then came the one girl he could not dismiss so easily—Aramia, Lady Callista's daughter.

She held out her hands to him. "Titus," she said, "it's good to see you again."

They had known each other many years—Lady Callista had sometimes brought Aramia to the castle so that Titus would have someone his own age to play with. They should have made perfect playmates: She was patient, uncomplaining, willing to try new things. Not to mention that, like him, she had never known her father. But Titus, a demon child in the years immediately after the loss of his mother, had tormented her instead.

He locked her into cupboards when they played hide-and-seek, snuck stinkbugs under her blouse when they played outside, and asked her why she was ugly when her mother was so beautiful.

But she had only shrugged and said, "Maybe my father was not so beautiful."

In recent years their paths had not crossed often. But guilt was like a bog. Whenever he did see her, he would realize he was still neck-deep in it.

He kissed her on both cheeks. "How have you been, Aramia?"

"Oh, same as usual. You know Mother, still trying to make a

swan out of me," she answered, not managing to be completely dismissive about it.

She had never been ugly—plain, perhaps, but not ugly. But even otherwise attractive women faded into insignificance next to Lady Callista. He could not imagine what it must be like to live entirely in the shadow of her beauty.

"But you are already a swan," he said, trying to cheer her up.

"I don't think inner beauty counts for much with Mother."

"Who said I was talking about inner beauty?"

This made Aramia smile. "That is very sweet, Titus, thank you. Would you like some snapberry punch? It's my own recipe, just a drop of snowmint essence as the secret ingredient."

He wished she had not called him sweet. He sank a little deeper into his bog. "You still enjoy tinkering with recipes?"

"I might as well be useful."

Since she could not be beautiful, she meant.

It was heartbreaking how much she wanted her mother's approval.

"I will have a glass."

She squeezed his hand. "Let me see what I can do so Mother doesn't pester you too much."

Aramia left to fetch the punch herself. By the time she returned, Alectus and Lady Callista had found Titus. Aramia, true to her word, drew her mother away on the pretense of something that needed the latter's attention.

Alectus by himself was easier to take. With the enthusiasm of an overgrown child, he recounted the epic quest that had been his search for a new overrobe, entailing five emergency fittings in the past two days.

Titus listened to him prattle as he pretended to drink Aramia's ice-cold punch. He did not distrust Aramia, but one never knew what Lady Callista might be up to.

"Have a glass of Aramia's punch," he said to Alectus. "It will quite restore you."

"Ah, you like it then?" said Alectus.

"I do. And why do you look so surprised?"

Alectus laughed awkwardly. "Well, it is just that Your Highness does not like very many things."

"Yes, the burden of having been born with exquisite taste."

"I believe that is indeed the c     "

"Stop that! No, not you, Alectus, you may carry on. I am speaking to my bird."

Fairfax had been acting strange. Pecking on his shoulders, chirping directly into his ears, and just now, taking a sharp snip at his neck.

"Perhaps Miss Buttercup is hungry?" Alectus suggested.

It *had* been a while since Fairfax ate, and there was a great deal of food being passed around. Titus took out a wrapped biscuit from inside his robe—he did not trust Lady Callista's food, either—and held it up to Fairfax.

She pecked his hand—hard enough to hurt.

"What the—"

"Oh dear, I do believe that is the Inquisitor arriving," said Alectus breathlessly. "She said she might make an appearance, but I had not quite believed it. She socializes so rarely, Madam Inquisitor."

Titus turned cold. He had thought he would have a little more time.

The Inquisitor's chariot was plain black, unadorned except for the whirlpool emblem of Atlantis. The Inquisitor herself was also in black, her hair sleeked back into a knot at the top of her head.

She looked like death walking.

"If you will excuse me, Your Highness," said Alectus, and rushed off to personally welcome the Inquisitor.

Aramia came back to his side. "I shouldn't say this, but she gives me the jitters."

"I am surprised your mother tolerates her. She would have disowned you if you went anywhere in such an ugly overrobe."

Aramia chuckled softly. "Unfortunately, Uncle Alectus is very fond of the Inquisitor. Mother says the Inquisitor is the one woman Uncle Alectus would choose over her, so she has no choice but to be very convivial."

Indeed Lady Callista smiled most graciously as she greeted the Inquisitor. As the Inquisitor began to walk up the steps from the landing platform, Alectus hovered about her, like a child stalking an unopened present, entirely unashamed of his devotion.

The Inquisitor came directly at Titus, cutting a swath through the assembly. Nearly half of the guests bowed.

Aramia frowned. "Don't they know what they are doing? They are bowing down to a foreign power."

"It is practical," said Titus. "In their shoes, I might do the same."

"You wouldn't."

She had such a rosy view of him; it almost made him want to be a better person.

The Inquisitor was now before him. She bowed stiffly. Titus returned an equally rigid nod.

"Madam Inquisitor."

"Good evening, Your Highness."

"Have you met Miss Aramia Tiberius?"

"I have already had that pleasure. Now, Miss Tiberius, I would like a word with His Highness."

"Of course, Madam Inquisitor. May I offer you a drink before I go?"

"That will be quite unnecessary."

Aramia pursed her lips and left.

*For a supposed diplomat, your talent for diplomacy is abysmal, Madam Inquisitor.*

Titus did not give in to the impulse: right before a private interview was no time to antagonize the Inquisitor.

"Lady Callista has arranged a room here where we may have privacy," said the Inquisitor.

"Good. We shall need it when we return."

"Return?"

"Was it not you yourself who said that representatives of the Crown are welcome to inspect my subjects currently held at the Inquisitory?"

"Surely that can be arranged I—"

"I am a perfectly adequate representative of the Crown. And I am ready to see them now."

Behind the Inquisitor, Alectus all but trembled at Titus's interruption. The Inquisitor said coldly, "Now is not quite the time."

Before the menace in her eyes, Titus wanted to quail as Alectus did. "Any time, you said," he forced himself to speak. "And you have already inconvenienced me greatly with your demands upon *my* time."

"You are young and headstrong, Your Highness, and your demands ill-considered. Let us have no more of this foolishness."

Any sane person would have backed away. But he had no choice. The blood oath bound him to do his utmost. And utmost, of course, was synonymous with suicidal.

"I see I should have expected someone of your particular . . . background to display such untrustworthiness." The Inquisitor's teeth clenched at Titus's reference to her forger parents. "I have correspondingly changed my mind about speaking to you in private."

He walked away and approached a trio of young beauty witches. "I see all the most beautiful women present tonight are already acquainted with one another."

The three beauty witches exchanged looks among themselves. The apparent leader of the group smiled at Titus. "You are a very handsome stranger, sir. But we really are after the prince."

"That conceited prick? You are lucky he is too full of himself to notice you. Can you imagine the absolute bore he would be?"

"I wouldn't know about that, but you, Your H—I mean, sir, are anything but a bore."

He lifted a curl of her dark hair, feeling nothing of its texture, aware only of the force of the Inquisitor's anger, like needles upon his back. "Let me guess, your name is Aphrodite, after the goddess of love."

She laughed softly. "Excellent guess, sir, but it's Alcyone."

"A celestial nymph, I like that." He turned to one of her friends. "And you must be a Helen, the one mortal woman as beautiful as any goddess."

"Alas, I'm only a Rhea."

"Daughter of Earth and Sky, even better. And you," he said to the third beauty witch, "a Persephone who so overwhelms a god with desire that he is driven to abduction."

All the girls laughed. "That is indeed her name," said Alcyone. "Well done, sir."

"I am never wrong in these matters."

"May I ask, sir," ventured Persephone, "why do you have a canary with you?"

"Miss Buttercup? She is an exceptional judge of character. Has she made a peep since you welcomed me into your group?"

"No, she hasn't."

"Then you have her approval. Ah, I see from Miss Alcyone's expression that she sees a gorgon. Now watch, Miss Buttercup is turning around. She will lay eyes on the gorgon, and she will express her disapproval."

Fairfax issued a series of furious peeps. Was she warning him that he had gone too far?

"Your Highness," said the Inquisitor directly behind him.

Her tone. His stomach roiled—she was livid.

The beauty witches all curtsied. He did not turn around. "I trust you can see I am busy, Madam Inquisitor."

"I have changed my mind. Shall we to the Inquisitory?"

It was the last place he wanted to go. He hoped Fairfax was happy.

"My apologies, ladies," he said to the beauty witches. "I must desert you for a short time. I hope you are not leaving immediately."

He did not hear what they said in return.

It was time for his first Inquisition.

# CHAPTER · 15

BEING A BIRD GAVE IOLANTHE the freedom to look anywhere she liked. What she found out was that everyone watched them. Him.

At first she put it down to his rank and his attire—his deep-blue overrobe, heavily embroidered with silver thread, was magnificent. But this was an occasion that overflowed with magnificent clothes on men and women of superior rank. And the way they looked at him, footmen and prime minister, serving maids and baronesses alike, it was as if he'd cast a spell on them.

He had Presence.

The moment he stepped off his chariot, it was obvious that he was no ordinary adolescent. He was rude and inaccessible, but he exuded an enigmatic charisma that could not be ignored.

He would never convince Atlantis—or anyone for that matter— to take him lightly.

Perhaps he knew that. His heart pounded next to her—he'd put her inside his overrobe for the trip to the Inquisitory. The tunic he wore beneath the overrobe was of very fine silk, redolent of the herbs with which it had been stored, warm with the heat of his body.

She burrowed deeper against him.

"I will keep you safe," he murmured.

He meant it.

As long as he was safe, she was safe.

But how long would he remain safe?


Titus drove one of Alectus's pegasus-drawn chariots—the phoenixes were too sensitive to be brought near a place as sinister as the Inquisitory. Lowridge, his captain of the guards, and six soldiers from the castle rode behind him, each on a white pegasus.

Night had fallen. All the streetlamps and houses had been lit, which only emphasized the dark, desolate stretches of quick pine. The column of red smoke that marked the location of the Inquisitory glowed bright and eerie, a display of power that dominated the skyline night and day.

The original Inquisitory had been leveled during the January Uprising. Since its rebuilding, security had been airtight. The Inquisitor received no callers and gave no parties. The only way to get in, it was sometimes said, was to be dragged in.

The pair of pegasi that pulled Titus's borrowed chariot certainly wanted to bolt—almost as much as he did. One could not fly over territory under the Inquisitor's direct control; once they crossed its boundary, the pegasi had to trot on the ground. They whinnied, shied, and slapped each other with their tough wings. Titus cracked the whip near their ears to stop their jumpy antics.

Would that all *he* needed was a not-quite-lashing to pull himself together.

The new Inquisitory was a circular structure, the exterior one solid black wall, unbroken by a single window. Three sets of heavy gates led to an enclosed courtyard enveloped by an uncomfortably red-tinted light.

The Inquisitor's second in command, Baslan, was on hand to greet Titus. Titus could not decide whether he ought to be happy about the Inquisitor's absence or frightened that she was even now preparing for his Inquisition.

He tossed aside his reins and froze. Not ten feet from where he had pulled his chariot to a stop, a human skeleton poked out of the ground; the bony remains of its hand, the tips of the phalanges dark red, reached skyward as if seeking help from above.

"Interesting choice of decoration," he said, blood roaring in his ears.

"Half of the courtyard has been allowed to remain in ruins—a reminder for the servants of Atlantis to stay ever vigilant," answered Baslan.

The ruined half was pockmarked and strewn with blasted chunks of wall and broken pieces of glass that glittered red in the light. There were no other human skeletons, but Titus saw a dog skeleton and the top half of a doll, which made him recoil until he realized it was not a mutilated baby.

At the center of the courtyard stood a hundred-foot-tall tower. From the top of the tower, red smoke billowed.

Titus exhaled with relief when their path at last led away from the courtyard into the building. He stripped off his driving gloves. His palms were damp with perspiration.

They descended immediately; the aboveground rooms were obviously too good to waste on prisoners. The air below was musty, as was usually the case for subterranean interiors, but every surface was scrupulously clean.

All the hygienic measures in the world, however, could not diminish the oppressiveness of the place. With every step he took, the walls seemed to close in another inch. The air grew warmer and denser. It suffocated.

Three flights down, a desire to flee seized him. Thousands and thousands of mages had been held here in the first few years after the January Uprising. No one knew what had happened to them. But their despair had seeped into the very walls. Invisible filaments of it curled around Titus's ankles, driving chills up his tendons.

Three more flights down they emerged into a large circular space with eight corridors leading from it. The corridor they followed went on for a hundred and fifty feet. There were no bars, only solid walls and steel doors that were far too close together.

The cells could not be more than four feet wide.

Baslan stopped halfway down the corridor. With a tap of his hand, a narrow section of the wall turned transparent. A small, dimly lit cell appeared before them, empty except for a thin cot on the stone floor. A woman sat on the cot, sobbing—the housebreaker.

"Rise," proclaimed Lowridge, as his subordinates clicked their heels smartly. "You are in the presence of the Master of the Domain, His Serene Highness Titus the Seventh."

The woman looked up in shock. Then contempt. She spat. "You lie!"

This amused Titus, if grimly. "Can she see us?"

"No, Your Highness," answered Baslan. "The transparency is only one way."

"Who is she?"

"Her name is Nettle Oakbluff. She is the registrar of Little Grind-on-Woe."

Titus addressed the woman. "Why are you here?"

"I shouldn't be!" the woman cried. "I was trying to help Atlantis. I was trying to get them the girl!"

Titus glanced at Baslan, whose expression remained perfectly composed.

"You are a subject of the Domain. Why do you seek to help Atlantis?"

"There is money in it." Obviously a great deal of truth serum still flowed through the woman's veins. "I overheard my in-laws-to-be talking about it all hush-hush. They said Atlantis was itching for a really powerful elemental mage and that the agent who brought in this mage stood to gain a huge reward."

"And have you received said reward?"

Nettle Oakbluff blew her nose into a handkerchief. "No. All I got for my trouble is hours and hours of questioning. I want gold. I want servants. I want a villa overlooking the ocean in Delamer."

Her voice rose. "Do you hear me, Atlantis? You owe me that reward. If it weren't for me, Iolanthe Seabourne and her guardian would have disappeared without a trace. You owe me!"

She struggled to her feet. "You can't keep me here forever. My in-laws-to-be are important people. Oh, Fortune take pity on me, the wedding! Someone tell me what happened to the wedding. I need my daughter to marry the Greymoors' son and I demand—"

"She seems in fine fettle," Titus said to Baslan. "Next."

The wall was instantly opaque and soundproof, cutting off Nettle Oakbluff mid-tirade.

They walked some fifty feet down the corridor. The next cell Baslan revealed was similarly bare. A man sat on the cot, his back against the wall. He was unshaven, thinner and older than Titus remembered. But there was no question: he was Fairfax's guardian.

Titus took Fairfax out of the folds of his overrobe, keeping a tight grip on her tiny body. His other hand rested against the pocket where his wand was concealed. No one was going to snatch her from him—not without a fight to the death.

"I want him to see whom he is speaking to," Titus ordered. "I will not have another subject of mine think it is permissible to sit in my presence."

Reluctantly, Baslan complied.

Horatio Haywood blinked at the influx of light. He squinted at his visitors. There was apprehension in his eyes, but not yet the instinctive, cringing fear of the tortured.

"Rise," Lowridge again proclaimed. "You are in the presence of the Master of the Domain, His Serene Highness Titus the Seventh."

Haywood blinked again, rose unsteadily to his feet, and bowed. Only to lose his balance and stumble sideways into the wall. Fairfax was very still in Titus's hand, but her claws dug into his palm, and her heart hammered beneath the warm down of her chest.

Titus asked for Haywood's name, age, and occupation. Haywood answered obediently, a hint of hoarseness to his voice.

"How have you spent your time since your arrival at the Inquisitory?"

"I was hit with a paralysis curse before I was brought here and recovered only this morning. Since then I have been answering questions."

"Do you know why you are being held here?"

Haywood glanced at Baslan. "The Inquisitor is interested in the whereabouts of my ward."

"Certain parties in the know told me that your ward is nowhere to be found."

Was it Titus's imagination or did Haywood relax almost imperceptibly? His shoulders did not seem as tightly hunched. "I was unconscious, sire, and did not witness her escape."

"What was the means of her escape, exactly?"

"A pair of linked trunk portals that can be used only once, going only one way."

"Going where?"

"I do not know, sire."

"How do you know the other trunk is not buried at the bottom of the ocean?"

Haywood gripped his hands together. "I trust it is not. It is my understanding that it leads to safety, not calamity."

It had very nearly led to calamity.

Titus made an exasperated sound. "Not very productive to question you, is it?"

"There are many things I cannot recall, sire."

"This much memory erasure would cause undesirable side effects. You seem not to suffer from them. Did you entrust your memories to a memory keeper then?"

Haywood jolted only slightly. The Inquisitor must have already asked him the same question. "It would appear so, sire, though I cannot recall who, or when."

"But you know why."

"To keep my ward safe."

"I had no idea Atlantis was in need of a great elemental mage, and I should know these things. How did *you* know?"

"Someone told me. But I can't remember who."

There was frustration in Haywood's voice, but also relief. The sacrifice of his memories had not been in vain: he could not betray anyone in his ignorance.

"Was it her parents who told you?"

"I cannot recall," said Haywood.

"Are you her father?"

Fairfax jerked at his question.

"I am not, but I love her like one. Someone please tell her to stay away and not ever come near the Inquisitory. I'm sorry I couldn't keep her safe. I—"

The wall turned opaque. "Your Highness," Baslan said smoothly. "We must not keep Her Excellency waiting."

The prince held her tight, as if afraid she might do something stupid.

She wouldn't, not after all the sacrifices Master Haywood had made. And certainly not after his most recent pleas from inside the cell.

But for the first time she regretted that she was not yet a great elemental mage. She would tear the Inquisitory from its foundations and crush its walls into powder.

The prince stroked the feathers of her head and back. She wished he would put her back into his overrobe. She wanted to crawl someplace warm and dark and not come out for a very long time.

She was barely aware that they'd stopped again. The captain of the prince's guards once more proclaimed the presence of their sovereign.

"Who are you?" the prince asked.

"Marigold Needles, sire," answered a trembling voice.

Iolanthe nearly jumped out of the prince's hand. *Mrs. Needles?*

It was indeed kind, pink-cheeked Mrs. Needles, her face pressed against the transparent wall, a face at once frightened and hopeful.

"Why are you here?"

"I cleaned and cooked for Master Haywood and Miss Seabourne. But I'm only a day maid. I've never lived in their house, and I don't know any of their secrets!"

The prince glanced at Baslan. "Clutching at straws?"

"Straws sometimes lead to other straws," said the Atlantean.

"Please, sire, please," cried Mrs. Needles. "My daughter is about to have a baby. I don't want to die without seeing my grandchild. And I don't want to spend the rest of my life in this place!"

Iolanthe turned cold. What had the prince said? *Friendship is untenable for people in our position. Either we suffer for it, or our friends suffer for it.*

And Mrs. Needles wasn't even a friend, only a woman unfortunate enough to need the money cooking and cleaning for the schoolmaster would bring.

Mrs. Needles fell to her knees. "Please, sire, please help me get out of here."

"I will see what I can do," said the prince.

Tears gushed down Mrs. Needles's face. "Thank you, Your Highness. Thank you! May Fortune shield and protect you wherever you go!"

The wall turned opaque; they began the long climb up. Iolanthe trembled all the way to the surface.

"Is there time to admire the Fire of Atlantis?" asked Titus, as they reemerged into the courtyard.

"I'm afraid not, Your Highness," said Baslan. "Her Excellency is already waiting."

Precisely what Titus did not want to hear.

They crossed the courtyard. Before the heavy doors of the Inquisition Chamber, Lowridge and the guards were allowed to go no farther. Only Titus was conducted inside the enormous, barely lit hall—mind mages performed best in shadowy places.

The Inquisitor awaited, her pale face almost glowing, as if her skin were phosphorescent. From fifty feet away, he sensed her anticipation. A predator ready to strike; a hunter who had at last closed in on her quarry.

Cold skittered down his spine. It seemed the Inquisitor was determined to produce her finest work tonight.

As he approached her, she indicated the desk and two chairs beside her, the only pieces of furniture in the cavernous space. The two chairs were on opposite sides of the desk, one chair low and plain, the other high and elaborate. Either Titus chose the chair denoting greater status, and gave the Inquisitor yet another reason to bring him down a peg, or he submitted to the reality of the situation, selected the lesser chair, and endured the interview being looked down upon by the Inquisitor.

His solution was to step onto the lesser chair and perch on its back. Fortunately, the top of the back was flat. Had it had a few finials, like the dining chairs in which Mrs. Dawlish and Mrs. Hancock sat, he would have had to settle for sitting on the armrest, which would not give nearly the same jaunty, careless impression.

The Inquisitor frowned. Titus had ceded her the greater chair, but now he had the advantage of height.

She sat down and placed her hands, laced together, on top of the desk.

He drew a deep breath. *And so it begins.*

"Now, Your Highness, what have you been doing with Iolanthe Seabourne?"

He had prepared for this exact question, but still it jolted, as if he had gripped a live wire. "You mean the missing elemental mage you are looking for?"

"Last time we met, you did not believe she was an elemental mage."

"Lady Callista told me Atlantis is seeking her with all its might," Titus said with as much breeziness as he could muster. "She even encouraged me to look for her, since the girl is, after all, a subject of mine."

The Inquisitor ignored his insinuation. "You were at the village of Little Grind-on-Woe immediately after the lightning. After your visit, you changed your plans and left for England half a day earlier than originally scheduled. And when you arrived there, instead of heading directly to your school, you went to London, to a hotel where you maintained a suite of rooms as Mr. Alistair McComb, from which place you departed just as abruptly. Care to explain your movements, Your Highness?"

He wanted to taunt her. *And where was I between the time I arrived in London and the time I arrived at the hotel? Care to tell me that also?*

"I see you are fixated on the least of my doings," he said. "Very well, my abrupt departure from the Domain is easily enough explained: I am not at your beck and call, Madam Inquisitor. You cannot simply say to me, 'May I call on you this evening, Your Highness, to discuss what you have seen?'"

The Inquisitor thinned her lips.

"Besides, if you had taken the time to inquire from my attendants, you would have learned that I had decided to go back to school at an earlier time, *before* the lightning came down.

"Now, the hotel suite. I am a young man and have needs that must be met. Since that slum of a school Atlantis so strenuously recommended does not allow for such activities, I keep a place outside of school. As for why I left, I cannot imagine why I should remain once the deed is done."

"And where was your accomplice in . . . the deed?"

"Left before I did. No need for her presence once she had served her purpose."

"There was no report of anyone coming or going."

*Of course not, since she left with me.*

This time he had to swallow the words as they rose on his tongue.

"Were you watching all the service doors? A large hotel has many."

"Where did you find her?"

*In a certain house in Little Grind-on-Woe. Very well suited to wielding lightning, that girl.*

"In a certain—"

What was the matter with him? He was an accomplished liar. Truth should never approach his lips.

"—district of London. Have you ever been to London, Madam Inquisitor? There are nasty parts that teem with girls who must make a living on their backs. The bargains to be had there, you have no idea." He rubbed his thumb across his chin. "And frankly, after my encounter with you, I was in the mood to punish someone."

A small muscle leaped at the corner of the Inquisitor's eye. "I see," she said. "Your Highness gives precocity a whole new definition."

*Quite the opposite. I cannot afford to get close to anyone. And Fairfax will never have me now, will she?*

Alarm pulsed through him. What *was* the matter? Why was he overwhelmed with the need to confess?

Truth serum. He had been given a dose of truth serum. But how? He had taken nothing at the gala, not even Aramia's snapberry punch.

He might not have ingested Aramia's snapberry punch, but he

had most certainly touched the glass—held it in his hand for far longer than he would have, had someone else offered him that glass. The glass had not been ice-cold, as he had thought—he would have realized it had he actually taken a sip of the punch itself. The coldness had come from a gel brushed onto the outside of the glass, and the truth serum had made its way into him via his skin.

*That* was what Fairfax, pecking at him, had tried to warn him about.

He dreaded being slipped truth serum, so much so that he never took anything but water at the meals Mrs. Dawlish provided and rarely drank tea he had not prepared with his own hands. He even practiced telling lies while under the influence of truth serum. One drop. Tell a lie. Two drops. Another lie. Three drops. Keep lying.

But he had never suspected Aramia. She was the good one, gentle and self-effacing, tolerant, eager to please.

In hindsight everything was blindingly obvious. She longed for her mother's approval. If she could not be beautiful, she could still exploit Titus's guilt and make herself useful. She had said as much, had she not? He had felt not the least tingle of alarm, only sympathy so sharp it hurt.

*Friendship is untenable for people in our position,* he had told Fairfax. Had he thought it applied only to Fairfax?

The Inquisitor stared at him. "Your Highness, where is Iolanthe Seabourne?"

*Right here in this room.*

He was on guard, very, very much on guard. Yet he still felt his lips part and form the shape necessary to pronounce the first syllable of the truth. "I thought we had already established that I have neither interest in nor knowledge of your elemental mage."

"Why are you protecting her, Your Highness?"

*Because she is mine. You will have her over my dead body.*

"Because—"

He yanked himself from the precipice. A sharp pain slashed through his head, nearly tumbling him off his perch on the chair. He righted himself; the chair wobbled with his effort. "Because I have nothing better to do than run afoul of Atlantis, apparently?"

The Inquisitor's brow knitted.

"There is something you should know about me, Madam Inquisitor. I do not give a damn for anyone except myself. I dislike Atlantis. I despise *you*. But I am not going to harm a hair on my head over mere irritants such as yourself. Why should I care whether you find the girl or not? No matter what happens, I am still the Master of the Domain."

The words hurt. His throat burned. The inside of his mouth felt as if he had been chewing nails. And the pain in his head distorted the vision in his left eye.

The Inquisitor considered him. Gazing into her eyes was like looking at blood running down the street. "You mentioned Lady Callista a minute ago, Your Highness. I'm sure you are aware that Lady Callista and your late mother were close friends. Do you know what Lady Callista told me just after your coronation? She said your mother fancied herself a seer."

Titus swallowed with difficulty. "What does that have to do with anything?"

"One of the things Princess Ariadne predicted was that I would be the Inquisitor of the Domain."

"You are," said Titus.

The Inquisitor smiled. "I am, but Her Highness played a crucial part."

Titus narrowed his eyes. He had never heard anything of the sort.

"About eighteen years ago, a new Inquisitor named Hyas was appointed to the Domain. He was young, energetic, outstandingly capable, and superbly loyal to the Lord High Commander. The Lord High Commander couldn't have been more pleased with his performance. It seemed to everyone that Hyas was set for a long tenure.

"But three years into his appointment, he was abruptly dismissed. No one knew why—we serve at the Lord High Commander's pleasure. His replacement, Zeuxippe, was just as skilled and loyal. She held the post for only eighteen months, her removal no less abrupt and unceremonious. After that, I was promoted.

"For years, I remained as puzzled as everyone else concerning the events that led to my appointment. Yesterday I had an audience with the Lord High Commander. While I was in Atlantis, I called on my two predecessors and persuaded them to tell me their stories."

Titus made no comment on her "persuasion."

"Hyas was dismissed on charges of graft and corruption. He strenuously protested his innocence, but as some of the greatest treasures of the House of Elberon were found in his keeping, his objections fell on deaf ears. Zeuxippe's tale was even more ignominious, if that was possible. She was accused of improper advances against the Princess Ariadne.

"It was a pernicious charge. It destroyed not only Zeuxippe's career, but also her personal happiness: the love of her life left her after learning of the accusations. Now I am cynical—if mages were honest, there would be no need for Inquisitions. But I came away convinced of both Hyas's and Zeuxippe's innocence in their respective debacles. Which led me to the only conclusion possible, that Princess Ariadne was a deluded madwoman willing to do anything to make her so-called prophecies come true."

Titus leaped off his chair. "I did not come here to listen to such drivel."

He was furious. He could only hope his fury was sufficient to mask his dismay.

Everything—*everything*—rested on the accuracy of his mother's visions. If she had been a fraud who cheated to fulfill her prophecies—he could not even follow the thought to its logical conclusion.

The Inquisitor smiled slightly. "Lady Callista also told me that when they were children, Her Highness had a vision that one day she would die at the hand of her own father."

He blenched. His mother's death left wounds that had yet to heal. The Inquisitor was tearing off the scabs one by one.

"The common mage believes Her Highness's death to be the result of illness—her health had always been delicate and her passing at age twenty-seven unexpectedly early, but not implausible. You and I, however, both know that Prince Gaius, to demonstrate his desire to keep peace with Atlantis, executed Her Highness himself as a gesture of goodwill and submission. But now I wonder if Her Highness didn't participate in the uprising with an eye toward being punished, so that she could preserve the integrity of her prophecy."

He wanted to shout that his mother had never enjoyed her gift—that it had been a crushing burden. But did *he* believe it?

The Inquisitor smiled again. "I can't help but think what you are doing now has something to do with Princess Ariadne's wishes. Did she predict some magnificent destiny for you that would require you to risk life and liberty? Because as you said, Your Highness, you are too sensible a young man. I cannot believe you would throw away the best years of your life on your own initiative."

His heart pounded—from more than the upheaval of the Inquisitor's words. There was the truth serum, punishing him for not giving in to it, for not telling everything the Inquisitor wished to know. But there was something else also. Something that made him dizzy. He grabbed the back of the chair and looked at the Inquisitor.

"You should have been a playwright, Madam Inquisitor. Our theaters suffer from a shortage of sensational plots."

Her eyes locked onto his. "Such a loyal son. Was she as loyal to you? Or did she see you as but a means to an end?"

He hardened his grip so his hands would not shake. "You ascribe far too many motives to a simple woman. My mother was neither clever nor scheming. And she was nowhere near ruthless enough to use her only child as a pawn in some grand chess match with destiny."

"Are you sure?"

His head hurt, as if someone had scored his brain with broken glass. But nothing hurt as much as the possibility that his mother might have orphaned him to prove herself right.

Wrong. Something would hurt more: the idea that she was not yet done proving herself right, that from beyond the grave she was still manipulating Titus to justify the choices she had made in life.

"I am as sure as you are of Lady Callista's truthfulness."

"But you are not. I can see you are not. Her arrant disregard injures you. And why shouldn't you be distressed and indignant? A son's love for his mother ought not be perverted thus."

Was that what his mother had done? Exploited and defiled his love for her not for a noble goal that was greater than their individual lives, but for the mere fixation of being right?

He had always been alone in this. And he had always struggled against his own private doubts. Now doubts and loneliness threatened to swallow him whole.

He wanted to say something. But the sensation in his head—as if the rim of his skull was liquefying. He swayed. His hands clutched tighter onto the chair.

This was how the Inquisitor operated, he dimly understood. A calm, collected mind was far more resistant to her probing, so she first destroyed her subjects' composure. When they became distraught, she acted.

Her sobriquet among Atlanteans was the Starfish. A starfish inserted its stomach between the shells of a mussel and digested the poor bivalve in place. The Inquisitor did the same with the contents of a person's memory: dissolving the boundaries of the poor sod's mind, sucking all his scrambled recollections into her own, and sorting the wreckage at her leisure.

"Only fools stand in the way of Atlantis. Where is Iolanthe Seabourne?"

He would not allow her to get anything from him. He could not. If she had any suspicion he was not merely hiding Fairfax to thwart the Bane, but aimed for the Bane's complete overthrow, Atlantis would not suffer him to live. And Fairfax—Fairfax would disappear off the face of the earth.

But he felt the beginning of the Inquisitor's inimical surgery. Her powers sawed thick and jagged at his cranium. He tried to repel her. Tried to return himself to some measure of his usual coolness. He could not. All he could think was that his mother had done this to him.

"Where is the girl who brought down the lightning? Tell me!"

He did not realize until his nails were screaming in protest that he was clawing at the marble floors. He did not know when he had fallen down, only that he could not get up. His vision was turning black. No, it was narrowing into a tunnel. And at the very end of it was his mother, sitting on her balcony, absentmindedly stroking her canary through the bars of its cage.

The canary sang, urgently, beautifully.

Now he was truly hallucinating. Had the Inquisitor dug down deep enough to extract his memories? The pain in his head made his stomach burn.

The canary sang again.

Fairfax. It was Fairfax. They would get their hands on her within the hour, if he did not get her out of here.

But she was still free. She could do something: poke out the Inquisitor's eyes, or empty the contents of her bowels on the Inquisitor's head.

He laughed. But even to himself, he sounded quite deranged.

He raised his head and opened his eyes. Fairfax was right in front of him, fluttering madly.

CHAPTER · 16

THE PRINCE'S HEAD THUDDED AGAINST the floor.

Iolanthe cried, a hoarse chirp.

She'd been flabbergasted by the Inquisitor's revelations. Then terrified—what if the prince gave her up? Then pain had burst upon her, as if someone wielded a firebrand inside her skull. She'd convulsed, her wings twitching uselessly.

He remembered to take her out of his overrobe before he fell.

Until then, she'd thought that she was the only one who suffered, that he'd been wrong about the Inquisitor being unable to affect the minds of birds and reptiles. But as his knees gave out before her, she realized that she was not the Inquisitor's target, he was.

He was being tortured and she, perhaps because of the bond of the blood oath, shared his agony.

The sight of his hands clawing mindlessly at the marble floors—the way a man buried alive clawed the lid of the coffin—momentarily loosened the hold the pain had on her: he was in far worse shape than she was.

His glazed eyes frightened her. She'd never believed that he of all people, exquisitely controlled and perfectly prepared, could be so vulnerable.

Not only vulnerable: helpless.

Unless she helped him.

But she wasn't strong enough to disturb the foundation of the Inquisitory or even the walls of the Inquisition Chamber. And were she to unleash either fire or water, it would be obvious an elemental magic was at work.

Could she poke out the Inquisitor's eyes with her beak? The very thought made her gag. It was also impractical. She could get off the ground, but she couldn't fly fast or straight, which made her useless as a weapon.

She looked about desperately. A chandelier hung from a wrought-iron chain overhead. It had four branches, each holding a porcelain light sphere on a shallow cup.

An anti-shatter spell had been invented for glass, but not for porcelain. If she swung the chandelier, the light spheres would roll out—and plummet thirty feet to crash where the Inquisitor sat.

But she must not create too strong a gust, or the Inquisitor would immediately suspect the presence of an elemental mage.

Too strong a gust—she who couldn't even float a piece of paper.

A concentrated blast of air that wouldn't be felt at floor level. And all in one go, so that by the time the Inquisitor noticed anything awry, Iolanthe would have already accomplished the deed.

Could she do it?

A shard of pain slashed through her left eye. She shuddered. The prince jerked on the floor. He clamped his hands on either side of his ears. Blood oozed out from between his fingers.

The sight shocked Iolanthe senseless. She must get him out of here.

She tried to clear her mind, to concentrate until she was nothing but a singular purpose. But doubt retained its stubborn hold. She had never managed it, whispered a soft voice. She couldn't even when she was drowning in honey. What made her think she could now?

The honey had been make-believe. But this was real. His sanity was at stake. She might accuse him of lunacy, but she *would* peck the Inquisitor's eyes out before she'd let the woman destroy his mind.

Iolanthe blocked out everything else and allowed herself only to remember what it felt like when she manipulated fire—or lightning. That absolute conviction. That bone-deep sense of connection.

Uncertainty still licked at the edges of her mind.

Time was running out. The Inquisitor rose, her menace a thing that choked the air from Iolanthe's lungs.

Iolanthe closed her eyes. *Do it. Now. And do it exactly as I will you.*

A seemingly endless silence followed her command.

*How dare you defy me? Do it NOW.*

There came a dull sound of impact, followed by several sharp crashes and an unearthly shriek. Then all of a sudden, silence.

Iolanthe opened her eyes. The Inquisition Chamber was bright as day, the floor aglow with spilled light elixir, its luminance no longer dampened by the opacity of the porcelain spheres.

Doors burst open. Mages rushed in.

"Your Excellency!" shouted the Inquisitor's minions.

"Your Highness!" cried Lowridge.

The prince lay crumpled on the floor. Blood smeared his face, his collar, and the floor beneath his head.

Iolanthe barely avoided being trampled as she hopped toward him. She flapped her largely useless wings, bumped into one guard's calf, and then shot under another guard's groin to land, badly, on the prince's shoulder.

The captain of the guard checked the prince's pulse, his face grim with worry.

"Is he still alive, sir?" asked one of the guards.

"He is," said the captain. "We must get him to safety without delay."

But Baslan barred the way. "I demand an account of what happened to Madam Inquisitor."

Iolanthe noticed for the first time that the Inquisitor, like the prince, was on the floor. Anxious minions surrounded her. Iolanthe couldn't see her face, but she seemed as unconscious as he.[18]

The captain rose to his full height and towered over Baslan. "How dare you ask what happened to the Inquisitor? What has she done to our *prince*? If you do not remove yourself from my path this instant, I will consider this a provocation of war and act accordingly."

Iolanthe couldn't breathe. She'd been frantic with fear for the irreversible damage the Inquisitor might have caused the prince; it had not even occurred to her what a diplomatic nightmare she'd brought on by interrupting the Inquisition.

Baslan wavered.

But Captain Lowridge did not. With two of the guards' ceremonial spears and his own cape, he concocted a makeshift stretcher. The guards placed the prince onto the stretcher and marched out of the Inquisition chamber behind their captain.

The chariot was still in the courtyard. Captain Lowridge carefully deposited the prince's limp person on the floor of the chariot and took the reins himself. Atlantean soldiers blocked the exit. Iolanthe's wings twitched. If it came to that, did she dare bring down another bolt of lightning?

"Make way for the Master of the Domain." Captain Lowridge's voice was a rumble that seemed to carry for miles. "Or you will have declared war on him. And none of you will ever see Atlantis again."

The soldiers looked at one another. Finally, one shuffled a step to the side, and the rest followed. A sergeant opened the triple gates. Captain Lowridge sped the chariot outside, his guards behind on their mounts.

They cleared the boundaries of the Inquisitory in no time. Captain Lowridge whistled. At his command, the pegasi spread their wings and the chariot became airborne.

"The Citadel," he shouted at his subordinates.

"No," said the prince. Iolanthe started. She thought him unconscious still. "Not the Citadel. The castle."

His eyes remained shut, his voice was low and weak, but he was most certainly lucid.

"Yes, sire," answered the captain. He repeated the prince's order. "We make for the castle without delay."

"Canary," muttered the prince.

Iolanthe hopped onto his bloodstained palm. His hand closed about her. Another time she'd have protested the hold as too tight, but now she was only fiercely glad he had enough strength left to grip her so.

They raced for the expedited airway, the night traffic over Delamer yielding to the princely standard flying over the chariot. The kick of acceleration told Iolanthe they had left Delamer. She was never so happy to be almost asphyxiated. The prince grunted in pain as they were spewed out the other end.

She rubbed her head against the edge of his palm. Almost to safety—they would be all right.

"Your Highness, if you would," said the captain, once they were above the Labyrinthine Mountains.

The prince drew his wand and feebly muttered something. To the southeast a flare shot up in the sky, illuminating the highest towers of the castle.

"Thank you, sire."

The captain steered toward the direction of the flare. Iolanthe had forgotten that with the arrhythmic shifting of the mountains, even those who lived in the castle must look for it each time they left and came back.

The prince asked to be let off at the landing arch at the top of the castle, rather than in the courtyard. He allowed the captain to help him out of the chariot and leaned on the latter to walk.

His valet, his attendants, and a horde of pages ran up. They pressed in around him. He ordered them to leave him alone, sounding peevish in that way he did so well.

"Stand back, you idiots. I cannot breathe."

"The court physician is on his way," said an attendant.

"Send him away."

"But, sire—"

"Send him away or I will send *you* away. I will not have people say I needed to be patched up after a mere conversation with that gorgon."

But of course he needed to be patched up. He'd bled so much—and from his *ears*.

Nevertheless the prince prevailed. He barred the majority of the crowd outside the doors of his apartment. Most of the rest were allowed no farther than the anteroom.

The court physician, who had disregarded his wishes and come all the same, was not only denied entrance to the prince's bedchamber, but also awarded a tirade.

"Do you dare insinuate that I cannot talk to the Inquisitor for ten minutes without needing medical attention? What kind of a weakling do you take me for? I am the bloody heir of the bloody House of Elberon. I do not need a know-it-all sawbones after a chitchat with that Atlantean witch."

Even the valet was given the boot after he helped the prince take off his overrobe. "Go."

"But, sire, at least allow me to clean you."

"Who do you think cleans me when I am at school? I am not one of those old-time princes who cannot wipe their own arses. Leave."

The valet protested. The prince pushed him out of the bedchamber and shut the door in his face.

He swayed, caught himself on a small fruit tree that grew in a glazed pot, staggered into the water closet, and vomited.

Iolanthe chirped unhappily where she'd been left—just outside the closed door of the water closet. Faucets ran. Sounds of splashes came. The prince emerged ashen, but with most of the blood on his face washed off.

He picked her up and wobbled as he straightened. "You wanted to be in the bath with me earlier today, darling, did you not? Well, now you get your wish."

Once the amethyst tub had been filled, Titus climbed in fully clothed. He washed the blood from Fairfax's feathers, then recited the password. The next instant, he was sitting in a different tub, an empty one, his clothes and her feathers perfectly dry.

"Welcome to where I am *supposed* to go to school," he murmured.

The former monastery was a place of solitude and contemplation, a refuge from the pressures of the throne. It was also used as a site of learning, its clear air and distance from worldly distractions judged helpful to the studies of a princeling.

Titus did spend months here every year between Eton halves, reading, practicing, and experimenting. For someone who must keep secrets, it was a haven, as free from spies and surveillance as it was possible to be these days. There was no indoor staff except for those he chose to bring, and the outdoor staff came only once a week to maintain the grounds.

He climbed out of the tub, as clumsy as a sleepy toddler. One hand on the wall to steady himself, he inched down long, echoing corridors, stopping every minute or so to close his eyes and catch his breath.

Every time he did so, an ominous scene played upon the inside of his lids, of wyverns and armored chariots crisscrossing the sky in a choreography of deadly gracefulness. The vision had first come to him in the Inquisition Chamber, supplanting the image of his mother and her canary, just before a surge of horrendous pain rendered him unconscious.

And now it repeated itself whenever he closed his eyes for more than a few seconds.

Fairfax chirped as he opened the door of the repository. "Yes, I modeled my laboratory after this place. But this is much grander, is it not?"

The repository was ten times bigger, its shelves holding every substance known to magekind. He opened drawers and squinted—his headache gave him double vision.

"We are in trouble." He wished he would shut up, but the truth serum still pulsed in his veins and he was too weak to fight it. In any case, she would not remember a thing once she resumed human form. "I am afraid I have not convinced the Inquisitor of anything except my willingness to go to extraordinary lengths to conceal the truth from her."

Fairfax trembled in his hand. Or perhaps it was just him, shaking.

He poured an array of remedies down his gullet, followed by two bottles of tonics. They tasted like water that had been left out for a fortnight, thick with growing scum. He had not bothered to make them less disgusting, thinking he would be manly enough, in times of necessity, not to quibble over such minor details as flavor and texture.

He was wrong, as evidenced by another trip to the water closet to vacate the contents of his stomach.

Stumbling back out, he collected Fairfax from the counter where he had deposited her and headed for a different section of the repository, leaning against counters along the way to preserve his strength.

"I need to turn you back," he said, showing Fairfax a glass vial of white granules he had located. "You would have turned back on your own sometime during the night, but better you do it while I am still lucid."

He counted out three granules. She reached eagerly toward them. He blocked her beak. "No, not now, unless you plan to appear naked before me. Wait, that is your plan, is it not?"

He meant to leer at her but had to grimace when his head throbbed again.

She pecked hard at the outside of his hand.

"'The lady doth protest too much, methinks,'" he quoted. "Never mind. You do not know any Shakespeare, you ignoramus."

Fairfax in hand, he zigzagged to an adjacent room, where he sometimes slept when he stayed too late in the repository. He pulled out the sheet covering the thin mattress, placed her on the cot, laid the three granules before her, and spread the sheet over the whole cot again, burying her beneath it. His tunic and boots he peeled off so she would have something to wear. The tunic had not entirely escaped his bleeding, but considering the circumstances, it was pristine enough.

"Remember, it will be unpleasant and you will not be able to move immediately afterward. I will wait in the repository."

She chirped after a few seconds, perhaps trying to make sure he had vacated the premises.

"I am still here, shuffling along," he answered.

She chirped again. She was most likely telling him to hurry, but he chose to have a little fun with her—there was a severe scarcity of fun in his life. "*You* are anxious? Imagine how I feel, darling."

She chirped twice in a row. He wished he did not feel so wretched—carrying on an imaginary conversation with her would otherwise have been a highly rewarding use of his time.

"How can you help? If you will only . . ." He stopped.

He had been trying, with no apparent success, to bridge the chasm between them. But that was not *all* he wanted, was it? No, he was far more ambitious than even he had realized. He wanted her to . . .

"Fall in love with me." He heard, loud and clear, the words the truth serum compelled from him. "If you loved me, everything would be so much easier."

The transformation was horrendous, as if a hundred rodents were trying to gnaw their way out from underneath Iolanthe's skin.

Afterward, she lay in place, unable to move—and not merely because of her physical feebleness.

The things that boy wanted frightened her.

She should laugh at such ambitions on his part: nothing about him held any romance for her, not his crown, not his black heart, not his beautiful liar's face.

Yet she trembled inside, for what he wanted was not impossible.

It was not even improbable.

"I am not dead—or about to die," said Titus in response to Fairfax's gasp from the door.

She was at his side, her breaths ragged. "Then why are you on the floor?"

He had lost consciousness again after retaking most of the remedies. And it had seemed easier, after he had come to, simply to remain on the ground. "You had the nearest bed. How was the transformation, by the way?"

She did not answer, but only pulled him to his feet and half carried, half dragged him to the cot next door. "Are you sure you are not dying this instant?"

"I am very certain. I will die by falling, not lying comfortably in a bed."

"What?"

Damn the truth serum still raging through his veins. He should have censored himself—she was no longer a bird. "Make me some tea, would you? Everything you need you will find in the repository, in the cabinet underneath the globe."

She gave him a narrow-eyed glance but left, returning a few minutes later with two steaming mugs and a tin of everwell biscuits.

He tried to sit up.

She placed her palm firmly against his chest. "Stay down."

"How do I drink tea on my back?"

"Have you forgotten who I am?" A globule of tea the color and translucency of smoky quartz floated toward him. "This is how you will drink tea lying down."

Her expression was somewhere between anger and grief, but

closer to which he could not tell. "I can sit up for a cup of tea," he said.

"Don't. I was there. I know what the Inquisitor did to you. I saw you bleed from the ears."

He sucked in a breath. "You *remember*?"

"Yes."

Before he attempted his first transmogrification, he had read all the extant literature on the subject. Transmogrification was fairly old magic, so even though it had always been frowned upon and at times outlawed, there was no lack of records and studies.

In fifteen hundred years, there had been only two accounts of mages claiming memory from time spent in animal form. Most scholars considered those mages to have been either exaggerating or lying outright.

But Fairfax was clearly not lying—there was no other way she could have known what happened to him in the Inquisition Chamber except to rely on her own memory.

"How?"

"I'm not sure. I wonder if it has anything to do with the blood oath—that I had to maintain a continuity of consciousness so that I am never in danger of betraying my word."

He almost did not hear a thing she said as he recalled what *he* had said. *If you loved me, everything would be so much easier.*

She was still speaking, berating him for his stupidity in refusing to let the court physician treat him even though he had bled from his ears.

"I was not bleeding from the ears."

"Don't lie. I saw you."

"I cannot lie to you while under the blood oath, remember? The blood came from the veins on my wrists—I had extractors hidden inside my cuff braces. The court physician would have realized. That was why I could not see him. I cannot allow word to get back to the Inquisitor that I am not as badly hurt as I appeared to be."

The way she gaped at him, he could not tell whether she wanted to punch him or to hug him. Probably the former. He missed those brief hours when she *would* have hugged him. He never liked himself as much as when she had liked—even admired—him.

"How did you know you'd need extractors?" she asked, still suspicious.

"Before their minds broke, Inquisition subjects often bled from various orifices. I had hoped that when I bled, the Inquisitor would think she had gone far enough."

She clamped her teeth over her upper lip. "Did she stop?"

"No." He shook his head—and grimaced at the sharp pain brought on by the motion. "What happened in there? Did Captain Lowridge take it upon himself to break down the doors?"

Interruptions during Inquisition were *never* allowed. If Captain Lowridge had indeed cut in, for the man's own safety Titus would need to dismiss him immediately, so he could hide from the Inquisitor's wrath.

"No," said Fairfax. "Her minions rushed in first when they heard her scream. Captain Lowridge followed very closely on their heels, though."

He frowned. "What made her scream then?"

Iolanthe recounted her tactic, barely paying attention to her own story, still reeling from the revelation that the prince had planned the bleeding-from-the-ears part.

She ought to be more concerned that he was trying to make her fall in love with him, but all she could think about was the boy whose cat was killed on his lap, and who grew up terrified of the day he would be subject to the power of that same mind mage.

She recalled the precision of his spells, the result of endless, feverish practice. What of this nonspell, this pretense of bleeding? How many times had he rehearsed with extractors in his sleeves, falling down on the cold granite floors of the monastery, hoping that should an Inquisition come to pass, he would have a prayer of saving his mind?

"I moved the chandelier. The light elixir spheres fell out. My eyes were closed, but I believe one of the spheres struck the Inquisitor's person directly—I heard a thud before the crashes came. And then it was all to Captain Lowridge's credit for getting you out of the Inquistory."

She didn't expect him to be grateful, but she did expect him to be pleased. After all, he'd been deeply concerned about her inability to command air. Now she'd not only saved him, but proved herself that rarest of creatures, an elemental mage who controlled all four elements.

But his expression, after an initial shock, turned grim. He pushed the sheet aside and struggled to get up. "Why did you not tell me sooner?"

She gripped his arm to steady him. "I thought you were drawing your last breath."

He swayed, but his scowl was fierce. "Understand this: you will never again care whether I live or die, not when your own safety is in danger. My purpose is to guide and protect you for as long as I can, but in the end, only one of us matters, and it is not me."

He was so close, his heat seemed to soak into her. There was a small patch of dried blood he had not yet managed to wash off, an irregular-shaped smear at the base of his neck. And where he'd loosened his sleeves, she could see a puncture mark on the inside of each wrist, where the extractors had pierced his skin.

A bright pain burned in her heart. She might yet save herself from falling in love with him, but she would never again be able to truly despise him.

"We must get you out of the Domain this instant," he said, "before the Inquisitor realizes that someone else was in the Inquisition Chamber—someone with elemental powers."

He was already walking—tottering. She braced an arm around his middle.

"I need to go back to my apartment at the castle. The transmogrification potion is in my satchel. Get me to the bathtub upstairs. Then come down here and remove all evidence that might lead anyone to suspect your presence. The Inquisitor dared to come after my sanity; she could just as well invade my sanctuary."

She nodded tightly and walked faster, pulling him along.

At the bathtub, he bent down to turn on the faucets. "Go. And come back fast."

She ran and did as he asked. Sprinting back upstairs, she reached the bathtub as he materialized again, this time soaking wet, holding not a flask, but what looked to be a bottle of hair tonic.

"Where's the potion?"

He climbed out of the tub and pointed his wand at the hair tonic. *"In priorem muta."*

The bottle turned into a compartmented flask. She grabbed it. Drinking the potion in big gulps, she pointed her free hand at him and dissipated all the water from his sodden undertunic—the night was cool and he'd begun to shiver. Then she whisked away all the water he'd dripped onto the floor while downing the second solution.

"Clear thinking under pressure, as always," he murmured.

Assuming bird form was not only unpleasant, but disorienting, everything around her rapidly inflating to mountainous sizes.

He took her in hand. "Time to go."

✦ ✦

"You wish to be on a train headed not into Slough, but into London, sire?" asked Dalbert, sounding doubtful.

"Precisely." Titus checked his person, his clothes, and his belongings, applying one spell after another to reveal the presence of tracers and other foreign objects. He was clean.

"But, sire, in your condition—"

"All the more reason to leave without delay. You saw what the Inquisitor did to me. The House of Elberon means nothing to her. The farther I am from her, the safer I will be."

Dalbert still did not look convinced, but he acquiesced and lifted Titus's satchel.

A loud knock rattled the door of Titus's bedchamber. "Your Highness, Lady Callista to see you," announced Giltbrace from outside

Exactly what Titus had feared. He grabbed Fairfax's cage and gestured to Dalbert to keep quiet and follow him.

"Your Highness," came Lady Callista's voice. "The regent and I have been most distressed to hear of the seizure you unexpectedly suffered while touring the Inquisitory."

"Hurry," Titus whispered to Dalbert. "They will try to confiscate my transport."

They slipped into a secret passage accessed from Titus's dressing room and ran, Titus willing his stomach not to rebel again until later. The secret passage ended somewhere below the garret. He took the revolving steps three at a time, growing dizzier with each turn. Beneath came the pounding din of pursuit.

The garret, at last. They threw themselves into the rail coach, Titus bolting the door while Dalbert lurched for the controls. No sooner had Dalbert's hand fitted around the lever than a phalanx of guards burst through the door.

"Go!" Titus commanded.

Dalbert pulled. The rail coach shuddered and forcefully inserted itself into the pulsating bloodstream that was the English rail works.

The sound of steel wheels grinding on metal rails had never sounded so sweet.

Fairfax was safe. For now.

# CHAPTER ✦ 17

THE TRAIN HAPPENED TO TAKE them to Charing Cross rail station. Titus decided that one of the big, new hotels near Trafalgar Square frequently patronized by American tourists would serve his purpose very well.

He briefly bewitched a middle-aged lady and her maid. As the two followed dazed and obedient in his wake, he presented himself to the hotel clerk as Mr. John Mason of Atlanta, Georgia, traveling with his mother. Once he had his key in hand, he walked the lady and her maid out a different door, released them from the bewitchment, and bade them a cordial good night.

In his rooms, he applied layer upon layer of anti-intrusion spells, feeling no compunction in using the deadlier ones known to magekind. Deeming it secure enough for Fairfax to resume human form, he left her in the bedroom with a tunic from his satchel and a pair of his English trousers.

She padded out of the bedroom just as the dumbwaiter dinged.

"Your supper," he mumbled from where he lay slumped on the

settee, his arm over his eyes.

She found the door of the dumbwaiter. The aroma of chicken broth and beef pie wafted into the parlor. She set down the tray of food on the low table next to him. "Are you all right?"

He grunted.

"You don't want to eat anything?"

"No." He did not want to tax his stomach for the next twelve hours.

"So what now? Are we going on the run?"

He removed his arm from his face and opened his eyes. She was sitting on the carpet before the low table, wearing his gray hooded tunic, but *not* his trousers. Her legs were bare below mid-thigh.

The sight jolted him out of his lethargy. "Where are your trousers?"

"They had no braces and won't stay up. Besides, it's warm enough in here."

He was feeling quite hot. It was not unusual to see girls in short robes come summertime in Delamer. But in England skirts always skimmed the ground and men went mad for a glimpse of feminine ankles. So much skin—boys at school would faint from overexcitement.

He might have been a bit unsteady too, if he were not already lying down.

"You never answered my question," she said, as if the view of long, shapely legs should not scramble his thoughts at all. "Are we going on the run?"

"No, we go back to school tomorrow."

"What?"

"Had they managed to take you before we left the Domain, you would have been doomed. But now that danger is past, we must do everything in our power to preserve your current identity. As long as it remains intact, Atlantis can suspect me as much as it wants, but cannot prove anything."

"But you said you hadn't managed to convince the Inquisitor of anything. She will come after you again."

"She will, but not immediately. That interruption of yours was a blow to her. She will need some time to recover. Besides, I cannot disappear just like that. It is the law of the land that the throne cannot be left unoccupied. Alectus would be named the ruling prince."

And *that* would be the end of the House of Elberon.

She ladled herself a bowl of soup and dug into the beef pie. "So we have no choice but to carry on at school?"

"For as long as we can."

"And when we can't anymore?"

"Then we will be put to the test."

This earned him a look that was almost pure stoicism—except for a flash of sorrow. She had such beautiful eyes, this girl, and . . .

His thoughts slowed as he realized her eyes might be the last thing he saw before he died.

"You wouldn't have been involved in this at all if it weren't for your mother," she said, yanking him back to the present. "What if the Inquisitor is right?"

What if the Inquisitor had been? Much of his mother's brief life was a mystery to him, as were many of her visions. "Bear in mind the Inquisitor wanted to destabilize my mind as much as possible."

"Did your grandfather kill your mother?"

His face burned. "Yes."

Her gaze was steady. "Why?"

"To preserve the House of Elberon—he refused to go down as the last prince of the dynasty."

When given the choice by Atlantis between abolishing the crown altogether or offering his daughter, an active participant in the January Uprising, as a sacrifice, Prince Gaius had chosen the latter. It was not the most shameful secret of the House of Elberon's long history, but it came close enough.

"Did your mother really foresee her own death when she was a child?"

"I do not know."

"Did she tell you anything before she died?"

"Only that if I ever wanted to see my father, I had to bring down the Bane."

He would never have brought his father into the discussion, but the blood oath obliged him to tell the truth.

She chewed contemplatively. "If you don't mind my asking, who is your father?"

His cheeks scalded hotter, if possible. "I do not know that either."

"Your mother never mentioned him?"

"She mentioned him a great deal." His love of books, his beautiful singing voice, his smiles that could raise the sun at midnight. "But nothing that can be used to identify him."

How excited he had been at the possibility his mother's question implied. *Do you want to see your father?* He had thought it a question like *Do you want a slice of cake?*—with the cake to be produced within the minute.

Fairfax swirled a spoon in her soup bowl. "What did you say when you heard that you had to bring down the Bane?"

He had not been able to say much for the fear and disappointment that jostled within him. And the anger—that his own mother would trick him so.

"I said I was not going to fight the Bane because I did not want to die."

His mother had broken down and sobbed, tears streaming down her face to splatter upon her lovely sky-blue shawl. He had never seen her cry before.

"But you agreed eventually," said Fairfax quietly, her eyes almost tender.

He could still see his mother's tearstained face. Still hear her muffled voice as she answered his bewildered question.

*Why are you crying, Mama?*

*Because I hate myself for what I ask of you, sweetheart. Because I will never forgive myself, in this life or the next.*

Something in him had broken apart at those words.

"I was six," he said. "I would have done anything for her."

There existed something in this world that bound a mage tighter than a blood oath: love. Love was the ultimate chain, the ultimate whip, and the ultimate slave driver.

He reached into the satchel, which he had placed on the floor next to the chaise, and pulled out a thick book.

"I've seen that book. You brought it all the way from school?" asked Fairfax.

*"In priorem muta,"* he said. The book undisguised itself and became a plain, leather-bound journal. "My mother's diary. She recorded all her visions in here."

"It's empty," Fairfax said, after he had turned some thirty, forty pages.

"It will only show what I must see."

The diary had been left to him when his mother died, with the inscription *My dearest son, I will be here when you truly need me. Mama.*

He had opened it daily and come across absolutely nothing. Only after he had learned the truth of her death—that it had been murder, not suicide—had the first entry appeared. The one about him, on the balcony, witnessing the phenomenon that would and did change everything.

He kept turning the pages, but they remained stubbornly blank.

Something cold and terrible gnawed at his guts.

*I need you now. Do not abandon me. Do not.*

A few pages from the very end of the diary, writing at last appeared in her familiar, slanted hand. His hand tightened on the binding so his fingers would not shake from relief.

"You might as well read along with me," he said to Fairfax. "Many of her visions have to do with our task."

Fairfax left the low table and crouched down next to him.

*4 April, YD 1021*

*While Titus and I played in the upper gardens this morning, I had a vision of a coronation—one could not mistake those particular banners of the Angelic Host, flown only at coronations and state funerals. And judging by the colorful attire of the spectators thronging the street, I was witnessing no funeral.*

*But whose coronation is this? I caught three minutes of a long parade, that was all.*

*I came back to Titus tugging at my sleeve. He had found a ladybug he wanted me to admire. The poor child. I do not know why he loves me. Whenever he wants my attention, I always seem to be caught in another vision.*

"The date—it's just after the end of the January Uprising, isn't it?" asked Fairfax.

Titus nodded. Baroness Sorren had been executed the day before. They read on.

*10 April, YD 1021*

*The vision returned.[19] This time I was able to see, at the very end of Palace Avenue, the arrival of the state chariot. But I could not make out its occupant, except to see the sun dancing upon his or her crown.*

*For the rest of the day I could not concentrate on anything else. Poor Titus brought me a glass of pompear juice. After holding it for some time, I handed it back without taking a sip.*

*I need to know. I must know. The day after this vision occurred for the first time, Father requested that I exchange my life for Titus's future on the throne. I asked for time to consider it. He gave me three weeks.*

*If I am the person in the state chariot, then I will take Titus and go into hiding. The Labyrinthine Mountains are full of impenetrable folds and valleys. The nonmage world likewise offers plenty of means to disappear.*

*But what if I am not the person in the chariot?*

*12 April, YD 1021*

*I am not the person in the chariot.*
*Titus is. And he is tiny, barely bigger than he is now.*
*This time the vision lasted and lasted. I saw the entirety of his*

coronation, as well as the ceremony that invested Alectus with the powers of regency.

Either I have gone into exile by myself, or I am dead.

Because Titus is so young, many festivities that would otherwise take place are postponed until he comes of age. Still, for hours on end he receives well-wishers. My son, small, solemn, and all alone in the world.

Finally he is by himself. He takes out a letter from inside his tunic, tears it open, and reads. I could not see the writing on the letter, but the discarded envelope bears my personal seal.

The letter has a dramatic effect on Titus. He looks as if he has been kicked in the chest. He reads it again, then runs to take something out of his drawer.

*My diary.* This diary, which has never left my side.

He opens the diary. The first page reads My dearest son, I will be here when you truly need me. Mama. *The date beneath the inscription is two weeks from today.*

He turns the pages.

*Shock. My diary is empty— pages upon pages of nothing.*

*When something finally appears on the page, I am shocked again. It was the vision about a young man on a balcony, seen from the back, witnessing something that stuns him. I had experienced the vision several times but never sensed any significance to it.*

*Apparently I shall feel quite different about it in the near future. The description of the vision, less than two pages long when I last added to it, now stretches the full four pages I allot any one vision. Even the margins are packed with words.*

*The vision itself began to fade at this point, but I was able to read bits and pieces of my writing, which concern elemental magic, of all things. In the crammed paragraphs I reference other visions, which appear to have nothing at all to do with this one, even recounting a conversation with Callista, during which she told me in strict confidence what she had learned about Atlantis's interest in elemental mages, from the then Inquisitor himself, no less, who had been quite enamored of her beauty and charm.*

*The vision has faded completely. It is now past five in the morning. The sky outside my window shows the faintest trace of orange. I realize with a wrenching pain in my heart that my days are numbered.*

*But there is no time to wallow in self-pity. In the next two weeks I will write passionately about elemental magic, but I barely know anything about it.*

*I must quickly find out not only a great deal more about elemental magic, but why I should care.*

*But first I weep—because I will not see my son grow up. I will not even see him reach his next birthday. And he will only remember me as the dotty woman who did not drink the juice he had specially brought for me.*

The Inquisitor was the liar, not his mother.

A hot shame gripped Titus, that he had doubted his mother so harshly. That he had hated her as often and as much as he did.

He excused himself and hurried to the water closet, where he lost his battle with tears. He was still wiping them away when Fairfax called out, "Come here. I found another vision!"

"Are you sure? I have never seen more than one at a time," said the prince.

His eyes were red-rimmed, as if he'd been crying. She immediately looked back at the diary. "I was randomly flipping pages. I'm almost sure these pages were blank earlier when you looked at them, but they are not anymore."

He sat next to her. "This one is from almost a decade before the other one."

He began to read. She stole a glance at him, then did the same.

*7 May 1012*

> *A new vision today.*
>
> *The vision is of a library– or a bookshop. A woman, who has her back to me, wanders through the shelves and appears to be searching for a specific title.*
>
> *She stops and reaches for a tome that requires two hands to lift. The title on the spine reads* The Complete Potion.
>
> *(I know this book—a detestable volume full of pretension and remarkably empty on actual scholarship. My tutor used to torment me with it.)*

*The woman in the vision, with some difficulty, maneuvers the book to a desk and sets it down next to a calendar that shows the date, 25 August.*

*She opens the book and quickly finds what she is looking for. The subject is light elixirs. There is a stylus on the desk. She picks up the stylus and writes on the very edge of a page,* There is no light elixir, however tainted, that cannot be revived by a thunderbolt.

Iolanthe recoiled. These were the fateful words that had changed everything.

"Is this the advice that you received on Tuesday?" asked the prince.

Tuesday. Less than a week and more than a lifetime ago. She nodded.

"I guess we are about to find out who wrote it," he said.

*5 August 1013*

*A repeat of last year's vision, with no new information.*

*11 August 1013*

*I have seen this vision three times in the last two days. Yesterday I asked my tutor whether lightning could be used to mend an elixir. He laughed until he choked.*

*12 August 1013*

*Again the same vision. It grows vexing.*

*15 August 1013*

*Finally something new.*
*As the woman in the vision leans toward the stylus holder, I was able to make out, on the base of the holder, the inscription:* Presented to my dear friend and mentor Eugenides Constantinos.

*16 August 1013*

*I have found out that Eugenides Constantinos owns a bookshop at the intersection of Hyacinth Street and University Avenue. I will stop and take a look the next time I am in the area.*

Iolanthe sucked in a breath.

"What is it?"

"I know that place—my guardian used to take me there all the time. It had become a sweets shop by then, but it still had some of the old signs. The one I liked the best said something along the lines of 'Books on the Dark Arts may be found in the cellar, free of charge. And should you locate the cellar, kindly feed the phantom behemoth inside. Regards, E. Constantinos.'"

"'The warp and weft of Fortune weave in mysterious ways; only in hindsight does one see the threads of destiny taking shape,'" he quoted.

She exhaled slowly and read on.

*31 August 1013*

*A most fantastical day.*

*I slipped out of a command performance of Titus III, evaded my ladies-in-waiting, and hurried to the Emporium of Fine Learning and Curiosities, Constantinos's shop. As I walked into the shop, the vision repeated itself an unprecedented seventh time.*

*This time, I saw clearly the distinctive ring on the hand wielding the stylus.*

*When the vision had faded, I lifted my own hand in shock. On my right index finger is an identical ring that had been wrought for Hesperia the Magnificent. There is not another like it in all the mage realms.*

*The woman is me.*

Iolanthe's hand came up to her throat.

*I laughed. Well, then.*

*Once I had a vision of myself telling my father that a particular Atlantean girl was going to be the most powerful person in the Domain.*

*Then, when I saw the girl in truth, I told him what I had seen myself tell him—since one cannot deliberately change what has been seen to happen. He was terribly displeased to be faced with the possibility that he, a direct descendant of Titus the Great, would one day no longer be the absolute master of this realm.*

*But this time I would offend no one.*

*I found the book, dragged it to the table, lifted the stylus from its holder, and vandalized the book as I had done in the vision.*

*Only when I was finished did I remember the desk calendar. In the vision it is always 25 August. But today is 31 August. I looked at the calendar on the desk. 25 August! The device had stopped working a week ago.*

*I am not often cheered by how right I am: the ability to see glimpses of the future is frustrating and hair-raising. But at that moment, I was ever so thrilled.*

*On impulse, I opened the book again, turned to the section for clarifying draughts, and tore out the last three pages. The recipes given on those pages are riddled with errors. I was not going to let some other poor pupil suffer from them.*

They turned the page, but there was nothing else. They kept turning pages. Still nothing. The prince eventually closed the journal and put it back into his satchel.

He glanced at Iolanthe.

She realized she ought to say something, but she did not dare to speak aloud her thoughts—for fear she might truly find the long arm of destiny clasped tightly about her.

For fear she might come to accept the idea that her fate and the prince's had been interwoven since long before their births.

"Tell me about the vision in which she saw you dying," said Fairfax, returning to her supper. "Did you also read it in that diary?"

Titus slowly lay himself back down. Damn the truth serum. And damn the blood oath that prevented him from lying. One might as well blind a painter or chop off the fingers of a sculptor—he was an artist with his lies. "Yes."

"When will it happen?"

"I am described as in my late adolescence. So . . . any day now."

She blinked a few times, looked down at her food, then back at him. "Why?"

"There is no why. Everybody dies."

"You said that the diary only shows what you need to know. Why is it necessary for you to learn that you'll die young?"

"So I will prepare accordingly. It concentrates the mind, knowing that time is limited."

"It could have had the opposite effect. Another boy might have abandoned the whole venture altogether."

"That boy must not worry about meeting his mother in the after-life with nothing accomplished in this one. Besides, you cannot escape your destiny. Look at how much effort has been expended in helping you elude the ineluctable—and look where you are now."

A pot of tea had come with the supper tray. Her gaze dropped to the teapot. Tea jetted out of the spout by itself, arcing a graceful parabola in the air before filling a cup without a drop spilled. She wrapped her hands around the cup, as if she felt cold and needed a source of warmth. "So I might be alone at the end, facing the Bane."

The thought haunted him almost more than his impending death. "As long as I live and breathe, I will be with you. And I will shield you."

Her fingers flexed, then tightened around the teacup. "I never thought I'd say this, but I want you to live forever."

He did not need to live forever, but he would like to live long enough to forget the taste of fear. "You can live forever for me."

Their gazes met—and held.

She rose, went into the bedroom, and came back with a blanket. As she tucked the blanket in around him, forever became a distant thought—he would gladly exchange it for a few more moments like this.

"Sleep," she said. "The great elemental mage of our time will stand guard over you."

A few sparks of fire floated below the ceiling, providing just enough illumination to see. Iolanthe gazed at the prince's sleeping form, one arm slung over his head, the other kept close to his person, his wand in hand.

Gathering the sparks nearer herself, she took out his mother's diary and flipped through the pages again. Nothing, except for one particular page which bore a small skull mark that she hadn't noticed before at the bottom right-hand corner.

When she reached the end of the diary, she turned the pages backward. Still nothing. She sighed and returned the diary to his satchel.

In her heart she was beginning to understand that it was truly written in the stars, her destiny. Yet it still seemed utterly impossible that she would ever find the audacity to face the Bane, she who had lived such a small life, so tightly focused only on the well-being of her own family.

Especially if the prince was right about his death.

Upon his passing, the blood oath would cease to be binding. She would be free to walk away from this mad venture, snatch Master Haywood, if she could, and disappear into hiding.

There was nothing to stop her.

Except the knowledge that he had given his life to the cause, and she would have abandoned the entire foundation he had built.

Not to mention the question that was beginning to tug at the edge of her mind: if she had the power to overthrow the Bane, could she live with never trying, just keeping herself and Master Haywood safe in some pocket of the Labyrinthine Mountains, while Mrs. Needles and countless others like her rotted in Atlantean prisons?

Could she live with herself, cowering, while the world burned?

## CHAPTER 18

IOLANTHE WOKE UP HISSING WITH pain. Her fingers felt as if they had swollen to three times their normal size, her skin about to burst from the pressure.

But they *appeared* no different. She stared at her hands in puzzlement. When she closed her hands, her knuckles protested. She opened and closed her hands a few more times. The discomfort went away rather rapidly, leaving her bewildered.

"What is the matter?" asked the prince from where he lay, his voice rough with sleep.

"You're awake. How is your head? Want me to find you some breakfast?"

"No breakfast, thank you. And my head is terrible, but that is par for the course. What is the matter with you?"

"I'm not sure. My hands hurt a minute ago, but not anymore. Is it a side effect of transmogrification?"

"No, but it might be a side effect of your breaking the otherwise spell, though."

"What otherwise spell?"

"The one that was laid on you earlier, to make you believe you could not manipulate air."

"Maybe I was just late developing it."

He shook his head. "I read your guardian's letter to you and—"

She cocked a brow. She had never offered him the letter to read.

"Well, you already know I am unscrupulous."

She sighed. "Go on."

"These are his exact words. 'I can't help but wonder how your power would have manifested itself. By causing the Delamer River to flow in reverse? Or shearing the air of a sunny day into a cyclone?' Which tells me that you did have power over air as a toddler."

"But I thought you couldn't apply an otherwise spell when the subject already knows about something."

"Power over air is the easiest to disguise. You cannot explain away the sudden appearance of fire or water, or stones flying off a wall. But movement of air can always be blamed on a breeze from the window. And this way he could pass you off as an Elemental Mage III—much less noticeable."

"I still don't see why my hands should hurt now, after I broke through the otherwise spell, if that's what it was."

"Do something with air. Make the curtain flutter."

She tried, but the curtain moved only the tiniest bit. "I don't understand. I swung the entire chandelier last night."

"Now you are no longer in the midst of extraordinary circumstances.[20] An otherwise spell is not easy to cast off completely, when it has controlled you for so long. But you are already much further along than you used to be—the pain is likely a physical manifestation of the potential you have unlocked struggling against what is left of the otherwise spell."

She tried again to flutter the curtain; the result was not much more impressive. It was disheartening. She'd thought her control over air would be easy and absolute from this point onward. "So what do I do now?"

"Train harder. All of elemental magic is mind over matter. You must keep pushing yourself." He sat up and winced in pain. "We all must keep pushing ourselves."

Mrs. Hancock's smile was as pleasant as ever, her day dress as brown and sacklike. "Your Highness, if you would follow me to my parlor."

Titus braced a hand on the banister—she had caught him as he was going up the stairs. "What is it with you Atlanteans? Can you not see I have a pounding headache?"

He was not lying: the inside of his skull felt like a nonmage demolition, all crowbars and sledgehammers. He was also feeble from hunger, having had nothing more than a cup of tea since his Inquisition.

"I wouldn't dream of disturbing Your Highness unless it was of vital importance," said Mrs. Hancock serenely.

"Who wants to see me?"

"The Acting Inquisitor, sir."

"Who the hell is the Acting Inquisitor?"

"His name is Baslan."

Baslan was not usually referred to as Acting Inquisitor, but as vice-proconsul or something of the sort. Titus rubbed his temples. "Is the Master of the Domain not important enough for the Bane's lackey now? I have to see the lackey's lackey?"

"You are ever so gracious, Your Highness," murmured Mrs. Hancock, as she reached out and straightened a frame of embroidered iris that had been knocked askew by a careless boy.

She led the way to an austere parlor of bare floor and unpadded chairs, and not a petal or stem of the printed flowers beloved by Mrs. Dawlish. Her drawer pulls, however, were carved with the stylized whirlpool symbol. Baslan's spectral image—a piece of Atlantean magic that the Domain's archmages had yet to duplicate—paced in the parlor, heedless of walls and furniture.

He snapped to at Titus's entrance. Titus plopped himself into the nearest seat and shaded his eyes with his hand—the sunlight streaming in from Mrs. Hancock's window burned like acid on his retinas. "What do you want?"

"I need an account of Your Highness's actions last night inside the Inquisition chamber."

A question that did not involve Miss Buttercup in any conceivable manner was not one Titus had expected. "*My* actions? Bleeding from all major orifices and suffering horrific damage to my vision, my hearing, and my cognitive abilities."

"You seem remarkably healthy for all the inflictions you listed," said Baslan.

Titus coughed. He turned his face to the side and spat blood all over Mrs. Hancock's skirts—a good trick if he did say so himself. Mrs. Hancock squealed—at last a genuine reaction—and waved her wand madly to get rid of the stains.

He glared at Baslan. "What did you say?"

Baslan looked baffled. He opened his mouth, then closed it again.

"The Acting Inquisitor need not hesitate," said Mrs. Hancock. "If His Highness doesn't already know what happened, he will very soon."

Baslan still wavered.

Titus made as if to rise. "You have wasted enough of my time."

"The Inquisitor has been unconscious since last night." Baslan's voice was shrill. "I demand to know what you did to her."

Titus knew that mind mages abhorred disruptions during a probe, but he had had no idea a disruption could be *that* catastrophic. Or was it because what Fairfax had thought of as dainty light spheres had not been so dainty? What if one such light sphere falling from a great height would have given the Inquisitor a concussion even under normal circumstances?

"Her mind is gone?" he asked, knowing that was too good to be true.

"Her mind is not gone," Baslan snarled. "She is only temporarily incapacitated."

"That is too bad. It would have been justice from the Angels for all the minds she has destroyed."

Baslan clenched his hand, restraining himself with difficulty. "You will tell me what you did to Madam Inquisitor."

Titus looked at him aslant. "So *that* was the reason you sent Lady Callista to the castle last night. And here I thought she was at last beginning to care about my health."

And *that* was why they had tried to prevent him from leaving. Not because they wanted to strip him of his canary, but because the physicians needed to know what had caused the Inquisitor's unconsciousness before they could formulate a treatment.

He smirked and pulled out his wand, adorned with seven diamond-inlaid crowns along its length. "This is Validus, the wand that once belonged to Titus the Great. I know Atlanteans are culturally isolated and largely unaware of histories beyond their own, but I trust that you, Acting Inquisitor, must have heard of Titus the Great."

Baslan's lips thinned. "I am aware of who he was."

"Titus the Great left behind a unified Domain. But to his family, he also left behind the Titus Benediction, a tremendous protection allied to the power of Validus, which would let no harm come to the heir of the House of Elberon."

He tapped the wand twice against his palm. Mrs. Hancock rose to her feet, Baslan took a step backward, both staring at the light now emanating from the seven crowns.

"Yes, you behold one of the last of the blade wands. An unsheathed blade wand is one of the most powerful objects around. And Validus unsheathed invokes the Titus Benediction—which I did before I fell unconscious. After that, all the might the Inquisitor aimed at breaking me would have deflected onto herself."

Baslan was still staring at Validus as Titus sheathed it. Titus pulled himself to his feet. With all the hauteur he could muster— not a great deal as he could scarcely remain upright—he sneered at the Atlanteans.

"And that is why you do not trifle with the Master of the Domain."

Iolanthe put her arm around him as he was about to start up the stairs.

His reaction was a low growl. "I told you not to come back until I gave you the all clear."

He was pale, and there were drops of blood on his sleeve. Even knowing the blood for the trick it was, her heart still flinched. "You might have needed help."

"Did I not also tell you never to worry about me?"

Stupid, stubborn boy. "If I hadn't interfered earlier, you'd be a drooling imbecile by now. So shut up and let me make my own decisions."

He almost smiled. "That does not sound right. I am the brains of the operation. You are only supposed to provide the muscle."

She wanted to touch his cheek, but did no such thing. "When there is enough muscle, it develops a mind of its own."

Birmingham, the house captain, bounded down the stairs. "What's the matter, Titus? You look like you are about to give up the ghost."

It still jarred Iolanthe to hear the prince called by his name. She almost snarled at Birmingham to not be so familiar. "Bad oysters at the diplomatic reception," she said instead.

Birmingham sucked in a breath. "Those can be deadly. You'd better hope the danger is past."

"I think I am going to puke again," the prince mumbled.

"Hurry. I'll secure you a chamber pot." She'd found one in the hotel. The prince had to explain to her what the object was for. The very idea of it. "Toodles, Birmingham."

Once they were in his room, she borrowed his wand and flicked it. There came the unmistakable sound of someone dry-heaving.

The prince winced, though he looked impressed at the same time. "What was *that*?"

"Learned it from a pupil in Little Grind. This was how she convinced her mother not to give her turnips at supper anymore." She set a sound circle and gave the wand back to him. "Now you lie down."

"I need to see what intelligence Dalbert might have sent."

"Lie down. I'll do it for you."

"I—"

"If Dalbert sends intelligence, I need to know how to receive it. Remember, you won't always be here."

*You can live forever for me.* The wistfulness in those words, the calm acceptance of what could not be changed. There was no glory for him in chasing after the impossible, no reward beyond a promise kept.

"Must you remind me?" He stretched himself out on his bed. "Put a piece of paper under the machine in that cabinet by my desk."

She had no trouble finding the somewhat porcupinelike device and successfully placed the paper on the domed tray beneath on her second try. The device clacked. When it stopped, she removed the paper and brought it to him.

"What news might Dalbert have? And what did Mrs. Hancock do with you? Did she ask that you produce Miss Buttercup?"

"No one asked about Miss Buttercup." He took the report from her hand and scanned it. A little color returned to his face. "So it *is* true: the Inquisitor remains unconscious."

"She is?"

"Has been since last night."

"From what I did?"

"From what you did, except they thought I was responsible for it, so I gave them a fairy tale about the powers of my wand."

He was still looking at the report, oblivious to what he'd just said. She suppressed an urge to giggle. "Did they believe you? All boys tell such tales about their wands."

He glanced up, his eyes first blank, then lit with mischief. "Maybe they do, but *I* actually possess a superior wand—the finest of its kind, no less. The sort of fireworks my wand can produce will leave any girl breathless."

They both burst out laughing. His entire aspect was transformed, like a desert come to life after a rainstorm. She had to turn away, her eyes filling with abrupt tears.

*You can live forever for me.*

She looked out the window, her back to him. It was a sunny afternoon. The small meadow behind the house hopped with junior boys at their various games—balls, sticks, and a kite three of the boys were trying to set aloft.

A life simple, peaceful, and bucolic all around him—and he would have only ever gazed upon it as if through a looking glass.

"Won't the regent contradict your account?" she heard herself carrying on the discussion, as if their present danger were the only thing that mattered. "Your wand is a family heirloom. If it has special powers, he'd know about it too, wouldn't he?"

"All Alectus can say is that he does not know. He will be the first to admit there is a store of knowledge that is only passed down the direct line of inheritance."

"So we're safe as long as the Inquisitor remains unconscious?"

"It would seem."

"What happens when she wakes up?"

"Something will give."

She turned around. "What will give?"

"Time will tell," he said, with a calm that was not resignation, but a fierce will. "We assume the worst and prepare accordingly."

The room was hung with crimson curtains and deep-blue tapestries. Vases of gilded ice roses bloomed almost to the painted ceiling. At the center of the far wall, under a triple archivolt, Princess Aglaia occupied her bejeweled throne.

Each classroom in the teaching cantos of the Crucible had been decorated in the taste of the ruling prince or princess who created it. Princess Aglaia, Titus's great-grandmother, had liked dramatic uses of color and ostentation. Princess Aglaia had also been one of the most learned heirs of the House of Elberon.

Titus took a seat on a low stool before the throne. "I seek your knowledge, Your Highness."

Princess Aglaia stroked the fat Persian cat in her lap. "How may I help?"

"I would like to know whether a mage can have a vision—as a seer—for the first time when he is sixteen years of age."

The spectacle of the wyverns and the armored chariots weaving in the sky, menacing and purposeful, no longer burst upon his mind as vividly as it had at first. But it still came, faded and blurred around the edges.

Princess Aglaia set an index finger against her cheek. "It would be highly atypical, but not unheard of. When the first vision occurs after the onset of adolescence, however, it is usually followed by a quick succession of additional visions—every hour, if not more frequent. Has your mage experienced that?"

"No." He had undergone nothing of the sort. "What if the first vision took place in a situation of great distress? Would that make additional visions less likely?"

"Describe the situation of great distress."

"A no-holds-barred Inquisition in full progress."

The cat purred. Princess Aglaia scratched it between the ears, looking thoughtful. "Curious. I am not certain a vision can happen when the mind is under such duress. And how did the mage in question emerge from a no-holds-barred Inquisition with enough lucidity to recall the vision?"

"The Inquisition was interrupted."

"When?"

"Quite possibly at the time of the vision, if not soon afterward."

"Ah," said Princess Aglaia. "Now it makes sense."

"How so?"

"I do not believe your mage had a vision at all. What he had was a rupture view. You see"—Princess Aglaia leaned forward, eager to share her erudition—"mind mages are a curious breed. You cannot simply pay mind mages to do your dirty work. They have to *want* to take part. The talents of mind mages are inborn, but the power they achieve is directly proportional to their dedication to a cause."

The Inquisitor was certainly fanatically devoted to the Bane.

"Mind mages fear interruption during their work for two reasons. One, their fully extended mind is quite vulnerable to permanent damage. Two, the thoughts they use to whip themselves into a frenzy of power might become visible as a rupture view. Your mage did not have a glimpse of the future, but instead a picture of the inner workings of the mind mage."

This was a most unexpected revelation. But Titus's thrill lasted only a second. "Does the rupture view happen only one way, or is it mutual?"

"It is most assuredly mutual. There have been instances when a mind mage's master chose to interrupt an Inquisition deliberately, when he believed the mind mage might not be strong enough to break the subject, in order to obtain a rupture view."

Which meant the Inquisitor, when she regained consciousness, would have the image of Princess Ariadne and the canary imprinted in her mind. She would need no time to find out that Princess Ariadne had never owned a canary in her life.

And then she would remember that she and Titus had not been entirely alone in the Inquisition Chamber.

It was only Kashkari, Wintervale, and Iolanthe for tea.

"His Highness is still puking?" asked Wintervale.

"Not anymore," said Iolanthe. "All the same, he doesn't want to smell fried sausages. He'll have a few water wafers in his room."

Wintervale gestured at the spread of food on his desk. "Well then, tuck in."

"How was your trip home, Fairfax?" asked Kashkari. "And will your family come for the Fourth of June?"

Iolanthe took a sip of tea, buying herself a few seconds to think. At least she knew for certain her family would not be coming for the Fourth of June, whatever that was. "They start for Bechuana-land this week, actually. And you, gentlemen, how is life away from home?"

"I am always in favor of life away from home," answered Wintervale with a sigh.

"What do you do on holidays then?"

"Wait for school to begin again."

What did one say to something like that? "Is it as bad for you, Kashkari?"

"No, I miss home—a round trip to India takes six weeks, so it's only during the summer that I get to see my family. I wish I didn't have to attend school so far away."

"Why *did* you decide to attend school so far from home?" She'd seen a few other Indian boys in uniform, so at least he wasn't the only one.

"The astrologer said I should."

"Astrologer?"

Kashkari nodded. "We have these complicated charts drawn up

when we are born. For every major decision in life, we consult the astrologer—preferably the one who drew up the chart—and he tells us the auspicious and sometimes the necessary paths to take."

It sounded remarkably like what mages did with their birth charts. "So you are not here because you want to be, but because it was in the stars."

"Some things are preordained."

The inflection of Kashkari's voice reminded her of the prince's, when the latter spoke of the futility of trying to escape one's destiny.

Wintervale reached for a piece of sausage. "I think you put too much stock in the stars."

His elbow knocked over his tea mug. They all leaped up. Kashkari reached for a towel next to Wintervale's washstand. Iolanthe lifted a stack of books out of the way.

Behind the books stood a small, framed picture—a family portrait, a man, a woman, and a young boy between them. Iolanthe nearly dropped the books. The boy was obviously Wintervale nine or ten years ago. His father looked vaguely familiar, but his mother's face she recognized instantly.

The madwoman who'd tried to suffocate her in the portal trunk.

"Your family?" she asked, hoping her tone wasn't too sharp.

"Except my father is no more. And my mother hasn't been the same since he died."

That was one way of saying his mother was a murderous lunatic. "Is that why you don't like holidays?"

"She's actually all right most of the time. I just never know when she won't be." Wintervale took the towel from Kashkari and wiped away the spilled tea. He tossed aside the towel, poured more tea for himself, and sat down. "I think we should do something about your bowling technique, Fairfax. You've great attack, but your arm and shoulder don't quite align as they should."

Through Titus's half-open door, the din of thirty-some boys at leisure washed in wave by wave: boots and brogues stomping up and down the stairs; junior boys hauling trays of dirty dishes, plates and silverware jangling; the house officers, in their common room across the passage, debating the differences between the Eton football game and the Winchester football game.

He sat on his bed, his back against the wall. The Crucible lay open on his lap, and a stranger's face stared at him. If he had ever doubted the efficacy of the Irreproducible Charm that had been cast on Fairfax, here was his proof. He was usually competent with pen and ink, but the rendering he had attempted of her face was outright unrecognizable.

He tapped his wand against the page. The ink lifted from the illustration in a swirl and returned to the reservoir of his fountain pen. Sleeping Beauty now lay on her bed without a face, amidst all the details of dust and cobweb he had added over the years. He tapped his wand again, and her original features returned, pretty and insipid.

A rap at his door. He looked up to see Fairfax closing the door behind her. She pointed at the wand in his hand. He set a sound circle.

"When were you going to tell me that the woman who tried to kill me is Wintervale's mother?"

He enjoyed the sight of her on the warpath, her eyes narrowed with indignation—a girl who emanated power with her very presence.

"I did not want your views of Wintervale, who is perfectly sane, colored by what you think of his mother."

"What would have happened if I were to run into her?"

"You would not. She does not come to school, and none of us are ever invited to visit her house. Besides, even if you do, she has no idea what you look like."

She was far from mollified. "Is this something you would have wanted to know, were you in my place?"

"Yes," he had to admit.

"Then extend me the same courtesy."

He sighed. It was difficult for him, having so long held everything close to the chest, to share all his secrets and hard-won intelligence. But she had a point—and not everything needed to wait until he was dead.

"Besides, you give me too little credit if you think I am going to judge a boy by his mother. If I can bring myself to see you in a sympathetic light, Wintervale has nothing to fear."

Warmth crept up the back of his neck. "You see me in a sympathetic light?"

She drew back and cast him a scornful look. "Sometimes. Not now."

He patted the bed. "Come here. Let me change your mind."

She made a face. "With more fairy tales of your wand's powers?"

He smiled. Her arrival might have turned over the hourglass on what remained of his life, but before she came, he never smiled. Or laughed.

"You are still my subject, so sit down on the command of your sovereign. He will show you his domain."

He taught her how to get in and navigate the Crucible by herself—not only the practice cantos, but also the teaching cantos, which she hadn't even known existed.

The teaching cantos was a small palace built of pale-pink marble, with clear, wide windows and deeply receded loggias. Inside, a double-return staircase led to a gallery that encircled the soaring reception hall. Along the gallery marched doors of different sizes, colors, and ornateness.

The first one they came to was black and glassy, an entire slab of obsidian that glittered with grape-sized diamonds arranged in constellations.

"This is Titus the Third's classroom."

"Titus the Third himself is inside?"

Titus III ranked as one of the most remarkable rulers of the House of Elberon, alongside Titus the Great and Hesperia the Magnificent.

"A record and a likeness of him. He was the one who constructed the Crucible, so his is the first classroom."

Next to the obsidian door was a plaque that bore Titus III's name. And beneath that, a list of topics that stretched all the way to the floor.

"He was an expert on all those subjects?"

"Most of them—he was a learned man. But his knowledge was for his time." The prince tapped on the list, and a bramble of annotations spread over the original engraved letters.

Iolanthe peered closer. On the subject of potions, a number of comments had been left.

> *Archaic recipes. Go to Apollonia II for simpler, more effective recipes.—Tiberius.*
>
> *Do not go to Apollonia II for recipes unless you intend to pluck eyes out of live animals. Titus VI—I know, shocking—has a number of very reliable recipes.—Aglaia.*
>
> *Aglaia has adapted Titus VI's recipes to more modern tools and processing methods.—Gaius.*

"So this is how you have been educated in subtle magic, by your ancestors."

"Many of whom were capable mages, though only a few are also good teachers."

The gallery turned. And turned again. She stopped paying attention to the individual doors and studied the boy next to her. He looked slightly less ravaged, though he still walked hesitantly, as if worried about his balance.

And everything would only become more difficult.

This was why he wanted her to love him, because love was the only force that could compel *him* onto this path—and hold him to it.

There came a prickling sensation in her heart, a weight with thorns.

They were approaching the stairs again. The last two doors belonged to Prince Gaius and Prince Titus VII, respectively. "Your mother doesn't have a place here?"

"She was never on the throne. Only a ruling prince or princess is allotted a spot in the teaching cantos."

Prince Gaius's door, a gigantic block of basalt thickly studded with fist-sized rubies, bore an unmistakable resemblance to that of Titus III's—except everything had been done on a showier scale. On his plaque, he listed one of his areas of expertise as Atlantis. "Have you spent much time here?"

The prince cast an icy look at his grandfather's door. "I do not call on him."

Sometimes he was sixteen years old. And sometimes he was a thousand, as cold and proud as the dynasty that had spawned him.

She tapped on the door of *his* classroom. "And what do you teach?"

Next to Prince Gaius's, his door was almost laughably plain—and looked exactly the same as the door to his room in Mrs. Dawlish's house. "I teach survival—for you. When I am gone, this is where you will come if you still have questions."

Suddenly she understood the dread in her heart. If the prophecy of his death had been properly interpreted, it would mean he had very little time left. A year, perhaps. A year and half at best. How would it feel to push open that door, knowing he was gone, to speak with "a record and a likeness" of him?

She made herself say something sensible. "Would you mind if I asked your grandfather a few questions—in case he knew something about Atlantis that could help us free Master Haywood?"

"Go ahead. Although—"

"What is it?"

He didn't quite look at her. "I think you should first consult the Oracle of Still Waters."

A flagstone-paved path led out from behind the pink-marble palace, flanked on either side by tall, stately trees with bark that was almost silky to the touch. Pale-blue flowers drifted down from the boughs, twirling like tiny umbrellas.

Iolanthe caught one of the blue flowers. "Are we still in the teaching cantos?"

The prince nodded. "In the practice cantos, every time you leave, it is as if you have never been there. But the Oracle will advise you only once in your lifetime, and until her story was moved to the teaching cantos, where there is continuity, my ancestors could never get any meaningful answers from her."

"And she will only help you to help someone else, right?"

"Right—and she can see through you. When I pretended that I wanted to help the Bane remain in power, she laughed. When I said I wanted to protect my people, she laughed again. And when I asked how I could help you get to me, she told me to mind my own business, because you had no interest in my schemes."

He could joke about it now, but she wondered how the Oracle's blunt, unhelpful answers must have struck him when he desperately needed guidance and assurance.

The path led them to a clearing. The Oracle, at the center of a clearing, was not a pond, as Iolanthe had thought, but a round pool six feet across built of fine, creamy marble. The water was as beautiful as the light elixir she'd made with her lightning.

"Lean over the edge and look at your reflection," said the prince.

As she did so, the water ruffled. A pleasant, feminine voice greeted her. "Iolanthe Seabourne, welcome."

Iolanthe drew back in surprise. "How do you know my name, Oracle?"

The water danced, as if laughing. "I wouldn't be any good if I didn't know who had come to ask for my help."

"Then you also know why I have come."

"But there is more than one person you wish to help."

Iolanthe glanced behind her shoulder. The prince stood at the edge of the clearing, out of earshot.

"Think carefully. I can help you only once."

She rubbed her thumb along the raised rim. "Then help me help the one who needs it the most."

The pool stilled to an almost mirrorlike smoothness. Not a ripple distorted Iolanthe's reflection. All at once her reflection disappeared, as did the reflection of the cloudless sky above. The surface of the water turned ink dark and swelled like a rising tide.

The Oracle's voice turned deep, rough. "You will best help him by seeking aid from the faithful and bold. And from the scorpion."

"What do you mean?" But of course, one was not supposed to ask oracles such questions.

The pool turned clear again. Water receded from the edge, hissing with steam. The marble beneath her hand, cool to the touch a minute ago, was now hot, as if it had been in the sun for hours.

"As for your guardian, he will not long remain in the custody of the Inquisitor," said the Oracle, her voice low. "Good-bye, Iolanthe Seabourne."

They had entered the Crucible sitting a respectable distance apart on the bed. But Titus opened his eyes to find her head on his shoulder, his hand holding hers on the cover of the book.

He did not immediately release her hand. He should, but somehow he remained exactly as he was. His breath came in shallow, almost ragged. Her hair brushed against his jaw, as if she were tilting her face to look at him.

A hot urge pulsed through his veins. One second. Two seconds. Three seconds. If he counted to five, and she still did not move . . .

Four seconds. Five sec—

Her fingers tightened around his. But the next moment she was already rising and walking away. At the opposite wall, she turned around and crossed her feet insouciantly at the ankles, as if nothing had happened. Nothing *had* happened, but almost five seconds was an awfully long time to teeter on the brink.

He collected himself. "What did the Oracle say about your guardian?"

"That he won't be in the Inquisitory for much longer."

"How will he escape?"

"Do oracles ever answer such questions?"

A loud knock came, not on his door, but hers. "You there, Fairfax?" asked Cooper. "I could use some help with my critical paper."

"My flock bleats. I'd better shepherd." She opened the door. "Cooper, old bloke. Have you missed me?"

Titus already missed her.

When she had left, he opened the Crucible to the illustration for "The Oracle of Still Waters." Her face looked back at him from the surface of the pool. As he had hoped, the pond's ability to capture the likeness of anyone who looked into it was immune from the reach of the Irreproducible Charm.

Titus V had built the trick into the pond because he had wanted all the great and terrible mages who dwelled inside the Crucible to resemble him. Titus VII didn't even like to look at his own face in the mirror, but he was immensely grateful that his ancestor had been so silly.

Now he could work her likeness into any story of his choosing.

Now he could fight dragons for her.

And now he could kiss her again.

CHAPTER ✦ 19

PART OF A BRITISH BOY'S education consisted of memorization. In repetition class, pupils recited the forty or so lines of Latin verse they had been assigned to memorize.

Titus seldom viewed anything through the same prism as his classmates did. But on this mind-numbing exercise, he and they were in agreement: it was a colossal misuse of time. To make matters worse, although a boy could leave as soon as he had said his lines, sprinting out of the classroom like a puppy that had been kenneled too long, he could not say those lines until he had been called upon to do so. And Frampton invariably kept Titus waiting until almost everyone else had gone.

On the day Titus first returned to class after a weeklong convalescence, however, Frampton called on him second, immediately after Cooper, who always provided a perfect recital to set the standard for the rest of the class.

Titus, who had come to rely on listening to the lines repeated dozens of times during class to memorize them, stumbled badly.

Frampton tsked. "Your Highness, you are shortly to assume the reins of an ancient and magnificent realm. Surely the thought ought to compel you to do better."

This was new. Frampton might have delighted in making Titus cool his heels, but he had never been openly antagonistic.

"The success of my rule does not rely on my ability to recite obscure Latin verse," Titus said coldly.

Frampton showed no sign of being humbled by the rebuke. "I speak not of the memorization and delivery of specific lines, but of the understanding of duty. From everything I have seen of you, young man, you have a poor grasp of obligation and responsibility."

Next to him, Fairfax sucked in a breath. She was not alone. The entire class was riveted.

Titus made a show of examining his cuff links. "It is irrelevant what a lackey such as you thinks of my character."

"Ah, but times change. Nowadays princes from thousand-year-old houses may very well find themselves without a throne," said Frampton smoothly. "Next, Sutherland. Let's hope you've prepared better."

Titus wasted no time in leaving. As soon as he was back in his room at Mrs. Dawlish's, he inserted a piece of paper under the writing ball. No new intelligence awaited him. Not very surprising—only three hours ago Dalbert had reported that there had been little change in the Inquisitor's condition.

But if the Inquisitor remained unconscious, why had Frampton gone on the offensive? Simply to remind Titus that he was now persona non grata in Atlantean circles for having incapacitated one of the Bane's most capable lieutenants?

He was jittery. More than a week after the Inquisition, he still had no idea how to interpret the rupture view of a skyful of wyverns and fire-spewing armored chariots. Fairfax's march to greatness had stalled since her breakthrough with air. The only concrete progress he could point to was an escape satchel that they had prepared and stowed in the abandoned barn.

They could not go on like this, at the mercy of events beyond their control. He had to find a way to neutralize the Inquisitor, exploit the rupture view, and spur Fairfax to firmer mastery over her powers.

He turned to his mother's diary, hoping for guidance. If there was a silver lining to the dark cloud of the Inquisition, it was that his faith in her had been fully restored. The threads of destiny wove mysteriously, but he had become convinced that Princess Ariadne, however briefly, had had her hand on the loom.

He lifted the pages carefully, one by one, feeling that peculiar tingle of anxiety in his stomach. It was not long before he came to a page that was not blank.

*26 April, YD 1020*

Exactly a year before her death.

*A strange vision. I am not sure what to make of it.*

*Titus, looking much the same age as he does when he sees that distant phenomenon on a balcony, but wearing strange—nonmage?—clothes, is leaning out of the window of a small room. It is not a room I have ever seen at the castle, the Citadel, or the monastery, plain but for an odd flag on the wall—black and silver, with a dragon, a phoenix, a griffin, and a unicorn.*

The made-up flag of Saxe-Limburg. As far as Titus knew, there was only one in existence.

*It is evening, or perhaps night, quite dark outside. Titus turns back from the window, clearly incensed. "Bastards," he swears. "They need their heads shoved up their—"*

*He freezes. Then rushes to take a book down from his shelf, a book in German by the name of* Lexikon der Klassischen Altertumskunde.

There was nothing else.

Titus read the entry two more times. He closed the diary. The disguisement spell resumed. The diary swelled in size, its plain leather cover metamorphosing into an illustration of an ancient Greek temple.

Beneath the picture, the words *Lexikon der Klassischen Altertumskunde.*

*A Dictionary of Classical Antiquities.*

So one evening in the not-too-distant future, he would curse from his window, then rush to read the diary again. That knowledge, however, did little to extricate him from his current quagmire.

Three knocks in rapid succession—Fairfax, back from class.

"Come in."

She closed the door and leaned against it, one foot on a door panel. She had learned to walk and stand with a cocky jut to her hips. He had to rein himself in so his gaze did not constantly stray to inappropriate places on her person.

"You all right?" she asked.

"No further news on the Inquisitor. But it does not mean they cannot tighten the noose in the meanwhile." He tossed aside his uniform jacket and his waistcoat. "I have to go to rowing practice."

A boy well enough to attend classes was well enough for sports. Fingers on the top button of his shirt, he waited for her to vacate his room.

She gazed at him as if she had not heard him, as if he were not headed out for a few hours on the river, but to some distant and perilous destination.

All about him the air seemed to shimmer.

Then, abruptly, she turned and opened the door. "Of course, you must get ready."

Mrs. Hancock was in the corridor, making sure the boys were in bed for lights-out, when Titus placed one last piece of paper under the writing ball. The machine clacked. He waited impatiently for the keys to stop their pounding.

The report read:

> *The Inquisitor has yet to regain consciousness, but the latest intelligence has her responding better to stimuli. Atlantean physicians are optimistic she will continue to make headway. Baslan is rumored to have already scheduled a day of thanksgiving at the Inquisitory, so confident is he of his superior's imminent recovery.*

He jumped at the knock on his door.

"Good night, Your Highness," said Mrs. Hancock.

He barely managed not to snarl. "Good night."

Of course the improvement in the Inquisitor's condition and Frampton's new belligerence were related. Of course.

He looked through his mother's diary again, but it was blank. He paced for a few minutes in his room, angry at himself for not knowing what to do. Then he was inside the Crucible, running down the path that led to the Oracle.

It was night. Dozens of lanterns, suspended from trees at the edge of the clearing, illuminated the pool.

"You again, Your Highness," said the pool, none too pleased, as he showed himself. Flecks of golden light danced upon her darkened surface.

"Me again, Oracle." He had visited her many times, but she

had yet to give him any advice.

Her tone softened slightly. "At least you seem sincere—for once."

"How can I keep her safe, my elemental mage?"

The pool turned silvery, as if an alchemist had transmuted water into mercury. "You must visit someone you have no wish to visit and go somewhere you have no wish to go."

An Oracle's message remained cryptic until it was understood. "My gratitude, Oracle."

The pool rippled. "And think no more on the exact hour of your death, prince. That moment must come to all mortals. When you will have done what you need to do, you will have lived long enough."

In the distance, obscured by rising dust, an army of giants advanced, as if an entire mountain range was scudding across the plain. The ground beneath Iolanthe's feet shuddered. Boulders wobbled; pebbles hopped like so many drops of water on hot oil.

The wall that she had been building, from quarried blocks of granite originally intended for a temple, would have enabled the townspeople to attack the vulnerable soft spots atop the giants' skulls. But the wall was nowhere near completion.

The giants bellowed and banged enormous hammers against their shields. She'd already stuffed cotton into her ears, but the clangor still startled her. Ignoring the din as best she could, she focused her mind on the next block of granite. It didn't look particularly impressive in size, but it was five tons in weight. With the greatest difficulty, she'd managed to roll a three-ton block end over end to the base of the wall. But she couldn't even lift a corner of this block off the ground.

The prince had assigned her three stories. In one, she needed to produce a cyclone to protect a poor family's crops against a blizzard of locusts—but she could only come up with breezes. In another, she was to part the waters of a lake to rescue magelings who'd been stranded at the bottom in an ever-shrinking air bubble—had it been real, she'd have lost a great many magelings on her watch. And the wall—this was her sixth attempt at erecting the wall; she had yet to stop the giants.

Now when she woke up in the morning, the pain in her hands extended all the way to her elbows. She tried not to imagine what it would feel like when that same swollen sensation took over her entire body.

She kept on doggedly at her task until a giant hefted the very same granite block above his head and hurled it into the marketplace, setting off a long chain of screams.

She sighed. "And they lived happily ever after."

No more giants. No more boulders. Instead of the deafening roar of battle, rain fell steadily and softly. She was back in the prince's room and—

His hand was clamped over hers on the Crucible. His head rested on his other arm, his face turned toward her, his eyes closed. In the gray, damp light, he looked as tired as she felt. And thin, his face all angles. Granted, his was a remarkable bone structure—chiseled, one might say—but no one so young should be careworn to the point of gauntness.

Without quite realizing what she was doing, she reached out and touched his cheek. The instant her fingertips came into contact with his skin, she snatched her hand back. He did not react at all. She licked her lower lip, reached out again, and traced a finger along his jaw.

When she drew her hand back this time, she saw a note by his elbow.

*I am in the reading room.*

The teaching cantos consisted of more than classrooms. On the ground floor it also had a large library, referred to as the reading room. He'd been spending every spare minute there.

She looked back at him, this beautiful and just slightly warped creature. "I don't care what the visions say," she whispered, "I will not let you die. Not while I have a breath left."

He was in the stacks, sitting cross-legged on the carpet, three books open before him in a semicircle, another dozen in a tall pile to the side.

Iolanthe picked up the book at the top of the pile. Her eyebrows nearly met her hairline at the title, *How to Kill a Mage at Five Miles: A Primer on Distance Spell-Casting.* "I've been wondering what you read in your leisure time."

"A bit of light fare," he said without looking up, "before I get back to *Magical Properties of a Still-Beating Heart*."

She smiled down at the top of his head. "So what *are* you looking for?"

"Something that will let me put the Inquisitor into a permanent coma. She *will* awaken. She *will* put me under Inquisition again—without you by my side. My only hope is to find a way to attack while her mind is extended and vulnerable."

How quickly she'd hardened—she barely blinked at his answer. "You'll be in the same room with her. How will *How to Kill a Mage at Five Miles* help?"

"I like reading it—something I cannot say for books dealing with mind magic. And that is a tongue-in-cheek title, by the way. Distance spell-casting is a perfectly legitimate target-hitting sport in many mage realms."

"So the book doesn't teach you to kill?"

"It is like archery. If you strike someone at the right distance and speed, your arrow will kill, but that is not why English ladies enjoy it at their country house parties." He took the book from her. "How was the wall, by the way?"

"Not built."

He shook his head. "Not good. You must be able to take on the Bane, and I must be able to take on the Inquisitor."

That, in a nutshell, was their problem. "I can go back in again after supper, but now I need to write my critical paper."

"Can you write me one too? It does not have to be good."

"I'll bet most other fugitives from Atlantis don't have to write two sets of critical papers."

He smiled. "Thank you."

Her heart slipped from its mooring, as it always did when he smiled. "Only this once. And you owe me."

As she turned to leave, he said, "English household management magazines."

"I beg your pardon?"

"That is what I read in my leisure time."

"You like household management?"

"I like the authoritative answers the magazines give. Dear Mrs. So-and-So, all you need to have hair that shines like the moon is to mix olive oil and spermaceti in a proportion of eight to one and apply liberally. Dear Miss So-and-So, no, you will not wish to serve soup at your wedding breakfast. One or two hot dishes if you must, the rest should be cold."

Solvable problems, that was what he liked. The pleasure of ordinary concerns. The resolute lack of real danger.

*Someday,* she thought. *Someday.*

Iolanthe felt like a seed after a good long spring shower, soaked to bursting—yet somehow unable to break through her shell. Her capacity for elemental magic might be grand, but her *ability* stubbornly refused to improve.

At least the latest news offered some consolation. After a brief interval during which she'd seemed on the verge of consciousness, the Inquisitor had slipped deeper into her coma.

Iolanthe settled into a familiar cadence of classes and sports, a rhythm she had dearly missed in Little Grind. Sometimes it was almost possible to believe she was living only a slightly skewed version of normal life.

With the lengthening of the days, lockup happened much later in the evening, and boys were allowed outside as long as one last shimmer of the sun still remained above the horizon. For hours every day, she pitted herself against the boys on the pitch—where she could apparently do no wrong.

This athletic prowess earned her a ridiculous level of approval. She had always been careful to fit in wherever she went. But it was more than a little ironic that she had never been as popular as a girl as she was now as a boy, as someone who bore little resemblance to the real her.

This particular evening, after practice, many of the boys stayed behind to watch a match between the two best school clubs. Iolanthe packed up her gear and started toward Mrs. Dawlish's. She enjoyed the camaraderie of her teammates, but she was always the first one off the pitch at the end of a practice: as much as she refused to believe the prophecy of the prince's death, somehow it felt more ominous when she was away from him.

Kashkari fell into step beside her. They walked together, discussing a Greek assignment that was due in the morning. She remained somewhat wary of Kashkari, but no longer felt nervous in his company—he was most likely not a spy of Atlantis, only a shrewd and observant boy.

"What about dative or locative?" asked Kashkari.

"You can use the accusative, since they are going to Athens—makes it Athens-ward," Iolanthe answered.

She'd discovered that her grasp of Greek, inferior in her own eyes, was considered quite proficient by the other boys.

"Accusative, of course." Kashkari shook his head a little. "I wonder now how we got by when you weren't here."

"I have no doubt the devastation was widespread, the suffering universal."

"Indeed, it was the Dark Ages in the annals of Mrs. Dawlish's house. Ignorance was thick on the ground, and unenlightenment befogged all the windows."

Iolanthe smiled. Kashkari grinned back at her. "If ever I can do something for you in return, let me know."

*You can pay a little less attention to me.* "I'm sure I'll be banging on your door as soon as I take up Sanskrit."

Eton didn't have such a course, but mages in upper academies were usually required to master a non-European classical language. Iolanthe, in her before-lightning days, had aspired to Sanskrit for its wealth of scholarship.

"Ah, Sanskrit. I dare say my Sanskrit is as good as your Latin—my family put me to it when I was five," said Kashkari, rolling up his sleeve to check his elbow, which he had scraped on the ground in a fall during practice.

On his right arm, just beneath his elbow, he sported a tattoo in the shape of the letter *M*—for Mohandas, his given name, she supposed.

"What about Latin? Your Latin is good. Did you have a tutor for it before you came to England?"

He nodded. "Since I was ten."

"Was that when you knew you'd be sent abroad for schooling?"

"On my tenth birthday, in fact. I remember that day because my relatives kept telling me about the night I was born, all the shooting stars."

"What?"

"I was born in the middle of a meteor storm."

"The one in November of"—she still had trouble with the way the English counted years—"1866?"

"Yes, that one. And then they'd tell me about the even greater meteor storm in '33."

"There was one in 1833?"

"The most magnificent meteor storm ever, according to—"

"Look, it's Turban Boy and Bumboy."

Iolanthe looked across the street to see Trumper and Hogg, snickering to each other.

"Somebody ought to give them a thrashing," she said, not bothering to keep her voice low.

"Do you thrash for your prince every night?" said Hogg, moving his hips obscenely.

Other boys on either side of the street were stopping to see what was going on.

"Ignore them," Kashkari said calmly.

"Go home to your idol-worshipping, sister-marrying family," said Trumper. "We don't want your kind here."

That was it. Iolanthe gripped her cricket bat and crossed the street.

"What a big stick you carry," sneered Hogg. "Is that what the prince likes to use on you?"

She smiled. "No, just what I like to use on your friend."

She swung the bat. Not very hard, since she didn't want to kill Trumper, but still it connected with his nose in a very satisfying way.

Blood trickled out of Trumper's nostrils. He howled. "My nose! He broke my nose!"

"You too?" she asked Hogg. "How about it?"

Hogg took a step back. "I—I have to help him. But you are going to regret this for the rest of your life."

Several boys from nearby houses had stuck their heads out of their windows. "What's going on?" they asked. "What's that caterwauling?"

"Nothing," said Iolanthe. "Some idiot walked into a lamppost."

Trumper and Hogg took off amidst a volley of laughter—no one, it seemed, liked them.

When Iolanthe returned to Kashkari's side, he looked at her with something between alarm and admiration. "Very unhesitating of you."

"Thank you. I hope they'll think twice now before insulting my friends in my hearing. Now what were you telling me about the meteor shower in 1833?"

Titus winced as he pulled himself out of the scull in which he had spent the past three hours rowing up and down the Thames. Fairfax was on the pier, waiting for him.

"Is something wrong?" he asked as they walked out of earshot of the other rowers. She usually did not come to the pier.

She tapped her cricket bat against the side of her calf in an agitated cadence. "Thirty-three years before I was born, there was another meteor storm, wasn't there, an even more spectacular one? Were there no prophecies then concerning a great elemental mage?"

"There were. Seers fell over themselves predicting the birth of the greatest elemental mage of all time."

"And?"

"And he was born in a small realm in the Arabian Sea. When he was thirteen, he caused an underwater volcano long thought extinct to erupt."

Fire was a flamboyant power—as was lightning. But the ability to move mountains and raise new land from the sea was power on a different magnitude altogether.

She emitted a low whistle, suitably impressed. "What happened to him?"

"The realm was already under the dominion of Atlantis. The boy's father and aunt had both died while taking part in a local resistance effort. When agents of Atlantis arrived to take the boy away, his family decided that they would never allow it. They killed him instead."

This time her response was a long silence.

"What were the consequences to the boy's family?" she asked, her voice tight.

"To the family specifically, I am not sure. But the Bane's displeasure was great, and the entire realm suffered a battery of retaliatory measures. My mother believed that the Bane's failure to obtain the boy caused a loss of vigor on his part, which in turn led to a slackening of Atlantis's grip on its realms.

"Mages did not quite notice at first—not for decades—but when they did, they began to test the leashes. There were minor infractions, which became rebellions, which became full-scale uprisings."

"The January Uprising."

"Baron Wintervale timed it to take advantage of the general chaos. The Juras was already a bloodbath, with heavy casualties on both sides. Atlantis was also having trouble with both the Inter-Dakotas and the realms of the subcontinent. And there were rumors of discontent in Atlantis itself. The leaders of the January Uprising thought they would be the straw that broke the camel's back."

"But they themselves were crushed instead. Atlantis must have found a way to harness a new power."

"Or an old one. My mother believed that the Bane had to deplete his own life force, something he had been careful to preserve throughout the long centuries of his life. Which would explain why he is so desperate to locate you."

She turned the cricket bat around a few times, her motion growing more steady and deliberate. "I am not his to be had. And someday, he might just regret coming after me—after us—and not leaving well enough alone."

It was not until Titus was in his room, changing, that he realized the significance of what she had said: she meant to wrap her hands around the reins of her destiny. Around the reins of *their* destiny.

An unfamiliar emotion surged in his chest, warm and weightless.

He was no longer completely alone in the world.

Titus stood a long time outside Prince Gaius's door. Beyond awaited his mother's murderer, who had died comfortably in his bed, in the full of old age.

Even now anger and hatred simmered in him. But the Oracle had said that he must visit someone he had no wish to visit, and he could not think of anyone, other than the Inquisitor, whose presence repelled him more.

He shouldered open the heavy door. Music spilled out, notes as sweet and succulent as summer melons. A handsome young man sat on a low white divan, surrounded by plump blue cushions, plucking at the strings of a lute.

"Where is Prince Gaius?" Titus demanded.

"I am he," answered the young man.

*But you are supposed to be an old man.* All the other princes and princesses looked as they had close to the end of their lives. Hesperia in particular, though the gleam in her eyes remained undiminished, was as wrinkled as a shelled walnut. "How old are you?"

"Nineteen."

Only a few years older than Titus. "And you are qualified to teach everything you listed outside your door?"

"Of course. I am a prodigy. I was finished with volume two of *Better Mages* by the time I was sixteen."

Titus had not yet progressed halfway through volume one of *Better Mages*, the definitive text on higher magic. Gaius teased another few bars of music from his lute, each chord more plummy than the last.

"How can I help you?" asked Gaius, who clearly believed in his own superiority, but was not particularly tedious about it. In fact, there was a glamour to his assurance—a charm, even.

The hard, grim old man Titus remembered had once been this winsome, carefree youth.

"Do you know anything about your daughter, Ariadne?"

"Please," laughed Gaius, "I am not married yet. But Ariadne is a lovely name. I should like a daughter someday. I will groom her to be as great as Hesperia."

He had hated the petitions that landed on his door yearly for him to abdicate in her favor. There had been a huge chasm between father and daughter.

"Do you know anything of your future?"

"No, except I am set to knock Titus the Third out of the triumvirate of greats. There is nothing anyone can do to dislodge the first Titus and Hesperia, but I should easily surpass the third Titus's achievements. What do you think they will call me? Gaius the Grand? Or perhaps Gaius the Glorious?"

They had called him Gaius the Ruinous. And he had known it.

"Care to hear a piece I wrote myself?" asked Gaius.

He began without waiting for a reply. The piece was very pretty, as light and sweet as a spring breeze. His face glowed with enjoyment, blissfully ignorant that he would later ban music from court and destroy his priceless instruments one by one.

When he was done, he looked expectantly at Titus. Titus, after a moment of hesitation, clapped. It was good music.

The prince—who would someday have no music, no child, and only tatters of his youthful dreams—graciously inclined his head, acknowledging the applause.

"Now, Your Highness," said Titus, "I would like to ask you some questions about Atlantis."

# CHAPTER · 20

IN THE DISTANCE, SWORDS, MACES, and clubs bewitched by the Enchantress of Skytower continued to hurtle toward Risgar's Redoubt. Titus went through a cascade of spells to lock, steady, amplify, and focus his aim. The missiles must be struck down when they were more than three miles out, beyond the outer defensive walls of the redoubt. The moment they crossed over the walls, they would dive to the ground to wreak havoc on lives and property.

It was enjoyable, the repetition of the spells. It would have been meditative had his aim been perfect. But his success with moving objects hovered stubbornly at 50 percent. He would hit a few targets in a row, then miss the next few.

"That's it for this flock," shouted the captain. "Eat something quick if you need to. Visit the privy. The next flock will be here in no time."

Fairfax appeared next to him on the rampart, paying little attention to the soldiers rushing about. "Sorry it took so long. Rogers' verses were in terrible shape."

He had heard an Eton education described as something that taught boys to write bad verses in Latin and just as awful prose in English.

"You ought to charge a fee for your help."

"Next Half I will. You wanted to see me?"

He always wanted to see her. Even when they were both in the Crucible together, the sad truth was that they saw far too little of each other, with most of her time spent in the practice cantos, and most of his in the teaching cantos.

He took her elbow and exited the Crucible. "Remember what I told you about the rupture view?"

She nodded. "The image of wyverns and armored chariots you saw in your head when I interrupted the Inquisitor."

"I cannot be completely sure, but after speaking to my grandfather, I think it is the outer defenses of the Commander's Palace in Atlantis."

"The one in Lucidias?"

Lucidias was the capital city of Atlantis. He shook his head. "That compound is called Royalis—it used to be the king's palace, when Atlantis still had kings. The Commander's Palace is in the uplands. My grandfather had a spy who managed to send back a message in a bottle that traveled a thousand miles in open ocean. He indicated the rough location of the palace and noted that it had several rings of defense, one of wyverns, one of lean, swift, armored chariots, and another of huge chariots that carried dragons."

"You didn't mention dragons being carried."

"No, my view was too brief to notice all the details. I knew fire was coming out from some of the chariots, but I did not know what was producing the fire. It makes sense—several of the dragon species with the hottest fires either cannot fly or cannot fly well. By putting them on aerial vehicles, Atlantis can better exploit their fire."

She rose from her chair, went to his tea cabinet, and pulled out the small bag of chocolate macaroons he had recently purchased on High Street. Slowly, she ate three macaroons, one after another.

"It sounds as if you mean to tell me we will have to go to the Commander's Palace. Would it not be to our advantage to lure the Bane out to a less hostile location?"

He extended his hand toward her—he needed something to fortify him too. "What do you think of our chances at this less hostile location?"

She placed a few macaroons on his palm. "Next to nil."

He took a bite of a macaroon. "And you think so because?"

"He is invincible. He cannot be killed—or so mages say."

"And they are right—for once. Twice the Bane has been killed before eyewitnesses. Once in the Caucasus, where mages are experts at distance spell-casting. The second time when he was on the subcontinent to quell an uprising.

"In both cases, he was said to have been destroyed—brains and guts all over the place. In both cases, by the next day he was walking around, right as rain. And in both cases, the Domain sent spies to verify the accounts; they returned baffled because the witnesses were telling the truth."

She fell back into her seat. "He *resurrected*?"

"Or so it seems. That was the reason my grandfather was interested in the defenses at the Commander's Palace. If the Bane was truly invincible, he could sleep in the open and not fear for his life. But the Bane does fear something. And so does the Inquisitor—or she would not have been thinking about the defenses of the palace, which are vulnerable to great elemental powers."

She bowed her head.

Sometimes, as he lay in bed at night, he imagined a future for her beyond her eventual confrontation with the Bane. A popular, well-respected professor at the Conservatory of Magical Arts and Sciences—she had mentioned the goal several times in the school records Dalbert had unearthed for Titus—she would try to live a quiet, modest life.

But wherever she went, thunderous applause would greet her, the great heroine of her people, the most admired mage in her lifetime.

It was a future that did not include him, but it gave him courage to think that, by doing his utmost, perhaps he could still make it come true for her.

Tonight, however, that future was dimmer and more distant than ever.

She lifted her face. "Is it over the Commander's Palace that you would fall?"

To his death, she meant.

He swallowed. "It is possible. My mother saw a night scene. There was smoke and fire—a staggering amount of fire, according to her—and dragons."

"Which stories in the Crucible have dragons?"

"Half of them, probably. 'Lilia, the Clever Thief,' 'The Battle for Black Bastion,' 'The Dragon Princess,' 'Lord of the—'"

"What about 'Sleeping Beauty'? My first time in the Crucible you said you'd take me to her castle someday to fight the dragons."

He had deliberately not mentioned Sleeping Beauty. "The dragons there are brutal. I put in the toughest ones as part of my own training. And I still get injured, even though I have been doing this for years."

"I want to go after supper," she said.

"You already did two sessions in the Crucible today; you will not be in top form for the dragons."

Her voice brooked no dissent. "I imagine by the time I get to the Commander's Palace, I'll be quite tired too. I might as well get used to deploying my powers under less than optimum conditions."

He wavered. He had no good reason to refuse her, but if she succeeded . . .

He was being irrational. Her first time she would not even get inside the castle's gates, let alone climb all the way to the garret. He had nothing to fear.

"All right," he said, "if you insist, we will go after supper."

A thick ring of tangled briar girded Sleeping Beauty's castle. The prince pointed his wand and blasted a fifty-yard-long tunnel through the bramble.

The white marble of the castle's walls, lit by lamps and cressets, gleamed at the end of the tunnel. Inside the tunnel, however, only fantastically shaped shadows flickered. Iolanthe called forth globes of fire to float before her, shining their light on the path.

Her heartbeat was at an almost painful velocity—naturally brave she was not. She took a couple of deep breaths and tried to distract herself. "Why do you put the most brutal dragons here, rather than in a different story?" she asked him.

He blinked, as if the question had startled him. "It is convenient."

As far as she knew, every story was equally convenient to access in the Crucible. "Is it because you get to kiss Sleeping Beauty afterward?"

She was only joking. Or at least half joking. But he opened his mouth—and said nothing.

She stopped, flabbergasted by his implicit admission. "So . . . you want me to fall in love with you, while you play kissing games with another girl?"

It was the first time she had ever mentioned this particular scheme of his in the open.

He swallowed. "I have never done anything of the sort."

Since he hadn't doubled over in pain, she had to accept his answer as truthful. All the same, what wasn't he telling her?

An unearthly shriek split the night, nearly tearing her eardrums.

"They have smelled us," said the prince, his voice tight.

Overhead, flame roared, a comet of fire that shed pinpricks of orange through the thick tangle of thorns above. The heat of the flame made her turn her face away and shield it with her arms.

"What are they, exactly?" she asked, forgetting Sleeping Beauty for the moment.

"A pair of colossus cockatrices."

She'd seen dragons at the Delamer Zoo quite a few times. She'd seen dragons at the circus. And once she'd gone on a safari with Master Haywood to the Melusine Archipelago, to see wild dragons in their native habitats. Still her jaw slackened as she emerged from the tunnel. Standing before the castle's gates were two dragons with roosterlike heads, whose dimensions dwarfed those of the castle's walls. "Are they a mated pair?"

Colossus cockatrices, wingless, were ground nesters. To protect their eggs, the combined fire of a mated pair, thanks to a process that was still not clearly understood, became one of the hottest substances known to magekind.

The prince didn't need to answer. The cockatrices before the castle entwined their long necks—exactly what a mated pair did—and screeched again.

An explosion of fire sped at them, its mass greater and hotter than anything she'd ever known. Instinctively she pushed back.

Her shriek nearly rivaled that of the cockatrices. The agony in her palms, as if she'd plunged her hands into boiling oil.

*"Fiat praesidium maximum!"* the prince shouted. "Are you hurt?"

The fire stopped abruptly, barricaded a hundred feet away. She looked down at her hands, expecting to see blisters the size of saucers. But her palms were not even reddened from the heat. "I'm fine!"

"This shield can take two more hits. Should I set up another shield?"

"No, I want to see what I can do."

The dragons took a fifteen-second rest, then attacked again. She tried to stop the fire from reaching the shield, but failed miserably. The shield cracked, distorting her view of everything behind it.

Fifteen seconds. Attack. The shield blocked the fire, but dissipated in the wake of it.

She reminded herself that she was dealing with illusions. But the stink of the cockatrices, the crackle of the brambles burning behind her, the torch flames that leaped back from the dragon fire, as if in fear—they were all too real.

She threw up a wall of water as the cockatrices screamed again. The water evaporated before the fire had even touched it.

Ice. She needed ice. She was not adept at ice, but to her surprise, a substantial iceberg materialized at her command.

The ice melted immediately.

Changing tactics, she used air to try to divert the fire. But all she did was split the fire mass in two, both halves hurtling straight toward them.

Now she had no choice but to pit herself directly against the dragons.

Ordinary fire was as pliant as clay. But this fire was made of knives and nails. She shrieked again with pain. But was she doing anything to the fire? Was she slowing it? Or did it merely seem to arrive at a more leisurely pace because the agony in her hands distorted her perception of time?

Slow or swift, it swooped down toward them.

"Run!" she yelled at the prince.

For the first time in her life, she fled before fire.


She opened her eyes to find herself back in the prince's room, seated before his desk, her hand on the Crucible. The odor of charred flesh lingered in her nostrils. The skin on her back and her neck felt uncomfortably hot, as if she'd been out in the sun too long.

The prince knelt before her, one hand clamped on her shoulder, the other on her chin, his eyes dark and anxious. "Are you all right?"

"I—think so."

He set two fingers against the pulse at the side of her throat. "Are you sure?"

Not at all. "I'm going back in."

She might not have been born with natural courage, but she did loathe failure.

There was no fire burning in the bramble tangle and no tunnel going through: the Crucible always returned to its original state. The moons had risen, twin crescents, one pale, one paler.

"Does your shield spell have a countersign?" she asked the prince.

He hesitated, as if he wanted to tell her again to save the dragons for another day. Instead he gave her the countersign. She practiced the spell. When she thought her shield sturdy enough, she blasted a path through the brambles.

Walking through the tunnel, they discussed tactics and agreed that in order to eventually counter dragon fire, she must first achieve safety.

"Let's both put up shields, mine on the outside of yours," she said. That way, if her shield proved less than stalwart, they'd still have his for protection.

"Good idea."

"But if my shield is good enough, then I'll keep going."

He nodded. "I will stay on this side and distract the cockatrices— if they alternate their fire between the two of us, it will give you more time to figure out what to do. But for this time, do not go beyond the front steps of the castle."

"Why?" But then she remembered. "Is it because you don't want me to see Sleeping Beauty?"

"That is not—"

"Is she pretty?"

"She does not exist."

"In here she does. Is she pretty?" She disliked herself for the pestering questions, but she couldn't seem to stop.

"Pretty enough." He sounded strained.

"Do you enjoy kissing her?"

*Better than you enjoy kissing me?*

"I have not kissed her since I met you." Suddenly it was the Master of the Domain speaking, his tone hard, his eyes harder.

Misery and thrill collided in her. Had he declared that he'd given up other girls for her? Or was she being a complete fool?

"Now will you concentrate on the task at hand?" he went on impatiently.

She took a deep breath and counted to five. "Let's fight some dragons."


The colossus cockatrices, maddened by the scent of intruders, streamed their fire.

Iolanthe and the prince each called for a shield. Hers held. She summoned more shields, marching toward the cockatrices. They were chained to the castle gate and could neither come at her nor give chase. As soon as she moved past their fire range, she'd be safe.

The castle gate beckoned. She started running. Cockatrices had poor eyesight. With their fire blocked, they'd try to assault her with claws and tails, but not being predators, they'd be clumsy at it.

The ground shook as the colossus cockatrices thrashed and stomped, but she dashed past them. From somewhere behind, the prince shouted at her to be careful. She sprinted across the wide courtyard and up the steps. But she did not stop there, as he'd requested. Instead, she pushed open the huge, thickly reinforced doors of the castle and stepped into the great hall.

The interior of the castle was gloomy. A few guttering torches threw out faint circles of light, leaving large swaths of the great hall darkened and forbidding.

Could shadows move against shadows? She squinted, her fingers tightening on the prince's spare wand. Behind her came a soft sound like drapes fluttering before an open window.

Before she could spin around, something heavy and spiked slammed into the side of her skull, one particularly sharp spur burying itself deep into her temple. Her face contorted. Her muscles convulsed. Her scream lodged in her throat.

She fell with a resounding thud. A black, reptilian creature landed beside her, folding its wings with barely a swish. A sharp claw reached out and slashed her throat.

But she was already dead.

Titus shouted the first three words of the exit password before he realized that *she* had been the one to take them into the Crucible. For him to take her out now, he must be in physical contact.

He threw a battery of spells at the wyvern, driving it off her body. A second wyvern swooped down. He dove toward her, grabbing her hand just as the creature's spiked tail crashed toward him.

They were back in his room. Her eyes flew open, but they were the eyes of the possessed. She shook, the kind of frenetic convulsion that would cause her to stop breathing before he could get to the laboratory and find a proper remedy.

He slapped their hands on the Crucible and prayed frantically.

Iolanthe stared dumbly at the dark, star-sprinkled sky with its two moons. Who was she? Where was she?

Of their own accord, her hands clutched her throat. She was—she'd been—

Terror rose in her, a dark, drowning tide. She screamed.

And was instantly thrown into the coldest water she'd ever known, the shock of it like knives upon her skin. She gasped, her erstwhile horror forgotten. So cold, the burn of ice frozen to her body.

Someone yanked her out of the water and held her tight. She began to shiver. Her teeth chattered. She would never be warm again.

He rubbed his hand along her back, the friction needle points of heat. "Sorry, I had to do that. You were going into convulsions."

"What—what happened?"

His kneaded her arm. "You died in the Crucible. There are two wyverns in the great hall—I tried to warn you, but you did not hear me.[21] I am sorry. I should have told you sooner."

The fault was not his; she'd been an idiot who'd turned the topic to Sleeping Beauty and wouldn't let go. "Where am I now?" she asked, still trembling.

"Next to Ice Lake."

"Isn't that where the kraken lives?"

"Yes. We have to go soon. It would already have felt the—"

The lake sloshed behind her.

"And they lived happily ever after!" they shouted together.

The last thing she saw was an enormous, mottled tentacle, splashing toward her.

Her heart was still pounding.

She took her hand off the Crucible. "It's a dangerous book."

"You do not know the half of it," said the prince. "At least you seem better now."

She felt more or less normal. "So if I survive the convulsions, dying in the Crucible has no other effect?"

"What do you think about wyverns?"

The moment he said the word, her hands shook. She braced them against the edge of the desk, but the shaking only transferred to her arms.

"That is the effect of dying in the Crucible. I have never gone back to Black Bastion. The mere thought of Helgira still makes me"—he took a deep breath—"well, incoherent, to say the least."

She chewed the inside of her cheek. "I'm going back in."

"What?"

"I can't be afraid of wyverns. I can't go into hysteria in front of the Commander's Palace."

"At least wait until tomorrow."

"I'm not going to be less afraid tomorrow." She touched his hand. "Will you come and help me?"

*I can't be weak when the time comes. I can't let you fall.*

"Of course." He sighed. "Of course I will help you."

She stood with her hand on the ominously heavy doors of the great hall, the prince by her side. Behind them the colossal cockatrices bellowed impotently. Inside awaited the wyverns that had slaughtered her only minutes ago.

He laid his hand over hers. "They would have already smelled us. Wyverns are fast and crafty. They do not need to wait between breaths of fire. And as you already know, the ones in there are not chained."

She nodded.

"We go in on the count of three."

She nodded again, scarcely able to breathe.

"One, two, three."

He blasted open the doors. She shot a starburst of flames that illuminated every corner of the great hall, depriving the wyverns of shadows in which to hide.

They fought back to back. She paid only remote attention to what he did, her mind bent on controlling the dragons' fire. The wyverns spewed without cease, but their fires were less hot. The corporeal shield in which the prince had encased her further reduced the heat.

It still hurt. But the sensation was more like the abrasion of rough stones than the stab of red-hot knives. She welcomed the pain—if she hurt, then she was still alive.

At last she managed to direct one wyvern's flame to attack the other. The scorched wyvern screeched and returned the favor. As the dragons became bogged down in their own feud, the prince grabbed her hand. They ran up the grand staircase, throwing shields behind their shoulders, and pushed shut the blessedly fortified doors that led to the gallery.

She panted with her hands on her knees. It was not an unqualified victory, but at least she'd no longer be irrationally terrified of wyverns—only rationally afraid.

"Are there any more dangers in the castle?"

"No, that is it." He reached for her. "Now we can go back."

She backed away. "Since I'm already here, I might as well take a look at Sleeping Beauty."

Even the elation of victory could not quite dispel the acidness of jealousy.

"No!"

For a boy who had so much self-control, he was practically shouting.

"Why not?"

Did he flush? It was hard to tell. They were both hot from the heat of the battle. "My castle, my rules," he declared flatly.

She flattened her lips. "Fine."

Tension drained from his shoulders. She exploited his moment of inattention and ran, throwing up a wall of fire behind her.

"Stop!"

He swore. She dashed halfway down the long portrait gallery and up the next flight of stairs, three marble steps at a time.

She was being stupid, of course. But she couldn't help herself. She wanted to see the girl he used to kiss before she came along. And did he stop at kissing? Or did he do a great deal more to that pretty, grateful, pliant girl?

The stairs led to a gilded landing—the gold barely visible under the dust—which opened into a ballroom with moth-eaten velvet curtains. A row of maids, polishing cloths still in hand, dreamed peacefully.

This was where the fancy dress ball to celebrate Sleeping Beauty's coming-of-age would have taken place.

Past a room in which a wig master snored gently on a great pile of hair, and another room that contained dozens of dressmaker's dummies, each sporting a different costume, she sprinted up the stairs.

The castle was endlessly vertical. Cobwebbed corridors, windows falling off their hinges, paintings grimy with age. She ran past them all, headed ever higher.

A door burst open. Before she could recoil in alarm, the prince barreled out and tackled her. They fell onto a thick rug, sending up a cloud of dust. She shoved at him.

"No," he said, his eyes adamant.

She meant to heave him out of her way. For having another girl—however fictional—before her. For not living forever. And for taking away her freedom in making her fall in love after all.

Except, somehow, her fingers spread over his face. Her thumb traced the rise of his dirt-smeared cheekbone, smudged a drop of sweat trickling past his temple, then down to press into the corner of his lips, chapped from the heat of dragon flame.

So little time. They had so little time left.

Pulling him toward her, she kissed him. He turned stone still with shock. She pushed her hands into his hair and kissed him more fervently.

Suddenly he was kissing her back, with a hunger that both thrilled and frightened her.

And just as suddenly they were back in his room, sitting on two sides of his desk, touching nowhere.

"We cannot," he said quietly. "I had thought love would bind us together in one purpose. I was wrong. The situation is more complicated than that. You must leave me behind at some point, when I am of no more use. And that is not a decision to be made or unmade under the influence of unnecessary emotions."

*Unnecessary emotions.*

Heat prickled her cheeks and the shells of her ears. Her windpipe burned, as if someone had shoved a torch down her throat.

The utter humiliation of it, to be rejected like this, all in the name of the Mission . . .

But even worse was the absolute certainty in his voice. He lived his life counting down toward its end. She might as well have fallen in love with someone on his deathbed.

"Please," she heard herself speak past the lump in her throat, "don't be so melodramatic. Don't confuse a simple kiss with eternal adoration. I am surrounded by handsome boys—have you not noticed how gorgeous Kashkari is?—but you are the only one I can kiss without getting into trouble.

"Besides, have you forgotten that you are my captor? I can never love you when I'm not free. That you think I could only shows how little understanding you have of love." She rose. "Now if you'll excuse me, I need to be in my room before lights-out."

The colossus cockatrices roared uselessly outside. The wyverns had been contained in a corner of the great hall. Titus made the long, long climb to the garret of the castle, his footsteps heavy with fatigue and dejection.

Sleeping Beauty was deep in her slumber. He sank onto one knee and cupped her cheeks with his hands.

Very gently, he bent his head and kissed her.

She opened her eyes; they were the color of midnight. Her hair, too, was pure shadow.

He knew the texture of her hair, because he had once cut it himself. He knew the taste of her lips because he had kissed her—and as of today, been kissed by her.

"Iolanthe," he murmured.

She smiled. "You know my name."

"Yes, I know your name." And here, inside the Crucible, was the only place where he dared to call her—even to think of her—by that name.

"I have missed you," she whispered, her arms rising to entwine around his shoulders. "Kiss me again."

He had changed her dialogue just before he entered the Crucible. These were the precise words he wanted to hear. But they echoed hollowly against the walls of the garret, meaningless sounds that neither soothed nor reassured.

"Ignore what I said earlier, when I was annoyed," she went on, her fingers combing through his hair.

But he couldn't. He knew how much time she spent with Kashkari—they were always walking to or from cricket practice together. And how stupid of him to suppose that she could forget, even for a moment, that she was here against her will.

"And they lived happily ever after," he said.

Now he was back in his empty room. He rose from his chair and laid a hand upon the wall between his room and hers, as if that could propel his thoughts across everything that separated them and make her understand that it was not her kiss that frightened him, but his own reaction to it.

Because if he loved her, he would never be able to push her into mortal danger.

Yet he must, or he would have lived his entire life in vain.

## CHAPTER 21

UPON THE PLAYING FIELDS, a cricket game was in full progress, penned in by a crowd nine deep. West, the future captain of the school team, struck a ball directly out of bounds, giving his club six runs. The spectators roared with approval.

"Johnny, you must introduce me to West," a girl to the right of Titus said to her brother. "You simply must."

"But I've never been within a hundred feet of him," protested Johnny, a portly junior boy.

"Johnny, my dear," said his stern-looking mother, "is that all the enterprise you possess? If your sister wishes to meet West, then you will endeavor to make it happen."

Fourth of June was Eton's biggest annual fete, a daylong celebration marked by speeches in the morning, a cricket game in the afternoon, a procession of boats in the evening, and a display of fireworks at night, the whole heavily attended by Old Etonians and the families of current pupils.

Titus had forgotten what a horde of sisters and mothers always descended, inundating the school in a tide of pastel. Ruffles, ribbons, bustled skirts abounded. Thousands of silk-flower-trimmed hats bobbed and joggled. The air was heavy with perfumes of rose and lilies.

Such femininity struck him as exaggerated, almost caricatureish. These days, a girl was most beautiful to him in short hair, a uniform, and a derby set at a rakish angle.

He scanned the mob. Fairfax had not returned. She had banded together with Kashkari and Wintervale, who also had no family in attendance, for a picnic. Titus could have joined them, but he did not.

He and Fairfax had not exactly been avoiding each other. They spoke daily concerning news from the Domain, her training, and his search for a spell to permanently incapacitate the Inquisitor. But their interaction had become formal, structured, questions that changed little from day to day, and answers that varied even less.

It was probably for the best.

But he could not help wishing otherwise. All the more so since Dalbert was on leave—his dying mother wished him to accompany her to a spiritual retreat on Ondine Island, near her place of birth. Without Dalbert's daily reports, Titus felt as if he stood blindfolded in a minefield.

At least the last bit of news Dalbert reported before he left had been the most welcome yet: the Inquisitor had been transported to Atlantis, likely due to further deterioration of her condition.

A commotion behind Titus made him turn around. A group of men were pushing through the crowd, much to the consternation of those being shoved out of the way. To his displeasure, Titus recognized the coat of arms on the livery of the men coming toward him as the invented heraldry of Saxe-Limburg, his fictional place of origin. Behind the men came Greencomb, Alectus's secretary, dressed in a nonmage suit.

"Your Highness." Greencomb bowed. "The regent and Lady Callista humbly beg the honor of your presence."

"They are *here*?"

"Indeed. It is a day for family, sire."

Alectus and Lady Callista had never attended previous Fourths of June. Titus frowned. This was exactly the sort of land mine that blew up in one's face when one gave leave to one's indispensable spymaster. What new devilry was Lady Callista plotting?

Greencomb indicated a large white canopy that had been erected at the edge of the field. With the attendants parting the crowd before him, Titus headed toward the canopy, Greencomb trailing behind.

Murmurs went through the gathering. He had never been the center of attention at Eton, but now boys who had known him for years were taking second and third looks.

The occupants of the canopy came into view. There was Alectus, looking as eager and useless as ever. Lady Callista, to his left, was gathering a crowd of gawkers. And to Alectus's right—

Stood the Inquisitor.

Like everyone else, she had been wrangled into nonmage clothes. Tiered, gathered silk skirt over a large bustle, a feathered hat, and a fringed parasol, all in black. She looked ridiculous but perfectly healthy.

Their eyes met. She smiled, the smile of a predator ready to pounce. She had recovered. She knew that he had enjoyed the help of an elemental mage. And she had come to put him under Inquisition again.

Fear strangled him. But his feet continued to carry him forward. He was the heir of the House of Elberon and he did *not* lose his composure in public.

The regent had brought a retinue of twenty, and the Inquisitor almost as many minions. Whispered questions passed among the spectators concerning Titus's origin and true rank. He would have laughed at "Is he the next Kaiser?" if his innards were not knotted tighter than a noose.

As he approached, the regent and the Inquisitor bowed, Lady Callista curtsied. Titus inclined his head. The murmurs of the spectators climbed half an octave. They had expected that he would be paying obeisance, not the other way around.

"Words cannot express my delight," he said. "Will you be leaving soon?"

That hushed the crowd. Into the silence came Cooper's loud stage whisper. "What did I always tell you, Rogers? He isn't a piddling prince. He's a *grand* prince."

Lady Callista laughed softly, as if Titus had said something funny. "Your Highness, indeed, all too soon we will be leaving. So we must enjoy to the fullest what time we have together. The regent and I—and I am sure the Inquisitor too—are eager to meet your friends."

Only then did Titus notice Nettle Oakbluff amidst the Inquisitor's minions. She scanned the gathering with the wild-eyed greediness of a gold rusher, ready to find the one nugget that would lead to riches and glory. Next to her was Horatio Haywood, wan and unsteady on his feet.

Titus broke into a cold sweat. The Inquisitor had realized that he must keep Iolanthe Seabourne nearby. The Irreproducible Charm prevented her image from being drawn and disseminated. But it could not prevent her from being recognized by those who knew her.

Thank goodness she was away at her picnic with Kashkari and Wintervale.

Would that distance be enough to keep her safe?

"We have been provided a list of all your known associates, sire," said Lady Callista, smiling. "We are determined to greet them all."

Iolanthe and Wintervale lay on a small knoll by the Thames. Kashkari had been with them earlier, but had left for a walk.

Fat, fluffy clouds drifted across a perfect blue sky. The river shushed and soughed against its banks. Warm sunlight fell gently upon Iolanthe's skin.

She opened her eyes, grimacing. She must have fallen asleep. And even after such a short nap, her hands—her entire arms, in fact—hurt. She tried to tell herself that it was a good thing—more pain probably implied a more fierce struggle between her potential and what remained of the otherwise spell. But it was taking too long, and her mastery over air was still questionable.

"Damn it," exclaimed Wintervale, startling her.

"What's the matter?"

He sat up. "Remember what Kashkari said about the tennis tournament?"

"That today is the perfect weather for bouncing a vulcanized rubber ball on grass?"

"That and he wants to hold it next Sunday," said Wintervale gloomily. "I forgot I have to take a short leave that day."

Iolanthe's foot twitched—boys usually only took leaves to visit their families. "I thought your mother was in Baden-Baden."

"No, she came back last week. I didn't say anything about it—idiots like Cooper won't understand why she chooses to remain home on the Fourth of June."

"Oh," she said.

"You don't have to look so alarmed, Fairfax," said Wintervale, looking a little put out. "Most of the time she is all right. In fact, she—already back, Kashkari? You didn't go far."

Kashkari sat down between them. "The strangest thing happened. I hadn't gone five minutes before someone appeared out of nowhere and said that I'd stepped out of school boundaries and I'd best turn back. I walked north a couple of minutes, then turned west again; a different person popped up to tell me I couldn't pass."

Iolanthe frowned. The resident houses relied on a number of daily checks to make sure boys weren't absent without leave, but nobody patrolled Eton's ill-defined boundaries.

"That's ridiculous," huffed Wintervale. "This is a school, not a prison."

"Gentlemen! You have been summoned."

They started at Sutherland's booming voice. He had not come alone; with him was Birmingham, their house captain.

"I've never seen such pomp and circumstance in my life," complained Birmingham, a broad nineteen-year-old with a well-developed mustache. "Frampton made me come personally, in case Sutherland isn't enough of a messenger to fetch you three."

"Fetch us to what?" asked Kashkari.

"To the traveling court of Saxe-Limburg," answered Sutherland. "I always thought Titus was one of those princes with an acre to rule. Guess I was wrong."

"His family came?" Iolanthe was alarmed. He hadn't mentioned anything.

"What?" cried Wintervale at the same time. He, too, knew that there was no such thing as the traveling court of Saxe-Limburg. Or Saxe-Limburg altogether.

"Just a great-uncle, but what a dame he brought," said Sutherland.

He turned to Birmingham. "Did they ever say whether Helen of Troy is the great-uncle's wife?"

"I'll wager she's just his mistress—Europeans." Birmingham remembered himself and turned to Wintervale, who, like the prince, was also said to be from a small European principality. "No offense."

"None taken," said Wintervale, still looking flabbergasted.

"Let's go, gentlemen," said Sutherland. "It took us a while to find you. His Highness must be getting impatient."

Titus's skin crawled.

The Inquisitor was not conducting an Inquisition—the sheer size of the crowd presented an obstacle to a mind mage wishing to examine one particular mind in detail. But sitting next to her was still nerve-racking. Half a dozen of her minions had their eyes trained on him, making sure that he did not attempt anything that might impede their quest.

But all that he could have endured if Fairfax were somewhere in Siberia. Instead she must be on her way to him, escorted by Sutherland and Birmingham.

The day grew warmer; his shirt stuck to his back. Human nature being what it was, the line of people waiting to be presented to the court of Saxe-Limburg had grown exponentially, boys and Old Etonians making up connections to Titus, hoping to get closer to the once-in-a-generation beauty that was Lady Callista. The sisters and mothers—didn't English women usually pay no mind to

Continental princelings? Yet they stood patiently in the queue, their white parasols like so many pearls on a string.

Unfortunately, the length of the line would not matter when Fairfax arrived. She would be instantly swept to the front.

If his heart pounded any harder it was going to crack one of his ribs.

Was that Cooper back at the head of the line again? Had he not already been presented? This was *fun* for Cooper. The ostentation-loving dunce was having a ball.

Titus wanted to throttle him.

Or—perhaps he could make use of the idiot.

As Cooper bowed before Lady Callista again, Titus called out loudly, "What are you doing here, Nettle Oakbluff? And you too, Haywood. Does the Inquisitory give holidays to its detainees now?"

Then he sneered at Cooper. "Stop being such a useless twit, Cooper. You are taking someone else's place. Scram. No, wait. Go find Birmingham and Sutherland. Why are they not back yet? They are insulting me with their incompetence."

Sutherland could not stop talking of Lady Callista's beauty. Birmingham was unimpressed with Sutherland's effusiveness.

"I won't deny she is beautiful, but she must be our mothers' age and probably more."

"So what?" Iolanthe said, giving Sutherland a nudge. "As long as she is not *my* mother."

"Exactly." Sutherland laughed. "Fairfax here is a man after my own heart. Although I do wish they hadn't sat her next to that witch. That woman makes the soles of my feet cold."

Iolanthe almost came to a standstill. *That woman.* "You mean the prince's wet nurse?"

Birmingham and Sutherland snickered.

"A rock would give milk before she does," said Birmingham.

"My balls would have permanently shriveled if I'd had to drink from her teats," declared Sutherland.

Iolanthe approximated the sound of chuckling. The Inquisitor. When had she recovered? And what was she doing at such a public forum, receiving the prince's friends, no less? Could she take a sledgehammer to his mind when there were thousands of people swirling around?

Cooper barreled into sight. "Ah, there you are. I've been tasked to find you."

"Did Frampton send you too?" Birmingham sounded none too pleased at this implied snub against his competence.

"No, the prince himself sent me," said Cooper proudly.

Iolanthe's alarm instantly tripled. The prince never did anything without a reason. He must be well aware that Sutherland and Birmingham had already been dispatched. Why Cooper in addition?

"Quite the day for you, Cooper," she said. "You've always liked him being princely."

"Words cannot describe how *grand* he has been. The man was born to lord over others."

Birmingham snorted.

"Did anyone else come from the court of Saxe-Limburg besides his great-uncle, the beautiful lady, and the hair-raising lady?" Iolanthe asked.

"Yes, hordes of lackeys." Cooper thought about it. Iolanthe could almost hear the gears of his brain rattling. "Maybe not all of them are servants. The prince addressed two of them by name and said something like, 'When did the transitory let out its detainees?' You reckon some of them could be political prisoners?"

"You idiot." Birmingham had had enough of Cooper's prattling. "Who would bring political prisoners to a school function? And what in the world is a transitory, anyway?"

"I'm just telling you what he said."

Iolanthe could not hear anything else over the roar in her head. This was the prince's message: Master Haywood and Mrs. Oakbluff had been brought to Eton to identify her. And the moment her disguise was stripped, she would be taken away.

*Run!* bellowed her voice of self-preservation. *Vault somewhere. Anywhere. Get away.*

But what would happen to *him* if she ran? Should his closest chum disappear from the face of the earth just as witnesses arrived to identify Iolanthe Seabourne, even Prince Alectus might be able to put two and two together. It would be back to the Inquisitory with him. And this time, there would be no one to intervene when the Inquisitor began cutting through his mind.

Unless—

No. The very idea was insane.

But she had to. She had no other choice. There was no one else to help her.

"Ahhh!" she cried, and cupped her abdomen with both hands.

"What is it?" said the boys simultaneously.

"My stomach. I shouldn't have had that ginger beer. I'll bet that hag made it out of ditch water."

"Run for the lavatory," Birmingham advised. "When ginger beer turns on you, it turns on you hard."

"Want me to come with you?" Cooper asked cheerfully.

"And do what? Wipe my arse? You are the prince's personal envoy, so you've got to personally take my message to him. Tell him I'll be along as soon as I've had my rendezvous with the crapper."

She started running before she'd finished speaking.

Only to barrel into Trumper and Hogg a minute later, blocking her way.

"Oh, look who doesn't have any friends or cricket bats today?" said Trumper.

Hogg sneered, smashing one fist against the palm of his other hand. "You can kiss your pretty face good-bye, Fairfax. After we're done with you today, you'll look like chopped liver."

She swore—and punched Trumper in the stomach. He howled. Hogg threw himself at her and closed his arm around her throat in a chokehold. She rammed her elbow into his kidney. He yelped in pain and stumbled back. To Trumper, again joining the fray, she delivered a knee to the groin. Trumper emitted a high-pitched shriek and collapsed in a heap.

She ran again and ducked into an empty alley between two houses. Hands braced against the rough brick wall behind her back, she vaulted.

Only to open her eyes and find that she hadn't moved an inch.

Her destination was within her vaulting range. There was no reason she should have failed. She tried again. And again. And again.

To no avail.

Atlantis had turned the entire school into a no-vaulting zone.

# CHAPTER · 22

IOLANTHE SPRINTED.

If Kashkari had been telling the truth—and she had no reason to doubt him—then Atlantis had not only established a no-vaulting zone, but also made sure that one would not be able to simply walk out.

But not all no-vaulting zones were created equal. Permanent ones, like the one the prince had established in his room, took tremendous time and effort. A completely new, and most likely temporary, no-vaulting zone sometimes had areas of incomplete denial that could be exploited—or so she'd recently learned in the teaching cantos.[22]

She did not stop until she was before the wardrobe in Wintervale's room. Paired portals, unless specifically allowed, did not work inside a no-vaulting zone. When one was inside and the other out, however, they were sometimes overlooked by a first-iteration no-vaulting zone, especially one that covered such a huge area.

She opened the wardrobe, pushed Wintervale's coats aside, squeezed in, and closed the door. But when she opened the door again, she was still in Wintervale's room at Mrs. Dawlish's.

Her fingertips shook.

Unless . . . unless the portal had a password. Most didn't: the magic undergirding portals and that which governed the use of passwords were not terribly compatible. But the prince had definitely used one for the bathtub portals connecting the castle to the monastery.

But how was she to find out the password now? The prince was out of reach. And were she to set out to search for Wintervale, there was every chance she'd be seen and brought to the Inquisitor before she could come back and use the portal.

She perspired—it was dark and stuffy inside the wardrobe. Her lungs felt as if they were about to collapse. Her hands, braced on either side of her person, barely kept her upright.

Like a bright flare at night, the Oracle's counsel came to her. *You will best help him by seeking aid from the faithful and bold.* She'd thought of those words daily, and never had they made any sense.

Now they did.

"*Fidus et audax*," she said, Latin for "faithful and bold."

And this time, when she opened the door of the wardrobe, she was in Wintervale's house in London.


Iolanthe stepped down. The dark-blue wallpaper and the rich Oriental carpet both looked unfamiliar—she'd remembered very little of the decor. The space behind the wardrobe, where the prince had shoved her when Wintervale came at his mother's summons, was tiny. She and the prince must have been pressed together like a pair of shirts going through a clothes wringer.

But the window and its deep ledge looked exactly right—except she'd thought it faced the street, when in fact it overlooked a small garden in the rear of the house.

The corridor outside was thickly carpeted, the walls covered in a pale-gold silk. There were several other bedrooms on the floor, but they were all empty.

"Lee, is that you?" came a feminine voice behind her. "What is the matter? Why are you home?"

The madwoman. Wintervale kept insisting she was only sometimes mad. Iolanthe prayed that today was one of her more lucid days.

She slowly turned around, her hands held up, palms out. Wintervale's mother was in another tightly cinched English dress. And for all that she'd spent the spring in a spa town, she did not appear rejuvenated: her eyes were sunken, her cheeks hollow, her skin as thin and fragile as eggshells.

The moment she realized it was not her son standing before her, however, her gaze turned feral. She pointed her wand at Iolanthe. "Who are you? What are you doing here?"

"I am the one you swore a blood oath to protect, from the moment you saw me." Iolanthe pushed the words past her rapidly closing throat. "Last time I was here, you tried to kill me. This time, you will help me."

The corner of the madwoman's eye twitched. "I said I was *asked* to swear a blood oath." She laughed softly, the sound of nightmares. "I never said I did."

Titus prayed.

He had meant for her to flee, and judging by what Cooper said, she had run for it. But had she gone far enough? He wanted her halfway around the world by the time the Inquisitor broke him.

The Inquisitor *would* break him. For all her days in a coma, she seemed to be haler than ever. Her eyes were sharp, her complexion glowing, her attention as focused as a beam of light that had passed through a magnifying glass.

Mrs. Hancock arrived with the staff from Mrs. Dawlish's house: cooks, maids, laundresses, and charwomen. Much to the complaints of those standing in the queue, they leapfrogged to the head of the line.

The Inquisitor leaned forward with anticipation.

Of course a *girl* living in Mrs. Dawlish's house was going to be subject to more suspicion than a boy. And several of the maids and laundresses were about the right age.

It so happened that a kitchen maid had the day off to visit a sick sister in London. The Inquisitor was displeased. "We asked for all the members of the staff to be accounted for."

"They were as of last evening, Madam Inquisitor," said Mrs. Hancock calmly. "But the girl received a telegram early this morning, and

Mrs. Dawlish, my superior, gave her leave without first consulting me. Rest assured she will return in good time."

Mrs. Hancock herded Mrs. Dawlish's staff away. Cooper shouted, "There he comes, our Fairfax, fresh from the powder room, as promised."

*What?* Titus felt as if he had been whipped. *Why?*

From the edge of the crowd, Fairfax made her jaunty way toward him, head held high, hat set at a dashing angle, whistling.

*Whistling.* Had she lost her mind? *Run, you fool. And do not look back.*

Guilt overwhelmed him: she had come because of the blood oath. There could be no other explanation. He prayed again—desperate, jumbled prayers—for the multitudes to close ranks and keep her out. Instead, she sliced effortlessly through the horde, like a clipper on an open ocean.

*You are the stupidest girl in the world.*

Mrs. Oakbluff stared at her. Haywood stared at her. The Inquisitor stared at *them*. The least twitch of recognition . . .

She continued to advance, prettier than all the silk-clad sisters. It was a wonder she had managed to pass herself off as a boy for so long; she would not fool them another minute.

Perhaps she did not intend to. Perhaps she meant to pit her powers against the Inquisitor's here and now. She would not stand a chance. Among the Inquisitor's minions were battle-hardened elemental mages with far greater experience than she.

She only stopped when she reached Greencomb the secretary. A second later Greencomb announced, "Mr. Archer Fairfax."

Fairfax stepped before her greatest enemies and bowed.

Titus's disbelief reached an excruciating peak. How was it possible that she had not yet been yanked away? What was going on? Yet he dared not glance at either Oakbluff or Haywood, for fear of giving himself away.

"I understand you are His Highness's faithful companion, Mr. Fairfax," said Lady Callista.

She had already smiled long and hard this day. Her expression had become stiff and tinged with fatigue.

"I am a frequent beneficiary of His Highness's largesse," said Fairfax. "It seems only fitting that when he requires companionship, I am there to provide it."

Lady Callista's eyes widened ever so slightly at Fairfax's neutral statement on their friendship.

Fairfax bowed again and prepared to yield her place to the next person in line.

"Who are your parents?" asked the Inquisitor, who had not spoken to any of the boys presented so far.

"Mr. and Mrs. Roland Fairfax of Bechuanaland, ma'am."

"Where in Bechuanaland, precisely?"

"A hundred twenty miles outside Kuruman. Have you been to Bechuanaland, ma'am?"

"No," said the Inquisitor. "But should the opportunity arise, I will be sure to call on your parents."

Titus felt as if a giant spider was crawling down his spine. If the Inquisitor were to mount a personal investigation, then Titus's thin veil of deception would not stand a chance.

Fairfax's sangfroid did not falter. "They will be honored to receive you, ma'am."

"We shall see," said the Inquisitor.

Fairfax bowed one more time and walked away.

Safe for now.


As Iolanthe left, she dared a glance in Master Haywood's direction. He looked dazed and exhausted, and it took everything in her not to throw the scene into chaos and make away with him.

Mrs. Dawlish's house was deserted. But Wintervale's mother was in his room, standing before his desk, writing something.

It had been a frozen moment of horror in Wintervale's house as Iolanthe realized her mistake. Then Wintervale's mother had said, *I won't try to murder you again. What help do you need?*

Iolanthe had been stunned. But there had been no time to ask questions. She'd hurriedly explained her needs, brought Wintervale's mother to Mrs. Dawlish's house, and sent her off with a description of the two mages at whom she should aim a barrage of invalidating spells, so that as Iolanthe stood before Master Haywood and Mrs. Nettle, they would neither be able to access old memories, nor gain new ones while under the spell.

She knocked very softly. Wintervale's mother turned around. "It's you."

"Thank you for helping me," Iolanthe said. *And please don't lose your sanity now.*

"I had better go," said the not-quite-so-mad woman. "Forgive me. And please do not mind what I said earlier—his choices are not your fault."

"Whose choices?"

But Wintervale's mother was already stepping into the wardrobe, a piece of paper in hand. When Iolanthe opened the wardrobe again, it was empty except for a note on the inside of the door.

*Dear Lee, I am blocking this portal for now, until I find a more secure means for you to access the house. Love, Mother.*

As it turned out, Fairfax was not the last boy from Mrs. Dawlish's house to be brought before the Inquisitor, nor the second to last. A junior boy had slipped away to buy tobacco in town. A boy in his final year was found in a compromising position with a maid in the headmaster's household—and dragged back for his inspection.

But even after all the boys had been accounted for, the wait continued as the absent kitchen maid remained absent. Lady Callista had come prepared with snow-white linen and a picnic grand enough for a state banquet. Titus touched nothing, not even a drop of water.

At six o'clock, he rose to join the other rowers for the procession of boats that was to take place at half past. A company of the Inquisitor's lackeys followed him, jogging along the bank, never letting him leave their sight.

Upstream, the boats were pulled ashore, and the rowers tucked into a special supper. Titus forced himself to eat, so as to appear unconcerned before his minders. Afterward, the rowers took to the boats again to row back downstream. Upon their return, the fireworks would begin.

Night had fallen. The trees along both banks of the river had been lit with miniature candles; the water glittered with their reflections. It would have been a pretty sight had he been in the mood to appreciate it.

Halfway down the river he realized that the mages who had shadowed him were gone. He veered between a bone-melting relief and a stark suspicion that this was the beginning of some new trickery.

Only when he saw that the white canopy had also disappeared did he allow himself to exhale. If the Inquisitor had planned to take him in tonight, she would have waited for him.

Pushing past the throngs of spectators gathered for the fireworks, he headed back to Mrs. Dawlish's.

Fairfax was not in her room—the entire floor was empty. But she did leave him a note on her desk. *Off to the fireworks. The boys insist.*

He returned to his own room, set the kettle to boil, pulled out a tin of biscuits from his cabinet, and slumped down on his bed.

For now, he was safe. But the next Inquisition would happen sooner or later. To protect Fairfax, he must go on the run. The only question was whether she would be safer coming with him or staying behind at Eton.

The kettle boiled. He looked into his cupboard for his favorite leaf, grown in the mist-covered mountains of the West Ponives, a mage realm in the Arabian Sea—and remembered that he had already finished his store. On an ordinary day, he would have settled for a bit of Fairfax's Earl Grey. But tonight he wanted—needed—the comfort of the familiar before he made decisions that would affect what remained of his life.

He went to Fairfax's room to vault to his laboratory—and could not. His shock was almost as great as what she must have felt when he tossed her into Ice Lake. Going into the empty house officers' lounge, he tried again—and again found himself in the same spot. He ran downstairs into the street—and still could not vault.

This was Atlantis's doing. It went without saying that if he managed to find the boundary of this no-vaulting zone, he would find it heavily guarded. And his flying carpet had been packed away as part of Fairfax's survival kit, now beyond his reach.

He took a deep breath and told himself he had no need to lose hope. There was always the wardrobe in Wintervale's room.

But when he opened the door of the wardrobe, he saw a note pasted on the inside. *Dear Lee, I am blocking this portal for now, until I find a more secure means for you to access the house. Love, Mother.*

His last option, ripped from him. He stumbled back into his room, numb with panic.

Distantly, there came the sound of fireworks exploding and enthusiastic cheering. Like a sleepwalker, he drifted to his window, only to see Trumper and Hogg on the grass, each with a brick in hand, getting ready to throw them at his and Fairfax's window.

His anger boiling over, he slashed his wand in the air. They promptly fell over. He clenched his hand, willing himself not to do anything else. In his current state of mind, he might maim them permanently.

He turned around. "Bastards. They need their heads shoved up their—"

He froze. It was exactly what he had said in his mother's vision. He hurried to his copy of *Lexikon der Klassischen Altertumskunde*. In his hands it turned back to Princess Ariadne's diary. Almost immediately he located the rest of the entry.

> *It is evening, or perhaps night, quite dark outside. Titus turns back from the window, clearly incensed. "Bastards," he swears. "They need their heads shoved up their—"*
>
> *He freezes. Then rushes to take a book down from his shelf, a book by the name of* Lexikon der Klassischen Altertumskunde.
>
> *Everything blurred.*
>
> *When I could make out clear images again, I was no longer looking at the same small room, but at the library of the Citadel. Is it the same evening? I cannot be sure. Titus appears again, this time in a gray*

*hooded tunic, moving stealthily through the stacks. (Someday he will be the Master of the Domain. Why this furtiveness in his own palace?)*

*Again everything dissolves—to coalesce once more into the interior of the Citadel's library. Many more mages are present, most of them soldiers in Atlantean uniform—how far the fortunes of the House of Elberon will have fallen—surrounding what looks to be a body on the floor. Alectus and Callista are there too.*

*"I can't believe it," Callista murmurs.*

*Alectus looks as if he'd lost his own sister. "The Inquisitor, dead. It is not possible. It is not possible."*

Did this mean if Titus took himself to the Citadel tonight, it would somehow result in the Inquisitor's death? The prospect was dizzying.

What had the Oracle said? *You must visit someone you've no wish to visit and go somewhere you've no wish to go.*

To go to the Citadel, he would have to pass through Black Bastion, Helgira's fortress.

*My visions are usually not so disjointed. At this point I am not sure whether this is one vision or three separate ones. I will record them as one for now and hope for clarification later.*

He turned the page. There was no more text. He turned another page and froze. At the bottom right corner of this page, there was a small skull mark.

*He* had left the mark, on the page that bore the vision of his death.

Were these two visions but part of the same larger vision? By going to the Citadel this night, was he going to his end?

*Think no more on the exact hour of your death, prince. That moment must come to all mortals. When you will have done what you need to do, you will have lived long enough.*

He changed into the gray tunic the vision had specified, set his hand on the Crucible, and began the password.

CHAPTER · 23

IOLANTHE WAS DRAGGED OUT OF Mrs. Dawlish's by boys who had come back to the house for supper. They could not understand why she wanted to stay in her room, and she, preoccupied, had failed to complain early on of headaches or fatigue.

She made sure she always stood or walked where it was darkest, kept a wary eye for the presence of Atlanteans, and an even warier one for the possibility of Master Haywood and Mrs. Oakbluff being led about like a pair of bloodhounds.

But no one arrested her. She made it back to Mrs. Dawlish's house and headed directly for the prince's room.

He was not there. She spent a petrified moment thinking he'd been taken after all, until she noticed his uniform jacket on the back of a chair—and the still-warm kettle next to the grate.

So he'd come back, taken off his jacket, boiled water for tea, and then—she felt the kettle again—between a quarter to a half hour ago, gone somewhere else.

But where? He could not vault anywhere. Atlantis monitored

the periphery of the no-vaulting zone. And Lady Wintervale had blocked the wardrobe portal on her end.

Birmingham's voice rang out in the hall, reminding the boys that it was time to prepare for bed. Soon Mrs. Hancock would come around to knock on all the boys' doors, making sure they were in their rooms at lights-out.

She checked the common room; he was not there. The baths were already locked. Only the lavatory was left.

Wait, she told herself. But half a minute felt like a decade. She swore and made for the lavatory, a facility she used only when it was entirely or mostly unoccupied. It was now shortly before lights-out: the place was not going to be empty.

She took three deep breaths before going inside, and still she almost ran out screaming. The trough was packed shoulder-to-shoulder with boys emptying their bladders—the last thing she wanted to witness, even if it was from the back.

"You want my place, Fairfax?" asked Cooper as he stepped back from the trough, refastening his trousers.

"No, thank you! I'm looking for Sutherland. He has my classical geography book."

She knocked on the stalls. "You in there, Sutherland?"

"Good Lord, can't a man visit a privy in peace anymore?" came Birmingham's grumpy reply from the last stall.

All the boys laughed. Iolanthe contributed her own nervous guffaws and escaped with unholy haste.

On a different night she might not have worried so much—if the prince didn't have some secret plans brewing, he wouldn't be Titus VII. But this day they'd faced their nemesis and escaped by the skin of their teeth. He must be dying to find out how she'd pulled off the deed. Not to mention they desperately needed to come up with a coherent strategy, together, to counter the Inquisitor's next move.

She returned to the prince's room. There was one place she hadn't checked, the teaching cantos. The Crucible was on his desk; she placed her hand over it. Once she was in the pink marble palace, she ran to his classroom.

A note on his door said, *F, I will be gone for a short while. No need to worry about me. And no need to worry about lights-out. T.*

Instead of reassuring her, his vagueness about his destination and purpose made her even more uneasy.

She opened the door—and paused on the threshold. Inside the classroom, illuminated by a dozen torches, woody vines rose wrist-thick from openings on the floor, intertwined in knots and arabesques on the walls, and spread open upon the ceiling. Clusters of small golden flowers hung from this canopy. A bank of French windows opened to a large balcony and a dark, starry sky.

There were no tables or chairs upon the carpet of living grass, but two elegant bench swings set at oblique angles to each other. The prince sat on one of those swings, in his Eton uniform, his arms stretched out along the back of the bench.

"Tell me what I like to read in my leisure time," he said.

"Who gives a damn! Where are you?"

As if he hadn't heard her at all, he repeated his demand.

With a pinch in her heart she remembered it wasn't really him, only *a record and a likeness*. "Ladies' magazines, English."

"Where did you last kiss me?"

The memory still burned. "Inside Sleeping Beauty's castle."

He nodded. "What can I do for you, my love?"

He'd never before called her that. Her chest constricted. Was he saving all such endearment for after his death? "Tell me where you've gone."

"You are, presumably, speaking of a time in my future. I have no knowledge of the specifics of the future."

"Where is your spare wand?" She hoped she wouldn't have to take matters into her own hands. But she planned to, as he'd taught her, *assume the worst and prepare accordingly*.

"In a box in my tea cabinet, the same box I asked you to pass to me before our first session in the Crucible. It will open only at your touch—or mine. Password: Sleeping Beauty. Countersign: *Nil desperandum*."

"In an emergency, what should I take from your room other than the Crucible and the spare wand?"

"My mother's diary, currently disguised as *Lexikon der Klassischen Altertumskunde*. Password: Better by innocence than by eloquence. Countersign: *Consequitur quodcunque petit*."

She asked him to repeat all the passwords and countersigns and committed them to memory.

Back in his room, she'd just found his spare wand when Mrs. Hancock called, "Lights off, gentlemen, lights off."

He'd told her not to worry about lights-out, but she needed a plan, in case his went awry. She could imitate the prince's voice and then, hoping Mrs. Hancock bought her imitation, turn off the lights, step out, and enter her own room before Mrs. Hancock's eyes.

Except she wasn't much of a mimic.

The knock came at the prince's door. Before Iolanthe could make a sound from her suddenly parched throat, the prince's voice rang out. "Good night."

Her heart almost leaped out of her mouth. She spun around. He had not come back. She couldn't be entirely sure, but the stone bust he kept on his shelf appeared to have answered for him.

"Won't you turn off your lights, Your Highness?" asked Mrs. Hancock as Iolanthe shoved the wand up her sleeve and grabbed the Crucible and *Lexikon der Klassischen Altertumskunde* from his desk.

The gas lamp went out by itself. Iolanthe opened the door just enough to let herself out.

"I will be turning my lights off right away also, ma'am," she said to Mrs. Hancock, smiling.

"See that you do, Fairfax. Good night."

"Good night, ma'am."

Her heart still pounding, she turned off the lights in her room, drew the curtain, summoned a smidgen of fire, and set it in the depression of a candleholder. Sitting down on her bed, she opened the diary first: she'd quickly know whether it had anything to tell her.

What she found terrified—and enraged—her. His mother specifically mentioned Atlantean soldiers and the presence of Lady Callista, known agent of Atlantis. And he'd taken off without so much as a word to her. It was almost as if he *wanted* to march to his doom.

She stormed into his classroom in the teaching cantos and tersely repeated the answers to the questions meant to ascertain her identity.

"If I need to go to the Citadel, right now, and I have no other means of transportation, what should I do?"

His record-and-likeness frowned. "No other means of mobility at all?"

"None. I am in a no-vaulting zone. And I have no vehicles, flying carpets, beasts of burden, or portals."

"And you absolutely must go?"

"Absolutely."

"You may use the Crucible as a portal, but only if it is a matter of life and death, and only after you have exhausted all other options."

"You told me the Crucible is not a portal."

"I said it is not *used* as one. And with good reason. To use the Crucible as a portal requires that a mage physically inhabit the geography of the Crucible. When you get hurt, you get hurt. When you are killed, you die. It is doable, but I advise strenuously against it."

She wanted to yank him off his swing and shake him. "If you advise strenuously against it, why have you done it yourself, you nitwit?"

He was perfectly unruffled. "I do not believe I have prepared for that question. Rephrase or ask a different one."

She forced herself to calm down. "Tell me how the Crucible works as a portal."

"It serves as an entrance into other copies of the Crucible. There were four copies made. One I keep with me at all times, one is at the monastery in the Labyrinthine Mountains, one in the library at the Citadel, and the fourth has been lost."

"So you enter this copy of the Crucible, say a password, and you are whisked inside the copy of the Crucible at the Citadel. Then you just say 'And they lived happily ever after' and you are standing in the Citadel itself?"

"I wish it were that simple. When Hesperia turned the copies of the Crucible into portals, she tried to make safe passages, but a great deal of the original structure could not be overridden.

"The story locales of the Crucible are normally each instantly accessible, like drawers in a chest. But when the Crucible is used as a portal, the locales join into one continuous terrain. Only one point of entry and exit exists at the center of this terrain, on the meadow not far from Sleeping Beauty's castle. To reach any other spot, you must travel, on foot, on beasts of burden, or via magical means, as long as those means were known at the time of the Crucible's creation—which means no vaulting.

"To make matters worse, Hesperia, concerned that pursuers might follow her into the Crucible, located the actual portals in some of the most dangerous places in the Crucible: Briga's Chasm, Forbidden Island, and Black Bastion."

Black Bastion, where he'd been killed by Helgira's lightning.

"Which one goes to the Citadel?"

"Black Bastion."

Well, *of course*. "The whole of Black Bastion or a specific place inside?"

"The prayer alcove inside Helgira's bedchamber."

She already felt nauseous. "How do I get to Black Bastion?"

"The map at the very front of the Crucible should tell you the layout of the land when it is used as a portal. From Sleeping Beauty's castle, Black Bastion is about thirty-five miles north-northeast."

She rubbed her throat. The collar of her shirt was suddenly too restrictive. "All right, give me the password and the countersign to using the Crucible as a portal."

He gave both, but added, "You must swear to me, on your guardian's life, that you will not use the Crucible this way unless you yourself are in mortal danger."

She hesitated.

He rose and took her hands. His own, calloused from countless hours on the river, were warm and strong. "I beg you, do not, *do not* put your life in danger, particularly not for me. I will never forgive myself. The only thing that makes this entire madness bearable is the hope that you may yet survive, that one day you may live the life you have always wanted."

Tears stung the back of her eyes. She looked away and said, "And they lived happily ever after."

Titus shook. He cursed himself, but the shaking would not stop.

He had been twelve, cocky about his prowess in the Crucible after having vanquished the Monster of Belle Terre, the Keeper of Toro Tower, and the Seven-Headed Hydra of Dread Lake. His death at Helgira's hand had obliterated any further thoughts of invincibility. In fact, it had been two months before he could use the Crucible again, and even then only to partake in the easiest, simplest quests.

In the years since, he had conquered his fear of the Crucible, but never his terror of Black Bastion.

The wyvern beneath him sensed his growing panic and decided to take advantage. It rolled and plunged, attempting to shake him loose. Practically joyous for the distraction, he jabbed his wand into the beast's neck. It screeched in pain.

"Fly properly or I will do it again."

Last time his approach had been blatant, at the forefront of a mob of attackers. He would not repeat that mistake. Helgira's saga began with one of her lieutenants arriving at Black Bastion on a wyvern. Titus had wrangled a wyvern from Sleeping Beauty's castle and would try to pass himself off as a soldier coming to warn Helgira of an impending attack.

The torch-lit silhouette of Black Bastion was beginning to be visible, a solid, foursquare fortress that crowned a foothill of Purple Mountain. He murmured a prayer of gratitude for the darkness—he could not see Helgira yet. The last thing he remembered from his previous foray was her slim, white-clad person, standing atop the fort, her arm raised to call down the bolt of lightning that would strike him dead.

In the aftermath, his convulsions had nearly snapped his spine. Even the thought of it made him shake again.

Black Bastion drew ever nearer.

This time, if he were killed, he would remain dead.

The landing platform was five hundred feet away. The wyvern was not trained to carry riders and had no reins. He wrapped his arms around its neck and pulled. It brayed, but slowed to a speed better suited for dismounts.

Soldiers surrounded him the moment his feet touched the platform. "We've been attacked!" he cried. "The Mad Wizard of Hollowcombe promised the peasants land and riches in exchange for our lives."

Dozens of weapons were unsheathed. The captain of the guard held a long spear—one that could follow a fleeing opponent for a mile—at Titus's throat. "You are not Boab."

"Boab is dead. They killed just about all of us."

"How could they kill Boab? Boab is—was a great soldier and an even better mage."

Titus's mouth was dry, but he doggedly repeated the plot of the story. "Treachery. They gave us drugged wine."

"Why were *you* not drugged?"

"I wasn't at the celebration. A peasant girl, you see. I thought she liked me, but she turned on me. I heard her talk to the people coming to kill me, so I stole her brother's clothes and this wyvern to come warn m'lady."

He hoped his gray tunic would pass for peasant attire.

The captain did not trust him, but he also did not dare not bring Titus to Helgira. With eight spears trained on him, Titus marched down the ramp to the bailey and into the great hall of Black Bastion.

The hall was crowded. There was singing and dancing. Helgira, in her white gown, sat at the center of a long table upon a great dais, drinking from a chalice of gold.

He stopped dead. Four spears pressed hard into his back. Still he could not move a single step.

Instead of turning angry, the captain chuckled. "Gets 'em bumpkins every time, she does."

But Titus was neither bowled over by Helgira's beauty nor petrified anew by fear. He was transfixed because Helgira was *Fairfax*.

She was twenty years older, but in her features she was identical to Fairfax. Her lips were the same shade of deep pink, her hair the same jet-black cascade he remembered so well.

*This* was the reason Fairfax had looked eerily familiar when they had first met.

Helgira perceived the arrival of the soldiers and signaled the musicians to halt. The dancers melted to either side of the hall, clearing a path.

Titus sleepwalked, staring at Helgira. Only after the captain smacked him on the side of the head and yelled at him for disrespect did he lower his head.

Before the dais, he sank to his knees, kept his eyes on the ground, and repeated his tale. The toes of Helgira's dainty white slippers—with lightning bolts embroidered in silver thread—came into his view.

"I am well pleased with you, warrior," she murmured. "You will be given a bag of gold and a woman who will not turn on you."

"Thank you, m'lady. M'lady is mighty and munificent."

"But you committed a grave breach of etiquette, young man. Do you not know that no one is allowed to gaze upon me without my permission?"

"Forgive me, my lady. My lady's beauty stole my sense."

Helgira laughed. Her voice was high and sharp, completely different from Fairfax's.

"I like this one—such pretty words. Very well, henceforth I grant you the privilege. But know this: I always exact punishment for any transgression."

With that, she unsheathed the knife at her belt and brought it down on him.

Iolanthe, sitting on her cot in the dark, almost screamed. It was as if someone had slashed her with a knife. She gripped her arm. There was no blood, but the pain was still there, making her grit her teeth with it.

What was happening? Could she possibly be sensing the prince's pain again?

A sharp, almost metallic smell wafted to her nostrils. No, it couldn't be. Her agitation must be playing a trick on her.

Something dripped to the floor.

A strangled bleat tore from her throat. She summoned a flicker of fire. Directly across from her, blood poured from the Crucible, forming a blackish puddle that drizzled steadily from her desk onto the floor.

She whimpered again. A second later, she leaped from her bed. With a wave of the prince's spare wand, she cleared away the blood—all mage girls above the age of twelve knew how to handle blood of this quantity. At least the book itself hadn't been stained, its pages dry and clean.

A thunderous crash came from her left. Instinctively she threw up a shield—and saved herself from shards of flying glass and the brick that been thrown into her room.

She stared at the brick a moment before stealing to the side of the window. She could just make out two figures behind the house. Her mind had been so much occupied with things not remotely related to school that she had trouble understanding what she was seeing. The prince was bleeding to his death out there, and here Trumper and Hogg wanted petty vengeance.

The next brick shattered the prince's window. Soon everyone would come running, including Mrs. Hancock. The last thing Iolanthe wanted, on the night the prince had gone to the Citadel to make mischief, was to have him reported as missing from school at the exact same time.

She stunned Trumper and Hogg, who promptly wilted into the grass. Next she applied a levitation spell. When her elemental magic proved insufficient at moving boulders, she sometimes cheated with the help of levitation spells. As a result, her authority over stone remained debatable, but now she could effortlessly suspend two beefy senior boys three feet aboveground and maneuver them into the coppice at the edge of the small meadow.

With a few kicks, she redistributed the glass shards, which had fallen on the floor in a straight line against her shield, into a more irregular pattern. The Crucible in hand, she ran out of her room just as doors began to open up and down the corridor.

"Did you hear that?" startled boys asked one another. "What happened?" "Anyone else hear breaking glass?"

She turned on the lights in the prince's room and mussed up his cot. Unfortunately, the Crucible was clean as a whistle, with not another drop of blood to give. She picked up a piece of glass shard, cut the pad of her left index finger, and squeezed a few drops of blood on the prince's sheets. Then she smeared a streak of blood on her own face, shoved the Crucible into the waistband of her trousers—she had yet to change into her nightshirt—and set a spell to keep it in place.

Next, with the door wide open, she bellowed at the top of her voice, "Faster, Titus. Catch those filthy bastards!"

As she'd hoped, Mrs. Dawlish's boys came running.

Helgira's knife sliced through Titus's left arm. The pain stunned him.

"Where is Mathi? Give this man some medical attention." Helgira caressed him lightly under his chin. "Notice I spared you your wand arm."

Titus swallowed. "My lady is magnanimous."

She was already walking away. "I want to see Kopla, Numsu, and Yeri. The rest of you ready the bastion for battle."

He stared at the furious reddening of his sleeve. He had not thought this through. What would happen to the blood he shed when he used the Crucible as a portal?

Mathi, a plump, middle-aged woman, came forward and pulled Titus to his feet. His hand clamped over the gash in his arm, he followed her to a small room with bitter-smelling poultices cooking over a slow fire. A cot lay in the corner. Unevenly sized jars of herbs lined the shelves.

The moment Mathi turned her back, Titus rendered her

unconscious. He caught her with his good arm and laid her down on the cot. Mathi was probably the best healer for miles around, but he still did not want her primitive medicine.

Teeth clenched, he cleaned his wound. Then he took out the remedies and emergency aids he had brought with him, and poured two different vials on his wound and a packet of granules down his throat.

His wound began to close. He threw a battery of spells at his tunic to clean and deodorize it. It would not do to arrive at the Citadel looking and smelling like a massacre.

When he was more presentable, he set a keep-away spell on the dispensary's door and set out for Helgira's prayer alcove.

He asked his way toward Helgira's quarters, using her promise to give him a woman as an excuse. Good-natured winks accompanied his progress for much of the way. Helgira's handmaidens, however, refused to let him into her personal chambers. So he pulled out his wand and fought his way in.

The prayer alcove was located in Helgira's bedchamber. He had just crossed the threshold when Helgira crashed in on his heels. There were two alcoves in the bedchamber, both curtained. He had no time to find out which was the prayer alcove, but leaped across her bed to the one that had the more elaborate curtain, muttering the password as he hurtled toward it.

If he chose wrong, he would smash into a three-foot-thick wall and die at the hands of a woman who had Fairfax's face.

He did not smash into a three-foot-thick wall.

The other end of the portal was, of course, the prayer alcove in Helgira's bedchamber—in the *Citadel's* copy of the Crucible. Had Titus not been running for his life, he would have remembered to be slower and more cautious.

As it was, he flew out of this prayer alcove into the midst of this Helgira's bedchamber.

This Helgira lifted her wand.

"Watch your feet!" Iolanthe shouted as Wintervale and Kashkari reached the door.

They caught themselves on the door frame and held on as they were bumped from behind by the arrival of Sutherland, Cooper, and Rogers.

But most of the boys had their slippers on and Cooper, who'd come barefoot, had Rogers toss him a pair of the prince's shoes and trooped in after the others.

Exclamations of disgust and outrage filled the room.

"My God, there is blood," cried Rogers.

"They've injured him," Iolanthe said. "And I thought it was bad enough they almost brained me."

More exclamations of disgust and outrage burst forth. "Bastards!" "We are not going to let anybody get away with something like this!" "Did you see who did it?"

"Trumper and Hogg, of course—the prince went after them

already," she said. "They tried to harass me earlier today, but I gave them a sound thrashing."

"Hear, hear," said Cooper.

"I'm not going to stand by and do nothing," said Kashkari, rolling up his sleeves.

As he did so, the tattoo on the inside of his right arm became fully visible. It was not the letter *M*, but the symbol ♏, for Scorpio, his birth sign in both western and Vedic astrology.

*You will best help him by seeking aid from the faithful and bold. And from the scorpion.*

Kashkari opened what was left of the prince's window and hoisted himself onto the windowsill. His action broke the floodgate. Iolanthe had to fight for her turn to go down the drainpipe. Seven more boys followed, two of them climbing out of their own windows; several didn't even use the drainpipe, but leaped down to the ground, their long nightshirts billowing like sails—before Mrs. Hancock caught someone still on the windowsill.

"Which way did they go?" asked Cooper.

"That way," said Iolanthe, pointing at a direction opposite the coppice where she had stowed Trumper and Hogg. "Let's catch them before they get back to their own house."

Ignoring Mrs. Hancock's yells for them to come back, she and the boys broke into a run.

When they were some distance from the house, she stopped everyone and divided all the boys into pairs, ostensibly so that they'd have both a greater chance finding Trumper and Hogg and a lesser chance being discovered by the night watchmen.

Kashkari she paired with herself. When she'd sent the other boys into various directions with instructions to wait behind Trumper and Hogg's house if they could not be located elsewhere, she tapped Kashkari on the shoulder and headed back toward Mrs. Dawlish's.

"I thought you said they went in the opposite direction," said Kashkari.

She prayed hard that the Oracle would once again prove herself right. "Long story. Remember when you said if I ever needed help?"

"Of course. Anything."

"I need your complete discretion. What you do tonight, you will never repeat to another soul. Do I have your word?"

Kashkari hesitated. "Will I harm anyone?"

"No. And you have my word on it."

"All right," said Kashkari. "I trust you."

*And I am putting our lives in your hands.* "Listen closely. This is what I need you to do."

Before this Helgira could pulverize him, Titus sank to one knee. "M'lady, I bear a message from my lord Rumis."

He had studied Helgira's story closely before he first set out to battle her. Following his ignominious death at her hand, he had tried to forget all about her. Now, however, certain important details dropped back into his head.

Such as that, for years, Helgira had carried on a secret platonic love affair with the great mage Rumis.

Helgira's expression softened into amusement. "My lord Rumis has quite the sense of humor then, sending his manservant into my bedchamber unannounced."

"He has an urgent request and no time to lose."

"Speak."

"He asks that m'lady outfit me with a steed and send me on my way."

Since he had entered this copy of the Crucible via a portal, the same rules applied. He must physically travel to the exit. A wyvern would ensure speed.

Helgira sighed. "Tell your master that although his request makes little sense, I trust him too much to delay you with questions."

"Thank you, m'lady."

"You may rise. I will have a wyvern waiting for you." Removing a cuff from her wrist, she placed it around his. "And this token from me will grant you safe passage through my lands."

Titus came to his feet. "Thank you, m'lady. I take my leave of you."

As he reached the door, she asked, "Is your master well?"

He turned around and bowed. "Very well, m'lady."

"And his wife, healthy as ever, I suppose?"

Rumis's wife was said to have outlived both Helgira and Rumis. "Yes, m'lady."

She looked away. "Go then. May Fortune be at your back."

Her expression so reminded him of Fairfax's that he could not help stare one more moment. "My master sends his most fervent regards, m'lady."

The wyvern was swift—too swift.

In a few minutes Titus would arrive at his destination. And perhaps in a few more minutes, he would use the execution curse on the Inquisitor.

A ruling prince was required to master the execution curse. If he sentenced any subject to death, he was to perform the deed himself, so that he must look the condemned mage in the face as he took the latter's life.

Titus had never thought he would use the curse. He was a liar, a schemer, and a manipulator, but not a murderer.

Not like his grandfather.

For Fairfax's safety, he was willing to give up his life. But was he also willing to give up what remained of his soul?

The wyvern landed on the meadow. He pushed aside his agitation to concentrate on what needed to be done. Under normal circumstances, when a mage exited the Crucible, it did not matter whether he had filled his pockets full of objects from the tales. Nothing could be brought out; the slate was wiped clean. But using the Crucible as a portal changed all the rules. The book would not close, so to speak, if he left with something that belonged inside.

He had already decided he would keep Helgira's cuff on his person. Should he escape the library of the Citadel unscathed, he would need a ready steed, and he could not find a better one than Helgira's. All he needed to do to keep the wyvern in place and waiting, her groom had informed him, was to take the stake at the end of the long chain attached to the beast's leg and push the stake into the ground.

The wyvern, however, did not seem to like the spot Titus had selected, on the bank of the stream that bisected the meadow. It bellowed plaintively, its claws clutching at the edges of Titus's tunic.

"What is the matter? Do you smell something?"

Wyverns had extraordinarily sensitive noses and could smell prey from miles away.

"You cannot be hungry, can you? I thought they fed you fresh meat all the time."

The wyvern hissed.

"I would not worry. Nothing menacing ever comes to the meadow. Not that I have seen, in any case."

Then again, he had never before physically inhabited the Crucible and did not know how it behaved in this state. He looked around. Everything was familiar enough, including Sleeping Beauty's castle on the hill.

Or was it? The castle glowed not with the usual coppery light of torches and lamps, but with something akin to the blue-green luminescence of deep-sea creatures.

This copy of the Crucible had been his grandfather's. It would seem Prince Gaius had made changes. While one could not alter the underlying thrust of a story—Sleeping Beauty, for example, would never come downstairs on her own and help her rescuer battle the dragons—almost all the incidentals of a story could be modified.

Turning Sleeping Beauty into Fairfax was only the latest of the changes Titus had made in his particular copy of the Crucible. There had not been wyverns in the great hall when the Crucible first came to him. Nor had the pair of dragons that guarded the castle gate been colossus cockatrices.

The changes Prince Gaius had made, however, felt more unsettling. But Titus could not pay much attention—not when he had murder on his mind.

Or ought to, in any case.

"And they lived happily ever after."

He was now in the Citadel, next to the Citadel's copy of the Crucible, which sat on a pedestal at the exact center of the dimly lit library. He slipped between the shelves.

The doors opened, and in came Alectus's voice. "And here we are, the library. Very soft lighting, exactly as Madam Inquisitor requested."

Titus held his breath.

"It will do," said the Inquisitor coldly. "You may leave us."

Who were *us*?

Titus had hid himself behind the end of a set of shelves. He peered around the edge, but could only see Alectus bowing and scraping on his way out.

"You should not have been so solicitous, sire," said the Inquisitor, her tone so soft and deferential Titus barely recognized it. "I would have handled the Inquisition at the Inquisitory itself."

"But we both know how sensitive a mind mage is to her surroundings, my dear Fia," replied an extraordinarily mellifluous male voice. "The Inquisitory still holds too much pain and fear for you."

"But it is a far safer place for you, my lord High Commander."

Titus's knees buckled. *My lord High Commander.* The man was the *Bane.*

"I am already overwhelmingly in my lord High Commander's debt for wresting me from death's grasp and restoring me to full health. How can I forgive myself exposing my lord High Commander to the likely perils of this place? Hesperia built it—it must be full of traps and snares."

"Fia, Fia, speak not from fear. Our mages have already inspected the library from top to bottom—sometimes a room is just a room. Now stop worrying about me and concentrate. To think, all these years we've misapplied your rare and wonderful talents, using you like a hammer when you are a fine scalpel. We will waste no more time. Tonight we slice past all the layers of magic Haywood has applied to hide his memories. Tomorrow, our young prince."

Titus shuddered.

"I cannot wait, my lord. And to think, since his mind will be perfectly whole afterward, he won't even be able to raise a diplomatic ruckus."

Titus leaned against the shelf, unable to support his own weight.

The doors of the library opened again. "Won't you care for some refreshments, my Lord High Commander, Madam Inquisitor?" said Lady Callista.

She held the large tray herself, sauntering toward the Bane and the Inquisitor.

"We have only just now enjoyed your bounteous banquet—my compliments to you, Lady Callista, the Citadel has the world's finest cooks. We might need a little time to recover our appetites."

The Bane was the ideal guest, honey-tongued and suave, not at all what Titus had expected.

"If only we'd had a little more notice of my lord High Commander's visit, we'd have put on a more suitable feast."

The Bane probably had not arrived until the Inquisitor sent news that she had failed to secure Iolanthe Seabourne with her ambush. Between the two of them, they were determined not to fail again.

"I will set the tray here," said Lady Callista, "and let my lord High Commander and Madam Inquisitor continue their preparation."

She withdrew. Not a minute later an Atlantean soldier entered and, two steps inside, knelt. "My lord High Commander, Madam Inquisitor, we have the detainee Horatio Haywood."

The Oracle had foretold that Haywood would not remain long in Atlantis's grasp. Did it mean Titus must be the one to whisk him to freedom? But then who would kill the Inquisitor? He could not do both at once.

The blood oath called for him to do his utmost to help Fairfax in her goal of freeing her guardian. He clenched his teeth.

The duration of the time-freeze spell decreased steeply when more than one mage was on the receiving end. What would last three minutes on one person would last only thirty seconds covering three mages. And if he had to cover four mages, he'd have at best ten seconds.

Would that be enough time to drag Horatio Haywood to the Crucible and disappear inside?

Haywood shuffled in with two guards. Four mages to cover. Titus's wand shook. Did he dare? Would his gallantry get himself caught, and result in Fairfax being yanked out of her bed in the dead of the night?

Titus saw his wand lifting. He could not believe what he was about to do. One. Two. Thr—

Haywood vanished before his eyes.

# CHAPTER · 24

IOLANTHE HUFFED WITH IMPATIENCE.

Sleeping Beauty's castle did not look terribly distant from the meadow, but to reach it on foot, even running at full speed, took far too long. And she'd already wasted enough time earlier, looking for a safe spot, worrying about the Crucible possibly bleeding again, before finally realizing that at this hour of the night, the Crucible could bleed a bucket and no one would notice a book lying in long grass.

But as the castle drew nearer, her impatience turned to fear. The thought of facing the wyverns alone turned her lungs weak—and the single moon in the sky was a relentless reminder that this was no make-believe. But she had to have a steed. Either that, or walk an entire day to reach Black Bastion.

At the edge of the briar forest, she saw the tunnel the prince had left behind. So he had been here. Had he got a wyvern too?

No roars greeted her ears as she sprinted through the tunnel. No warning streams of fire passed overhead. Even the air didn't stink as much. At the other end of the tunnel she saw why. The colossus cockatrices were gone, the pylons anchoring their chains snapped.

She hesitated only a moment before she resumed running. The doors of the great hall were wide open. She entered firing shield spells before her, but nothing attacked her. Only one wyvern was inside, slumped on the marble floor.

Its chest rose and fell. Either it was sleeping, or much more likely, the prince had blasted it unconscious.

She was faint with relief.

Now she could worry about surviving Black Bastion.

It took Titus a stunned second to realize what had happened.

*Tempus congelet,* he mouthed the time-freeze spell.

The entire Citadel was a permanent no-vaulting zone. With Haywood's disappearance, the library would be searched from top to bottom. He must get out this moment.

He sprinted. Fast. Faster. Still somehow not fast enough, like running from monsters in nightmares. And then he was out of the stacks, and in the midst of a bizarre tableau of frozen mages.

Still running, he pointed his wand at the Inquisitor. *"Mens omnino vastetur!"*

It was the strongest, most illicit spell of cerebral destruction he'd been able to find, not the execution curse. Likely he would regret his leniency later, but he was not a murderer. Not yet.

When he skidded to a stop before the stand that held the Citadel's copy of the Crucible, he was scarcely two feet from the Bane, who looked fifty years old, not two hundred. His features were confident, attractive—and familiar, somehow.

There was no time for the usual long password into the Crucible. Fortunately, he did not need to utter it, when the Crucible was already held open, so to speak. "I am the heir of the House of Elberon, and I am in mortal danger."

The next instant he was back in the meadow, under a night sky that was rapidly disappearing behind the clouds. Upon its hill Sleeping Beauty's castle glowed, eerily phosphorescent.

He panted with relief. But the air he breathed in—he grimaced at the pungency of it. Blood. He murmured a spell for light. Almost at once he saw a thin, sharp stake that had been pulled out of its mooring, a length of chain attached to it.

The stake that he had used to keep Helgira's wyvern waiting for him. He increased the intensity of the light and broadened its radius. Something dark lay on the grass. He ran toward it and stopped in his tracks, his stomach twisting. It was not a whole wyvern, only one bloody wing, crumpled like an old jacket.

Wyverns were terrifically agile creatures, both in body and in mind. They had vicious teeth, vicious claws, and vicious spikes— and could fly for hours at speeds in excess of one hundred miles an hour, with bursts of more than one hundred forty miles an hour. Titus could not think of a single beast both swift and brutal enough to hunt wyverns.

Yet one had.

He began to run toward Sleeping Beauty's castle. He needed another steed right away. With Haywood's disappearance, Atlantis might very well not wait until morning to come after him. He must get back to school as soon as possible, let Fairfax know what had happened, entrust the Crucible to her, and hide himself in the Crucible until such time as she could move him somewhere safer.

He could only pray his own copy of the Crucible was not such a perilous place as this one was proving to be.

The ground sloped up. He ran harder to maintain speed. His legs protested. His lungs too. In the nearly pitch-dark night, the thick, rich smell of wyvern blood continued to linger in his nostrils, feeding his nausea.

He stepped on something at once hard and soft. Instinctively he leaped away. The smell of blood intensified. He had been hot from running; now he was cold, his perspiration beads of fear rolling down his neck.

He tapped on his wand. A light flared, shining on a black limb in the grass—the lower portion of a wyvern's leg.

From the direction of the castle came an unearthly roar. The ground trembled, a vibration he felt in his shins. His heart raced as if it could escape; his breaths overshadowed all other sounds of the night.

Had this been a regular session in the Crucible, he would have hurried forward to find out just what fearsome creature now prowled the castle. But this was real. And he could not afford to end up in pieces all over the landscape.

On his way from Black Bastion to the meadow, he had passed over a market town not too far to the north. If he was not mistaken, it was the setting for "Lilia, the Clever Thief."

He had not practiced in that particular story in years, but he remembered it opened with the town being terrorized by an untamed wyvern. Not at all what he needed at this juncture, but as nonmages would say, better the devil you knew.

The wyvern would not respond.

Iolanthe had gone up to the costume room next to the ballroom, found a white dress that looked as if it could have been worn in times of antiquity, and slipped it on over her nonmage clothes. Then she'd snatched a black wig from underneath the sleeping wig master and set it on her head with a heavy application of adhesive spells, so it wouldn't fly away while she was airborne.

She'd read "The Battle for Black Bastion." She knew that Helgira had put out a call for assistance at some point. She would pretend to be one of the mages coming to aid her.

Her disguise in place, she approached the wyvern with extreme caution, leaped atop it, grabbed onto its skinny, scaly neck, and steeled herself to be violently tossed about.

Only to have the wyvern drool a little.

This was not a problem for which she'd prepared herself. On

the one hand, she was thrilled that the prince had used the heaviest spells. On the other hand, she was faced with a comatose steed when she needed a lively one that would fly fast enough to rip off all but the most meticulously adhered wigs.

"*Revisce.*"

Nothing.

"*Revisce forte.*"

More of the same.

"*Revisce omnino!*"

Still nothing. This last was supposed to be a spell that came just short of making the dead walk.

She smacked the heel of her hand against her forehead. The next second the wyvern let out a glass-shattering screech and shot up. She screamed and threw her arms around its neck.

The wyvern careened about the great hall with her hanging from its neck. She didn't know whether it had been traumatized by the prince's spells or whether it was her weight that made it frantic. Either way, it was doing its best to shake her loose.

She swung one leg up its back. The wyvern flipped upside down. She yelped and lost her footing.

The wyvern, one of the most ferociously intelligent beasts, must have noticed how her legs swung out as it banked a rapid turn. It threw itself at a pillar, pulling away only at the last possible second. She had to yank her legs up to her chest to avoid smashing them on the pillar—and losing her grip on the wyvern.

The beast tried again. She tucked herself into a fetal position and cleared the pillar by less than an inch.

All of a sudden she remembered that she now controlled air—how could she have forgotten? Time to make this struggle a little less one-sided.

She willed a gust of headwind. The wyvern was not expecting that. With its wings spread wide, it was pushed by the current to a nearly vertical position.

She hooked her legs around its body—finally, a better perch. Now how to get the creature out of those doors without any reins.

Well, the prince kept calling her the great elemental mage of their time. She had better come up with something.

Once the wyvern had leveled, and once she was sure her seat was secure, she hit the wyvern with a hard current that forced it to bank left. Then, a three-pronged approach that more or less hurtled the beast toward the front doors of the great hall.

Her efforts were inexact. The wyvern did head in the general direction of the doors, but it broke through the large rose window above instead, exiting the great hall in a shower of splintered wood and broken glass.

A messy business, rescuing princes.

It must be the fatigue of running five miles at the end of a day during which he had eaten only a handful of biscuits since breakfast. There was no other reason for Titus not to have vanquished the wyvern after a quarter of an hour.

He ducked into an alley. This was not good. Instead of fighting the wyvern, he was running away from it. So he could catch his breath, he told himself. It could not possibly be that he was afraid. Of dying uselessly. Stupidly. Of never seeing Fairfax again.

He crept along the edge of the alley. No sounds emanated from the cowered populace, or the wyvern. He held out his hand to feel his way—the sky had become completely overcast, the night impenetrable. His fingers came into contact with another wall.

He was in a *blind* alley.

He barely managed to throw up a shield as a stream of fire shot toward him—the wyvern had trapped him. He swore. He had not made this kind of mistake since he was thirteen, a lifetime ago.

*"Aura circumvallet."*

The wyvern spewed more fire, but his spell acted as a holding pen for the fire. He shot two jets of flames at the wyvern's belly. Subtle magic could not duplicate the scale of elemental magic, but he was decent at it.

The wyvern flew up to avoid his fire. He ran. But the beast again blocked his way at the mouth of the alley. He shot two more streams of fire. This time the wyvern was prepared and shielded itself with the outside of its wings. Dragon fire might singe its wings, but ordinary fire lacked the power.

He dove under one wing. The wyvern's spiked tail came at him. He threw himself to the ground and rolled away. Still the end spike opened a nasty gash on his side.

He screamed in pain. And with that pain came an angry rush of energy. *"Flamma caerula."*

A blue sizzle shot out of his wand into the wyvern's belly. The beast twitched and roared. The momentum of the struggle at last shifted in Titus's favor. Several minutes later, the wyvern was carrying him toward Black Bastion, while he applied salve to his person to stop the bleeding.

He wished his injury had not happened. *If you are cut, you bleed,* Hesperia had told him long ago in her classroom. He could only hope his blood was not dripping out of the Citadel's copy of the Crucible. All those mages in there, looking for the cause of Haywood's disappearance—a bleeding book in their midst would not go unnoticed.

The wyvern could not fly fast enough for him. He kept looking behind himself, watching for pursuers. Theoretically he knew he had no cause to worry: the knowledge that the Crucible could be used as a portal was passed down only to those in the direct line of succession. But sometimes others in the family gleaned such information by trickery or by accident—the Usurper, most famously.

The weather was turning uneasy. High winds ripped. Shearing currents blew the wyvern left and right. Then came a gust of headwind so vigorous, the wyvern was nearly flipped backward.

Titus flew lower, searching for calmer air. He did not find it. Nor did he find it at a greater altitude. A string of expletives left his tongue, only to be drowned by a roar that shook every bone in his

425 ♦

body—the exact same roar that had sent him fleeing from Sleeping Beauty's castle.

The wyvern screamed. Despite the uncooperative winds, it accelerated, as if driven by sudden fear. Titus pulled the hood of his tunic over his head, covered most of his face with the edges of the hood, and turned around.

The night sky was empty, save for a luminescent dot. He uttered a far-seeing spell. All at once, a huge winged creature loomed—so monstrously sized it would make colossus cockatrices look like sparrows. Even more grotesquely, the beast shimmered against the turbulent sky above.

A phantom behemoth, the steed of Angels.

Was *this* the change Prince Gaius had made to the story of Sleeping Beauty?

Phantom behemoths were not real. It had been concluded centuries ago that they were creatures of legend, born of the awe and fright of mages witnessing colossus cockatrices for the first time. But when a mage used the Crucible as a portal, everything inside became real.

He countermanded the far-seeing spell. The phantom behemoth faded again to a dot in the sky. It was still miles behind him.

The beast roared once more. The biggest winged creatures did not always fly the fastest. But judging by the roar, the phantom behemoth was closing in so swiftly, Titus might as well be running on foot.

He turned around again and tried to see if the phantom behemoth carried a rider. A smaller creature was tethered to it, a giant peregrine—which looked like a flea next to the phantom behemoth. The peregrine most certainly carried a rider. In the eerie glow of the behemoth, the rider's eyes were entirely colorless.

The Inquisitor!

And the rider who sat on the enormous head of the behemoth, with his handsome and oddly familiar-looking face, was none other than the Bane.

Iolanthe didn't know how she managed to bring down the wyvern on Black Bastion's landing platform without killing them both.

But her feet were on solid stone, and the wyvern was being skillfully led away by a pair of grooms, without erupting into a rage that would roast mages in a hundred-foot radius.

She expected to be challenged immediately, but everyone on the landing platform who wasn't busy with the wyvern sank to one knee, with murmurs of "M'lady."

Who knew help was so desperately needed at Black Bastion?

She descended into the bailey. More people paid obeisance to her. And even more dropped to their knees as she marched through the great hall. Who did they think she was? Helgira herself?

She kept pushing farther into the fort. Each time she was faced with a choice of directions, she chose the one that looked more sumptuous.

Opposition came in the form of a nondescript maid. As Iolanthe stepped into Helgira's richly decorated apartment, the maid cried, "That is not our lady!"

"No?" Iolanthe raised a brow. She snapped her finger, and a bolt of lightning flashed outside the window.

The maid appeared horribly confused.

Iolanthe snapped her finger again and another, even more impressive lightning bolt sizzled across the width of the sky.

"Forgive me, my lady." The maid sank to her knees, shaking.

Iolanthe ignored her. Inside the bedchamber, she passed through the prayer alcove to the Black Bastion in the Citadel's copy of the Crucible.

This Black Bastion was much calmer, its inhabitants preparing for bed rather than war. Iolanthe thought its mistress away from home until she saw a woman standing before a window, her long black hair fluttering in the strong breeze.

Helgira.

A woman who lived in warlike times should be more alert to her surroundings. Iolanthe could be an assassin, waiting in the shadows. Helgira, however, remained oblivious to Iolanthe's presence, her breaths emerging in a series of trembling sighs and gasps. "An Angel . . . I have been blessed. I have been blessed."

She was probably in a bout of religious mania. But out of curiosity, Iolanthe used a far-seeing spell to look out the window.

The soles of her feet prickled. A phantom behemoth. No wonder

Helgira was dazed. In every chapel and cathedral Iolanthe had ever visited, they had been painted on the ceiling, the steeds of the Angels.

But wait. There was a wyvern, a few miles closer to her, and it carried a rider. She redoubled the far-seeing spell. The rider's features were still too faint, but she recognized the gray hooded tunic that Princess Ariadne had specified in her vision.

Titus.

It took Titus a moment to remember that he had directed the mind-ruining spell at the Inquisitor while the latter had been under the time-freeze spell. Mages under time-freeze spells were safe from the vast majority of assaults. Little wonder then the Inquisitor was well enough to accompany her master on his pursuit of Titus.

He urged his wyvern to fly even faster, wishing he had brought a pair of goggles. His eyes burned from the relentless wind, his ears ached.

The next second the ache turned into agony, as if someone had threaded a needle between his ears. He screamed. Then he felt it, a sensation like a finger poking inside his head, rubbing against the ridges and folds of his brain.

Was this what the Bane and the Inquisitor had been talking about, a more subtle way to use the Inquisitor's talents? It was obscene.

That she was able to do it from several miles behind him frightened him. Her health hadn't been the only thing improved by her trip to Atlantis. Her powers, too.

He could guess what she wanted. For the moment, not secrets buried deep, only his identity, since they could not see his face. But once she had it, what would prevent her from going deeper right then and squeezing everything out of him?

It was now or never.

He double-tapped his wand, unsheathing it—he had not lied about the fact that it was indeed a blade wand. Then, wrapping his sleeve around the wand so the light from the crowns could not be seen, he turned around, his other hand holding the hood shut below his eyes.

The spells left his lips like a paean to the Angels, syllables cascading with a deadly beauty. Such spells were of no use at all in close range, like trying to fell someone with a feather. But as he straightened his arm and aimed, the puff that left his wand would gather strength and momentum, until it became an unstoppable force, all the more lethal for its invisibility.

He wrapped his arms around the wyvern's neck. In the nick of time—a fresh turbulence tossed the beast upside down. It shrieked. Titus hung on, but only barely, his fingers slipping from the smooth scales. The wyvern fell for an eternity before it righted itself, the two of them both shaking with fright.

A tornado materialized directly in his path.

This was not natural weather. An incredibly powerful elemental mage was at work.

The Bane.

Why had Titus not known that the Bane was an elemental mage himself?

He yanked the wyvern to the left just as a second tornado appeared, also to the left. He swore. Urging the wyvern to the right, he narrowly fitted them between the two tornadoes, ducking as a chunk of debris hurtled by mere inches from his head.

Fairfax might someday be the greatest elemental mage in the world, but today that title belonged to the Bane, who delighted in toying with him.

The finger poking inside his head abruptly disappeared. He peered over his shoulder and deployed a new far-seeing spell, just in time to see the Inquisitor topple from her giant peregrine.

The Bane's mouth rounded with a scream. The Inquisitor's body stopped falling and rose instead, all the way into the Bane's arms. And then it disappeared.

*What if you die while you are using the Crucible as a portal? Would your body not rot inside, since you can't get out?* he'd once asked Hesperia in the teaching cantos. *The Crucible keeps no dead,* Hesperia had replied. *It will expel the body.*

His mother's vision had proved true again. In the library at the Citadel, Atlantean soldiers would surround their superior's corpse while Alectus and Lady Callista spoke words of shock concerning her death.

He had done it. He had killed the Inquisitor after all. He

straightened, relief and nausea rising within him, entwined. He did not know whether to cry or to vomit.

A hissing, crackling rumble behind him, however, made him forget both. He wrenched the wyvern higher and barely avoided a trail of fire as broad as a highway.

The phantom behemoth was still half a mile behind him. No real dragon spewed its fire so far, so fast. But that was the advantage of mythological creatures: they were a law unto themselves.

Fire fell like a meteor storm. The grassland below burned. Rising smoke racked him with coughs and made his eyes water. It was only by his sense of hearing that he dodged the next tornado; and only by the hair standing on the back of his neck that he somehow evaded a quieter tongue of flame that had stolen upon him.

In front and to either side, walls of tornadoes towered, howling with violence. Behind him bellowed a mountain of fire, so much of it, as if a portion of the sun had been torn loose.

Was this it—fire, smoke, and dragons? Would he fall to his end, as his mother had foreseen?

He had done what he needed to do. He had lived long enough.

*Be safe, Fairfax. Live forever.*

The fire the phantom behemoth breathed! The mass was staggering. The beauty. The splendor. As a lover of fire, Iolanthe had never seen finer. That was, until she realized the fire was directed at Titus, her Titus. His wyvern weaved between the raging torrents, clinging to safety by a hairbreadth.

Helgira sank to her knees. "The will of the Angels is a joy to behold," she murmured.

*You mud-eating primitive! That is no Angel; that is Atlantis.*

Iolanthe said nothing; she only lifted her wand to render Helgira unconscious.

*I will not let you die. Not while I have a breath left.*

Huge tornadoes reared like a cliff, obscuring her view of him. The phantom behemoth emitted a roar that made windowpanes rattle, then spewed forth fire enough to melt Purple Mountain.

She strode onto the terrace outside Helgira's bedchamber and raised her hands. All the power that had been building inside her raced toward her fingertips.


The fire would irreparably damage the wyvern's wings, leading to certain death. The tornadoes? Almost certain death, but people had been known to survive tornadoes.

Titus urged the wyvern forward. Perhaps they'd find a gap.

Or perhaps not: the tornadoes formed an unbroken barrier.

And then the barrier was no longer so unbroken. One tornado weakened, then dissipated altogether, leaving a cloud of falling debris.

He wheeled the wyvern toward the gap.

No, they were not going to make it before the gap closed.

A tailwind—so freakishly strong it almost sheared him off the wyvern's back—*threw* them through the gap.

Another elemental mage was at work.

Helgira.

He reapplied the far-seeing spell. There she was, in her long white dress, standing on the terrace atop her fort, her black hair whipping in the wind. In the light from the fort's torches, she resembled Fairfax exactly.

He urged the wyvern toward her.

The air whistled. Boulders the size of houses flew at him. They must already be in the foothills of the Purple Mountain, not too far to go.

But the boulders were relentless, a storm coming from all sides. He steered the wyvern blindly, relying more on intuition than sight.

*I'm so close. Help me!*

Something struck the wyvern on the head, a smaller rock, but enough to send it plunging, and he with it.


*I won't let you fall.*

She did not. She held the wyvern aloft and propelled it with a tailwind the Angels would be pleased to have breathed.

As for the phantom behemoth and the would-be murderer who sat upon it—enough was enough.

She raised her hand toward the overcast sky. The clouds crackled with electric charge. Blue flashes leaped from cloud to cloud. From the farthest horizon, lines of energy rushed toward Purple

Mountain, meeting at the zenith of the sky, seething, roiling.

Waiting for her.

She pointed her finger at the phantom behemoth.

Down the lightning came, beyond beautiful, beyond powerful.[23]

All the boulders in the air fell. The phantom behemoth fell, striking the ground with a force that jolted her entire person.

After another minute, the hardy little wyvern regained consciousness and, finding itself still airborne, began to flap its wings again.

Titus landed on Helgira's terrace, kissed the wyvern on its scaly neck, and dismounted. Helgira, panting, regarded him with both tenderness and fury. All at once he knew she was not Helgira, but Fairfax. She had come, his most stalwart friend, and she had saved him.

He closed the distance between them and wrapped his arms around her. "Thank you. Thank you. Thank you. I thought this was the night the prophecy came true."

"No, not tonight." One of her hands was in his hair, the other tracing his jaw. "Not ever, if I can help it. But not tonight, at least."

He could not begin to describe the sensation of being alive, being safe, and being here, with *her*.

His lips hovered barely an inch above hers. Their breaths mingled.

"Love will make you weak and indecisive, remember?" she murmured.

What a fool he had been. For a journey like theirs, love was the only thing that would make him strong enough.

"Do not ever listen to an idiot like me," he answered.

"Well," she said, "I guess it doesn't count if it happens in the Crucible."

With that, she pulled him to her and kissed him. Tears stung the back of his eyes. He had survived. *They* had survived. He held tightly on to her, on to life itself.

Titus would have liked to remain forever—or at least another minute—in this state of euphoric closeness. But with a sigh, Fairfax let go of him. "I've got boys running all over Eton to cover our tracks. I need to get them back to bed."

Titus made sure he left behind Helgira's cuff. And just to be careful, after they returned to the Black Bastion in his copy of the Crucible, he sealed the portal: he still preferred to err on the side of caution, even in the midst of risking his life.

In this fort, where he had caused such a ruckus, there was consternation at his reappearance, followed by flabbergasted looks as Fairfax climbed onto a wyvern behind him. But that was the advantage of being mistaken for the lightning-wielding mistress of Black Bastion: she did not need to explain herself to anyone.

Even better, as the wyvern took to the air, she wrapped her arms about him and laid her head on his shoulder.

Was this what happiness felt like?

She recounted how she had managed to pass before the Inquisitor unscathed, and that Kashkari had been "the scorpion." He told her what he had seen and heard in the Citadel, including Horatio Haywood's mysterious disappearance.

"Thank you," she said, banding her arms tighter around him.

"What for?"

"For being willing to rescue my guardian."

"Now we no longer know where he is."

"We'll find out," she said, her voice scratchy with fatigue. She ruffled his hair. "And you—you are all right with having killed the Inquisitor?"

"I would rather someone else had taken her life. But I will not miss her."

They dismounted on the meadow before Sleeping Beauty's castle. She shed the wig and the gown she had borrowed and turned once again into a lithe, cocky boy.

He drew her to him and rested his cheek against her hair. "Is it true that if it happens in the Crucible, it does not count?"

She held him tight. "My rescue, my rules."

He kissed the shell of her ear. "Then let me tell you this: I live for you, and you alone."

CHAPTER ♦ 25

Kashkari had followed Fairfax's directions beautifully. He had tied, blindfolded, and gagged Trumper and Hogg with strips of their own clothes. Then, once they had regained consciousness, he had thrown a barrage of German at them, as Fairfax had asked, in order to make them think that he was Titus, generally known to be a native speaker of German.

When Fairfax and Titus arrived on the scene, he shook their hands and then left with Fairfax to join the other boys. Titus did the same after rendering Trumper and Hogg unconscious again and dropping them on the front steps of their house, stripped to their drawers.

All the boys stood together and admired his handiwork. Now that their night's task—and fun—was done, they started back for their own beds, yawning. At Mrs. Dawlish's, the front door was open, the downstairs lights on, and Mrs. Dawlish and Mrs. Hancock both waiting. Mrs. Dawlish wearily waved them up. "Go to bed now. We'll deal with the lot of you tomorrow."

"Except you, Your Highness," said Mrs. Hancock. "Would you mind coming with me to my office?"

Fairfax stepped in front of him. "We all went. The prince shouldn't be singled out."

Titus briefly rested his hand on her shoulder. "Go. I will be fine."

In Mrs. Hancock's office, it was Baslan's spectral projection again, pacing into shelves and walls.

"You may leave us," Baslan said to Mrs. Hancock.

"I would like to remind you, sir, that I am a special envoy of the Department of Overseas Administration, not your subordinate," Mrs. Hancock said, smiling.

Baslan gave Mrs. Hancock a cold stare.

Titus plunked himself down on Mrs. Hancock's best chair. He enjoyed squabbles between agents of Atlantis. "What do you want this time, Baslan?"

"You will address me as Inquisitor, Your Highness."

Inquisitor. So Titus's nemesis was truly dead. He gave his stomach a moment to settle. "Inquisitor, Baslan? Is everybody at the Inquisitory called the Inquisitor these days?"

Baslan flinched at Titus's suggestion. "Madam Inquisitor can no longer carry out her duties. She has departed this earth."

Titus found that he did not need to pretend to be shocked. He was shocked, still. "It cannot be true. I last saw her only hours ago. Right here at Eton. She showed no signs of imminent death."

"To our lasting regret, it is quite true."

"How did it happen?"

"That is strictly private. I need Your Highness to give an account of your whereabouts tonight."

"And that is not strictly private?"

"No," said Baslan without any sense of irony.

Titus crossed his arms before his chest. "After your lot finally let me go in the evening, I retreated to my room to enjoy a little peace and quiet. I was there until lights-out. Not long after lights-out, two boys threw a rock into my window. I chased them down, gave them what for, and dragged them to the front door of their house."

"Are there corroborating eyewitnesses?"

The question was for Mrs. Hancock. "The prince was in his room at lights-out—I knocked myself. Both the prince and his neighbor's windows were broken. As for the rest, I will go check right now."

"And you will confiscate all the prince's books," ordered Baslan.

Mrs. Hancock rolled her eyes but did not remind him again about their separate jurisdictions.

Titus exhaled. A very good thing that Fairfax had his mother's diary. And that he had stowed his copy of the Crucible, disguised as a volume of devotional poetry in medieval French, at the school library, until he could move it to the laboratory.

Baslan held up the Citadel's copy of the Crucible. "What do you know about this book?"

"Oh, that. I play Big Bad Wolf to Little Red Riding Hood. She likes it rough, did you know? I did not."

"I beg your pardon?"

"What else are you going to do with such a contraption? Of course Sleeping Beauty is probably prettier, but I am not going to fight dragons for any girl. And the chit who lives in the woods is agreeable enough, but those dwarfs in her cottage are perverts. They always want to watch."

Baslan's face turned splotchy. "Did you use such a book as a portal to get into the Citadel tonight and make away with Horatio Haywood?"

Titus laughed. "Listen to yourself, Baslan. Are you mad?"

Baslan's throat worked. "As you are no doubt aware, Atlantis is seeking a young woman who can summon lightning. We encountered her tonight."

"Why did you not take her into custody?"

"She was in this book. We want to know where she is now."

"Still in there, obviously. Have you never heard of Helgira?"

"Who?"

Titus rolled his eyes. "Helgira the Merciless, one of the most famous mythological, folkloric characters known to magekind. Oh, I forgot, Atlanteans do not know anything."

Baslan clenched his teeth. "Atlanteans are not ignorant, but we do not pay attention to stories of lesser lands."

"Well, then, how did you enjoy your encounter with Helgira?"

Baslan fumed, but had nothing else to ask Titus. Mrs. Hancock returned shortly with Trumper and Hogg, still mostly naked.

There followed a scene of great comedy, at least to Titus. Trumper and Hogg, half-frightened, half-opportunistic, neither quite noticing they were speaking to a phantom projection, accused Titus of not only abduction, but of innumerable acts of violence and perverse cruelty on their persons, and therefore providing incontrovertible evidence that if anyone had killed the Inquisitor, it could not have been Titus.

Mrs. Hancock returned once more, carrying an armload of books. "I have His Highness's collection here, Inquisitor. Will you send a courier for them or shall I?"

Titus rose. "I will leave you two to discuss details. Good night, Inquisitor. Good night, Mrs. Hancock. And good night, Messrs. Trumper and Hogg—it was my *pleasure*."

The no-vaulting zone was gone in the morning. And when the prince's spymaster returned, reports flew out of the writing ball.

The Inquisitor was indeed dead. As was, apparently, the Bane—though no intelligence on whether he had been killed outright by Iolanthe's lightning or by the subsequent fall. The double deaths caused both panic and rejoicing in the Citadel—which turned into ashen fear a short while later, as the Bane walked back into the Citadel looking younger and more vibrant for having been resurrected a third time.

Inquisitory personnel initially accused Lady Callista of tampering with evidence—the blood that came out of the Crucible had all been cleared away by the time they'd arrived. But she'd wept over how awful the blood looked on the floor, and all of a sudden everyone agreed that of course she had every right to keep her own home free of such upsetting sights.

The news that mattered most to Iolanthe, however, concerned the punishments that were to be meted out to the boys who'd left Mrs. Dawlish's home that night: twenty lashes to Titus, five each to everyone else. What if she'd be required, as she'd heard rumored sometimes, to lower her trousers in the course of the punishment? She'd lasted this long; she did not want to be found out as a girl for such a silly reason.

But Titus came out of his punishment smiling. Birmingham not only didn't require the removal of trousers, he didn't even hit Titus—the lashes were given to a rug instead. In addition, Birmingham congratulated him warmly on making Trumper and Hogg into laughingstocks before the whole school.

Still Iolanthe practiced her memory and confusion charms. But her time with Birmingham turned out to be very pleasant. They had a cup of tea together and a lively chat on Homerian epics—something near and dear to Birmingham's heart.

The rest of the term passed just as agreeably. The house cricket team did not win the school cup, but it contended for the first time in years. Wintervale made the roster for the school match against Harrow, which thrilled the entire house. Iolanthe, to the prince's head-shaking amazement, won ten quid for writing the best Latin essay in the entire school. She promptly spent the money on ices and fancy cakes for everyone—and a very nice monogrammed shaving set for Kashkari, toward which the prince chipped in half of the cost.

The last Sunday before the end of Summer Half, Kashkari finally organized the tennis tournament he had been talking about for a while, in honor of Birmingham and a few other senior boys who were leaving to attend university.

There was one trophy for the junior boys and another for the senior boys. A group of Iolanthe's friends watched the junior boys from her room. When it was time for the senior boys to compete, they left en masse, eager to defeat one another.

The prince was the last person remaining.

She tilted her head at the door. "Shall we?"

He closed the door and took out a plate from her cabinet. *"Flamma nigra,"* he said. A black flame crackled into being.

"What's this?"

"Give me your hand."

He plunged their combined hands into the black flame. The flame was the temperature of a sun-heated stone, licking at her skin with the playfulness of a puppy. After a few seconds it turned purple, then deep blue, then sky blue, then the pale blue of a vein seen through the skin. At last it turned transparent and dissipated.

She stared at her hand, then at him. "That was—that was the blood oath?"

He lowered his head, almost as if he were feeling shy. "Yes. You are free."

"Do you understand what you have done?" she asked, her voice unsteady.

"How can I not? I have been thinking of nothing else for weeks. The enormity of it is still beyond my understanding."

"Then why? Is it because we had made one attempt on the Bane's life?"

That had been the terms of their agreement, *one and only one attempt*. But surely that didn't count, since the Bane did not remain dead.

"That was part of it."

"What's the rest of it?"

He hesitated briefly. "The choice was made for me. I was never asked whether I was willing to walk this path. I do not want to take that choice from you—friends do not enslave friends. You should decide for yourself."

Her eyes prickled with the beginning of tears. "What if I decide to take off on my own?"

He looked down for a moment. When he looked back again at her, this boy who had told her that he lived for her and her alone, his gaze was not without fear, but also not without hope. "That is your right."

Below, boys were calling their names. Like a sleepwalker, she drifted to her open window. "We'll be down this minute."

Outside, everything looked the same, summer sky, summer grass, summer boys. Yet everything was different. Her life was her own once again, to do as she willed.

She turned around to the boy who had just become her truest friend in the world. "Do I need to decide now?"

"No," he said. "Take your time."

"Come on, Fairfax. You too, prince," shouted Wintervale. "We are waiting for you to draw lots."

"Coming!" she shouted back. Then, more softly, "We'd better go play some tennis."

At the door, he laid a hand on her shoulder. "No matter what you decide, knowing you has been the greatest privilege of my life."

She closed her own hand over his and blinked back tears. "Likewise, prince."

"And just so you know, I am going to annihilate you at tennis."

She laughed even as she wiped at her eyes. "You can try, Your Highness. You can always try."

## ✦ EPILOGUE

TITUS WAITED.

Cape Wrath was beautiful this time of the year. The sun shone bright enough to turn the sea from its usual moody gray into a deep, dark blue. A few sheep, their biscuit-colored wool still short after the spring shearing, grazed on the green headland. The lighthouse glistened, white and serene.

But he was no longer capable of appreciating the loveliness of his surroundings.

She was late.

She had left school two days before he did. She knew the exact hour she must meet him here, at the only remaining entrance to his laboratory. It was now past that time.

If he did not leave now, he would miss his train.

He continued to wait, a black pain strangling his heart. He could no longer imagine life without her.

They had perhaps thirty seconds left.

Twenty.

Fifteen.

Ten.

"Sorry! Sorry! Don't go without me!"

It was her, valise in hand, hurtling toward him. His heart almost bursting with joy, he grabbed her hand. They sprinted together toward the lighthouse.

Explanations spilled from her. The train from Edinburgh to Inverness had been delayed en route because a section of the tracks had been covered by a small-scale landslide. She, the great elemental mage of their era, who could now move tons of soil at a snap of her fingers, had to remain in her seat while railroad workers cleared the tracks with shovels. Shovels!

But all he heard was poetry, verses of hope and friendship and courage and everything else that made life worth living. She was here. She was here. *She was here.*

She panted with exertion. "And I couldn't leave the train, since I had to get within a hundred miles of Cape Wrath before I could vault. More than that on my own in a day might kill me."

"You cannot vault a hundred miles at a go."

"I split the distance into four segments, and did some blind vaulting in the middle."

He pushed open the door to the laboratory and thrust the potions at her. He was turning her into a tiny turtle this time—just in case anyone still wanted to confiscate his canary. "Blind vaulting, are you mad?"

She threw aside her valise and gulped down the potions. "Of course I am. I am here, am I not?"

He was choked up. "I am—I am glad you are here."

She smiled at him. "Ready?"

Perhaps she was only asking him whether he was ready for her to transform. But when he answered, he answered for all the possible futures that awaited them.

"Yes," he said. "I am ready."

1. (p. 5) FOR CENTURIES, historians and magical theorists have debated the correlation between the rise of subtle magic and the decline of elemental magic. Were they merely parallel developments or did one cause the other? An agreement may never come, but we do know that the decline has affected not only the number of elemental mages—from approximately 3 percent of the mage population to less than 1 percent—but also the power each individual elemental mage wields over the elements.

Presently, quarry workers still regularly lift 20-ton blocks of stone, the record of the decade being 135 tons by a single mage. But most elemental mages make few uses of their dwindling powers and are capable of little more than parlor tricks; all the more astonishing as we look back upon the great elemental mages of an earlier age, those individuals who set mountains in perpetual motion and destroyed—and created—entire realms.

—From *The Lives and Deeds of Great Elemental Mages*

2. (p. 35) THE DOMAIN'S classification as a principality rather than a kingdom has often confused mages. It is certainly not a microrealm: at more than one hundred thousand square miles in area, it is one of the largest mage realms on Earth—and historically, one of the most influential.

Legend has it that the night before his coronation, Titus the Great, the unifier of the Domain, had a dream in which a voice cried, "The King is dead and his house fallen!" To avoid that fate, he had himself crowned Master of the Realm, styled His Serene Highness, a prince instead of a king. The ruse worked: He lived to a ripe old age, and his house has endured. Today, when most other monarchs and princes are figureheads without actual power, the House of Elberon remains that rare phenomenon among mage realms: a ruling dynasty.

—From *The Domain: A Guide to Its History and Customs*

3. (p. 47) THE SEPARATION of mage and nonmage populations has never been absolute, on account of vestigial mage communities that either opted not to join a larger mage society or subsequently left.

The nonmages, with their burgeoning advances in science and technology, may someday pose a threat to magekind. But throughout history, the greatest menace to mages has always been other mages. Never was a successful witch hunt mounted without the cooperation of mages willing to turn on their own. For that reason, mages who dwell among nonmages are subject to the strictest regulations.

The Exiles from the January Uprising presented a curious

scenario. By the time the revolt had been quelled, there were no other mage realms to which its sympathizers could flee: Atlantis was the master of the entire mage world. So they chose instead to live among nonmages and to plot their return therein.

—From *A Chronological Survey of the Last Great Rebellion*

4. (p. 49) THESE DAYS, the term "beauty witch" has become quite diluted.

On one hand, the leading ladies of stage and fashion are sometimes referred to as beauty witches. On the other hand, it has also become a euphemism for prostitutes, much to the annoyance of real beauty witches who consider themselves far above such common strumpets.

For the purposes of this book, we shall cleave to the classic definition of "beauty witch": a woman of great beauty and elegant taste who is well versed in music, literature, and art and who can converse intelligently on most topics under the sun. She may or may not depend economically on the generosity of a protector, but she has no profession other than that of her personal attractions.

—From *Sublime Loveliness:*
*The Seven Most Celebrated Beauty Witches of All Time*

5. (p. 62) SOON AFTER the advent of vaulting, mages realized that this revolutionary new means of travel presented a serious problem to the security of public institutions and private households alike. A mage who has seen the interior of a building can vault back into it anytime,

which quite defeats the purpose of having walls in the first place.

A series of ingenious—and sometimes laughable—solutions came into being. Who can forget the Nevor-Same™ Home, which changed the colors of a house's walls and furnishings after every visitor? Randomly, one might add, leading to some of the ugliest interiors ever to assault a mage's eyes.

Nowadays we enjoy advanced and discreet spells to protect our dwellings from ill-intentioned vaulters. The spells listed in this section, when implemented properly, are guaranteed to repel any unauthorized attempt to vault into your home.*

*None of these spells, singly or in combination, work when a quasi-vaulter is involved. Therefore we are terribly glad that quasi-vaulters have become virtually impossible to find.

—From *Advice to the Novice Householder*

6. (p. 81) NEW ATLANTIS'S rise as a dominant mage power was, in many ways, a surprising event. The island, while big—nearly twice the size of the Domain—is ill-suited to large-scale civilization. The volcanic frenzy behind its creation was too recent, its interior too steep and angular. Much of the ground is basalt, arduous to walk upon, impossible to cultivate. Sea life, astonishingly abundant when mages first set foot on the island, came dangerously close to irreversible depletion at several points in its eight-hundred-year history.

Two hundred of these eight hundred years, in fact, were known as the Famine Centuries. The isolation of the island, the relative primitiveness of long-distance transportation of the era, and widespread corruption among members of the royal clan made aid campaigns mounted by other mage realms largely ineffectual. At the end of the Famine Centuries, population on the island had plunged by at least 70 percent.

The Bane is believed to have been born during the last decade of the Famine Centuries, into a devastated, lawless society. Whether he would have still become the single most influential mage on earth had he come of age in a more prosperous realm, we can only speculate. But there is no doubt that the chaos and deprivations of his youth influenced his desire for order and control throughout his career.

—From *Empire: The Rise of New Atlantis*

7. (p. 86) MAGELINGS WITH elemental powers present additional challenges to parents and caregivers; there is no disputing that. Most young children give in to temper tantrums at least once in a while. But a toddler elemental mage in a screaming fit is liable to shift a house from its foundation or choke the air from a playmate's lungs—without ever meaning to. And even when elemental magelings grow older, they might still inadvertently let their powers get the better of them.

In this chapter we aim to present a comprehensive list of training techniques for disrupting the direct connection between an elemental mageling's anger and his or her instincts to turn to the elements. It has been repeatedly pointed out that violence is hardly the best substitute, but until we learn how to perfectly control small children's emotions, their tiny fists will remain preferable to their—at times—disproportionally immense powers.

—From *The Care and Feeding of Your Elemental Mageling*

8. (p. 87) A QUICK word on countersigns before we move on to our first section of spells.

The spells in this and many other textbooks do not have countersigns. But no one ever became archmage using spells that can be found in public libraries. Heirloom spells and cutting-edge spells, considered far more powerful, usually operated with an incantation that can be said aloud—and therefore overheard by others—and a countersign that is never uttered, to preserve the secrecy of the spell.

By the same token, countersigns are also sometimes used with passwords, to maximize the latter's effectiveness and security.

—From *The Art and Science of Magic: A Primer*

9. (p. 92) IT TOOK more than fifty years after vaulting was first achieved for the general mage population to accept that vaulting is not a universal ability. Until then, it was believed that with earlier and better training, and an ever-burgeoning collection of vaulting aids, every mage could be taught to vault. Nervous parents regularly enrolled children as young as three in vaulting classes, for fear that should the tots start any later, they would grow up to be *emus*—flightless birds—disdained by their peers. Medical

literature of the day recorded multiple instances of dangerously premature labor, brought on by expectant mothers hitching too many vaults in misguided attempts to inculcate the process in the minds of their gestating babies.

But before society at large could accept that vaulting was not possible for every mage, it had to first accept that mages who could vault often did not vault very far. In the heady early years of vaulting, mages were convinced that their vaulting range would continue to improve, as long as they continued to practice. When these pioneers began to be thwarted by personal limits, they attributed it to late starts, incorrect training, and a flawed understanding of the principles of vaulting—and encouraged the next generation to push harder and more astutely.

The best data currently available suggests that between 75 to 80 percent of adult mages are capable of vaulting. Of those, more than 90 percent have a one-time vaulting range of less than fifteen miles. Only a quarter can tolerate consecutive vaults; the rest must wait at least twelve hours between vaults.

Moreover, it is now known that vaulting exacerbates pre-existing medical conditions. Expectant mothers, the infirmed, the elderly, and those recovering from serious illness should refrain from vaulting. In rare instances, vaulting has been known to cause grave consequences in otherwise healthy individuals.

—From *The Mage's Household Guide to Health and Wellness*

10. (p. 96) DO YOU need a wand? The short answer is no, you do not. The working of a spell requires only intent and action, and it has been conclusively proven that mouthing or speaking the words of a spell constitutes action.

Why then do we still use wands? One reason is heritage: We have wielded wands for so long, it seems almost rude to stop. Another is habit: Mages are accustomed and attached to their wands. But more practically, the wand acts as an amplifier. Spells are more powerful and more effective when performed with a wand—reason enough to find one that fits well in your hand.

—From *The Art and Science of Magic: A Primer*


11. (p. 105) NOT MUCH will be said of otherwise charms here, given that they are both too advanced for the scope of this book and, more importantly, illegal.

Love philters are often mistakenly pronounced as the best known examples of otherwise magic. The effects of love philters, however violent, are temporary. The effects of true otherwise charms, on the other hand, are semipermanent to permanent. And they seek not to alter emotions and short-term behaviors, but perceived facts. In other words, they are campaigns of misinformation.

Fortunately, it is not easy to implement otherwise spells. If Mr. Stickyfingers is a known thief, no otherwise spell will change that perception. Nor will otherwise magic help someone already suspected of lying. Otherwise spells are only effective when (1) the intended audience is entirely unwary and (2) the misinformation disseminated does not run counter to established facts.

—From *The Art and Science of Magic: A Primer*

12. (p. 121) LAST WEEK'S confirmation by the Citadel that Princess Ariadne is indeed expecting her first child ended months of speculation—and raised even more questions.

The decree governing succession to the crown specifies only that an inheritor should be a firstborn child of the lineage of Titus the Great. No mention is made of legitimacy.

With a few notable exceptions, most princely bastards have refrained from staking a claim to the throne. But the *Observer*'s sources believe that Princess Ariadne intends to declare her firstborn an heir of the House of Elberon.

The declaration, should it come, would not be challenged on grounds of legality. But most mages surveyed by the *Delamer Observer* are of the opinion that they deserve to know the paternity of a future ruling prince or princess. The princess's steadfast refusal to name the father of her child has damaged her erstwhile pristine reputation. Rumors brew and froth, many casting doubt on both the princess's character and her fitness to rule.

—From "The Princess's Hurdle," *The Delamer Observer*,
8 June, Year of the Domain 1014

13. (p. 133) THE FOLLOWING is a reproduction of a January Uprising-era underground pamphlet.

*We have ill news from our friends on the Subcontinent. The offensive in the Hindu Kush has failed catastrophically. Survivors report of Atlantean aerial vehicles of a type never before seen, armored and enclosed chariots that repel every known assault spell.*

*To make matters a hundred times worse, the armored chariots spray a deadly potion in their wake. The potion is clear and odorless. Many of the resistance fighters on the ground first believed it to be natural precipitation and believed the demise of their colleagues to be casualties of battle. But afterward, when massive civilian deaths were tallied in the armored chariots' flight paths, our friends had no choice but to conclude that Atlantis had unveiled a terrifying new weapon, death rain.*

—From *A Chronological Survey of the Last Great Rebellion*

14. (p. 143) IT CANNOT be stressed enough that blood magic is not the same as sacrificial magic. Sacrificial magic, needless to say, has always been taboo in mage realms. Mages who choose to break the taboo usually do so among nonmages, manipulating local religious rituals to suit their own ends.

Blood magic does not require the taking of lives or the severing of body parts. Furthermore, its spells, contrary to popular belief, do not drain the body. Only a very minute amount of blood is needed

to power a spell, and that blood must come from willing participants. Forcibly spilled blood neither keeps secrets nor binds anyone
in oaths.

—From The Art and Science of Magic: A Primer

15. (p. 168) IT BEARS remembering that advances in magic do
not always follow a linear progression: Some developments com-
monly regarded as modern are but recent rediscoveries of what
had come before. Court physicians for the rulers of Mesopotamia,
for example, had formulated entire classes of prophylactic spells.
The spells were eventually lost to war, fire, and other ravages
of Fortune, but records survived to attest to their miraculous
effectiveness.

To consider a more current example, magical historians have
argued for years that the venture-book, perhaps the most successful
magical application in a generation, is but a commercial adapta-
tion of devices that had been employed for centuries by the House
of Elberon to instruct and train its young heirs, especially in times
of adversity. Newly unveiled documents concerning the Last Great
Rebellion seem to indicate that Prince Titus VII indeed had at his
disposal devices that performed many of the functions of present-
day venture-books, except better.

—From "Everything Old is New Again," The Delamer Observer,<br>2 December, Year of the Domain 1151

16. (p. 216) THE COALITION for Safer Magic and the League of Sensible Parenting—henceforth referred to as the undersigned—hereby petition the Ministry of Education to remove all mentions of mage-to-animal transmogrification from textbooks intended for primary and secondary educational establishments.

Each year, dozens of young magelings, piqued by the allusion in these textbooks, attempt such transmogrifications. They concoct dreadful, frequently toxic potions, misapply spells, and cause fires and explosions at home and at school—not to mention harm to their persons. In this past winter alone, there has been a mageling unable to breathe normally from having grown gills; another turned nearly blind after acquiring bat vision; and a third who lost all his hair by molting. That the cases have been reversible do not mitigate their severity.

—From Petition No. 4391, lodged with
the Ministry of Education, 21 April, Year of the Domain 1029


17. (p. 224) THE BANE'S public embrace of mind mages marked a watershed event in his ascendance. Until then, mind mages, even those valued as tools of torture and extraction, had always been kept out of view, not acknowledged and certainly never honored.

But the Bane brought them out into the open and gave them some of the highest offices of his empire. And not just those of Atlantean birth but mind mages from many realms, in the secure knowledge that their first loyalty would always be to him, who elevated them to positions of trust and distinction, and not to the native realms that had treated them with fear and loathing.

—From A Chronological Survey of the Last Great Rebellion

18. (p. 264) THE POWER of a potent mind mage is often compared to that of a drill, boring through the skull to reach its quarry. But the truth is slightly more complex. In a probe, the mind of a mind mage, though dominant, is in a sense as exposed as the mind of its prey, as vulnerable as it is devastating.

—From The Art and Science of Magic: A Primer

19. (p. 288) AS ANYONE who had read a story of misunderstanding knows, overhearing part of a conversation, without the proper context, can lead to devastatingly mistaken conclusions.

For that reason, among seers, those who see future in long, unbroken stretches are considered far more gifted than those to whom only quick flashes are revealed, as short, chaotic glimpses are much more prone to misinterpretation, if they can be deciphered at all.

Even rarer are seers who can view the same set of future events repeatedly, allow them to notice greater texture and details with each iteration. Such visions become the most unambiguous signposts along the otherwise unpredictably swerving road that is the forward progress of time.

—From When Will It Rain and How Much:<br>Visions Both Luminous and Ordinary

20. (p. 301) IT IS difficult to predict how powerful a child elemental mage will become. A toddler elemental mageling who can shift the foundation of a house in a rage may be able to lift no more than a quarter-ton block of stone as an adult.

Sometimes the reverse is true. An elemental mage who can move no more than a quarter-ton block of stone under normal circumstances may very well manage to lift something twenty times heavier when his or her life depends on it.

—From *The Lives and Deeds of Great Elemental Mages*


21. (p. 356) THE WYVERN is the rare carnivore that consents to being domesticated. But wyverns born in captivity tend to be slower and less ferocious. This is fine for mages who wish to keep wyverns as pets, but unsatisfactory for mages who race wyverns or for those looking for a fierce guard dragon.

Wyverns born and raised in the wild and subsequently tamed are, therefore, far more desirable. It has become the established practice of stable masters to sneak eggs from their prized wyverns into the aeries of feral wyverns, then later track down the juvenile wyverns at a stage just short of maturity to tame and bring back into the fold.

—From *The Dragon Watcher's Field Guide*


22. (p. 378) THE ESTABLISHMENT of a permanent no-vaulting zone requires a heavy initial investment of time—it cannot be hurried.

The setting up of a temporary no-vaulting zone, however, requires not time, but labor.

A few friends on a camping trip can manage a temporary no-vaulting zone around their tent in about an hour. A few dozen friends can do the same for a small public park, to have themselves a party—provided they first secure the permits, of course. Armies, with their much larger number of mages on hand, have been known to turn small cities into temporary no-vaulting zones overnight.

—From *The Art and Science of Magic: A Primer*

23. (p. 435) THE GOLDEN age of elemental magic is generally considered to have ended nearly a millennium ago with the passing of Leopold Sidorov and Manami Kaneshiro, who spent their careers in a virulent rivalry and died in a duel that killed both, along with a number of unfortunate spectators.

Hundreds of years went by without the next truly great elemental mage coming along. It had become accepted wisdom that another one would never be witnessed when Hesperia the Magnificent came into her powers, one of the greatest among the great.

It rather gives us hope that we might yet see an immensely formidable elemental mage in our lifetime.

—From *The Lives and Deeds of Great Elemental Mages*

# ♦ ACKNOWLEDGMENTS

Kristin Nelson, for the six drafts we went through together.

Donna Bray, for knowing the way to perfection. It's a destination that one never reaches, but I had no doubt she set me on the right path.

Everyone at Balzer + Bray, for their incredible dedication and expertise.

Colin Anderson, for the smashing cover art.

Erin Fitzsimmons, for the genius art direction.

Janine Ballard, for the invaluable read.

Flannery Keenan, for her honest opinion.

Dr. Margaret Toscano, for the fantastic Latin spells.

Maili Ryan, for her peerless fact-checking skills.

Ivy Adams, for all the laughter.

My family, for giving me both the support and the space I need. A special thank-you to my firstborn, the most unwavering champion anyone could ask for—and a pretty darn good fanboy besides.

And if you are reading this, thank you. Thank you from the bottom of my heart.

Turn the page for an excerpt from

# THE PERILOUS SEA

BOOK TWO

IN THE

ELEMENTAL TRILOGY

# CHAPTER • 1

THE GIRL CAME TO WITH a start.

She was being pelted with sand. Sand was everywhere. Beneath, her fingers dug into it, hot and gritty. Above, wind-whipped sand blocked the sky, turning the air as red as the surface of Mars.

A sandstorm.

She sat up. Sand swirled all about her, millions of sepia particles. By reflex she pushed at them, willing them to stay away from her eyes.

The sand stayed away.

She blinked—and made another pushing motion with her hand. The flying particles receded farther from her person. The sandstorm itself showed no signs of abating. In fact, it was worsening, the sky becoming ominously dark.

She had power over sand.

In a sandstorm, it was much better to be an elemental mage than otherwise. Yet there was something disconcerting about the discovery:

the fact that it *was* a discovery; that she'd had no idea of this ability that should have defined her from the moment of her birth.

She also had no concept of where she was. Or why. Or where she had been before she awakened in a desert.

Nothing. No memory of a mother's embrace, a father's smile, or a best friend's secrets. No recollection of the color of her front door, the weight of her favorite drinking glass, or the titles of books that littered her desk.

She was a stranger to herself, a stranger with a past as barren as the desert, every defining feature buried deep, inaccessible.

A hundred thoughts flapped about in her head, like a flock of birds startled into flight. How long had she been in this state? Had she always been like this? Shouldn't there be someone to look after her if she didn't know anything about herself? Why was she alone? Why was she alone in the middle of nowhere?

*What had happened?*

She pressed two fingers against her breastbone. The pressure inside made it difficult to breathe. She opened her mouth, trying to draw in air faster, trying to fill her lungs so that they wouldn't feel as empty as the rest of her.

It was a minute before she gathered enough composure to examine her person, praying for clues—or outright answers—that would tell her everything she needed to know about herself. Her hands were not forthcoming: a few calluses on her right palm and little else of note. Pulling up her sleeves revealed blank forearms. A look at the skin of her abdomen likewise yielded nothing.

"*Revela omnia,*" she said, surprised to hear a deep, almost gravelly voice.

"*Revela omnia,*" she said again, hoping that the sound of her own speech might trigger a sudden cascade of memories.

It didn't. Nor did the spell bring to light any secret writing on her skin.

Surely her isolation was only an illusion. Nearby there must be someone who could help her—a parent, a sibling, a friend. Perhaps that person was even now stumbling about, calling for her, anxious to locate her and make sure that she was all right.

But she could hear no voices carried upon the howling wind, only the turbulence of sand particles hurtled about by forces beyond their control. And when she expanded the sphere of clear air around her, she uncovered nothing but sand and more sand.

She buried her face in her hands for a moment, then took a deep breath and stood up. She meant to start on her clothes, but as she came to her feet, it became obvious that she had something in her right boot.

Her heart somersaulted when she realized it was a wand. Ever since mages realized that wands were but conduits of a mage's power, amplifiers that were not strictly necessary to the execution of spells, wands had turned from revered tools to beloved accessories, always personalized, and sometimes to a silly degree. Names were woven into the design, favorite spells, insignia of one's city or school. Some wands even had their owners' entire genealogy engraved in microscopic letters.

She would dearly love to see her family history laid out before her, but it would be more than good enough if the wand had an *In case of loss, return to* _____ inscribed somewhere.

The wand, however, was as plain as a floor plank, without any carvings, inlays, or decorative motifs. And it remained just as bare when examined under a magnifying spell. She had no idea such wands were even made.

An oppressive weight settled over her chest. Loving parents would no more give a child such a wand than they would send her to school in garments made of paper. Was she an orphan then? Someone who had been discarded at birth and brought up in an institution? Elemental magelings did suffer from a higher rate of abandonment, since they were so much trouble in their infancy.

Yet the clothes she wore, a knee-length blue tunic and a white undertunic, were of exceptionally fine fabric: weightless yet strong, with an understated gleam. And though her face and hands felt the heat of the desert, wherever she was covered by the tunics she was perfectly comfortable.

The tunics did not have pockets. The trousers underneath, however, did. And one of those pockets yielded a small, rectangular, and somewhat crumpled card.

```
A. G. Fairfax
Low Creek Ranch
Wyoming Territory
```

She had to blink twice to make sure she was reading correctly. Wyoming Territory? As in the American West? The *nonmage* portion of the American West?

She tried several different unmasking spells, but the card provided no hidden messages. Expelling a slow breath, she put the card back in her trouser pocket.

She had thought all she needed was a name, the tiniest of clues. But now she had a name and a clue, and it was worse than if she'd had no insight at all into her past. Instead of staring at a blank wall, she was looking at a single square inch of tantalizing color and texture, with the rest of the mural—the people, places, and choices that had made her who she was—remaining firmly out of view.

Without meaning to, she slashed her wand through the air, all but growling. The swirling sand retreated farther. She sucked in a breath: eight feet from where she stood, a canvas tote lay half-buried in the sand.

She launched herself at the bag, yanking it out of the sand. The strap was broken, but the bag itself was undamaged. It was not terribly big—about twenty inches wide, twelve inches high, and eight inches deep—nor was it terribly heavy—fifteen pounds or there-abouts. But it was quite remarkable in the number of pockets it had: at least twelve on the outside, and scores upon scores inside. She unbuckled a large outside pocket: it held a change of clothes. Another of a similar size stored a rectangle of tightly packed cloth that she guessed would expand into a small tent.

Pockets on the inside were carefully and clearly labeled: *Nutrition, each pack one day's worth. Vaulting aid: five granules at a time, no more than three times a day. Heat sheet—in case you require warmth but need to remain unseen.*

*In case* you *require warmth.*

Would she have addressed herself in the second person—or was this evidence that someone else had been intimately involved in her life, someone who knew that such an emergency bag might come in handy someday?

Thirty-six pockets of one entire interior compartment were stuffed with remedies. Not remedies for illnesses, but for injuries: everything from broken limbs to the burn of dragon fire. Her pulse quickened. This was not a camping bag, but an emergency tote prepared in expectation of significant, perhaps overwhelming danger.

A map. The person who had meticulously stocked the bag must have included a map.

And there it was, in one of the smaller exterior pockets, woven of silken threads so slender they could barely be discerned with the naked eye, with mage realms in green and nonmage realms in gray. At the top was written, *Place the map on the ground—or in the body of water, if need be.*

She lay the map flat against the sand, which, with the heat of the sun blocked by the turbulent sky, was rapidly losing its warmth. Almost immediately a red dot appeared on the map, in the Sahara Desert, a hundred miles or so southwest of the border of one of the United Bedouin Realms.

The middle of nowhere.

Her fingers clutched at the map's edges. Where should she go? Low Creek Ranch, the only place she could name from her former life, was at least eight thousand miles away. Desert realms typically didn't have borders as tightly secured as those of island realms. But without official papers, she would not be able to use any of the translocators inside the United Bedouin Realms to leapfrog oceans and continents. She might even be detained for being somewhere she shouldn't be—Atlantis didn't like mages wandering abroad without properly sanctioned reasons.

And if she were to try nonmage routes, she was about a thousand miles from both Tripoli and Cairo. Once she'd staggered to the coast of the Mediterranean, assuming she could, she would still be at least three weeks from the American West.

More words appeared on the map, this time above the very desert in which she was stranded.

> *If you are reading this, beloved, then the worst has happened and I can safeguard you no more. Know that you have been the best part of my life and I have no regrets.*

*Long may Fortune shield you.*
*Live forever.*

She passed her hand over the words, barely noticing that her fingers were trembling. A dull pain burned in the back of her throat, for the loss of the protector she could not recall. For the loss of an entire life now beyond her grasp.

*You have been the best part of my life.*

The person who had written this could have been a sibling, or a friend. But she was almost entirely certain that he had been her sweetheart. She closed her eyes and reached for something. Anything. A name, a smile, a voice—she remembered nothing.

The wind shrieked.

No, it was her, screaming with all the frustration she could no longer contain.

The sandstorm shrank away, as if afraid of what she might do.

She panted, like a runner after a hard sprint. About her, the radius of clear, undisturbed air had increased tenfold, expanding a hundred feet in each direction.

Numbly she spun around, searching for what she dared not hope to find.

Nothing. Nothing. Absolutely nothing.

Then, the silhouette of a body in the sand.